Long Shadows

Stuart Bone

Copyrights

Novel - © 2018 Stuart Bone

All rights reserved. This book is sold subject to the condition that it shall not, by way of trade or otherwise, be lent, re-sold, hired out or otherwise circulated without prior consent. No part of this text may be reproduced, transmitted, downloaded, reverse engineered, or stored in or introduced into any information storage and retrieval system, in any form or by any means whether electronic or mechanical, now known or hereinafter invented, without the express written permission of the author.

Front cover design - © istock.com/ChrisGorgio

Author's website: www.stuartboneauthor.com

For Lesley
Friend and confidence builder

Chapter 1

Derek sighed deeply as he walked out through the main gates at the end of a very long day. As much as he loved his job working as head gardener, he disliked 'Help Out Wednesdays.' It was Margaret's latest idea to get the residents of the retirement home out into the grounds for some fresh air and a bit of gentle exercise. It wasn't one of her best ones, Derek felt, as he replayed images from the afternoon in his head.

It had been a total disaster. Last Wednesday only four residents came out to help him, this week it was fifteen and way too many for Derek to control on his own. Geraldine Peterson was pretty speedy on her walking frame and had pulled out half a row of Begonias before Derek could stop her. Bill Henderson, confused when Derek told him the rose needed a clip, had smacked Rose Delaney around the ear. While she was helped back to her room, old Percy Fanshawe thought it a good idea to mow the narrow grass path between the two main flowerbeds at the back of the house. Still, they'd managed to find Mrs McAllister's big toe before the paramedics took her away and with her poor circulation she hadn't felt a thing.

Dora hadn't helped the situation either. She was sat with her group of friends on two of the benches, watching, laughing and catcalling the entire time.

"Ooh Derek, could you give my lady garden the once over?"

"Hey Derek, how would you like to come and propagate my seedlings?"

"Derek, my nickname's Clematis because I'm great up

against a wall."

He'd tried his best to ignore them, although that wasn't easy. Why did old women sit with their legs open? It wasn't nice to look up from weeding a border to see a ninety year old growler staring back at you.

Still, having to call the paramedics out today should surely be enough to convince Margaret that 'Help Out Wednesdays' was an idea that needed to be forgotten. Derek really didn't have the time to watch over the residents anyway. He was busy enough what with tending the grounds, acting as 'Odd Job Man' whenever something inside the old house started leaking or cracking, while also trying to oversee his enthusiastic assistant, Ash and prevent him destroying the flowerbeds with his over-zealous weeding.

He was also busy with his favourite part of the job, designing. Margaret wanted him to create a new area in the grounds using the large, oval, Victorian-style, white gazebo she'd recently purchased second hand on eBay as a centre piece. She needed designs and costings by next week and Derek was behind schedule. Still, Margaret was currently loved-up again with her latest online date so perhaps she'd be happy to give him a bit more time.

No, that's not going to happen, he thought to himself, as walked down the lane towards the village. Margaret was bringing her new boyfriend over to his and Angela's house tomorrow night for a meal. They'd been seeing each other for about three months now and, from past experience, Derek knew that was usually the time Margaret's relationships turned sour. The last guy she was dating had admitted he was still married on their three month anniversary. The one before that had often sort Derek out in the grounds of the Home and at three months had suggested a threesome outdoors somewhere, requesting Derek wear nothing but his Wellington boots and a pair of soiled gardening gloves. God knows what was going to happen with the latest guy. This one Derek hadn't even met yet. He was a businessman who only passed through the area every couple of weeks. As relationships went this arrangement seemed to work for the two of them but something was bound to crop up and Derek was sure it would happen tomorrow night.

It was at moments like this that he sometimes regretted the move to Tenhamshire but the feeling usually passed quickly. It did now as he walked by the impressive local church and began making his way down the high street of Baddlesbury. The village was beautiful with the centre being a mix of timbered, medieval houses built by wealthy land owners who'd got rich during the boom in the wool trade. These old houses now leaned awkwardly against each other for support and cast crooked shadows across the narrow pavements. Derek had visited here two years ago during an eventful coach holiday and when he and Angela decided to set up home together and start a new life, Tenhamshire, and Baddlesbury in particular, had seemed the perfect place to do it.

Of course it helped that their friend, Margaret, another passenger on that fateful trip, had already moved here and taken ownership of a rather rundown Retirement Home, installing her mother, Dora into the largest suite. She needed a gardener to tend the grounds and Derek had just completed his garden design course at college. He moved here a year ago to start the job and Angela joined him six months later after arranging her new job at an auction house over in Cunden Lingus. Everything seemed perfect, almost too good to be true.

Derek continued walking through the high street, nodding at

several village residents that he recognised by sight while weaving in and out of the tourists who were stood on the pavement, taking photographs of the old houses on their mobile phones. Just past the newsagents, he turned left through a driveway between two old houses that were attached together on the floor above. After passing under the building the driveway widened and became bathed with sunlight. The road curved sharply to the left and continued round to a large, redbrick coach house that had once belonged to a member of the local gentry in the nineteenth century. It had recently been converted into three separate properties. Derek made his way to the dark green door at the far end. Angela wasn't home from work yet, her car wasn't in one of their two designated spots. The bay nearest the front door had a small, silver-grey hatchback parked in it. Derek opened the door and walked into the hallway.

"It's only me," he called.

"I'm in the kitchen, love."

Derek walked through to the back of the house. The room that overlooked the back garden contained a large, white, shaker-style, u-shaped kitchen, complete with central island. Every time Derek entered this room, which also had space to house Angela's Victorian, pine farmhouse table and array of eclectic antique dining chairs, he couldn't help feeling impressed. Just this one room was about the size of his old, one-bedroomed apartment that he rented out back on the outskirts of East London and Essex.

In the kitchen area a woman was bent over the stainless steel range cooker. She stood up, holding a white, enamelware dish between oven gloves.

"I made a Shepherd's Pie," she said, placing the dish onto a trivet on the island and spreading some grated, cheddar cheese across the top.

"You don't have to keep cooking for us, mum," Derek told her, "Angela and I are quite capable of rustling something up when we get in from work."

"It's no problem," she replied, returning the dish to the oven, "I've been in ages anyway so I thought I'd make myself useful."

She stood up again after closing the oven door and pushed her hair behind her ears.

"You know, I'm still not entirely happy with this colour," she said, squinting at her distorted reflection in the chrome tap as she looked at her bob from all angles, "I think this shade of brown is a little too dark for me. Ginny said I could get it adjusted if I wanted to."

"Who's Ginny?"

"Well, she's the colourist, obviously, up at the hair salon in the square. I might pop up there tomorrow, after I've been to the newsagents. Mary said that sewing magazine I wanted should be in."

"Who's Mary?"

"She works in the newsagents. Don't you know anyone in this village, Derek? It's important to fit it when you're living in a small community you know."

Before he could respond, Derek heard the front door open again.

"I'm home," Angela called.

"Kitchen."

A moment later Angela entered the room, looking miffed. Her ice-blue eyes were narrowed and she'd obviously just ruffled the front of her highlighted, light-brown hair as it was sticking up at odd angles.

"Bloody traffic jam just outside of Cunden Lingus on the way home tonight," she said, placing her handbag and brown leather, satchel-like briefcase onto the central island, "When I finally got to the front of the hold-up there was just a line of cones and some old bloke leaning on a shovel. Honestly, I felt like getting out of the car and kicking it from under him."

"I think someone needs a glass of wine," Derek said.

Angela smiled, wearily.

"I think so too," she replied.

"Right," Derek made his way over to the wine rack, "I'm gagging. Shall I get one for you too, love?"

He winked and Angela laughed.

"Bastard," she said, "Oh, sorry Ursula. Have you done dinner again? You know you don't have to."

Ursula waved her hand.

"It's no bother," she told her, "I've made a shepherd's pie."

She looked at her watch.

"Right, I'm going to go and freshen up. Can one of you watch that broccoli on the stove and turn it down if it starts bubbling?"

She left the room. Angela lifted the saucepan lid while Derek uncorked a bottle of Rioja. Back when they'd met on the coach trip, Derek's wine habits had been the occasional glass of sweet, German white but Angela had slowly introduced him to a new palette and now he preferred a glass or two of red of an evening.

"Mmm, what a great aroma," Angela said, as she stuck her nose into the top of the glass Derek passed to her.

"Oh, that's me," he replied, "I've dabbed a little organic fertiliser behind my ears."

Angela rolled her eyes.

"Dinner smells great too," she said, "I have to admit, your mother's a great cook."

She put her glass down and took three dinner plates out of the integrated plate rack.

"I really enjoy a home-cooked meal. It's nice to come home and not have to make anything...she is still leaving though, right?"

"She was looking at an apartment today," Derek replied, "I've only just got in myself and haven't asked her about it yet."

"Well talk it up, whatever it was like."

"Angela! I'm not having my mother living somewhere she doesn't want to be."

"Well, just so long as she doesn't like being here too much. Ursula's great but this is our home Derek, the first one we've owned together. I mean the few months we rented were great but I was so excited to move in here back in March. By April Ursula had joined us. It's June now, Derek."

"Well her house sold quicker than she thought. It won't be long, I promise."

"I hope you're right. She's taken over the guest room **and** the third bedroom with all of her sewing stuff. That was our office. I've got some work in my briefcase that I'd like to look over tonight but I'll have to wait until we're in bed. That's the only quiet time I get."

"That says a lot about our sex life."

Angela laughed.

"You know what I mean," she told him, "I don't see why all of Ursula's sewing stuff couldn't have gone into storage as well as her furniture. She's filled the room with fabrics and cotton threads. Why does a woman need two sewing machines and one of those headless mannequin things?"

"She likes to keep busy."

"That torso mannequin gives me the creeps," Angela continued, "Especially when Ursula attaches the arms and legs to it. Mind you it's better than her hanging the limbs up in the window. Our postman's never got over the shock."

Ursula returned to the kitchen.

"After dinner I must get on with that dress for Theresa Jennings," she told the room.

"The what, for who?" Angela asked.

Ursula checked the broccoli and quickly turned off the heat, tutting at the other two as she drained the saucepan.

"This needs serving up now. Derek, give the gravy another quick blast in the microwave will you," she turned to Angela, "I'm making a dress for Theresa Jennings. She admired my grey two-piece in the post office the other day and we got chatting. She wants a dress for her daughter's wedding in August and I said I'd be happy to make one for her. You must know Theresa."

Angela shook her head. Ursula tutted again.

"Honestly you two. Theresa lives in the old rectory up by the church. Derek, you pass her house every day for work, you must have seen her. Her husband owns one of the antiques shops up on the market square, the one beside the tourist information centre. You really should get to know the community that you live among."

Angela shot Derek a look. The microwave pinged and he took the gravy out.

"Did you see that apartment today, mum?" he asked, brightly, as he passed her the steaming jug.

"Thanks love. Could you grab the shepherd's pie for me as

well and I'll dish up. Yes I saw two actually."

"Oh yes?"

"Mmm, the first one was tiny and right on a busy main road. That was a no no."

"Shame," Angela called over from the dining table, where she'd laid out the knives and forks.

"I know," Ursula replied, "Still, the estate agent took me to a lovely place afterwards. Spratling Kershaw is the name of the village, funny name, and they've just finished building a block of apartments there. Beautiful they are, in a stunning setting."

"That's great."

"It's not," Derek said, bringing two plates piled up with shepherd's pie over to the table.

"Why not?" Angela asked.

"Yes, why not?" Ursula added, bringing over the third and sitting down beside her.

"Because that's where Angela and I stayed on our coach holiday two years ago."

"So?" Angela said.

"So, it's a village in the middle of nowhere with no amenities."

"It was a beautiful apartment though, Derek," his mum told him, her eyes shining as she pictured it in her mind, "With two large bedrooms and a lovely lounge diner. Oh, and the views from every window were amazing."

"But you must have some amenities close by," he continued.

"She's got her car for that, Derek," Angela reasoned.

"For now, but what about when she can no longer drive. She's seventy."

"That's not ancient. Ursula's a very safe driver."

Ursula stood up.

"Oh, I forgot to get dessert out of the freezer, it needs to stand for ten minutes."

While she was over at the freezer Angela leaned forward in her chair.

"What are you trying to do," she hissed across the table, "We want your mother to get her own place don't we?"

"Yes," Derek hissed back, "But I told you I don't want her stuck somewhere she doesn't want to be."

"She does want to be in this apartment Derek, it's you that has the problem."

"I don't, I just…"

Ursula returned to the table.

"You know, with hindsight perhaps you're right about that apartment, Derek," she said, "It would be okay if there was a bus perhaps, even just a few times a week but there wasn't, I checked with the Estate Agent. It's a shame though, the apartment itself was so perfect. Oh well, I'll just have to keep on looking."

Derek smiled at his mother and made sure he didn't catch Angela's eye until after he'd finished his shepherd's pie.

It was quiet in the lounge after dinner. Angela, still in a mood, had decided she'd look over her work papers now rather than later. Ursula was sat in the armchair beside the patio doors, hand sewing two pieces of material together and taking full advantage of the early summer sunlight streaming in through the window. Derek sat in silence with a glass of Rioja. He felt Angela was being unreasonable. When she'd joined him here in Tenhamshire six months ago it had been her suggestion to ask his mum if she wanted to move to the county as well. Ursula had thought it a wonderful idea and Derek had been rather surprised at how quickly she'd put the old family home on the market. There were a lot of memories in that house. Okay not all of them were good but Ursula had continued to live there, even after her husband's fatal boating accident. Derek had wanted to drop out of university at the time to get a job and help her pay the mortgage but she'd insisted he stay on and get his qualifications, telling him everything would be fine. She'd been running an alterations business with a friend in the local shopping arcade but began taking on larger projects as well, making outfits for people and had made enough money to pay all the bills on her own. Perhaps he was a little overprotective of her now but he was proud of his mum and all the sacrifices she'd made for him.

Ursula held up the material she was sewing and sighed.

"I'm not sure this colour says 'Bride's Mother' do you? It's rather a dull beige."

"If it's what she wants," Derek replied.

"I know, but the pattern is very plain too."

"It's not your problem, Ursula," Angela threw in, "I'm sure you'll make it look lovely."

Ursula smiled.

"Thanks dear," she said, and began sewing again, "Perhaps Theresa can't afford to pay out for something more elaborate anyway. I expect her husband's antiques shop doesn't make that much money. I suppose it has more browsers than buyers. Of course you know what that's like, don't you Angela."

Derek tensed.

"You had an antiques shop, until the bottom fell out of the market."

Angela shot Derek a disgruntled look before sighing and replying,

"Yes, that's right Ursula."

Derek relaxed. Now wasn't the time to tell his mum the truth about Angela's past. She wouldn't understand.

"Antiques are a difficult market," Ursula continued, "Tastes change so quickly these days. Do you remember that lovely mahogany dining suite of your Nan's, Derek? I'd have got more money for that if I'd chopped it up and sold it for firewood."

Derek hoped his mum would change the subject now.

"Mind you, those antique hatpins I owned sold quite well. And most of my thimble collection is silver; that seems to hold its value. Not that I'm planning on selling those, or that emerald bracelet your father bought me that time. I also had…"

The doorbell rang. Ursula stood up.

"I'll get it," she said, "I want to put this piece back in my sewing room anyway. I shan't do anymore tonight. You know, the wedding is at Theresa's villa in Spain. Perhaps their shop's doing okay after all."

She left the room. Derek relaxed.

"Her sewing room? Did you hear that, Derek," Angela said, "Not, 'your office' or 'your bedroom' but 'her sewing room.'"

"It's just a figure of speech," he replied, "For God's sake Angela, my mother isn't moving in, alright? Why don't you change the record?"

"I will once she's exchanged contracts on a place and not before. This isn't a dosshouse for all waifs and strays."

Derek opened his mouth to respond but heard his mother talking to someone out in the hallway. Her voice was muffled but she sounded quite cheerful.

"Who's that do you suppose?"

"Probably Theresa whatserface. She's going to strip off in here and try her dress on while your mum pins a hem."

The door to the lounge opened and Ursula came in followed by a tall, slim, grey-haired man, carrying a holdall.

"Look who's here," Ursula said, smiling up at him.

"Hello Ange," the man said, "God this place is a bugger to find. Could I borrow twenty quid for the taxi?"

"Dad."

*

Derek sat in bed reading a seed catalogue but he wasn't really taking in any of the words. Angela was in the en suite. She was very quiet in there; well, she'd been quiet since the surprise arrival of her father. Derek hadn't met him before but he'd heard plenty of stories. He didn't think Angela had given him their address but he'd still managed to find them.

The door to the en suite opened and Angela stepped into the room, switching off the bathroom light. She got into bed, picked up a magazine and began flicking through the pages, rather rapidly Derek felt. Surely she wasn't still in a mood?

"That was a bit of a surprise, Bert showing up like that," he said.

"Mmm."

"Did he say why he's here?"

"He'll want something," Angela replied, casually, "Money usually. Still, apart from the cab fare tonight, he's out of luck this time. We don't have any to spare."

"Won't he just have come to see you?"

Angela snorted.

"No, Bert does nothing like that. He either wants something or is just lying low for a while. You wait and see," she closed the magazine and looked up at Derek, "Don't you dare give him anything, no matter what sob story he comes out with. And make sure your mother knows that too. And tell her to hide her valuables."

"You're not serious?"

"I am. Dad's a crook, always has been. You can't trust him an inch."

Derek returned to his catalogue but still couldn't concentrate.

"Do you think he's down here planning a job then?" he asked.

Angela burst out laughing.

"He's not one of the Great Train Robbers, Derek. Bert Jenkins is a petty thief, and not a very good one at that, otherwise he wouldn't have spent most of my and my brother's childhood going in and out of prison."

Derek had one other question he needed to ask.

"Does he know about your past?" he asked.

Angela put the magazine onto her bedside table.

"You mean does he know I used to earn my living as an escort? Yes he does Derek. People of that age can cope with that sort of revelation."

Derek didn't want to get into that argument yet again but there didn't seem any way to avoid it.

"I will tell my mother about you when the time is right," he said, slowly, trying to control his temper, "Now isn't that time. Let her get settled first."

"And when will the right time be Derek?" Angela replied, "When we first got together was wrong because you said she needed to get to know me first. When we'd been dating six months was wrong because she was getting over flu, when we decided to live together was also wrong because that was a Thursday and Ursula's never liked Thursdays."

"Now you're being ridiculous," he told her.

"Am I? You don't give your mum enough credit. She's not some innocent virgin you know."

"Fine!" Derek spat, "Tomorrow I'll tell her you were a prostitute when we met."

"Escort."

"And then right after that I'll come to work with you and you can tell all of your colleagues as well."

Angela folded her arms tightly in front of her.

"That's different," she whispered.

"Why is it? Why is it okay for you to constantly badger me into telling my mother about your past when you yourself pick and choose who you want to know about it?"

"Because my telling my boss would end up with me being sacked while your mum is family and I don't want her discovering the truth accidently like you did," Angela said, "Don't you remember that night on our coach holiday to Tenhamshire? We'd grown so close over the week and then that bloody coach driver blurted out the truth and we had an almighty row. We could have lost each other that night, well we nearly did. If it wasn't for that courier I…"

Angela left the sentence hanging as she heard the crack in her voice. Derek took her hand and squeezed it.

"I know what you're saying," he told her, gently, "I don't want mum to find out by accident either."

"Then you need to tell her Derek. Margaret and Dora both know, it's only a matter of time until someone blurts it out accidently. Don't let that happen to Ursula. Tell her Derek, and soon."

Angela smiled and kissed Derek on the cheek before turning over and switching off her bedside light.

"It's hard keeping secrets," she added, as she plumped up her pillows, "It's probably best not to have any."

Derek placed his seed catalogue down on his bedside table and picked up his mobile phone. He read the text message again.

Hi Derek. It was so nice to meet up. Perhaps we can do it again the next time you're down this way. Leanne. x

Some things should remain secret, he thought to himself, especially being back in touch with your ex-wife.

Chapter 2

When Derek walked downstairs the following morning Angela was picking up her car keys from the hall table.

"Are you going into work already?" he asked.

"Yes," she replied, "I've still got that reading from last night to do. Dad turning up meant I couldn't finish it."

"But aren't you going to speak to him," he said.

"About what?"

"Well, he's come all this way."

Derek glanced through the open doorway to the lounge where Bert was snoring away under a duvet on the sofa. Angela stopped messing with her hair while staring at her reflection in the large, rectangular, silver-framed mirror on the wall.

"Didn't you hear what I said last night? He's here to get money out of us only he doesn't straight out ask for it on the first night. We've got nothing to say to one another and I've got a busy day at work. Margaret and her new beau are coming for dinner tonight, remember; so I need to be home on time."

Angela kissed Derek on the cheek and opened the front door. It closed loudly behind her. The sleeping mass stirred.

"Where am I? Who's got the stuff?"

"You alright, Bert?" Derek called out, walking into the lounge.

"Oh, it's you, thank God," Bert said, relieved, "For a second there I thought the Pavlov brothers had found me."

"Right, well I think you're safe here."

"You're never safe when the Russian mafia are involved,

Derek."

There wasn't really a response to that.

"Did you sleep well?"

"Like a baby, Derek, like a baby," he replied, "Mind you I'm one of those people who could nod off on a washing line."

He yawned and stretched before rubbing his eyes, ice blue just like his daughter's.

"Of course, knowing you've put some space between yourself and the Hong Kong triads does aid a more restful sleep."

Derek couldn't help grinning.

"I thought it was the Russian mafia."

Bert tapped the side of his nose.

"I get about," he said, "I probably shouldn't have mentioned it to you actually."

"Your secret's safe with me."

Derek sat down on the edge of the sofa.

"Talking of secrets," he said, "My mother doesn't know about Angela's…well, past life shall we say. I haven't found the right time to tell her yet. So if you could…"

"Say no more, Derek, it's fine," Bert interrupted, "Your mother's a gentle soul; a real lady, I can see why you wouldn't want her to know."

I wish your daughter shared that opinion, Derek thought to himself.

Out in the hallway the door opposite the lounge opened and Ursula emerged from her bedroom, already washed and dressed and prepared for the day ahead.

"Morning," she called out, seeing the two men looking back at her, "Bet you wouldn't say no to a bacon sandwich, would you Bert."

"I certainly wouldn't Ursula," he replied, "Let me make myself decent first. You'd best give me a couple of hours."

Ursula laughed.

"Oh Bert, you are a one."

She headed into the kitchen and Bert climbed out of his bed. He was totally naked and didn't seem bothered by it, taking his time to straighten the duvet before bending over and rooting around inside his holdall for fresh underwear. Derek realised he was staring and quickly stood up.

"Erm, I'll just go see how mum's getting on."

He stood in the doorway to the kitchen, blocking the view; only moving inside the room once Bert had headed into the bathroom through the door beside the hallway mirror at the front of the house, fortunately wearing a pair of boxer shorts. Derek was so glad the front door didn't have a glass panel.

"I didn't know we had bacon," he said.

"I got a pack out of the freezer last night to defrost," his mother replied, "Well I thought Bert would much prefer a bacon sandwich than that muesli you and Angela eat. Do you think he'd like a sausage?"

"No he's got quite enough of that already."

"Sorry?"

"Nothing; actually mum, Angela says her dad is…well, not to be trusted."

Ursula laughed.

"Dear me, her own father; are you sure she said that Derek?"

"Yes!"

Derek felt like he was five years old again with his mother disbelieving his story. Of course at five he had been lying about how the crayon mark had got onto the wallpaper but he was forty-seven now and was confident he knew what his partner had told him last night.

"Look," he continued, "Bert has a bit of a colourful past; you know, taking a few things that weren't his to take."

Ursula turned round from the frying pan on the hob.

"I'm not an idiot Derek. I was there in the room when Bert was talking last night. I just choose to see the good in people. So long as Bert is kind to us I'm going to be kind to him."

"Yes but…"

"No buts. Now, shouldn't you be on your way to work? You wanted to get in early today didn't you?"

Derek looked at his watch.

"Shit!"

"Derek!"

"I didn't realise the time. I've got to get there before Tweedle Dum decides to start thinking for himself."

"You shouldn't call him that," Ursula admonished, "Ashley is your assistant and he's very keen to learn."

"And that would be great if he wasn't so accident prone. He rushes off all gung-ho about something which usually winds up in a big mess that I have to sort out. If he wasn't the matron's son I'd get rid of him. He's got no gardening knowledge at all, doesn't know his Allium from his Erysimum."

"Well you're there to teach him."

"I do try. Yesterday he asked me why we grew carrots in rows and not bunches. How was I meant to respond to that?"

Ursula giggled.

"He sounds sweet," she said.

Derek sighed and looked at his watch again.

"Damn, I haven't had time for breakfast or a coffee."

"Ahem."

Ursula held up a thermos mug and a paper bag.

"I came in and put the coffee machine on before I got dressed. Knowing you wanted to get to work early I made up two cheese rolls as well."

Derek grinned.

"Thanks mum."

"I was surprised when Angela joined me in the kitchen. She's up extra early today too. Refused a cheese roll; said she'd get something on the way to work. I hope she does. I think she was looking peaky this morning."

"I think she's just busy," Derek told her, "Anyway I must dash."

He took the rolls and coffee and kissed his mum on the cheek.

"We both want to make sure we're back in plenty of time tonight for the meal with Margaret and her new fella."

"Oh yes, that's right."

"Shit!"

"Derek, please, not at this time of the morning."

"Sorry, I forgot about Bert."

"What's the problem? We'll just be six for dinner, a nice, round number. I'm sure it will be a lovely evening."

Derek wasn't convinced. As he walked up the high street he couldn't help thinking that four out of the six members of tonight's dinner party knew about Angela's past. He and Angela weren't about to say anything but what if she angered her father? He might say something in retaliation. Perhaps Margaret would blurt out the secret accidentally. She did get tipsy after only a couple of glasses of wine. Derek sighed. A lovely evening, he didn't think there was a hope in hell of that happening.

*

Angela sat in her car at the drive-thru burger restaurant, eating something in a muffin that bared no resemblance to the image on the menu board. She hadn't needed to leave so early this morning but she didn't want to face her father. Bert was always trouble. The only good thing Angela had to say about him was that his visits were few and far between. He always put her on edge. Why she bothered to still see him after that time he'd stolen her savings she didn't know. Some kind of misguided loyalty she supposed. It was that loss of money that led to the worst time in her life. Angela shivered and shook her head. That wasn't a memory she needed to revisit right now. Suffice it to say each time he'd turned up again she'd given him money before it was stolen from her. It was easier that way and made his visits shorter, although it also meant he would always show up again when he needed more.

Not this time though. She and Derek didn't have any to give him. The money from the sale of her apartment had all gone into the coach house. Derek's old place usually provided a bit of extra income although he was currently between tenants and wanted to update the décor before renting it out again. Being so far away it was going to take a while to do. Angela didn't know why he didn't just sell it and buy somewhere closer to rent out. She'd suggested it often enough.

Oh well, so long as he was happy, which he was. Derek wasn't earning much as a gardener compared to his previous role as an accountant but he usually returned home of an evening with a smile on his face. It was the same for her. She loved working as a valuer at the auction house. She'd always had an interest in history and antiques but this job was certainly less lucrative than escorting had been.

Not that she missed it. Although her wealthy clients had taken her to some very exotic places around the world she was happier being here in Tenhamshire. It was a fresh start for both her and Derek. When they met they'd both been at a crossroads in their lives. Derek was newly divorced and studying at college to become a garden designer and she'd just decided to leave her escorting career behind her as she approached forty. She hadn't known what she was going to do next but had met Derek on the coach holiday and her life changed.

Angela smiled to herself as she thought about that eventful trip. As soon as Derek boarded the coach, something inside her stirred. It wasn't that he was drop-dead gorgeous although he was a good-looking man. In many ways his appearance had said Mr Average; average height, starting to get a little thicker around the middle, dark brown hair beginning to recede at the front, but her gut had told her here was someone special. She hadn't felt that way in a long time. They'd chatted on the coach and she'd loved the way his brown eyes crinkled whenever he smiled at her and his whole face lit up when he laughed. It was amazing really that they were together now. There weren't many men who would take up with a woman who used to earn a living escorting.

The smile fell from Angela's face. She was being hard on Derek about telling his mother the real story of her past, but the thought of Ursula finding out some other way scared her. She liked Ursula and hated having secrets from her. Margaret and Dora both knew about her past. Dora wouldn't say anything, even after a drink. Mind you that woman could down a bottle of gin and still remember all the words to those dirty songs she knew. Margaret barely touched alcohol and a glass or two of wine made her giggly and chatty. What if she blurted something out tonight? No, the sooner Derek sat his mum down and told her the truth, the sooner they could all move forwards with their lives.

    Angela put the half-eaten muffin back into the bag and threw it into the bin beside her car. She looked at her watch. It was time to get to work. She turned the key in the ignition but didn't put her car into gear. She sighed. She knew Derek thought her a hypocrite. He couldn't see why it was okay for her to nag him about telling his mum the truth about her when she refused to do the same thing with her work colleagues. She did understand where he was coming from. Angela was aware that lately she'd begun referring to what she'd done as escorting rather than as prostitution. While she'd never shouted what she did from the rooftops, Angela had been proud of how she'd made a lucrative career out of sex, but now she'd left that behind her and was working in a 'proper job,' she was beginning to see the last twenty years as an embarrassment. Why would you then tell people you work with about that embarrassment? They didn't need to know but Ursula did, she was family. Well, not officially family. It's not like Derek had asked her to marry him but they were together and that was almost the same thing for her.

    Angela leaned her head back against the headrest. She remembered those first few times she'd slept with someone for money. It had made her feel dreadful; used and dirty but she kept telling herself it was only to get her through university. After that, everything would be fine and she could get on with her life. She'd had so many plans for what to do after passing her history degree, but then Bert had turned up on that fateful visit where her money had gone missing and all those plans dissolved into nothing.

She'd continued her life of prostitution but now worked hard to make it into a business and eventually had a select list of a few, well-to-do clients that she would visit regularly. Some of them didn't even want sex, just an attractive, young woman on their arm who could hold her own in conversation. It was those later years that made her feel proud, a time when she'd been able to use her knowledge and qualifications and not just her body. Why should she feel embarrassed about that? But she did now. She couldn't help it.

Angela pulled out of the car park and drove through the outskirts of Cunden Lingus. She realised that it was really thanks to her prostitution, and to one of her lucrative clients, that she was where she was today.

Alistair St John Pilkington had been well-known and respected in antiquing circles. After his much-loved wife died he'd sought the company of an attractive woman he could dine out with and talk to. Angela fitted the bill. She'd liked Alistair. He was an old-fashioned gentleman and never referred to her as an escort, prostitute or even as a girlfriend. In public she was a family friend, 'kind enough to accompany an old codger like myself about town.' They met up about six times a year but never slept together. Through him Angela was able to develop her knowledge of antiques. He was always patient and obviously enjoyed sharing his experience. He helped her buy and sell different pieces and Angela loved the thrill of an auction.

It was after meeting Derek that Angela spoke with Alistair and explained her predicament. She wanted to leave prostitution behind her and get a job, something that could hopefully lead to a career. She was willing to start at the bottom and work her way up. In no time at all he'd arranged a place for her at a small auctioneering firm in London where she could use her skills and knowledge and also learn about how an auction house worked. The owner, impressed with Angela's enthusiasm and work ethic had been sorry to see her leave a year later but had given a glowing recommendation to Jacobson & Lee Auctioneers in Cunden Lingus. It was just after starting her new role here in Tenhamshire that Angela learned Alistair had died. She didn't go to the funeral, it wouldn't have felt right. She mourned him in her own way.

However, without her 'backer' she was now on her own in the world of antiques and that was really why she was fearful of anyone she worked with discovering her secret past. There was no reason that they should but if they did and she lost this job it would be virtually impossible now to find another. Alistair couldn't help her anymore and Angela's past would prevent her ever getting another role.

She turned onto the main road that ran through the centre of Cunden Lingus, her mind still thinking about the past. It hadn't been an easy decision to make, selling herself for money but, at the time, it felt like she had no other option. Angela had been offered a place at university and saw it as a chance to break free and do something with her life, but she couldn't afford to go. The days of grants had long gone. Then she'd recalled an incident from a few years before. A dodgy friend of her father's had propositioned her when she was fifteen, offering her money for a blow job. Disgusted, she'd told her father all about it but he'd just laughed it off, saying, "That's Denny for you." He'd not given her any support and left her with a feeling that this was how all men saw her; purely as a sex object. But maybe that could be turned to her advantage, a way to help her get through university. That was how it had all started; all due to an acquaintance of her father's propositioning her and her father's reaction to it leaving her feeling worthless.

As she turned into the car park at Jacobson & Lee Auctioneers, Angela realised her thoughts had come full circle. She was back onto Bert again. Having him in her house now was just a reminder to her of where her life had gone wrong.

*

Derek was sat in the largest of the outbuildings on the left-hand side of the main house at the retirement home. Most of it he used as storage for all of the gardening equipment, including the sit-on lawnmower that Derek always made sure was locked up securely, knowing Dora liked to sneak out this side of the building because she knew it was out of bounds for residents. He didn't trust her not to take it out for a spin around the country lanes. The staff entrance was this side of the house too as there was a room just inside the door that they used as a changing-cum-restroom.

At the far end of the outbuilding was a small, brick and glass add-on that Derek used as a kind of office. There was a phone extension and a small desk which Derek was sat at now, trying to work on the designs Margaret wanted to see completed next week. Outside his assistant, Ash was washing out terracotta plant pots, sat in full sun, going hammer and tong with wiping the dirt off of the outsides, his tongue hanging out in concentration and sweat pouring down his forehead from his long, blonde hair that was pulled back into a ponytail. Derek sighed and counted down.

"Three, two, one."

The terracotta pot slipped in Ash's hands and smashed against the side of the galvanised bucket full of soapy water, smashing into several pieces. Ash looked forlornly at the piece of the base that was left in his hand for a moment before throwing it over his shoulder and picking up another pot, starting exactly the same process over again.

Ash was best described as gangly. He had large hands and feet and long limbs that he seemed to have difficulty controlling. He was a nice, polite young man and when he wasn't breaking something, Derek found him pleasant to be around. Nothing fazed him and whether someone was being polite or nasty to him, he always gave back that big, lopsided grin of his.

A movement beyond where Ash was sitting caught Derek's eye. An old woman had emerged from the staff entrance and was staring guiltily around her in all directions. When Derek had first met Dora on that fateful coach trip she'd been waiting on a second hip replacement operation and had used a wheelchair on the daily excursions. Now all she needed was a stick to get around with and whenever he came into close contact with her, Derek always made sure he knew exactly where it was, otherwise the experience could end painfully.

Now able to move around freely Dora had lost a few pounds but she was still well on the side of hefty. With the Home providing a free hairdresser, she now sported a dark shade of red in her short, wavy hair, rather than the cheap purple rinse she used to have. She was definitely up to no good and after closing his pad of drawings, Derek stood up and went out to see what she was up to.

He crept up to her quietly and it wasn't until he was almost by her side that she realised someone was there. Dora jumped but then breathed a huge sigh of relief.

"Oh Derek, it's just you. I thought it was one of the nurses."

"Well I am staff," he replied.

"Outdoors and unskilled, that doesn't count."

"Charming."

"You know what I mean."

Dora looked about her again.

"What are you up to? Derek asked.

Dora tried to look innocent.

"Me? I'm not up to anything."

"Of course you are. You're always up to something, usually with your sidekick. Where is Sir Jasper today?"

"I have no idea. I'm not his keeper."

Dora looked about her again.

"You're being a lookout aren't you," Derek said, "Sir Jasper's in there doing something and you're watching out for any approaching staff. Oh God, you're not sneaking Syrup of Figs into the gravy again are you? With the extra toilet usage last time that rusted, old sewage pipe burst and ruined my dahlias."

Dora giggled.

"I know, that was funny."

"Well you'd better not be doing that again. I've no problem reporting you to…"

"Calm down Derek, God you're like an old woman at times. We're not doing anything like that."

"Well what are you up to?"

Dora sighed resignedly.

"Alright, Sir Jasper's trying to sneak into the staffroom."

"He's not going to hide in the cupboard to watch the nurses changing out of their uniforms again is he? You know how that ended last time."

Dora grinned.

"Yes he wasn't expecting Nurse Kenny to be the one changing. Then he leant against the cupboard door and fell out, just as Kenny bent over to pull his trousers up."

A faraway look appeared in Dora's eyes.

"Imagine having buttocks that firm they could break someone's glasses like that. I wish I could fit inside that cupboard."

"Is that what he's doing now because he'll end up hurting himself and…"

"Will you calm down Derek," Dora told him, "We're just hunting for a bit of information about Tommy Jefferies, that's all."

"Is he the old man who thinks he looks like Elvis; wears that oversized black wig and is always curling his lip?"

"Well that's actually due to a stroke but yes, that's who I'm talking about."

"Why are you looking for information about him in the staffroom?"

"Well you don't think my Margaret's going to let me look at his Resident's file do you? No, he had the doctor into him again last night and Sir Jasper and I are trying to overhear the nurses talking. We don't think he's got long left and I'm thinking of having a fiver on ten to ten thirty tonight that he pops off."

Derek shook his head.

"This death sweepstake you run is sick, do you know that?"

"It's just a bit of fun, Derek," Dora replied, "We've got to have a few laughs in this hole."

"But betting on death?"

Dora shrugged her shoulders.

"Death visits here more often than relatives do. It's a fact of life Derek. How many people second guess the sex of a new baby when they discover a woman is pregnant? We're just at the other end of the scale. Aside from the odd bet the only interesting thing going on around here is trying to discover what Dental Flossie does when she disappears to her room at eight o'clock each night."

"She's probably going to bed."

"Yes but who with?"

Derek pulled a face.

"Hey, old people are allowed to have sex you know," Dora told him, "It doesn't stop when you start collecting your pension."

She sighed.

"Mind you, I don't think that's Flossie's thing. No, she's up to something in that room. I'm determined to find out what it is. That might be something to have a bet on; how soon until I discover the truth about her."

"You know the matron is trying to ban this gambling ring," Derek told her.

Dora laughed.

"Moron can't find her arse with both hands, she's hardly likely to discover our gambling syndicate."

"Her name is Maureen, Dora."

"I know what name suits her," she indicated Ash out in the yard, who'd just managed to tip the bucket of water over himself, "It's no wonder that lad of hers is like he is, poor boy."

"Ash is a nice guy, just a little over eager," Derek told her, "And Maureen is a sweet lady."

"Who's completely out of her depth as matron here. I don't know how she passed her nursing exams let alone become the head honcho. She almost killed me not long after I arrived here."

"You're exaggerating."

"I am not," Dora said, indignantly, "Moron shoved one of my suppositories down my throat at medicine time. I nearly choked to death. She was too busy concentrating on getting an aspirin up my arse to notice me turning blue. Thank God Kenny was there, that's all I can say. Actually every night I thank God for Kenny."

A man walked up to Dora from the passageway behind her. He was of similar height to her, about five feet five and his white hair was short all over and spikey on top. He had a small, regimental moustache and while he also had a stick, he barely rested it on the ground as he walked along.

"I can't get in there yet," he said to Dora, "I'm going to have to try again later."

He spotted Derek.

"Oh, ah, hello there," he said, nervously pushing his glasses further up the bridge of his nose, "I was just wondering where the delectable Dora was. Quite by chance I was passing through the hallway when…"

"He knows, Sir Jasper," Dora interrupted.

"Ah."

"But he's not going to say anything, are you Derek?"

Derek sighed.

"Okay," he said, "I haven't seen anything, but don't let me catch you again, otherwise I'll be going straight to Margaret."

"Don't worry young Derek," Sir Jasper said, "We'll make sure you won't catch us again."

He and Dora both started laughing.

"Come on Sir Jasper," Dora said, "I think we deserve a nice

cup of tea before trying again later. We should try and tackle Flossie too. Find out what happens at eight pm."

They turned to head off back inside but Dora stopped.

"Isn't my Margaret coming down to yours with her fuck buddy tonight Derek," she asked?

"Dora!" Derek winced, "He's her boyfriend."

"A boyfriend is around each week and you go out on dates with him. A guy that turns up once or twice a month and heads straight for the bedroom I think you have to go with fuck buddy. Still, as long as she's getting some. Anyway, she's coming to yours tonight isn't she?"

"Yes she is," Derek replied.

Dora nodded.

"Good, well, next time you could try asking me along. I am allowed to go out if I want to you know. I've not seen your new place down the road yet."

Derek was startled to realise that he and Angela hadn't invited their friend over.

"Oh, right, yes we will," Derek said, "Sorry it's just been a bit manic, what with mum moving in and then Angela's dad showed up last night as well and..."

Dora turned back to Sir Jasper and said,

"You go on ahead, I'll catch you up."

She walked back to Derek.

"You haven't told your mother about Angela yet have you," she said.

Derek shook his head.

"Not yet, no. I told her Angela used to run her own antiques shop until the bottom fell out of the market."

Dora tutted.

"You shouldn't have done that. I've met your mum, she's a

nice lady and she deserves to know the truth."

"Don't you start," Derek said, "Angela keeps on at me about that."

"So she should. You can't very well say you've accepted her past if you keep trying to hide it."

"I have accepted it," Derek told her, indignantly, "I can accept it and still not like it or agree with it. How would you feel if it was the other way round? What if Margaret told you she was getting paid for sex with this guy she's been seeing?"

"I'd say 'hallelujah, can we now afford satellite telly in the main lounge.'"

"You wouldn't. Besides, I secretly think Angela is regretting her past too. She's worried it will come out at work."

"Well she's allowed to regret it, if she wants. It was her life and she went through it. You're not allowed to regret it, you're meant to support her if she feels bad. That's your job. You know, there's a lot more to a relationship than just being together, believe me. My Billy and I had a wonderful marriage but only because we worked at it constantly and were honest with each other. You're here in Tenhamshire having a fresh start. Well to do that successfully you've got to let go of the past, and you can only do that by accepting it."

"I have accepted it."

"Then tell your mother," Dora told him, forcefully, "Because if you don't you're going to lose that lovely girl. "

She nodded and then closed the door, leaving Derek standing on the step, feeling like he'd just been chastised by his grandmother. A crashing sound behind him brought Derek out of his reverie. Ash was lying on the floor on a bed of freshly cleaned, but now smashed, terracotta pots. He saw Derek looking at him.

"Slipped," he called over.

Chapter 3

Derek received a text from Angela as he drove back from the garden centre with some new plant pots. Her boss had called her in for a meeting at five o'clock so she wasn't going to be able to get home as early as she'd thought and could he deal with dinner. He dealt with it straightaway and phoned his mum.

He arrived home that evening to the aroma of Ursula's special spicy coating for chicken in the air. As he walked towards the kitchen he heard giggling. Looking in he spied Ursula and Bert sat close together up on stools by the central island, their backs to him and their heads almost touching.

"Oh Bert," he heard his mother say, "That's a whopper and no mistake."

"Alright what's going on in here," Derek called out loudly, as he walked into the kitchen.

Ursula and Bert both turned round on their stools to face him with puzzled expressions on their faces.

"Bert's just been telling me some stories about his life," Ursula said.

"Oh right, sorry."

"Not that I believed that last whopper," she continued, grinning back at Bert.

"Honestly Ursula, on my son's eyes, that's exactly what happened."

Ursula giggled again as she got down off of the stool.

"Everything's ready for dinner, Derek," she said, "The chicken pieces are going in the oven in ten minutes, I've stirred some chives into the sour cream for the jacket potatoes and there's a mixed leaf salad and a Caesar Salad ready prepared in the fridge. Bert helped me make the cheesecake this afternoon; oh and there are also some strawberries and cream."

"Thanks mum, that's great."

"Bert kindly bought the chicken pieces."

"Thank you too, Bert. Sorry if I upset your plans today mum. You were going to get your hair colour changed weren't you?"

"Oh, no I've decided to keep it for a bit. Bert says he thinks it suits me."

She smiled at Angela's dad before speaking to Derek again.

"Right, now you're home to entertain Bert I'm going to go and get ready."

"You look lovely as you are Ursula," Bert called after her, as she walked towards the hallway.

Ursula giggled again.

"Now that is a whopper of a lie," she said, and left the room.

Derek turned his attention to the grinning Bert and decided he was very quickly outstaying his welcome. Ursula had never shown any interest in dating in the twenty-seven years since her husband's death. It had been a tragic accident and Derek wondered if his mother had ever truly got over it. She'd got on with her life but had barely spoken about the accident ever again. It always seemed to upset her. While Derek wouldn't mind if she started seeing someone he didn't particularly want it to be Bert. Still, the man was currently a guest in his house so he forced a smile on to his face and said,

"What have you been up to today?"

"Oh your mum took me on a tour of the village and then kindly drove me into Cunden Lingus as I needed to go to the bank. Then we came back here and spent some time pumping in the bedroom before preparing dinner."

"Well that sounds like a full day…sorry…you did what in the bedroom?"

"I pumped up your airbed," Bert told him, "Ursula said that seeing as we had guests tonight I oughtn't to leave my duvet out in the lounge. She's very thoughtful your mother. We moved some bits out of the sewing room and put them in your mum's bedroom so that I could put the airbed down on the floor. And very comfortable it is too, Derek."

Angela's not going to like her dad getting too settled here, Derek thought to himself, mind you, I'm not too keen either.

"Actually Bert," he said, "I need to go and get changed myself, so…"

"No problem Derek," Bert told him, "I'm perfectly fine on my own. How was your day? It's your boss who's coming for dinner tonight isn't it?"

"Yes," Derek replied, "Although she's a friend as well. Margaret and her mother, Dora, were also passengers on the coach holiday where Angela and I met. Margaret's late father ran a very successful business but sold it when he became ill, leaving the two of them rather well off."

"Really?"

Derek realised he was telling the wrong person that someone had money.

"Yes but Margaret was looking for a new start, a fresh challenge. I'm not sure running a retirement home was her first choice but the place came up for sale and she's ploughed her money into that."

"What, all on her own?" Bert asked.

"Well I think she has some silent partners, a couple of doctor friends who are quite happy to get paid a return each year but mostly it's been Margaret. She's done loads. The Home's an old manor house with a number of acres attached to it. It was already a retirement home although rather rundown when Margaret bought it but she's already updated all of the health and safety bits, you know, rewiring, new heating, putting in ramp access and a lift. The place is beautiful on the outside, Georgian symmetry with two identical wings jutting out either side of the main entrance. The brickwork is a really dark red but in certain light that changes to brown and the whole house looks like it's made out of chocolate. I look after the grounds that haven't been rented out and I also design new areas as and when Margaret wants them. I really enjoy it."

"She sounds like a formidable woman."

Derek laughed.

"You wouldn't know it to look at her. Dora first described her to me as a mouse and I can see what she means. She can be very quiet and prefer her own company but when you see her in business mode well, that mouse can roar like a lion."

Derek looked at the clock on the wall.

"Well I really should get changed," he said, "Oh your chicken, when does mum want it in the oven?"

Bert held up his hand.

"Don't worry about that," he told him, "Your mum and I have got it all under control. When she's ready for it, I'll stick my meat in."

"That's what scares me."

"Sorry?"

"Oh, nothing," Derek said, "I'm just thinking aloud. I'd best go get changed."

"Okay. And don't worry about the cost of the chicken."

"Thanks."

"You can settle up with me later."

"Oh right, yes, of course."

*

Seven o'clock and Angela still wasn't home from work. She'd texted to say the meeting had gone on longer than expected and she was now stuck again in the roadworks so they should start dinner without her. Margaret and her boyfriend were due any minute. Derek felt nervous. Although Margaret was a friend he wasn't very good playing host on his own. Yes, Ursula and Bert were there but it was his and Angela's house and their dinner party. They were the hosts and Derek needed her by his side. It had been the same when he was married and Leanne had organised many a dinner party, either for friends or for business acquaintances. Derek had always been happy being coat collector and wine uncorker, leaving Leanne to greet the guests. He still hadn't answered her text yet. What had she meant by wanting to meet up again? Maybe it was just friendly but why did she end the text with a kiss?

Margaret arrived at seven-fifteen, all smiles on the arm of Paul, a rather short, bald man of about fifty who was wearing a three–piece navy blue suit with a light-blue shirt and tie. He was a little over dressed, Derek felt, who was standing there greeting the couple in a white shirt and black jeans.

"If we're a bit late it's my fault," Paul explained, as they walked through to the kitchen, Derek and Margaret both towering over him, "I was with one of my most annoying clients earlier who goes on and on, but she spends a lot of money with my firm so I have to pander to her. I must admit I do struggle with her tall stories."

"I can see why," Derek replied, before he could stop himself. "Sorry?"

"This is my mother, Ursula," he added, quickly, "And that's Angela's father, Bert over there. I'm afraid Angela has been delayed but she'll be here soon."

"Dinner smells wonderful," Margaret said, sitting down at the dining table and taking off her sparkly black cardigan that she'd had draped across her shoulders.

Derek noticed that Bert quickly sat down at the head of the table so that he was beside Margaret. What was he going to ask her? Mind you Margaret was no pushover and she'd soon see through him if he tried to spin her some con story. Ursula sat down at the opposite end to talk with Paul, leaving Derek to get the drinks.

"That's a glass of dry white for you is it Margaret?" he asked. She nodded, "And what can I get you Paul, wine, beer, or are you a short man…I mean would you prefer a whisky or brandy or…"

"A glass of white wine is fine with me."

Derek quickly turned round to hide his reddening face. He hoped Angela wasn't going to be much longer.

With drinks served Derek sat down across from Paul. Bert had engaged Margaret in conversation. Derek overheard him asking about the amount of medication the residents needed between them.

"Do you store a large stash at the Home?"

"No," Margaret told him, "We get a weekly delivery from the pharmacy."

"Oh, shame."

The timer on the oven pinged and Ursula stood up.

"That's the chicken ready," she said, "I'll serve up Derek. I'll leave you to make small talk with Paul."

Derek fought hard not to laugh out loud at his mother's choice of words.

"So Paul," he said, "Whereabouts do you live?"

"I'm based in a village in Surrey," he replied, "More a hamlet really, it's tiny."

"I suppose it would have to be."

"It's not far from Guildford, but I'm hardly ever there to be honest with you. This job means a lot of travel around the country for me. The rest of the team are based solely in the London office. With the amount of traffic on the roads these days I sometimes feel I've been given the short straw."

Derek bit his lip.

"But then if it wasn't for the travelling I would never have met Margaret."

Paul placed his hand on top of hers and gave it a squeeze. Margaret smiled back at him before resuming her conversation with Bert.

"We don't get a lot of time together," Paul continued, "But we do make the most of it when we do."

"Short and sweet."

"Exactly Derek, exactly."

Perhaps this evening was going to be rather fun after all.

Derek helped his mum bring the plates over to the table and just before he sat down, the front door opened. He headed out into the hallway.

"I'm so sorry," Angela said, shoving her handbag and briefcase into the third bedroom, "I was caught up by…what's that airbed doing in there?"

"Ah, well. Good news, the sewing room is now officially

being called a bedroom again. Mum's made Bert feel welcome," Derek told her, "But don't worry about that now."

"Oh my God! What's wrong with her?"

"Angela! She didn't want Bert's makeshift bed on show in the lounge."

"Well she could have just thrown the duvet and pillow in here, not set up a bed. He'll never bloody go now."

"Angela, look I'm sorry you've had a busy day and a horrendous journey home but we do have guests in the other room. Let's concentrate on them for tonight okay?"

Angela sighed, wearily. She smiled and kissed Derek.

"I'm sorry, you're right," she said, "Dinner smells wonderful. I assume you let Ursula cook."

"Of course. She's done her special chicken."

"Great. Well, let's enjoy a pleasant evening."

The two of them walked through into the kitchen.

"So sorry I'm late," Angela told the room, "Work commitments I'm afraid."

Margaret beamed at her.

"Angela, this is Paul," she said.

Paul turned round. The smile fell away from his face and the colour drained from his cheeks.

"Oh my God," he said, "You're that Angela."

"Oh, er, it's you Paul," Angela replied, obviously embarrassed, "Erm, it's…well…nice to see you again."

Margaret let out a little gasp. Derek closed his eyes. This was it. This was his worst nightmare come true. He always knew they'd bump into one of Angela's ex-clients one day. Mind you, he hadn't expected to be serving him dinner.

"Oh," Ursula piped up, brightly, "Do you two know each other then?"

The evening was about to get even worse. Derek couldn't move or say anything.

"Oh well," Angela began, "We used to erm…well…work together."

"How lovely," Ursula said, unaware of the growing tension in the room, "You must have lots to talk about."

Perhaps in other countries Paul and Margaret would have stood up and left the house there and then, maybe there would have been a huge row or a hearty laugh when the situation was explained, but this was England and they did what most English people would do in polite society, they tried to ignore the situation and sat down to dinner.

Derek was unable to meet Paul's eyes across the table. Sat beside him, Angela was facing Margaret and seemed unable to look at her friend too.

"There now," Ursula said, quite happy and contented, "Eat up everybody, while it's hot."

Everyone picked up their knives and forks and began silently pushing the food around their plates, all except Bert, who was obviously enjoying the situation and grinned inanely as he added sour cream to his baked potato and salad to his plate.

"So Paul," Ursula said, after a few moments of silence, "You're in the same line of business as Angela."

Paul dropped the bowl of Caesar Salad onto the table with a clatter.

"Erm, not exactly," he replied.

"Perhaps you suffered the same problems as she did," Ursula continued, "Angela kept at it until the bottom fell out, didn't you dear."

Paul looked aghast.

"I'm so sorry," he said to Angela, "I didn't realise that could happen."

"Still, she's back in the saddle now."

"Are you?" Paul asked.

"Well, obviously in a slightly different way," Ursula told him, smiling, "Now she sells her stuff to the highest bidder?"

"Really?"

Paul looked confused. Derek wanted the ground to open up and swallow him. Why couldn't he just shout out that Angela worked at an auction house and that his mother wasn't talking about selling sex?

"I suppose it's a bit less personal than before but it's good commission isn't it," Ursula continued.

"Pimping?" Paul questioned.

"I'm not sure that's the right term," Ursula said, looking momentarily puzzled, "Still, it's all much of a muchness really. You love it anyway don't you Angela?"

Angela was struggling to find words to respond. She sat there with a stunned look on her face. Derek wished he, or anyone else at the table, could find a way to shut his mother up but it appeared everyone else's mind was as blank as his. Ursula was obviously enjoying her conversation.

"You're always eager to get your hands on something old, aren't you dear," she continued.

"Well I assume they've always been the most grateful," Paul reasoned.

"And often the money's better the older you go," Ursula told him, "I know it also depends on the number and the condition. After all, if you have a pair they're usually worth more."

"Two at a time? Yes I should damned well think it is more expensive."

"But of course if the condition isn't too good then you can't charge as much."

Paul looked perplexed, as well he might.

"Surely it doesn't work that way round," he queried.

"Well, if it's got a large crack you're not going to get much pleasure out of it, are you."

Paul's mouth dropped open.

"I hadn't really considered that," he said, quietly.

"Anyway," Ursula continued, smiling, "Angela's knowledge and enthusiasm is so infectious that I'm thinking of having another bash myself."

If Paul had had hair his eyebrows would have disappeared into it.

"I mean I'm no expert," she continued, "And I didn't have much success on my old dining table but you should have seen me with my hatpins."

Derek closed his eyes again and hoped he'd wake up somewhere else.

"That's not really the sort of thing I was into," he heard Paul say.

"Was it not? Oh, then you probably won't be interested in what else I've got tucked away."

If Derek was already struggling to find a way to end this conversation, Paul's reply shocked him into further silence.

"Well, not necessarily. What are we talking about here?"

Derek opened his eyes. Margaret gasped again. He hoped his mum was about to rush out and bring in her silver thimble collection and then they could all laugh about the misunderstanding but Ursula just giggled.

"Well," she said to Paul, "I'll give you a clue. They're silver, decorative and once you've got them onto the tip you can…"

"I'm afraid I don't feel very well," Margaret said, standing up.

Derek and Angela both stood up quickly as well.

"Take me home Paul," Margaret told him, rather aggressively, "I really need to get back home. I'm so sorry everyone."

"No it's fine," Angela said, as Paul reluctantly stood up, "I'm sorry too."

Margaret nodded.

"We'll speak later," she told her, picking up her cardigan, "Come on, let's go."

Angela walked them out to the hallway. Derek heard some whispered comments but couldn't make out what was being said as his mum was busily clearing the plates.

"I hope I didn't make the chicken too spicy," she said, looking forlornly at the plates of food, "No one seems to have touched a thing besides Bert."

"It was delicious," he called down the table to her.

Ursula smiled shyly back at him. Angela returned to the room.

"Well, that was a total disaster," she said, looking squarely at Derek.

Derek looked back at her, puzzled. Was she blaming him for all this?

"Would anyone like some cheesecake?" Ursula asked.

"Not for me," Angela said, "I've got a splitting headache. I think I'll go to bed."

She turned and left the room.

"I'd love some," Derek heard Bert say, as he followed her.

Upstairs Angela was already getting undressed when Derek entered the room.

"Well," she said, "That was a complete travesty of an

evening wasn't it."

"I know."

"I hope you're happy Derek."

"What! I knew that look downstairs meant you blamed me for this. How dare you!"

Angela looked up calmly from where she was sitting on the bed, taking off her tights.

"If you'd only told your mother the truth…"

"And how would that have changed tonight? Margaret would still be devastated and you would still have been embarrassed."

Angela stood up and moved over to the dressing table.

"If you want to blame someone for tonight," Derek continued, "Then take a look at the reflection in that mirror. You're the one that slept with him for money Angela. Tonight's on you. Don't you dare try and lay your mucky past at my door."

Angela's shoulders slumped. She turned and faced him.

"And there it is, Derek. You couldn't have left it at 'Tonight's on you' could you. You had to call my past mucky."

Derek sat on the bed and put his head in his hands.

"I'm just angry at you trying to blame it all on me. I'm sick to death of everything always being my fault, that's all."

"The truth is," he heard Angela say, "Is that you haven't accepted my past yourself have you."

Derek sighed as he looked up.

"Don't you start," he told her, "I had Dora telling me the same thing today."

"Well perhaps you'll listen to her if you're not going to listen to me."

"Oh for fuck's sake," Derek was on his feet, "I'm here living with you and loving you, isn't that proof enough that I accept your past? Does it matter that I still wouldn't want all and sundry knowing about it? Can't I accept you but still be embarrassed by you?"

"Oh, so I embarrass you do I?"

"That's not what I meant. I meant what you used to do not... well not you."

"How eloquently put."

"Fine, have it your own way," Derek walked over to the door, "Sit there and blame me for everything, why not. I'm sorry for everything, alright? I'm sorry I made this evening happen, even though you asked Margaret and her fella over, I'm sorry I made you a prostitute, even though it was years before we knew each other, I'm sorry that I booked a holiday on a coach trip and met you."

The last sentence hung in the air. Angela's bottom lip began to tremble.

"You're sorry that you ever met me are you," she said.

Derek sighed again.

"That's it, I'm done. I can't even say anything without it being misconstrued. You know I fucking love you. I love you when a lot of men wouldn't, knowing what you used to do, but if that's not enough then I'm done. What else can I possibly give you?"

"How about some respect," Angela whispered.

Derek was too angry to respond. He turned and left the room. Halfway down the stairs he sat down and pulled his mobile phone out of his trousers pocket.

Hi Leanne. Will be at my apartment this weekend. Hope we can meet up. Derek x

Chapter 4

Derek slept in the lounge that night. He didn't want to alert Ursula and Bert to his argument with Angela so waited until they'd gone to their respective beds before hunkering down on the sofa. The next morning he made sure he was up before anyone else. Upstairs he dressed in silence. He knew Angela was awake and watching him. Before he left the room to go to work he said,

"I'm going to go back to my apartment later today and stay there for the weekend; get properly started on the decorating."

"Okay," Angela replied.

"I'll use the van from work. I've got to get some designs for Margaret finished as well. It'll be easier to do that back at home."

"Fine."

"I'll pack a bag at lunchtime."

"If that's what you want."

The silence continued for what felt like an age. Eventually Angela sighed and got out of bed but before she could speak, Derek strode past her and out of the room without kissing her goodbye.

*

Derek would rather have avoided Margaret today but he had to let her know he was leaving early. Right now he wasn't sure what was happening between him and Angela but maybe a break away from her and everything else in Tenhamshire would help him think straight. It would be good to catch up with Leanne again anyway, and her young son, Nathan. He was a really sweet little boy, in that lovely eighteen months old stage, before the 'terrible twos' kicked in.

Derek didn't like lying. The apartment wasn't in that much of a mess, not for renting anyway. It was after the previous tenants left that Derek had returned to check up on the state of the place and had bumped into Leanne and her son in town. They hadn't had the nicest of divorces but she was on her own again now, her new man having gone off to Australia. Leanne had suggested a coffee and, after a quiet start, the two of them had ended up chatting away together quite easily in the coffee shop. They'd got on better than they had in years. The divorce was in the past. Catching up on each other's lives, their conversation over a morning coffee progressed into a long chat over a sandwich lunch.

Nathan had been so well behaved the whole time. Okay he spilt his milk over Derek but that had just been an accident. It had made them all laugh anyway. It was then that Derek had decided to repaint the apartment. Talking with Leanne that day, he'd almost forgotten he'd moved away to Tenhamshire. He hoped he could recapture that feeling this weekend.

On his way to see Margaret, Derek was accosted by Dora in the main hallway.

"Are those workmen still out the front putting up the new sign?" she asked.

Derek had passed the van on the way in.

"Yes," he told her, and then a thought struck him, "You're not planning some sort of ambush are you?"

Dora looked affronted.

"Derek, I'm shocked and appalled by your opinion of me." Then she grinned.

"But that sounds like a great idea."

As Derek opened his mouth to reply, Dora interrupted him.

"Calm down, I'm not planning anything. I'm not in the mood anyway. We had a tragedy here last night."

Derek remembered the death sweepstake.

"Oh, is it Tommy Jefferies?"

Dora nodded.

"Yes," she told him, "It's such a shame."

"Well I'm sorry for your loss."

"Thank you."

"At least he's out of pain now," Derek added.

Dora looked momentarily confused.

"What do you mean?" she said, "The old bastard made it through the night. I'm a fiver down, that's the tragedy!"

"Oh for God's sake," Derek replied, indignantly, "I thought you meant he'd died. Well, it serves you right for cheating."

"I didn't. Sir Jasper found out nothing yesterday. While he did manage to hide out in the nurses' staffroom, all he heard one of them say was that she thought her breasts were getting bigger. It was too much for him and he fainted inside the cupboard."

"Well, at least it was only five pounds you lost."

"What do you mean, 'only'? I'm not made of money."

"Yes you are," Derek told her, "You're worth a fortune."

Dora waved her hand dismissively.

"Margaret gives me a small allowance each month but she's spent most of my Billy's money on this place. I'm sure that new sign out front cost an absolute fortune," she made a huffing sound, "A waste of money if you ask me. It's no different from the old one, except this one adds the word 'Welcome' to it. 'Welcome to God's Waiting Room.'"

"You've seen it then?"

Dora's eyes widened for a split second and then she let out a loud laugh.

"You almost had me there, Derek," she told him, "I think 'God's Waiting Room' sounds a darn sight better than 'The Whispering Wood Retirement Home.' Blimey, what a mouthful."

"Angela wanted a name for the coach house when we moved in," Derek told her, "Rather than just 'Number One, Coach House Mews.'"

"What did she want, 'Dunwhorin'?"

Derek winced. Dora laughed again.

"Come on, it's just a joke. I love that Angela was able to use man's basic need to make herself a good living, using them rather than they using her."

"Well let's not get into that again," Derek said.

Dora nodded.

"Right, that's not why I stopped you anyway. I wanted to know what happened at your place last night. Margaret and Paul came back early and they had words before he left. I know she's given him the push but she's been shut up in her office all morning and hasn't spoken to anyone. I don't know what happened."

Derek sighed.

"It turns out Paul and Angela had met before," he said.

Dora looked questioningly at him before realisation dawned. She laughed out loud again only this time she didn't stop. Eventually Derek had to help her into one of the chairs in the hallway.

53

"Oh my God," she said, after she'd got her breath back, "That's hilarious."

"None of us were laughing."

"That Paul, paying for it? The horny, little devil."

"It's not funny, Dora," Derek told her.

"The hell it's not," she replied, "I can just imagine it; you lot, all sitting round the table together, trying to ignore the situation."

She started laughing again. Derek felt the corners of this mouth start to twitch. Perhaps it was just Dora's infectious laughter or maybe the situation was funny. If you took out the prostitution part, one woman introducing her new boyfriend to a friend who had already slept with him was kind of funny. If it had happened to someone else wouldn't Derek have been laughing like Dora?

His lips creased into a smile and a giggle rose to the surface. Very quickly Derek found himself laughing alongside Dora until tears rolled down his face. Several residents crossing the hallway to the dining room looked at them with disgust but that only made them laugh even more.

"Oh God," Dora finally said, wiping her eyes with a handkerchief while fanning her face with the other hand, "That sort of thing could only happen to you and my Margaret, Derek. I know I've always wanted her to date more but honestly, she can't half pick 'em."

"I wish I could have seen the funny side last night," he told her, "I'm afraid Angela and I had words over it."

Dora nodded.

"I can understand it being a shock," she admitted, "But I suppose there's always the possibility of bumping into someone you've known intimately when you've slept with a lot of people."

Derek winced again, a feeling of disgust and embarrassment passing over him in a wave. Would there ever be a time when he didn't feel that way? Sometimes in the bedroom he couldn't always perform when an image of Angela with someone else entered his mind. She always told him she understood but really, it was no wonder they argued when they were both so frustrated. This weekend away to cool off was becoming more and more appealing. Still, now he saw the funny side of things he really ought to text Angela a nice message before leaving. It was sale day at the auction house and she'd be too busy to take a phone call, even if she wanted to speak to him.

"Margaret's problem is that she idolised her dad her entire life," Dora told him, "She still does. She wants to meet someone just like him but I'm afraid my Billy was a one-off. I thought this internet dating would be good for her but I think she's better off on her own."

"Perhaps she just needs a rest from dating for a while," Derek suggested.

"Or turn this place into a convent and have done with it." Derek smiled.

"And where would you go?" he asked.

"I'm going to hell Derek," Dora replied, "I've been told to go there often enough."

She winked and Derek laughed again. After being helped up from the chair, Dora headed off to the dining room to find Sir Jasper while Derek walked in the opposite direction, past the entrance to the kitchen and on through to the office area on the other side of the Home from where his outbuildings were. He knocked on Margaret's door and called through that it was him. He heard a 'Come in' and opened the door.

Margaret was sat behind her desk, staring intently at her computer screen. She wore half-moon glasses when at her computer and with her fair hair pulled back and up into a loose bun, she reminded Derek of his old headmistress. After last night he felt he was here to be punished. Mind you, hadn't Angela wanted him to take the blame?

"Come in and sit down Derek," Margaret said, "I won't be a moment. I'm just noting down a few ideas and figures."

Derek sat in the chair opposite her and waited quietly. It was a couple of minutes before Margaret took off her glasses and looked at him. She smiled.

"Well," she said, "That was an eventful evening wasn't it."

Derek smiled back.

"I'm sorry."

"You've got nothing to apologise for Derek."

"Well I'm sorry you and Paul had words last night."

"Oh you've heard about that have you?"

"If it's any consolation, so did Angela and I."

Margaret scowled.

"Of course that's not a consolation, Derek," she told him, "I don't want you two falling out. You're my best friends. These things happen. I'd have reacted the same way if Angela and Paul had just dated in the past rather than him paying her for… well, anyway; we weren't really that serious about each other now I come to look at it. No, it's time for me to concentrate on my work. That's what I was doing just now."

Margaret indicated the computer screen.

"Now that the Home has been made safe, secure and as medically advanced as it needs to be, it's time to think about the aesthetics. We've got to appeal to the wealthy and make this the place they choose to come and live out their twilight years.

I'm looking into upgrading the furniture and redecoration. I'm also considering the business potential of the outside."

"I'll get those plans to you re the gazebo on Tuesday, I..." Margaret nodded.

"Yes, yes, that's already been decided. I'm thinking about other business ideas. We rent a lot of acreage out to local farmers; what do you think about us taking it back and running our own farm instead?"

Margaret looked keenly at Derek. She was in business mode now rather than friend and the lion was just behind the eyes.

"Erm, well, I don't know. I couldn't look after it," Derek told her.

"I realise that. I mean have a proper farm, staffed by experienced people. I know you want to develop the old, walled Victorian garden and produce fruit and vegetables but with a farm we could grow even more of our own produce, raise animals, become self-sufficient, or perhaps sell our produce as a proper business. The animals may provide stimulation for our residents too, or perhaps we could charge the education authority to bring schools here on trips. I was also thinking about converting some of the outbuildings into self-contained apartments, or perhaps even having a wedding venue in the grounds somewhere. Maybe that could be incorporated into your designs for the gazebo area."

Margaret really was concentrating on her business. From what Dora had told him about Billy, Derek could see that Margaret was definitely her father's daughter. His head was spinning with all of this information.

"They all sound like ideas," was the only response he could come up with, "Erm I came here to ask if it was okay to leave early today. I want to head back to my apartment this weekend to get it ready for new tenants."

Margaret's eyes had been shining with her ideas but the glow left her.

"Well it's about time," she said, "I hope you're going to up the rent to claw back some of the money you're currently losing by leaving it empty. That's a valuable resource you're wasting there, Derek."

Derek blushed. He really hated all of this lying but he couldn't exactly mention his desire to visit Leanne and Nathan, not to Angela's best friend sitting in front of him. Margaret nodded.

"That's fine for you to leave early. Ash is around anyway isn't he, for watering and generally keeping everything alive?"

"I'd do a residents' headcount tonight if I were you."

"Sorry?"

"Nothing. Yes, he's around."

Margaret nodded again.

"Good. Well, I'll meet with you on Tuesday as planned to discuss the new area."

Their chat at an end Derek returned home to pack a few things for the weekend, leaving a note for his mother who appeared to have gone out with Bert again. He got back into the van and texted Angela. When her reply came later, Derek opened 'Messages' on his mobile. Angela's text appeared just above Leanne's. Leanne had ended her last message to Derek with a kiss. Angela's entire message was just a smiley face.

*

Sales day at the auction house was always busy but especially so for Angela today. After the general sale there was a specialist ceramics and glass auction, the area that Angela worked in. Charles, the man she worked with when valuing items was going to act as auctioneer. Angela considered him her superior. He'd spent his entire career at this auction house and there was little he didn't know about ceramics. He was sixty-five but looked older. Angela thought he had the appearance of an old-fashioned university professor; one of those men who, if he sneezed, would send up a cloud of dust from his body. About to retire, Angela tried to learn as much as she could from him. Although his knowledge was vast he didn't have a lot of patience and didn't suffer fools gladly. He was always happier when Angela dealt with members of the public who brought their goods in to be valued on open days.

"Most of the items are worthless pieces of shit," he would often tell her, a little too loudly, "And the owners aren't much better."

Fortunately Tenhamshire was a county with a vast array of manor houses and old families so there were still a lot of genuine antiques to be sold to keep her mentor happy. He liked and admired Angela and she adored him. He'd never married and his retirement plans consisted of writing a large tome on Earthenware through the ages.

Angela usually sat up with Charles on the rostrum to ensure he didn't miss a bid from the floor. She was often in charge of the internet bidding too as Charles had no interest in computers and technology. When Ben Jacobson, the main partner at the auction house, had decided to install a new computer system for internet sales he'd wanted a photograph of each member of staff to be added to the new company website alongside a short, personal biography. Charles was the only one who had refused to have his picture taken.

Today though, Angela was standing in front of the crowd and displaying the more delicate items on sale. Usually this job was performed by a sales assistant but as there was only Clive on offer Charles had asked Angela to do it instead.

"I'm not letting that oversized oaf near any of the pieces," he'd told her, "The man can't scratch his genitals without dropping a bollock."

Angela was quite happy to just hold things up today rather than be involved in the actual sale. Her mind hadn't really been on her work all morning. She hated fighting with Derek but it seemed to be happening more and more often. She'd been so excited to move into the coach house with him but then Ursula had come to stay. It wasn't Ursula's fault of course but Angela felt things would have been better if she and Derek had had more time together as a couple on their own. They certainly wouldn't have been as stressed out as they were now and last night's events would probably have been laughed off... eventually.

Angela sighed. If only Derek would tell his mother about her past then she would know he accepted her. That's why she couldn't go behind his back and tell Ursula herself. It had to come from him. She feared he didn't accept her. She'd been about to apologise to him this morning before kissing him goodbye but Derek had brushed past her before she'd had a chance. That rejection had hurt like a knife to the ribs.

In her life Angela had only ever trusted two men. The first one she tried not to think about too often. He was the reason she'd taken twenty years to trust again. Derek was different. At least she'd thought he was, but that brush off this morning had felt like an utter rejection and left Angela feeling more worthless and ashamed than she ever had with any of her escort clients. Now Derek was running off back to his old apartment. He'd said he was going home. Wasn't the coach house home? Would he return? Angela was startled to realise she didn't know the answer.

The ceramics auction was about to start. The building they were standing in was basically a large warehouse split up internally into separate rooms. A reception area greeted guests at the front and beside that was the valuers' room where members of the public could bring in their items they wished to sell and get an estimated price from the relevant expert. Directly behind this was the vast salesroom where Angela was currently stood. Beyond this, at the back of the building was a staircase leading up to a mezzanine floor where the boss, Ben Jacobson had his office and where there was also a staffroom with lockers and kitchen area. In the salesroom today it was standing room only for the potential customers. Angela made a huge effort to put her private problems out of her mind.

"Right now ladies and gentlemen," Charles said, into the microphone from up on his rostrum, "We have a number of items to get through in the ceramics and glassware sale today. We'll start with a rather lovely pair of Royal Worcester painted ewers. I must say, it's not often I'm lucky enough to get my hands round such a pretty pair."

A faint titter passed through the crowd. Charles sold these and several other items before moving onto the next lot.

"Next up is a figurine of a rhino in amber-coloured glass, maker unknown but definitely of the art deco period. Where is it? Oh it's up here. I'll pass it down to you Angela, my dear. That's right; let me give you the horn."

Laughter ran through the crowd but Charles didn't understand why. He did his best to carry on but the mood of the audience had turned playful.

"Lot forty-seven is a beautiful pair of French, silver and cut glass claret jugs."

Angela held them up carefully.

"These really are exquisite and well worth a good look," Charles continued, "Can everyone see Angela's jugs?"

The crowd laughed out loud again. Angela stood there, feeling her face turning red with embarrassment.

"Please everybody," Charles called out, clearly rattled, "Could you settle down. There's no reason for this laughter. This is a serious auction. You're not going to see a quality pair of jugs finer than Angela's. Take a few moments to admire their beauty."

"Why don't you jump up and down a bit darling?" one man called out, and the crowd erupted into laughter once more.

Charles banged his gavel for quiet although it took quite a while for the laughter to die down. After selling the jugs he moved onto the next item.

"This is number forty-eight in your catalogue, a mixed lot of Walter Moorcroft bowls. Now then, where are they? Ah, right in front of where I'm sitting. Okay ladies and gentlemen, if you could all look right under the desk in front of me, you should get an eyeful of my bowls. Oh please everyone, this mirth is ridiculous! This is a serious auction, not a performance at the local comedy club. Now then, my bowls are on display; who wants them. Oh, stop it now!"

Angela had never been so pleased for an auction to be over with. Charles remained in a foul mood. She watched him stomp past the crowd as he left the room, taking a swig from his George the fifth silver hipflask. Angela quickly grabbed her phone from her desk drawer and escaped the auction house and headed down to one of the sandwich shops in the high street for a late lunch. She had two messages.

The first was from Derek, telling her he was sorry they'd rowed last night and that telling Dora today had helped him see the funny side of the situation.

Well, Angela thought, that was a start.

However, he was still going to head down to his apartment as planned to sort out the decorating and he'd again described it as 'going home.' What did that mean? Angela knew she shouldn't have taken her bad mood out on him last night and it was good of Derek to apologise first, but it was only by text. After brushing her off this morning, Angela wondered if he still couldn't face her. Not sure how best to respond to the text, she sent him a smiley face image and hoped that conveyed the right message.

The second text was from Margaret. She too was apologising for yesterday. Angela was starting to feel guilty. All of these people were telling her they were sorry when she felt like it was all her fault. Margaret asked her if she wanted to meet for a drink in the village pub over the weekend, just the two of them as she knew Derek was going to be out of town.

Angela smiled as she sat eating her salad in the window seat of the sandwich shop. She knew Margaret was making herself available in case she wanted to discuss her relationship with Derek. Angela realised she hadn't been out on her own with Margaret since before the move into the coach house. A boozy catch up would be nice. She really did enjoy being here in Tenhamshire and having her best friend living close by. She knew she loved Derek and that he loved her too. They both wanted their relationship to work. Perhaps they both just needed to make a bit more of an effort.

There was an e mail message waiting for her from her boss, Ben Jacobson when she sat down at her desk after lunch. Someone wanted a home valuation done for a large number of antiques that his late mother had owned and could she travel down to Ryan Harbour on Monday? She'd been asked for personally. Was she already getting a reputation for herself in the world of antiques? Perhaps things were looking up.

Chapter 5

The apartment smelled musty. Derek opened all of the windows. It didn't make much difference; there was hardly a breeze blowing and the heat of the June day hung in the air. He sighed as he stared around the small lounge. This place had never been happy for him, the diminutive apartment he'd moved into in a converted, nineteen fifties house in Hornchurch after divorcing Leanne. She'd bought him out of the large, four-bedroomed house they'd both owned in Upminster and he'd moved in here. Why had he done that? Well, he hadn't needed a mortgage for this tiny one bed; that was the first reason, and it was close to his mum's house in Romford. Derek couldn't remember any of the other reasons. Still, at least it meant he'd kept a roof over his head when the redundancy came through from the accounting firm he'd worked for, just after the divorce had been finalised. It was here that he'd decided to start afresh and enrolled on the garden design course. Needing a break from the confines of the four, square walls he'd also booked himself onto a short, coach holiday in Tenhamshire. That's why he was living there now, with Angela; working at a job that he actually enjoyed doing.

The apartment still had a depressing atmosphere for him though. Previous tenants had been happy enough living here, the first one even showing an interest in buying it. It hadn't been the right time for Derek to sell but now he regretted that decision. There really was nothing that wrong with the décor but Derek knew he'd have to decorate now anyway to cover up his lying.

He walked into the tiny, square kitchen off of the lounge and put some bread, milk and cheese that he'd bought at the supermarket at the top of the road, into the fridge. He put a small packet of tea bags and a tin of baked beans into the cupboard beside the cooker. What would Angela, his mum and Bert be eating this evening? Something more substantial and a darned sight tastier, that was for sure. What the hell was he doing here? One big argument with Angela and he'd stormed off like a spoilt child. Running away, isn't that what he was doing? All he had to do was tell his mum about Angela's past life and everything would be okay.

But would it be? While Angela seemed to think so, Derek couldn't agree. This wasn't just about his mother. Wouldn't there always be someone else who came into their lives that needed to be told about Angela's life as a prostitute? Would they ever be able to put her past completely behind them? Was the relationship worth all this angst?

Derek sighed as he added water to the kettle. He was here for a break, he reasoned, a chance to forget all about Tenhamshire for a while. He liked being able to forget about Tenhamshire for a while.

The old, plastic kettle was a slow boiler so he phoned Leanne before making tea. She answered the phone straightaway.

"Hi Derek, I've just got in. Are you still coming down?"

"I'm already here," he replied, "I left work early today."

"Me too. Mind you I've had to bring a pile of stuff home with me to sort out later. Hang on just a minute. Nathan, no, put mummy's purse down. That's not a toy."

Derek could imagine the scene being played out at the other

end of the line.

"Sorry," she said, "The little bugger always makes a beeline for my handbag when I leave it on the floor. Nathan, no, why do you always manage to grab a twenty. Hang on Derek."

He could hear Leanne's voice at a distance and then a howl of indignation. The crying got louder and then Leanne's voice called loudly down the phone.

"Someone needs a nap, Derek. Why don't you pop over in half an hour for a coffee? His Nibs should be asleep by then."

Derek agreed and rang off. As he switched off the kettle at the plug, he smiled.

*

It felt strange to drive up to his old house, knowing it was no longer his. The house was a detached, nineteen thirties build; white with black, mock-Tudor beams and wide, circular bay windows to the front lounge and main bedroom upstairs. The avenue was full of similar houses, each set back from the tree-lined road, making the street seem wider than it really was. It was one of the better turnings in the area and Derek couldn't help feeling a tinge of sadness that he no longer lived here.

The garage attached to the side of the house wasn't big enough for a car and Derek had to squeeze the van onto the driveway behind Leanne's light blue BMW SUV. She opened the front door just as he was about to knock.

Leanne was dressed casually in jeans and t-shirt, but both items had well-known designer names on them. Her long, brown hair was pulled back in a ponytail but it had been carefully brushed and gelled so that not one frizzy strand poked out anywhere. The look was definitely stylised casual. She was obviously still finding time between being single mum and full time businesswoman to go to the gym. Derek had stopped going not long after they'd split up.

"Derek, you look like shit. Come on in."

Before he could reply, Derek caught a glance of his reflection in the hallway mirror as he stepped inside. He noticed the dark circles under his eyes from last night's lack of sleep. The blue shirt he had changed into back at the coach house was badly creased from the four hour drive in the van. He looked down at his shoes and saw he was still wearing his gardening boots, stained from months spent in dirt. How come he hadn't noticed any of these things before leaving the apartment?

"I'm sorry," he said, "It's been a strange day."

"Well come into the kitchen and have a coffee. I think you need one. Erm, could you take those shoes off first? Thanks. My God is that a hole in the sock. Talk about rustic living in the countryside."

Leanne led the way from the panelled hallway through to the back of the house and the kitchen. It was a smaller room than the one at the coach house, with the kitchen cabinetry down two walls in an L shape. There was just enough room for an island with two stools at the back. With the number of dinner parties she'd always hosted, Leanne had preferred a separate dining room where none of the guests could see the clutter of used pots and pans. The kitchen was brand new and was obviously a bespoke, top-of-the-range model. Derek sat up on one of the white leather stools while Leanne poured him a coffee.

"I'm glad you're down this weekend," she said, "I've got one of these plus one dinner invites for tomorrow night and I've been let down at the last minute. Would you mind stepping in?"

Derek hadn't expected to hear that. It was one thing catching up for coffee but a dinner party? Wouldn't that be like a date? Is that how Leanne saw things between them?

"Erm, well, I…"

"I wouldn't normally ask at such short notice," she told him, "But although it's a casual dinner it could prove useful, workwise. I want someone I can trust and someone that Nathan likes."

This really was sounding like a date but Derek had to admit, he felt flattered rather than worried. Mind you, why did it matter if Nathan liked him? They'd only met once before. Oh well.

"Of course," he told her, smiling, "I'll be glad to help out."

"Really? That's great."

She placed his coffee down and got up onto the stool beside him.

"So," she said, patting the side of his right thigh affectionately, "How's the quiet life in Tenhamshire? They obviously don't have any gyms near you."

"It's not as quiet as you might think," he replied.

He must have said it with some feeling as Leanne asked, "Is anything wrong?"

Derek shook his head.

"It's nothing," he told her, "Just a difference of opinion."

"And how's the job? Are you missing finance yet?"

Derek shook his head again.

"Come on, it's half year-end soon. You always loved a good audit."

He laughed.

"Not at all," he told her, "I love working in the grounds at the Home. I get to design new areas. It's great."

Leanne wrinkled her nose.

"Well I don't know how you stand it," she said, "Out in all weathers. What's wrong with being in a nice, warm, dry office?"

"Well, obviously it has its minuses as well as its plusses," Derek reasoned.

"No bonus, probably no pension plan. Well, you can't afford to pay into one now can you? What do gardeners earn?"

"It's not about money."

"Well I'd never have let you do that as a job if you were still married to me. This Angela must be some lady."

"She is," Derek told her, meaning it.

Leanne fell silent and sipped her coffee. Derek didn't want to create a bad atmosphere.

"It's not all sweetness and light," he conceded, "But I like my work. At the Home next Wednesday, there's a trip to Tenham House for the day. That'll be enjoyable."

"Haven't you been there before?"

"I'm not going, just the residents. I'll get a day away from them all. It'll be great."

Leanne laughed.

"They can't be that bad," she said, "Besides, you have a pensioner living with you."

"Only temporarily…How did you know about that?"

Leanne sipped her coffee.

"Your mum told me the last time she called."

Derek put his mug down.

"Mum called you? Why?"

"Ursula's always kept in touch," Leanne told him, "Not like every week but I usually get a call once a month or so. It's sweet. Well, we have known each other for over twenty-five years. I really ought to ring her first sometimes but, you know how it is."

"She's not staying long," Derek said, "Mum's looking at new apartments all of the time."

"She doesn't want to move into the Home you work at then?"

"Couldn't afford it even if she wanted to. The Whispering Wood Retirement Home is an expensive place to live and it's going to get a lot dearer too if the owner has her way. Nope, only someone such as a high-earning member of the legal profession could afford to live there."

Derek winked at Leanne. She tutted and then smiled.

"I'm not exactly a barrister or a judge, Derek," she told him, "I head up a legal team in an investment bank."

"Please, you make it sound like you run a small section. You're a director heading up a team of fifty. You're raking it in."

Leanne leant forwards to grab the cream jug. Her top moved up above her jeans at the back and Derek couldn't help staring, remembering the times the two of them were naked together upstairs in this house. He shivered as a thrill passed through him.

"You could have been part of all that Derek," Leanne continued, sitting back up again and adding some cream to her mug, "Many a time I offered to recommend you to a contact in finance. You're a smart man and a good accountant."

Derek shook his head.

"No," he said, "I didn't want the long hours and the stress. That's what my dad's job was like as he tried to create a lifestyle for us, but I hardly saw him. I liked working at Sanderford & Kelly. It was mostly nine to five."

"Those two old fossils," Leanne said, remembering, "I think the second half of the twentieth century and the new millennium passed them by. I wasn't shocked when they went out of business. I was just surprised it took so long."

She paused before adding,

"And you really don't miss that sort of job?"

Derek smiled as he shook his head.

"Not even one bit?" Leanne pushed.

"Not even one bit. To be honest, when I first began studying for my accountancy degree at university I didn't have any intention of going into a job like that."

Leanne was about to take another sip of her coffee but stood the mug down again.

"You never told me that," she said.

"No, well I did it more to please mum and dad. I knew a degree would prove useful to fall back on, particularly an accounting one but I wasn't planning on a finance career. That all changed after my dad's death though," Derek confessed, "Mum told me that dad had a few outstanding debts. Although she managed to pay them off herself somehow, I could see it was a struggle. She made sure I stayed on at university to get my degree and I felt that afterwards I owed it to her to go into a safe and secure job, so I put aside any thoughts of striking out on my own. Ironic really that I lost the 'safe and secure' job."

Leanne nodded.

"Still," she said, "At least that led you on to your new life. Without the redundancy you would never have moved to Tenhamshire. Well, there was obviously the divorce as well."

Derek's smile wavered slightly. Leanne was right, he wouldn't have moved to Tenhamshire. What would have happened if he and she had stayed together? She was still an attractive woman. Would it have only taken him accepting a more stressful, higher paying role at an investment bank for their marriage to have worked? The two of them could have still been sitting here together now but as a married couple and with their own child sleeping upstairs. Derek wondered if he should get Leanne to ask her question again. 'And you really don't miss that sort of job?' Perhaps he'd been too quick to shake his head.

*

"I think it's the next turning on the left," Ursula said, squinting at the hastily scribbled note in her hand, "That's what the estate agent told me over the phone."

Angela sighed as she switched on her indicator.

"Well I hope it is," she replied, "This is the fourth left turn we've tried."

This wasn't how she'd planned on spending her Saturday morning; trailing Ursula around an apartment viewing.

"Carla, the estate agent, seemed very eager for me to see this apartment today now that it's come back onto the market."

"She'll be worried about her commission," Angela told her, "With the previous buyer pulling out at the last minute, the agency will want to find a new buyer as soon as possible."

That was one of the reasons Angela had offered to drive today. Ursula had seemed very flustered after the phone call this morning, as if she'd been bullied into seeing this apartment. Angela was worried about who this estate agent was. Yes, she wanted Ursula out of her house but she didn't want her conned into buying something she didn't want.

"We'll give you our honest opinion about it," Bert called out, from the back seat.

Angela hadn't actually invited her father to come along but it was probably better to have him where she could see him. There was no telling what he'd get up to if left alone in her house. Mind you she could have done without Ursula asking him all about her childhood as they drove to the viewing. Twice she'd had to bite her tongue and not moan about how Bert was hardly there for the majority of it.

"Always had your nose in a book, didn't you Ange, history ones mostly," he'd said, as they'd driven through the high street in Tenham.

"They were the only ones you had trouble selling on after your plundering of the local library," she'd replied.

"I like to see children reading books," Ursula had told them, "Rather than always playing games on their mobile phones and those computer thingies, what are they called, maxi pads?"

"Ipads," Angela had corrected.

"That's it."

The conversation about her upbringing had fortunately stopped after the first wrong turning and now everyone was concentrating on finding the right route. Angela continued on down the road Ursula had just indicated she turn onto. They passed rows of semi-detached, nineteen sixties bungalows with large front gardens and long driveways. At the bottom was a dead end but just beside it was a driveway that disappeared off to the right.

"I think that's it," Ursula said.

"Really?"

It looked to Angela like a driveway to someone's house but she drove onto it. A few yards down it veered sharply to the left and continued on straight, past the backs of gardens that belonged to the houses on the main road they'd turned off of. There were no streetlights, Angela noticed. Was this the main entrance in to the apartment block? It wouldn't be safe at nights if you were walking. It looked dodgy enough in the daylight.

Just as Angela was about to say she thought this must be wrong, the road expanded into a large square area with garages and parking bays. At the far side stood a three storey apartment block, also built around the nineteen sixties; flat, square and with white weatherboarding beneath the wide windows on each floor.

"Well, erm, it has good parking," Ursula admitted.

Angela would quite happily have turned the car round there and then, and left, but a young woman in a black skirt suit ran over to them, waving, her long black hair blowing in the breeze. She was holding a see-through folder full of papers in her other hand but when she stumbled on her high heels the folder fell and papers flew around the car park. She was frantically picking them up when the three of them walked over to her.

"I must get every single one back," she told them, in a fast-talking, high-pitched voice, "Some of the sheets have private addresses on."

Angela, Ursula and Bert helped Carla find all the pieces of paper. Once the folder was full up again Carla breathed a huge sigh of relief.

"Oh my God," she said, "That would have been terrible if I'd not got them back. What am I like?"

Even in her high heels, Carla was still only about five foot three. She stood there, panting heavily in front of them, her ample chest going up and down. Bert appeared hypnotised by the movement. Carla looked at her watch.

"We really should get inside," she told them, "I've got

another client arriving in twenty minutes."

"I'm sure you won't even need ten minutes," Angela said, looking up at the building with disdain, "That's if you want to go in at all, Ursula. That's a long road into here and there were no streetlights."

"Oh there's another entrance at the front," Carla told them, brightly, "This is the back. The front faces the main road and there's a car park opposite it for the shops."

She grinned at Ursula.

"Very handy to have amenities close by when you're past it isn't it."

"If there's a car park on the main road, why on earth did you send us round to the hard-to-find back entrance?" Angela asked her.

Carla's face fell.

"Oh, I don't really know," she said.

She flicked through her folder of notes.

"I'm sure there was a reason," she said, "Ah, this is it."

She pulled out a page and read it aloud as she spoke.

"Show them the parking at the rear. For God's sake don't tell them it's on a busy main road otherwise you'll never get them in through the door…oh, I guess I should have read that bit to myself."

Angela grabbed Ursula's arm.

"Come on, we're leaving."

She pulled gently but Ursula didn't move.

"Oh we might as well look inside now we've come all this way," she said, "And poor Clara has come all this way too."

"She has another unsuspecting customer arriving in twenty minutes," Angela reminded her, "She has to be here, you don't."

"It might be worth a look," Bert told them, "I mean it's good

76

to see what you don't want as well as what you do. It could help focus your mind, looking at a shithole like this."

Carla beamed.

"That's the spirit," she said, and got the keys out of her pocket.

The apartment was on the second floor and there was no lift, just a narrow, winding staircase that left Angela wondering how anyone ever moved in or out with all of their bulky furniture. Carla was describing the stairwell to Ursula as 'charmingly bijou' from her notes, as she tripped up it in her heels.

Once inside, the apartment actually seemed quite spacious. The previous residents had already moved out and the place was empty of furniture and with no curtains at the windows to deaden the noise, Carla's voice echoed throughout the space. Angela remained in the lounge, only half listening to the sales pitch.

"As you can see the kitchen is modern and was updated only two years ago. Oh be careful of that cupboard with the metal-effect roller door on the front of it. The shutter is a bit stiff. I managed to trap a nipple under it earlier."

"Does it need kissing better?"

"Oh Bert, you are a card," Ursula joked.

Angela shook her head. There was no denying the apartment had been well maintained inside but it was so wrong for Ursula. Aside from the hard-to-find back entrance, Angela could hear the noise from the main road even with all of the windows closed. There was no character to the place either. It was just square room after square room inside a large, square box. Whilst Ursula had also looked at some brand new apartments, Angela had seen from the photographs of those that they had been thoughtfully designed, all brickwork and bay fronts with proper pitched roofs on top.

"It's this way to the bedrooms," Carla called out, "I've got a couple of beauties I want to show you."

"Are you okay Bert?" Ursula asked, concerned, "You've suddenly gone very red."

Angela thought about the coach house while she stared out of the lounge window onto the main road. That had a very modern interior but the outside was full of character. Although she really liked the place, left up to her, she'd have chosen somewhere with a few more features on the inside. Upon viewing she'd seen Derek's face light up when they'd seen the inside and knew it was the place he wanted. She went along with his enthusiasm for it and was genuinely pleased when their offer had been accepted. She knew once she'd added her own furniture it would become a great home for them and she believed it had. But now Derek kept referring to his old apartment as home in his texts and she wondered if the place was really right for them after all. Mind you if she told him of her fears it would surely only lead to another argument, with Derek saying she was over-reacting to a simple text message. She'd then get angry because she felt it **was** important and that he was mocking her.

Angela sighed. What was it about their relationship? They either didn't confide in one another or said too much and started arguing. There never seemed to be any middle ground. Were they trying too hard to please one another, or were they just trying too hard to make this relationship work. Surely it shouldn't be this difficult, not in the early years.

Angela shook her head. She didn't want to think that this had all been a mistake. She still loved Derek and knew that he loved her but something had to change, she just wasn't sure what that was.

"And now we're back in the spacious lounge diner," Carla said, entering the room with Ursula and Bert in tow, "So, what do you think?"

"Well it's a bit noisy," Ursula admitted, "And there are a lot of stairs for someone of my age. The parking area at the back is hazardous with no lighting and it's not really got the right feel for me. Sorry."

"No that's fine," Carla told her, making a note on one of her many pieces of paper, "I'll just pop you down as a maybe."

Chapter 6

Saturday morning saw Derek doing something he usually avoided if he could, clothes shopping. A casual dinner is what Leanne had said, but from old, Derek knew that just meant a tie was optional with the suit. As he tried on a couple of outfits he realised he was looking forward to tonight. It had been ages since he'd been to this sort of dinner. When he and Leanne had been married it was a weekly occurrence and often a strain but now it would make a nice change.

    As Derek paid for the suit and shirt on his credit card he smiled, imagining Leanne's reaction to this outfit when he knocked at the door tonight. He hoped Nathan would be awake so that they'd have time to get reacquainted. Their last meeting at the coffee shop that had extended to lunch as well had been so enjoyable. Derek hadn't seen Leanne laugh like that in a long time, when Nathan spilt his drink all over him. She had the cutest giggle. With Angela lately, all they seemed to do was row. When was the last time the two of them had had an evening out together?

    Derek nipped into the supermarket and purchased, what he thought was, an expensive bottle of red wine and then returned home to press the shirt, ready for tonight. Instead of measuring up and buying paint, he spent most of the afternoon cleaning the inside and outside of the van. He wasn't sure where the meal was tonight. Maybe they'd take a taxi but if Leanne wanted him to drive then he had to be prepared. He didn't want to show her up.

He felt a bit nervous, driving over to Leanne's house that evening, that sort of excited, nervous feeling. Should he have bought some flowers?

Don't be silly, Derek thought to himself, Leanne was taking him out for a meal, not cooking. He wasn't going to be spending the entire evening at home.

He was glad he'd paid a little extra and bought the better quality suit when Leanne opened the door. She was wearing a sleeveless, tight, black dress and had a burgundy wrap across her upper arms. She looked beautiful, elegant.

"You're dressed up," she told him, as she stood back and let Derek enter the hallway.

Derek smiled.

"Thank you. Well I thought I'd better, after yesterday."

"Oh, you've brought wine."

"Yes," Derek held up the bottle, "It's a Chateauneuf Du Pape. I hope that's okay."

"It's fine," Leanne replied, "But I'd rather you only have one glass."

She obviously wanted him to drive. Derek was so glad he'd cleaned the van. Or perhaps she wanted him to drive her flashy BMW.

"But you can always take it back home with you afterwards."

"Wouldn't that be rude?" he asked.

Leanne didn't appear to hear him.

"Anyway, Nathan's in here," she said, and showed Derek into the front lounge.

This room used to be the formal lounge when Derek and Leanne had still been married, and only used when they had guests. While the décor was the same the space was obviously now used as a playroom. Vibrant, wooden storage units had been built in either side of the fireplace and the parquet flooring was covered with an over-sized, red, nylon rug that had brightly painted letters of the alphabet on it. Nathan was sat there, surrounded by cushions and playing with a large, colourful book that had buttons on the front. As he pressed one so the book emitted a loud moo and he giggled. The TV was on in the background but he wasn't watching the cartoons that were currently showing.

"Hey sweetheart," Leanne said, picking him up, "You remember Uncle Derek? You threw your drink over him didn't you?"

She laughed. The blonde-haired, little boy stared back at his mum and laughed too. Derek hoped he wasn't about to give a repeat performance.

"He's all ready for bed and he'd normally be asleep by now but I wanted you to see him first."

"Yes, I missed him yesterday," Derek replied, smiling at the toddler.

The doorbell rang again. Leanne handed Nathan to Derek.

"That will be Nick," she said, and left the room.

A moment later Leanne returned with a man who looked about thirty, by Derek's reckoning. He was very handsome with the sort of cheekbones and strong jawline that most male models advertising watches in magazines seemed to have. His outfit was the mirror image of Derek's, except that he was bulging out of his shirt due to the muscles in his chest, while Derek was expanding around the middle.

"This is my personal trainer, Nick," Leanne said, "He's my plus one for tonight."

"Oh right," Derek said, as his hand was being crushed in a handshake by Nick, "Sorry, what?"

"This is Derek," Leanne continued, talking to Nick, "He's kindly stepped in to babysit at the last minute after Julia let me down...again."

"Oh, **you're** Derek."

Nick said that like he'd heard so many things about him and could finally put a face to the name. Was the next line going to be, "Yes, I can see what you mean now?"

Not that Derek was really thinking about that at the moment. He was too busy wondering how he'd agreed to babysit yesterday. Leanne said she'd been let down at the last minute. Derek assumed that had been by her date, not the babysitter. No wonder she didn't want him to drink his wine.

"Well, we'd best be going," Leanne said.

She kissed the baby Derek was still holding.

"Goodnight sweetheart. I'll be back later," she said, and then to Derek, "He doesn't need feeding but there's water in his bottle in the kitchen. It's past his bedtime now but let him get used to you before putting him to bed. He'll probably want a story. There are loads of books in his bedroom, our old, third bedroom upstairs at the back. That's where the changing mat and spare nappies are. I shouldn't be too late back."

With that Leanne and Nick swept out of the room and Derek was literally left holding the baby.

He thought he coped quite well while Nathan was awake. At first the young boy continued to play on the floor, just looking shyly up at Derek every so often and smiling. Derek had taken off his suit jacket and was sat on the old, leather sofa, not wanting to leave the room in case Nathan began crying. He watched the cartoons on the TV screen feeling scared and stupid about being left in charge of an eighteen month old baby. Nathan was used to going to a childminders but still, was leaving him with a random stranger a regular occurrence?

Eventually Nathan looked up and said, "Drink." At first Derek didn't hear him; too wrapped up in what Peppa Pig was doing on the screen but then Nathan called out again.

"Sorry, what, oh drink. Yes right, that's in the kitchen. Erm, shall we both go and get it?"

Derek stood up and held out his hand. Nathan got up and tottered over and the two walked out to the kitchen together, hand in hand. Derek couldn't help smiling.

Water found they returned to the front room and Nathan decided he wanted to sit up on the sofa beside Derek and watch the TV. The two of them laughed at the cartoons in the same places. Eventually Derek felt Nathan's head resting on his arm.

"Are you tired," he asked, "Are you ready for bed?"

The smell that permeated his nostrils told him that a change was required first. As he carried him upstairs, Nathan snuggled into Derek's shoulder and his heart melted. Derek held him a little tighter.

It had been a long time since he'd been asked to change a nappy, back when he and Leanne had still been married. One of her friends had gone all 'earth mother' and was only using the old-fashioned, reusable nappies. Derek had only popped round to her house to advise her on what best compost bin to buy. She'd asked him to change the baby while she was busily liquidising tofu and lentils for baby's lunch. That sort of diet created quite a mess in a nappy and Derek managed to throw up a little onto the baby. He was never asked to do it again…until now.

It was touch and go for a while but he managed to keep his lunch down. Nathan lay there quite happily, obviously used to the smell. Afterwards Derek put him into bed and picked a book off of the shelf to read. He kept glancing at Nathan who was lying down and twiddling a bit of his hair as his eyelids began to droop. Derek could have stopped reading sooner than he did but he was keen to discover whether little Bobby ever did find his lost sock.

Back downstairs again Derek made himself a coffee and a sandwich. He sat back in the playroom where he was closest to the stairs if Nathan called out as he wasn't able to get the baby monitor working. He left the TV turned down and let his mind wander back to how he'd ended up here this evening. He'd somehow slipped back inside his marriage without his ex-wife knowing about it. During their time together Derek had invested a lot of energy in trying to please his wife, whether she wanted him to or not. Today he'd spent out a large amount of money on a new outfit and a number of hours cleaning out his van, just in case either of those things was going to impress Leanne. Why the hell had he done that? As usual, Leanne hadn't even really noticed. Angela would have. With Angela, Derek would have owned up straightaway that he'd got the wrong end of the stick about babysitting and the two would have laughed about it together. If he'd told Leanne that, she'd have laughed in his face and called him a prat.

Derek sank back into the sofa and sighed loudly. Why wasn't he sitting in his own home with Angela? Why was he being such an idiot? Was he here trying to teach her a lesson? Was he trying to show that there was another woman that appreciated him and didn't go on at him all of the time? Well Leanne certainly wasn't that woman, she never had been. She wasn't attracted to him again. She was attracted to his free time so that he could babysit.

Why was he really here? Surely one row shouldn't have

caused him to run away from Tenhamshire. But it wasn't just one row was it. Okay, so it was always the same topic, Angela's past. Why couldn't Angela see that his being with her meant he was okay with it? Perhaps it was time to stop asking that question and accept that she needed more. They ought to sit down tomorrow and rationally sort it all out, without resorting to arguing. Derek reached for his mobile and phoned home. Ursula answered.

"Hello love," she said, "No Angela's gone out for a drink with Margaret. It's just Bert and I here, enjoying a night in."

Derek's mum's voice faded as she spoke to Bert. It was an annoying habit she had when on the phone, suddenly talking to someone else in the room with her and not listening to the person on the other end of the line.

"It's Derek. Ooh, you're being quite vigorous, aren't you Bert?"

"Mum? What's going on?"

Ursula giggled.

"If you keep rubbing it that hard you'll lose your grip on it."

"Mum? Mum!"

Ursula returned to the phone call.

"What Derek?"

"What the hell is going on there?"

"Nothing's going on. Bert's helping me polish up my silver thimble collection."

"Oh. Well, I'll be home tomorrow. I'm leaving here first thing."

"Good. I bought a leg of lamb while out with Bert today. We can have it lunchtime tomorrow."

"Great."

"We've had an enjoyable day today," Ursula continued,

"Angela drove me to see an apartment in Tenham this morning but it wasn't for me. This afternoon I drove Bert over to Pinstown to show him the historic high street. We were just driving through it on the way home when Bert asked me to pull over as he thought he'd left his wallet in one of the shops. Well, just after he'd gone I heard an alarm going off. I saw Bert running up the street towards the car through my rear view mirror. I thought it was a shop alarm but Bert told me to drive off quickly as it was apparently a sign that the police were about to close off the road, you know, for a suspect package or something. Bert got me out of there just in time. Wasn't that sweet?"

"Erm, yes. You know mum, perhaps it really was just a shop alarm and Bert had actually...never mind."

Derek rang off. It was probably best for his mum not to realise that she'd just been used as a getaway driver. He thought he'd text Angela a message so she knew he was coming home tomorrow. Ten minutes later, he was still attempting to compose it, trying to convey exactly what he wanted to say and in the right tone of voice so that nothing could be misconstrued. In the end he gave up and wrote, *Back home tomorrow for Sunday lunch. I've missed you. Talk soon. D. Xxx.*

Half an hour later he received a reply of three kisses.

Leanne arrived home at ten. She walked in on her own.

"Oh, you're still in here," she said, walking into the playroom, "You could have used the main lounge."

"I know, but it was comfortable in here. How was your meal?"

Leanne pulled a face.

"Not great," she said, "Just a bunch of bores all talking about themselves. I was glad to have the excuse to come home to relieve the babysitter."

Derek stood up.

"Yes, well, everything's been quiet so I guess I should…"

"No don't go yet," Leanne told him, "Your wine is still out on the hall table. Let's open it and have a glass. I've got something I want to ask you."

If it's to ask if I can babysit next weekend it's a no, Derek thought to himself, as he trailed after her into the kitchen.

Leanne uncorked the wine and poured out two glasses. The two of them sat up on the stools by the island as they had done the previous day.

"I've got something important to ask you," she said, after chinking Derek's glass and taking a sip, "I was wondering if you would become Nathan's guardian."

Chapter 7

"What?"

Derek wasn't sure he'd heard correctly. Leanne explained.

"I need to put provision in my will for Nathan's future in case anything happens to me and that includes who I want taking care of him."

"And you want me to do it?"

She nodded.

"I don't have anyone else, Derek," she told him, "Not that I'd trust anyway. My parents are both in their eighties and Nathan's father told me he wanted nothing to do with him or me before he fucked off to Australia."

"But what about your friends," Derek questioned.

Leanne snorted.

"Yeah right," she said, "Which of them would be suitable to raise my child? Sarah runs her one-bedroomed apartment as a cat sanctuary and regularly meets me for lunch with scratches up her arms and cat poo in her hair. Then there's Janice, the self-titled 'medical miracle;' a woman with one kidney, polycystic ovaries and a birthmark on her stomach that's the same shape as Tenerife. At her last dinner party she delivered a presentation on her Labiaplasty operation, complete with close-up photos and a video."

Derek smiled.

"I suppose compared to them I'm practically Father Christmas to a child."

"Well I wouldn't go that far."

The smile dropped.

"But surely you've got other friends apart from those two," Derek told her.

Leanne took a sip of her wine.

"Not really. The rest are more work-related colleagues. Like I said, I want someone I can trust to raise my son, not someone I just schmooze with at dinner parties, each of us using the event to try and further our careers. I only want you to consider it at the moment. Obviously you'll have to discuss it with Andrea."

"It's Angela."

"That's right. She might not be happy with the idea. You might already have plans for your own children."

"Angela can't have children," Derek admitted.

"Oh, right, I'm sorry. I didn't mean to pry or anything."

Derek was surprised he'd just blurted it out like that. When they'd first got together, Angela told him that she'd been sterilised a number of years before, due to what she did as a living. She'd got quite upset after telling him but Derek had just placed his arms around her and said it didn't matter. They were both over forty and had each other, that was enough. It seemed the right thing to say and it had stopped her crying. He'd have liked children with Leanne but it had never been the right time. Now, here she was offering him the son he'd always wanted. Leanne was still talking.

"Angela might hate children for all I know," she said, "And then that wouldn't really work out. I don't want to add stress to your relationship. A child might not fit in with your lifestyle or your work life."

Oh God, Derek thought, Angela's work again. Leanne couldn't make this decision without knowing all about Angela. Here was another person that needed to be told about her past.

Here was an actual example of what he'd feared; there was always going to be someone else that had to be told the truth. Angela's prostitution was never going to go away. They'd moved to Tenhamshire to start a new life together but how could they achieve that when the old one kept coming back to haunt them, casting its great big shadow over their happiness?

"Are you okay Derek?"

Derek realised he'd stopped listening. Leanne was staring at him.

"Sorry," he said, "It's just a lot to take in you know, you giving me a child."

"It's only in the event of my death Derek. Don't get too excited about it."

"You're right. I wasn't picturing that bus driver losing control of his vehicle, honestly."

Leanne smacked him playfully on the arm.

"Time for you to go," she said, standing up, "Anyway, go home and have a chat with Angela about it and then call me afterwards. I'm not forcing you into anything, Derek. If you decide you don't want to be a guardian then that's fine, no pressure."

Derek drained his glass.

"Yes, well I'll let you know."

He stood up.

"Thanks again for babysitting," Leanne told him.

"I enjoyed it."

Derek realised he really had.

His mind went into overdrive on the journey back to his apartment. He would love the opportunity of being a father; not that he wanted Leanne to die or anything but still, as a guardian in her will, wouldn't it be a good idea to remain a part of

Nathan's life so that if the worst did happen, he wouldn't be sent to two strangers?

The problem was how to tell Angela. She thought he was down here getting the apartment ready for renting out. She had no idea he'd been in contact with Leanne. They may not have done anything but he'd still been secretly seeing his ex-wife behind her back. It didn't seem to take much for the two of them to argue these days and this was a big thing. What if it put an end to their relationship? Derek couldn't help a sneaky thought entering his head that said, 'But if that happened, you could still be guardian to Nathan.'

*

The local pub in Baddlesbury had recently been taken over by a chain and renamed. Because the area had made its fortune in the wool trade the new owners decided to call it, 'The Spinning Wheel.' Although now set up as a gastro pub with trendy white leather padded seating and dark wood tables, it was still a place where one could enjoy a drink and a catch up. When Angela arrived, Margaret was already waiting for her, sitting in a booth beside Dora.

"She insisted on coming when she found out what I was doing," Margaret explained.

"Of course," Dora said, "Like I told your Derek, I'm not a prisoner I'm a resident and can come and go as I please."

"Within reason."

Dora tutted at her daughter. Angela smiled.

"It's lovely to see you both," she told them, as she slid onto the bench seat in the opposite side of the booth.

"I want to see your new house too," Dora added.

Margaret sighed.

"Honestly mum, wait until you're asked."

"If I did that the next time we'd all be in the same room together would be at my funeral."

"Well there's something to look forward to," Margaret said.

"That's nice, your own mother."

Angela laughed as she poured herself out a glass of Gavi from the bottle Margaret had already purchased. A lady at another table caught her eye and waved. Angela waved back.

"Who's that?" Dora asked, blatantly staring at the woman.

"I'm not sure," Angela replied, "Oh hang on, it's Theresa someone…Theresa Jennings. Ursula's making her a dress for her daughter's wedding in Spain. She lives in the old rectory near you."

"Oh I know her," Margaret said.

She turned round and smiled and waved before facing her friend again, the smile having disappeared.

"Nosey old cow," she whispered, "Came to look round the Home, telling me she was thinking of putting her old mum in there before deciding against it the following day. I found out later her mum had died years before. She just wanted to see the house. Has she been to yours yet?"

Angela shook her head.

"No, at least I don't think so."

"I bet she will. She'll arrange a fitting there and 'get lost' looking for the toilet."

"You'd best take that mirror down off your bedroom ceiling."

"Mum!"

Angela laughed.

"She'll see no surprises in our house. Besides, Ursula works from one of those torso mannequins once she's got a person's measurements. She fills it out to the right size using bubble wrap."

"That's a good idea," Margaret said.

"I wouldn't mind a new dress," Dora announced, "Perhaps I ought to get one made."

"I don't think there's enough bubble wrap in the entire county," Margaret told her.

"Well that's charming. I can't help my shape. Besides, men like their women with a bit of meat on them. Your father certainly did."

Dora smiled as she recalled a memory.

"I remember once when I climbed on top and…"

"Mum! I don't wish to hear about that."

"What? It's just sex. We're all adults here. I could tell you two a thing about sex and relationships. Well, maybe I can't. After all, I've never been friends with a woman who's slept with the same man I have."

Angela and Margaret looked shyly at each other. Dora laughed.

"Come on," she said, "Spill the beans. What did Paul like to do? What did he do differently to each of you? How much did he pay for services?"

"Mum! We're not going to have that sort of conversation."

"Just because **you** didn't charge."

"Enough!"

Dora grinned before taking a large swig from her glass of wine.

"I'm just trying to make light of the situation," she told them, "I think it's hilarious."

"Yes Derek told me in his text that you'd both had a good

laugh about it," Angela said.

"Well it's better to not let these things get too serious," Dora replied, "I can just imagine the looks on all of your faces when you and Paul were introduced."

Angela and Margaret looked at each other again and grinned.

"It was a bit of a shock," Margaret admitted.

"And yet we all sat down to dinner," Angela added.

The two women laughed.

"It was funny that Derek's mum had no idea," Margaret said, "She just kept on talking."

Angela sighed.

"You know I'm beginning to wonder if Derek is right and Ursula is that naïve."

"I don't think so," Margaret told her, "I think she was just concentrating so hard on making it a nice evening for all of us."

"Then if she's not naïve, why won't Derek tell her about me?"

Angela felt every conversation always came back to this point. Dora waved over at the barman.

"Oi John," she called, picking up the wine, "Another bottle of this over here."

She turned back to the two women.

"Are you still on about that," she said, "I spoke to Derek about it but really, if he isn't going to tell her, why don't you?"

Angela sighed again.

"Because if he won't tell her then that means he hasn't accepted my past, and therefore hasn't accepted me."

"That's bollocks," Dora said, "He adores you. We can all see that. Don't be too hard on him though. It's not many men that would have even dated you knowing what you used to do, yet here's a man who loves you and lives with you."

"Then why won't he tell her?"

Dora sighed.

"Because he's a man and he's got an ego. Of course he's going to feel embarrassed about it. Look at that group of men up at the bar now. Could you imagine if one of them told the other two about his new girlfriend and said she was an ex-prostitute? How do you think his mates would react? How many jokes would be made at the poor woman's expense? That's why he hasn't told anyone."

"But this is his mum we're talking about, not mates," Angela said.

The barman came over with a new bottle of Gavi.

"Your round Angela, isn't it?" Dora said, with a wink.

Angela fished her purse out of her handbag and thought about what Dora had just said. It did make sense. She and Derek were together. Did it matter if he remained embarrassed? She didn't want to tell the people she worked with about her old life and that was partly due to embarrassment too.

"You know, perhaps you're right," she admitted, once the barman had left, "Maybe I am being too hard on Derek."

"And on yourself," Dora told her, "You too, Margaret. All this online dating, trying to find Mr Right. Take a break and let love find you. It's the way it used to happen before we had all of this technology. That's how this lovely lady sitting opposite you found her man."

Angela turned round to look behind her. Dora laughed before continuing.

"Neither she nor Derek was looking for love when they both happened to book themselves onto a coach holiday but they found each other. It'll happen for you too, darling."

Margaret smiled.

"It's moments like this that stop me putting a pillow over your face at night."

Both Dora and Margaret laughed loudly.

The ladies enjoyed the second bottle of wine and then ordered food. While eating Angela received a text from Derek, telling her he was missing her and would be home tomorrow. She was so glad that he'd called the coach house 'home.' She sent him three kisses in reply.

After the meal Dora insisted they have one more bottle for the road and kindly let her daughter pay for it.

"I've got a favour to ask of Derek," Margaret said, as she poured out three glasses.

She still seemed quite sober, seeing as this was the third bottle but then Angela watched Dora chug her glass down and realised she and Margaret had barely had three glasses each.

"You know we've got the outing to Tenham House on Wednesday?" Margaret continued.

Angela nodded.

"Well I'm not going to be able to go and supervise one of the groups. I've got a gentleman arriving for a tour of the Home. He's looking for a place for his old dad and Wednesday is the only day he can come. I'm hoping Derek won't mind going in my place."

Angela had a shrewd idea what Derek would think about that but he'd still do it anyway, to help Margaret out.

"Tell you what," she said, "Why don't I take the day off work and come along as well, if that will help you out."

"Really?"

"Yes, we've just had our monthly ceramics auction at work so it's the ideal week for me to take a day off. I've got a new client to meet on Monday so Wednesday will be no problem."

"That'll be great," Margaret said, "Thank you."

"Besides," Angela replied, "I always think of Tenham House as the place where Derek and I admitted we were in love. It will be nice to return there together."

"You can be in charge of my group," Dora chimed in.

"Well I don't think we need punish her for helping out," Margaret said.

Dora feigned shock.

"My own daughter," she said.

Angela smiled. It might have been due to the alcohol but she felt happy. Derek was coming home tomorrow and she had a new client to meet on Monday for work. Everything was going to be just fine.

*

Derek still wasn't sure how to bring up the subject of Leanne and Nathan and had spent most of the drive home worrying, but when Angela opened the front door and smiled warmly at him, all thoughts and fears evaporated. They stood in the doorway and hugged for a long time.

"I've missed you," Angela whispered, "I'm sorry about going on at you all of the time to tell your mother everything."

They parted.

"But?" Derek asked.

"No buts," Angela told him, "I'm not going to badger you anymore. You tell her in your own time."

Derek smiled back at her but there was a distinct knot starting to tighten in his stomach. Angela was being so warm, kind and reasonable and he didn't want to ruin that by explaining about his deceit. Perhaps he could wait for a while until he explained about Nathan.

"Did you get much done?" Angela asked, as they walked into the hallway.

"Sorry?"

"With the apartment."

"Oh right. Erm, not as much as I'd have liked. I concentrated more on the designs for Margaret."

He stopped walking and put down his holdall.

"Look," he said, "I might just pop the van back up to the Home now. I can't leave it blocking the driveway where it is."

He turned and left the house. Back inside the van he took a deep breath. It was ridiculous to feel so guilty but Derek couldn't help it. Keeping his time with Leanne secret made him feel like he **was** having an affair. The guilt was so bad he'd panicked and had to get out of the house.

Driving up to the Home he began to calm down and tried to rationally work out what to do. For a start the apartment definitely needed to be decorated. Should he get some decorators in to do that and then pretend he'd done it? That would cost money; money that was in their joint bank account. Perhaps he could just rent the apartment out as it was. It's not like Angela ever went there herself. But that would mean the apartment appeared online. What if she saw the photos and saw nothing had been painted? He could just say they were old pictures but that was more lies.

Derek parked the van just inside the side gate so that he wouldn't risk bumping into anyone and began walking back to the coach house. Maybe he didn't need to say anything about Leanne right now. If he turned down her request to become Nathan's guardian then Angela would never need to know he'd even seen his ex-wife. But Derek couldn't do that, not after spending last night looking after that sweet, little boy. He remembered him snuggling into his shoulder as he was carried upstairs to bed. No, there was no way he could turn down this opportunity. For now Leanne and Nathan would just have to remain a secret. Telling his mum about Angela, that was the first thing to tackle but not today. Angela had just given him some breathing space and Derek was going to take full advantage of that.

After Ursula's delicious roast lamb and a couple of glasses of a rather nice Merlot, Derek was feeling much calmer. When Angela offered to help him unpack his bag he said yes and the two headed upstairs.

"I had a bit of a headache this morning," she told him, as Derek upended his holdall onto the bed, "After last night."

"Did you? It's not like Margaret to hit the bottle."

"Dora came."

"Oh, say no more."

Angela laughed.

"Actually I'm glad she was there. She helped relax us."

"I'm sure the wine helped," Derek said, with a wink.

Angela grinned.

"Yes, but she really helped me and Margaret laugh at what happened with Paul."

"She's good at doing that. I must admit I felt a little jealous of him on the night, you know, having been with you."

"That's silly," Angela said, "It's like me being jealous of Leanne."

Derek started and hoped Angela hadn't noticed.

"It's all in the past anyway, isn't it," she continued, "Ex-lovers I mean. Well, not just ex-lovers. I'm not jealous of the woman that runs the fish stall at the farmers' market who fancies you."

"Eh? Who?"

Angela looked up.

"Come on Derek, she's up in the market square Tuesdays and Thursdays. Whenever you're there she calls out suggestively to you, even when I'm there. She's the one with the hooked nose and only three fingers on her right hand."

"Oh her. My God, I'd be worried about your self-esteem if you were jealous of her."

"I'm not talking about appearance. She fancies you."

"She doesn't fancy me. I'm just a good customer, that's all. That's why she always allows me to select my own piece of fish."

"Yeah, right," Angela replied, "That's exactly what she means when she calls out, 'Mr Noble, come over here and handle my wet plaice.'"

"Well, when you say it like that…"

"Anyway, I'm not jealous of her. No, Dora really helped me see that I'm being too hard on you with telling your mum about me."

Derek stopped unpacking his toiletries and looked up, confused.

"Dora told me the other day that I needed to tell mum as soon as possible, that I'm not being fair on you."

It was Angela's turn to look puzzled.

"She said I wasn't being fair on you either; that most men wouldn't have even dated me knowing about my past."

Derek smiled.

"Either she's losing it or the wily, old mare's trying to sort both of us out."

Angela giggled.

"She's not losing it."

She picked up a crumpled shirt from the bed.

"This is nice, is it new?"

With a start Derek realised it was the shirt he'd bought with his suit. He'd left that hanging in the wardrobe back at the apartment and thought the shirt was with it too. He grabbed it quickly.

"No," he said, screwing it up even more, "It's an old one I bought just before I was made redundant. I found it back at the apartment."

"What, after all this time?"

"Yes!"

"Alright, calm down Derek, it was just a question."

"Sorry."

That's great, Derek thought, we finally find some peace with telling mum about Angela's past and now I get abrupt and defensive about a new secret.

"It was rolled up at the back of the wardrobe," he told her, trying to sound calmer, "I assume a previous tenant put it there. It's a nice one so I thought I'd bring it back and wash it."

"Perhaps we should have an evening out somewhere nice, just the two of us, so you can wear it," Angela said.

Derek smiled as he sat down on the bed beside her.

"That sounds good," he replied, "I thought the other day about how long it's been since we've been out together."

"That reminds me," she said, "How would you like to spend the day together next Wednesday?"

"Wednesday? That's my quiet day at the Home while the residents go out on their trip."

"Yes, well about that..."

Chapter 8

It's going to be a great day, Angela thought to herself, as she pulled into her parking space at the auction house on Monday.

Things were improving between her and Derek and the roadworks that had caused her delays last week had been removed over the weekend. Later this morning she was heading down to Ryan Harbour to value items at a house. She couldn't recall a Mr Saunders, the man that had asked for her specifically, but she did meet a lot of different people through her work.

Perhaps I'll treat myself to lunch while I'm down there, she thought, happily.

A new restaurant had recently opened up on the harbour front which had previously been an ailing old pub. It was receiving some rave reviews and Angela hoped it would help rejuvenate the area. She and Derek had visited the town on their coach holiday two years ago but when they returned last year, while Angela was on a trip down to see Derek before moving down permanently, the vibrant harbour front had seemed dead.

The one problem Angela had with heading out this morning was that her colleague, Charles, would have to deal with all of the valuations on his own, both the online ones and those from people that walked in off the street. When she entered the valuations room it was obvious that Charles was already in an intolerant mood. He was sat in front of the computer screen, scowling.

"Have you seen some of the excrement people think is valuable on this electric fax thingy?"

"E mail," Angela corrected, tentatively, "Why don't you leave those for me to go through."

"I've not seen this much horseshit in my life before. And I grew up on a farm!"

"You remember that I'm heading out this morning don't you," Angela said, "So you'll have to deal with the customers coming in."

"Yes, yes, I remember," Charles replied, waving his hand dismissively, "I can cope. Just so long as I don't get a load of moaners like yesterday. Honestly just because I tell people their items aren't worth three figures they take offence. The look on their faces you'd think I'd just told them their children were ugly. Actually one woman did bring in a very unsightly child yesterday with sticky-out ears and a neck brace. The poor, little bastard looked like a trophy."

"Right. Well, I'm going to get myself a coffee."

Angela headed off to the staffroom. Sally, a fellow valuer was already there, filling up the kettle.

"Morning Angela."

"Morning."

"You haven't got a ceramic penis have you?"

"No I always stand like this."

Sally looked confused for a second and then smiled.

"No, I meant for Trevor's specialist sale this Friday. We're short on items. I keep telling him an erotica sale is a terrible idea but he doesn't listen."

"He has some beautiful paintings and statues of nudes though," Angela told her, "And the phallic tribal art has an amazing history behind it."

Sally tutted.

"I think he's only putting this together so he can browse through his Victorian, pornographic postcards in public. Haven't you got anything that could be classed as 'erotic?' What about leftovers from your auction?"

"Don't talk to me about that sale," Angela replied, "With the audience laughing at the word 'jugs' I think Trevor's idea for his auction is a stroke of genius."

Sally sighed.

"I don't mind a double-entendre sense of humour but honestly, if I hear Trevor say once more, 'Let's flip her over and look for marks on the bottom' I think I'm going to scream."

Angela smiled.

"I can't think of anything that we could give you," she told her, "But I'll keep the sale in mind. I've got a big valuation job to do this morning, who knows, perhaps something will turn up there that could be classed as 'erotic.'"

"Or just plain rude," Sally added, "Let's face it, anything with breasts or a nob will make Trevor's eyes light up."

Back in the valuations room, potential customers were already getting their goods valued by the experts.

"Tell me madam, have you had it up against a wall?"

"Erm, well, just once, during a boozy holiday in Benidorm. Look do you really need that much information?"

"I was talking about your oversized mirror."

"Oh."

Angela made her way over to the ceramics table which, fortunately was deserted of actual people. However, Charles was busy replying to the e mails. The sound of his heavy tapping on the keyboard was a sign his mood hadn't improved.

As Angela joined him he pointed at the photograph he had up

on the screen.

"Woman here thinks her nineteen eighties monstrosity of a pink vase is a genuine Clarice Cliff. Not only is she miles off in date but she's spelt Clarice with a 'K'. It's shameful, it truly is. I'm telling her where she can stick her vase."

"Please Charles, let me deal with that. She might put in a complaint if she thinks your e mail rude."

"What do I care? I'm out of here soon."

"Yes but I'm not," Angela told him, forcefully, "This business will continue after you've gone and it needs all the customers it can get. We're not the only auction house in town. It won't help if the customers go elsewhere because you've pissed them off."

Charles sighed and pushed his chair back.

"Fine," he told her, "You tell her where to stick her vase in a nice way then."

Angela pulled her own chair forward and began dealing with the e mail queries. A woman came up to the desk with something in a carrier bag.

"I picked up this vase at a charity shop yesterday for a pound."

As the woman took off the newspaper, Charles rolled his eyes at Angela.

"I think it's nineteenth century Crackleware," she told him, "What do you think."

Out of the corner of her eye, Angela saw Charles take a deep breath before picking the vase up. She braced herself for his reply.

"No it's not Crackleware," he told the lady, "It's just cracked. I think madam, that for a pound, you've been robbed."

*

Angela was glad to leave the office later and make her way down to Ryan Harbour. Her appointment was for half past eleven and she allowed herself a little extra time for traffic and possible parking problems.

She drove down through the high street. At the bottom of the road the harbour front loomed up in front of her with the back of the new restaurant directly opposite. She turned right and travelled up a steep road, passing many large, Victorian houses that had beautiful views out to sea. The house she wanted was the last of these detached period properties. Beyond it was a fenced off area with a sign saying, 'New apartments coming soon.'

Although the house had a driveway, Angela parked on the road. There was a large Range Rover on the drive and she didn't want to block it in. For this age of property there was quite a large frontage. The garden area had been planted with several trees and there was a small lawn. While this gave privacy the view to the sea was obscured. As she walked up the curved drive, holding her briefcase, Angela noted the large, square-bayed windows on the ground and first floors. There was a recessed porch and the red, beige and black tiles on the floor in front of the huge, blue-painted front door were original to the property. It was very beautiful. After ringing the doorbell she turned round and looked at the view back down the driveway. She could see now why the trees had been planted. Walking back down the driveway the sea view would hit you as you emerged onto the pavement.

What an invigorating way to start each day, she thought to herself.

Behind her the door opened.

"Angela sweetheart," a deep and very recognisable voice said.

Angela felt her blood run cold. It couldn't be him, surely, not again. She slowly turned back and gasped.

"Surprise sweetie."

"Max," she squeaked, "What the hell are you doing here?"

He grinned at her.

"I'm waiting for a valuation, my darling," he gestured around him, "This is my late mother's house, the home I was brought up in."

"You lived here?"

Max looked at her, mocking surprise.

"Well of course," he said, "Didn't we bump into each other here a couple of years back? You were on a coach holiday and I was visiting mother. It was so delightful meeting up after so long, wasn't it? Now that poor mother has passed away I need to sell her house and all the things in it. I could have gone to several antiques experts or auction houses of course, but then I just happened to see your face on the website of Jacobson & Lee."

Angela closed her eyes. Why hadn't she done the same as Charles and refused to have her photo used online? She opened her eyes again. Max was still grinning at her. He looked the same as he had two years ago when she'd bumped into him on the high street here in Ryan Harbour with Derek. She was too shocked at the time to wonder what he was doing here. Although he was about fifty-seven now his thick, curly, dark brown hair showed no sign of grey or of being dyed. His moustache was the same colour and thickness and bristled as he grinned at her. At five foot six he wasn't tall but compensated for that by oozing confidence. When they'd first met, over twenty years ago Max had played a lot of rugby and had the physique to match. He carried a lot more weight now but was stocky rather than fat. If she didn't already know about his manipulative, cruel personality, Max, standing before her in his crisp, light blue shirt and beige trousers, smiling at her, with just a few crinkles around his large, brown eyes, would have been very attractive to her, and probably was to a lot of women who didn't know him. After what he'd put her through in the past though, Angela thought him the ugliest man she knew.

"I'm leaving," she told him, "You can have another valuer come out to you if you want, or you can go to another auction house entirely, I don't care. I'm leaving."

She turned and started to walk down the path.

"Oh I don't think you are," Max called after her, menacingly.

Angela stopped beside the Range Rover.

"There's really no need for you to rush off my sweet."

Angela turned back to face him.

"I'm not going to let you threaten me," she called out to him, "Not again."

Max leaned nonchalantly against the door frame.

"Now who said anything about threatening you? I just want someone to value some of my mother's finer pieces. You have such experience. I was very impressed by your biography on the website; all of your travels and study."

"It's all true."

"I don't doubt that, but there does seem to be a teeny bit of information that was left off…the fact that you're a whore."

Angela bit her bottom lip. She had to remain calm. She couldn't allow anger to take over. Rational thought, that's what was needed.

"I'm a valuer at an auction house," she replied, firmly, "What I did in my past has nothing to do with that."

She emphasised the word, 'past.'

Max pretended to look thoughtful.

"Hmm," he said, stroking his chin, "I'm not sure that's really correct. I wonder what affect your being a whore would have on your colleagues if they knew. Yes, I wonder how many sales the auction house would get if the customers knew their goods were being valued by a woman who's spent most of her career on her back."

He grinned at her, his eyes shining.

"Well not always on your back," he continued, "But that other stuff cost extra, didn't it sweetie."

Angela walked back up to the door.

"What I used to do to earn a living has nothing to do with my work colleagues and it certainly has nothing to do with you. Now, you've had your fun, you've made me squirm. I'm leaving and you can go to hell."

Max grabbed her tightly around the waist.

"You're not going anywhere," he hissed.

A little bit of his spittle hit her cheek. Angela could have vomited.

"Get your hand off of me," she told him, calmly, "You're not the only one who can make threats, remember? If you don't want to me to shout out 'rape' and 'help' at the top of my lungs to get the workmen at the site next door running to my aid then you'll let me go right now."

Max was staring daggers at her but then he smiled and removed his arm.

"Now," he said, "There's no need for this animosity. I want you to value my mother's antiques ready for sale, that's all. I'm not here to attack you. You know that's not my style. Besides."

He looked her up and down.

"You're no longer the enticing young thing you once were, are you."

"Ditto."

Max looked up sharply.

"I wasn't the one being paid," he spat.

Angela stepped back.

"You really need to go to someone else for a valuation," she said.

"Oh no. You're going to do it."

Angela sighed.

"No I'm not."

"You are. You are going to value the items today or I go to your boss and tell him all about your past."

Angela shrugged her shoulders.

"And where will that get you?" she asked, "He'll know you were a client."

Max's grin returned.

"I was never a client, you know that my darling."

Angela shuddered. Here was the only other man she'd ever trusted in her life besides Derek. What a mistake that had been. Those horrible memories of twenty years ago tried to force their way to the front of her mind. She felt her resolve dissipating. Panic was racing through her. Was he about to ruin her life again?

"My reputation will remain intact," he continued, "But yours will be in tatters. You'll be out of a job, won't you? Who else will hire you now that poor old Alistair Pilkington is dead?"

Angela gasped.

"How do you know about Alistair?"

Max laughed.

"I have my sources. Your saviour; the man that got you off the streets and into the antiques business isn't around anymore to bail you out. No, you'll be out of a job and what will that do to your relationship with Derek?"

Angela's panic was threatening to engulf her.

"Oh yes, I know all about him too," Max smirked, "Well, we met briefly didn't we?"

Angela stood up a little straighter.

"Derek knows all about my past," she told him, "You can't break us."

"Really? That's interesting. Does he know about me?"

"You just said you met him."

"Yes but does he know what I really was to you?"

Angela took too long replying. Max laughed.

"I thought not. Now, why don't you stop this strong, businesswoman act? It's cute but I know the real you, remember. So, you're going to come in here and value my mother's antiques. Then you'll return to your office with the marvellous news that you've got a new client that's going to raise a lot of commission for the auction house. Won't that do a lot for your career?"

"And what are you expecting in return?"

"Well, let's see, shall we?"

He stepped out of the porch and slowly walked all the way around Angela.

"I'm not short of offers of female company obviously," he told her, "But they don't all provide the sort of services you did; all those little extra enhancements that you were so willing to do to make me happy."

He stepped back up onto the porch and stared back at her.

"Hmm," he said, "How about a quick blow job? Right here, right now. It doesn't have to mean anything does it? Who's to know?"

Max grabbed his crotch.

"Why not take this, right now?"

Angela's eyes involuntarily stared downwards. Max started laughing again, loudly.

"My God, you were considering it, weren't you? You really are such an easy slut. You're a great loss to the whore world you know that."

Angela stepped forwards onto the porch.

"Actually," she told him, her face right up against his, "I was just wondering if, at your age, you can still get your rancid, little cock up."

Max stopped grinning.

"So," he seethed, "Perhaps the angry Angela I last saw twenty years ago in that hospital ward is still in there is she? Well, no matter. Is she willing to risk everything for my silence? We'll find out. You think this is about sex? I'll rephrase that. Do you think this is only about sex? My dear, I want to see how far you'll go to protect your reputation, your job and your Derek. You know the sort of acquaintances I have sweetie. You've been on the receiving end of them. That's why it was the hospital where we met for the last time. Well I say last time. Obviously there was that delightful chat two years back, with Derek."

"Have you been planning this since then?" she asked.

Max feigned innocence.

"Planning what, my sweet?"

Angela shuddered.

"Now then, that's enough chatter," he continued, "I need

some time to think about what you're going to do for me."

He raised his voice, menacingly.

"But right now why don't you just get on with your job. Get your fucking arse in here and start valuing."

He turned and walked into his house. Angela closed her eyes and sighed. Her shoulders drooped. She shook her head, opened her eyes and resignedly followed Max down the hallway.

Chapter 9

Derek's meeting with Margaret was going well. She liked his different ideas for the new area.

"I think flowers and shrubs for visual effect would be best either side of the new path," he said, "I can plan the shrubs so that we get colour from flowers and foliage all year round. For example, Mahonia has a nice yellow flower from November and Camelia will often bloom from December on into spring. I can plant daffodil, hyacinth and tulip bulbs as well and there'll be room to add bedding plants each year. I thought scented plants and flowers around the gazebo; perhaps some nice honeysuckle growing up it and lavender in boxes attached to the sides, set at the right height for the residents to see and smell them while they're sitting down."

"I'm still a bit worried about putting the gazebo in that space," Margaret admitted, "There is a bit of a slope."

"There's enough room to wind the path round so that it moves up gradually, although that will mean a longer walk for the residents and it will cost more to lay down the paths that way. Mind you, it will be less than paying the contractors to lower the whole area first. I've got some costings for both options on page four."

Margaret flipped over a page.

"Hmm, yes that's very helpful Derek. Leave it with me and I'll get a final decision to you as soon as I've done a few calculations of my own."

"No problem."

Margaret took off her half-moon glasses and clasped her hands in front of her.

"Now," she said, "How are you and Angela getting on? I hope you're over that silly situation with Paul last week."

Derek pulled a face.

"I thought everything was fine," he admitted, "Until yesterday. Angela came home early from work in a funny mood. She was very quiet but then snapped at each of us whenever we tried to talk to her. Then she'd apologise for doing so. She did it all evening. Perhaps I'm making too much of it. It was probably just a bad day at work."

"Is she still coming on the day out tomorrow?"

"As far as I know. She's still got the day booked off."

"Good. Perhaps a break from work is just what the two of you need."

Derek didn't see looking after a bunch of pensioners on a day out as a break from work but he didn't voice that thought with Margaret.

"I'm afraid I must head out now, Derek," Margaret said, standing up, "We've got the doctor out to Mr Jefferies again. He had a bad night. I don't think there's anything that can be done for him, to be honest with you. I believe we're about to lose one of our residents. It's just a matter of time. We're probably talking hours. I'm going to go up now and see the doctor and relieve Maureen for a while. She's been sat with him most of the night."

"That's a shame."

Margaret nodded.

"Yes," she said, "But it happens, especially in a retirement home. He is ninety-four."

They walked out of the office and back towards the main

hallway.

"Ninety-four," Derek mused, "Does everyone live to an old age in Tenhamshire do you think?"

Margaret laughed.

"It certainly seems that way. When I first took this place over, a lady of seventy-nine had just died. Everyone kept saying it was such a shock, she was so young."

"Well it bodes well for the rest of us."

"I think my mum's planning on outliving me," Margaret said, "Eighty-seven and no sign of slowing down."

"And how old is her sidekick?"

"Sir Jasper? He's eighty-nine."

Derek shook his head.

"My God, I hope I have their energy if I reach that age."

"Yes. Mind you, they egg each other on. They're like two peas in a pod."

Derek grinned.

"Do you think you're about to get a new dad?"

Margaret winced.

"Could you imagine mum as Lady Dora? She'd be even more unbearable. No, I was more than happy with the father I had."

Her face took on a melancholy expression.

"I still miss him," she said, "There are times, even now, when I turn to ask him a question about business only to realise he's not there to answer me. I think about him every day. Mind you, so does mum. No, I don't think there's any man out there that could replace Billy Bradley, for either of us."

"I think it's the same for my mum too," Derek agreed, "She was younger than I am now when she lost dad, and although it was a terrible accident, him dying on his boat like that, I do believe he must have been the love of her life and no one else could ever take his place."

Margaret touched Derek affectionately on the arm before heading off up the grand staircase to relieve Maureen. Derek headed out the front door and turned left. Around the opposite side of the house from his storage and office area was the old Victorian walled garden. This was another area that needed work and Derek relished the challenge of bringing the area alive again to be able to grow fruit and vegetables for the Home. So far he'd managed to patch up the original glasshouse (twice, after Ash was let loose with the leaf blower last autumn and managed to shoot gravel through the newly installed panes) and was using it to grow some tomatoes and to start off seedlings.

To get to it Derek had to pass through, what he called, the formal garden, complete with box hedges, cypress trees and a central fountain. Being this side of the house, a tall, Yew hedge had been planted surrounding the entire space to screen the area off for privacy from the main driveway that ran passed it at the front. When Margaret took the home over she thought this would have to be taken down in case a resident got overlooked inside the area. Derek had had the idea to cut out square windows within the hedge so that the nursing staff could see into it but the garden could still remain relatively private. It was also a lot cheaper than taking the whole thing down.

Derek liked the tranquillity of the space where the only noise was the gentle splashing sound of the fountain. Today he wasn't alone in there. As he passed through he saw Dora sat on one of the benches at the farthest edge of the area. He walked round to her.

"Why are you sitting so far away from the main part of the garden?" he asked her.

"Because if I hear the running water of the fountain it makes me want to pee. Besides, from here I can see who's coming," she told him, "I don't like being overheard when I'm having a private conversation."

"Right."

Derek was about to leave but turned back to face her.

"Hang on, no one else is here. Have you started talking to yourself?"

He sat down beside her.

"Tell me your name. What year is it? Who's the Prime Minister?"

Dora smacked him on the arm.

"You cheeky sod, I'm not going gaga. I know I'm alone. I'm…waiting for someone I want to talk to in private."

"Are you planning something for the outing tomorrow?"

Dora's face took on an innocent expression.

"Would I do something like that?" she asked.

"Of course you would."

Dora smiled.

"No, you're fine Derek," she said, "I'm just here waiting for Sir Jasper. He's on a reconnaissance mission. We're still trying to discover why Dental Flossie always disappears to her room at eight o'clock each evening. There's got to be a reason. We even managed to get inside her room, briefly, but there was nothing odd about it. Not that we had time to look through her things. It looked just like every other bedroom, smaller than mine but then Dental Flossie isn't made of money. There was a rumour that she lost a lot of savings in a dodgy pension plan. If that's the case, God knows how she can still afford to live here."

"Why do you call her Dental Flossie?"

"Well it's Florence but she prefers Flossie."

"Yes but why Dental Flossie?"

"Because there are two Flossies living here and you need to distinguish between them."

Derek scratched his head.

"Well which one is Dental Flossie?"

"The one with all her own teeth, obviously," Dora told him, like he was an idiot not to realise that.

"Do you all have nicknames?" he asked.

"Of course not. Only the residents who share a first name with someone else need a nickname. Saying that we've only got one Sir Jasper but I've heard him being called a few other names since I've been here."

"I don't think 'Dirty Old Man' is a nickname that will catch on."

Dora chuckled.

"True," she said, "We have a surprising amount of people who share the name Elizabeth. That's okay because there's one Betty and one who prefers Lizzie. We've got two who are called Cissie though. My friend, Elizabeth Shelton, we call her Pissy Cissie."

"You call your **friend** that?" Derek asked her, shocked, "Blimey I'd hate to think what you call the other one."

"It's not derogatory," she told him, "It's just that the day Sir Jasper and I souped-up the stair lift and Vera Alderton shot off like a rocket up to the first floor, Cissie laughed a little too hard and had an accident. You see?"

Derek did but couldn't think of a response. He stood up to leave but then remembered his chat with Margaret.

"I probably shouldn't be telling you this," he told Dora, "But the doctor's here to see Mr Jefferies again."

Dora tutted.

"I know that," she told him, "I've got another fiver on him popping off at nine thirty this evening. I really think I'm in with a chance this time."

"This death sweepstake is sick. Besides, I don't think he'll last that long."

"Want a bet on that."

Dora whipped out a notebook and pen from her cardigan pocket.

"What do you fancy?"

"Alright, a fiver on two o'clock this afternoon."

Dora noted it down.

"Done," she said, "You haven't got a hope. Oh God, here comes Moron."

She indicated with her head behind Derek. He turned. The matron had just stepped into the area through the entrance that led out to the walled garden. She was a short, dumpy woman with dyed, jet black hair that she always combed back into a tidy ponytail. She was about fifty and never wore any make-up, at least not at work. Her large round face showed no sign of a line and her complexion was what Ursula would describe as 'peaches and cream.'

"It's like being cared for by the Grim Reaper," Dora said, watching her, "Why don't you lend her your scythe, Derek and I'll give her Margaret's black coat with the hood."

"Why do you have such a problem with Maureen, she's…"

"Ssh, she'll hear you," Dora whispered, "Quick, talk about something else."

"Like what?"

"I don't know. Give me one of your boring plant facts."

"Oh that's nice."

"Just say something, she's almost here."

"Erm...well, okay. So, they're actually perennial if you keep them warm over winter."

"Really?" Dora replied, acting a little too interested, "That's what my Margaret says about the residents. Oh, hello Maureen, love."

Maureen smiled sadly at them as she approached.

"I've come out for a breath of fresh air," she told them, "But I'm glad I've seen you. I'm afraid there's bad news. Poor Tommy Jefferies passed away."

"What!" both Derek and Dora called out.

"It was about twenty minutes ago, while the doctor was still here," Maureen continued, "At least he's not suffering anymore."

Dora put her head in her hands.

"I don't believe this," she said.

Maureen stepped past Derek and placed her arms around Dora.

"It's okay to be upset," she said, "We're all going to miss him."

"It's such a loss."

"I know. There, there."

"Another fiver."

"Sorry?"

It seemed a good time to leave.

"I've got to go," Derek told them, "Work to be getting on with."

He left Maureen comforting Dora over her 'loss' and headed off to the glasshouse. He made sure that everything was well watered seeing as he wouldn't be around tomorrow but then a thought struck him. Perhaps the excursion to Tenham House would be postponed after Tommy Jefferies death? Derek sighed to himself.

No, he thought, I couldn't be that lucky.

Chapter 10

"Do you think I'm right to be worried?"

Derek was musing over what his mum had told him at dinner the previous evening.

"I mean mum tells me she had a lovely afternoon out with Bert, driving around the big houses on the Hereward estate in Tenham. She thinks sitting outside each one while Bert studied the security systems and wondered how many entrances the places had was a magical afternoon. She doesn't seem to realise Bert was casing the properties. What if her car was spotted? Could she get into trouble Angela…Angela?"

"Hmm?"

They were walking up the high street towards the Home. It was a beautiful, sunny day and the temperature was due to rise into the high twenties.

"What is wrong with you," Derek asked, "You've been lost in your own world since Monday."

"I'm not lost," Angela snapped, "Perhaps I'm just fed up with you wittering on about your mother all of the time!"

"Oh nice."

Why was Angela still so irritable? She'd been in great form the day he'd returned home from his apartment. They'd had a lovely Sunday lunch together and Angela had been laughing a lot, especially while Derek had been telling his mum how, even though Margaret knew him, he'd still had to formally apply for his job as head gardener.

"I showed her my CV, my qualification certificates and a

rather nice pair of testimonials."

"And she still employed you," Angela had joked.

Something had happened since then to change Angela's mood but Derek didn't know what that was.

Angela sighed.

"I'm sorry, Derek," she said, "I didn't mean to snap at you. I don't think you have anything to worry about regarding Ursula and Bert. Dad's always worked alone. If anyone's going to get locked up, it's him. He's used to it. I'm used to it."

They continued walking.

"I know I've been a bit short with people," Angela said, after a few moments, "Really, it's nothing. Charles has given his official retirement date in at work and I'm nervous about having sole responsibility for all ceramics valuations, that's all."

She didn't like lying like this but what else could she do? Mind you, technically it wasn't a lie. She **was** worried about not having Charles at work to rely on."

Derek rubbed her arm.

"You've got nothing to worry about," he told her, "You're great."

She smiled.

"Besides you took on a big valuation all on your own on Monday didn't you. That went well."

Angela's insides turned cold and she shivered.

"Erm yes, the valuation went well."

"Exactly. You said your boss is really happy to have this new client. You're already doing it all on your own."

Derek was smiling at her. He was so proud; she could see it in his face. She nodded at him in response but then quickened her pace so that she could turn away again. The thought of Monday made her feel sick. She'd managed to value everything, even with Max breathing down her neck the whole time. She was so frightened she feared he must have been able to hear her heart thumping. What was he going to do to her?

As it turned out, nothing on that day. Like he'd told her, he expected her to value the items and return to the office and she did. As she'd made to leave he'd put his hand across the opened doorway, barring her exit.

"I'll be in touch regarding our arrangement. For now, my lips are sealed about you but that could change. It all depends on how kind you are to a dear, old friend."

He'd stepped back after that and it was all Angela could do to walk down the drive and not bolt to her car. She didn't know what to do, what to say. She was so happy in her work and really didn't want to lose her job. It meant a lot to her. But it wasn't just the fear of being sacked. Her boss had taken her on because of a recommendation from the place in London that Alistair had arranged for her. Would they get into trouble if all this came out? Perhaps she could just resign and return there herself; escape to London. But what would happen with Derek? Would he go back with her? He'd want to know why. What could she tell him? Then there was Ursula. She'd just sold up and moved to Tenhamshire. How could she say they all had to move back again? Perhaps she'd have to leave them behind. Max knew some dodgy people. She wanted everyone to be safe. She had to protect them, whatever that involved.

They walked past the church and turned left down the lane that led to the main entrance of the Home.

How much time did she have to decide what to do? Max said he'd be in touch. When, how, and what did he want? What if it was only a few sexual favours? Could she bring herself to do them? The thought repulsed her but why? She'd been doing that sort of thing for years, sleeping with men she wasn't attracted to? But that was different, it was before Derek and she'd been in control of who she saw and what she did. Max was from before then; a time when Angela wasn't the woman she was today. And the things Max had liked her to do…she shivered.

But maybe this wasn't going to be about sex. She knew Max, he liked to be in control. This was a game to him. It was all about control and manipulation and so far, he was winning. Maybe he was watching her right now, or was employing someone to watch her. She wouldn't put it past him. He was a sneaky, evil bastard. How had she ever trusted him? If he was watching her now, how long had he been doing it for? He knew about her job in London and about Alistair. He could have been planning this for months, years. Angela took a deep breath and kept walking.

Two large minibuses were already outside the front of the Home. Kenny the nurse was loading bottles of water and fold-down wheelchairs into the back of one of them. Derek rushed off to help him while Angela made her way up the steps to where Margaret was standing with a clipboard. Here at the Home at least, Angela felt safe. She was among friends.

"Ah Angela, good," Margaret said, "We've had a few of our residents cry off at the last minute as they're worried a whole day out in this heat will be too much for them. That means we need to keep another member of staff back. You and Derek are alright looking after a group of five aren't you?"

"I should think so."

"I should warn you, it includes mum and Sir Jasper."

Angela nodded.

"It'll be fine…we are allowed to use reins on them aren't

we."

Margaret laughed.

"If only," she said. She passed a sheet of paper to Angela, "These are the names of your group. I've got Maureen looking after four on her own although I'm beginning to worry she's not up to it. She seems a little panicked by the responsibility."

She indicated where the matron was pacing up and down beside one of the buses, a cigarette between her lips and another smoking away in her left hand.

"I wish I was coming too, to be honest but we've got that man arriving today to tour the Home. Since we lost a resident yesterday that's another bed free. I know it sounds a bit uncaring but from the business side of things, we do need to keep the beds filled."

"It's not a problem," Angela told her, "I hope he likes the place."

She went to break the news to Derek.

"Here's our group," she told him, handing him the sheet of paper.

"Oh great," he said, after scanning it, "Not only the two biggest kids in the Home but Pissy Cissie as well."

"Who!"

Angela grabbed the list back.

"Elizabeth Shelton," Derek told her, pointing at the name on the sheet of paper, "That's what Dora calls her because there are two Cissies."

"Well we're only looking after one so you can just call her Cissie."

"Well of course I will, to her face," Derek replied, "I'm not an idiot. I do know people's names."

He indicated the pacing matron.

"Why's Moron looking so stressed?"
"Maureen!"
"Shit!"

Twenty minutes later and they were on their way. Derek was trying to memorise the faces in the rest of his group. Cissie was sitting beside Dora so that was fine and Dora had told him the Florence on his list was Dental Flossie, the one that disappeared to her room each night at eight o'clock. All Derek knew about her was that she had her own teeth. A Willy Jenson was the last member making up their group.

"Excuse me everyone," Derek called out, to the rest of the bus, "But I just need to make sure I know each member of my group. Now, which one of you is Flossie?"

Two women put their hands up. That was useful. What was he going to do next, ask which of them could take their teeth out?

"It's that one Derek," Dora called out, pointing to a small, grey-haired lady in a bright floral dress.

"Thanks," he said, and then consulted his list again, "Now, I'm also looking for Willy."

There was a smattering of giggles around the bus.

"Aren't we all dear," Dora called out.

The giggling got louder. Even Angela was grinning. Derek battled on.

"Yes, very funny," he told them, "But seriously, I must make sure I know each of your faces before we get to Tenham House."

"There are two of them too Derek," Dora called out.

"Well Mr Jenson is my one," he told her.

He expected a hand to be put up but it wasn't.

"Come on now, is my one here?" Derek asked, starting to

feel miffed, "Look, no one is getting off this bus until I've had a good look at my Willy!"

The whole bus erupted.

"Ooh Derek, don't be so selfish," Dora called out, "Give us all a look."

Derek sat back down in his seat, aware of the shaking coming from beside him as Angela tried to control her own silent laughter.

Tenham House had been the ancestral home of the Dukes of Tenham. The line no longer existed and the house and grounds were now owned by a heritage trust. The residents of the home were free to do what they wanted once there and Derek's group decided to stay outside in the grounds.

"We come here every year," Cissie told him, "There's nothing new inside. Besides, the wheelchair users can't even get up to the first floor."

Derek wondered why Margaret had kept up this trip when she took over the Home. Surely there were better suited places for the residents to visit. Personally he loved the grounds at Tenham House and was always keen to pick up ideas he could use at the Home, but even though the residents in his group didn't need wheelchairs, they weren't able-bodied enough to go tramping miles around the gardens. The first thing they did was walk down to the lake and commandeer a number of deckchairs. It was a pleasant spot to sit and watch the ducks and geese and swans on the water but after an hour Derek was bored and kept surreptitiously looking at his watch. He noticed Dental Flossie kept doing the same thing.

It wouldn't have been so bad if he'd been able to join in the conversation but most of his group were just listing their ailments; each one trying to better the others, like a game of

Disease Trumps. Dora, of course, was cheating and had already confessed to fibroids and two bouts of malaria. She might have won the competition if she hadn't mentioned her prostate operation.

Angela had gone into herself again. After getting off of the bus she'd started looking all around her as if she was searching for someone. She only stopped once they'd taken their seats. Now she was sat a short distance from the group, on the grass, staring at the lake but it was obvious she wasn't seeing anything.

An excited man ran up to their group. He was probably only about thirty but his dated, worn clothes made him seem older. His thick, black hair was badly in need of a cut and his blue, threadbare, woollen jumper; in this heat, made Derek feel even hotter. His green trousers were too long and the hem of both legs was smeared with dirt. He spoke to them in a jumpy voice, as if he was constantly trying to catch his breath and he kept pushing his glasses up the bridge of his nose every few seconds. His ID badge around his neck told them he was Greg, a volunteer at Tenham House.

"I was wondering if I could bother you for a few seconds," he asked them, brightly.

"Why ask when you've already started," Dora told him, grumpily, upset that Willy Jenson had just provided visual evidence of the removal of a testicle and had been declared winner of the ailments contest.

The young man smiled at her.

"Thanks," he said, "I just wanted to draw your attention to some of the changes the trust is currently putting into place here at Tenham House."

He handed a leaflet to Derek.

"We're putting an exhibition on about it next month, called 'The Future of Tenham House.'"

Derek's group began laughing.

"Our average age is about eight-five young man," Cissie told him, "What interest have we got in the future?"

He looked a little crestfallen.

"Well it's not really about the future," he said, "It's showcasing what we're planning to do in the future to help recreate the past. For example, later this year we're going to reinstate the old maze on its original site."

"Good," Sir Jasper called out, "That means you can get lost."

Dora chuckled. Greg remained determined.

"And we're also going to reveal a new portrait of the last Duke of Tenham next month," he continued.

Sir Jasper had just taken a mouthful of water from his bottle and it dribbled down his front as he spluttered.

"That unsullied, old tosspot," he said, wiping his chin.

"He was the only one never painted."

"He was the only one never laid. Why do you think the family line died out?"

"Did you know him, Sir Jasper?" Cissie asked.

"Of course," he told her, "Odd fellow. He used to write poetry in Latin and enjoyed walking in the woods."

"What's odd about that?"

"He did both without any clothes on."

Sir Jasper began talking about the Dukes in an unflattering light while Greg stood despondently beside Derek.

"The whole family were thieves," Sir Jasper said, "Stole land off of my family."

"Did they?" Cissie was enthralled, "When?"

"About six hundred years ago."

"And you're still angry about it?"

Sir Jasper sat up straighter in his deckchair.

"One doesn't forget a theft," he told her, regally, "Not that they were Dukes back then. We were both old families and our estates bordered each other. They got rich off of our land and used the money to ingratiate themselves with the reigning monarchs of the day. That's how they eventually became Dukes, by arse licking."

"I thought they proved themselves worthy at the Battle of Blenheim alongside Churchill," Dora threw in, "Didn't they become Dukes of Tenham at the same time that the Churchills became Dukes of Marlborough?"

"Exactly," Sir Jasper replied, a look of disgust on his face, "Queen Anne was handing Dukedoms out willy-nilly. If my family had been offered one we'd have refused it. I'm a Baronet and damned proud of it!"

The young man beside Derek couldn't stand it any longer.

"They were a noble family," he called out.

The chatter stopped.

"Are you still here?" Sir Jasper asked.

"Yes I am," Greg replied, "They were a noble family that did a lot for this county, the last Duke especially."

"What rot!"

"It's true. The last Duke was a great patron of the arts and will probably always remain the best known of the entire line."

"Crap," Sir Jasper replied, "His great grandfather was well-known for siring bastards all over this county."

Greg looked confused.

"How is that better?"

"It proved he was a man," Sir Jasper said, rubbing his walking stick with gusto.

Greg sighed.

"Well the last Duke was the only one to realise that it was important to maintain things for future generations. He created the vast library here at the house and then left it to the trust so that we could all enjoy the treasures and history that Tenham House has to offer. That's why he's getting his portrait."

Greg looked proudly at the group in front of him, as if he'd just proved he'd won the argument. They stared back at him.

"He still couldn't get it up though could he," Sir Jasper said.

The group turned away and began discussing who had the largest operation scar.

"Don't worry," Derek told Greg, "Why don't you concentrate on chatting to visitors who are a little younger."

Greg sighed.

"You find me a young person and I'll talk to them. Honestly, is everyone in this county over sixty?"

Derek was beginning to go off of this guy.

"I've already been ignored three times this morning and had one man rip up my leaflet in front of me."

If he put him in the over-sixties bracket again Derek thought he might do the same thing.

"Just keep trying," he told him, "Things can surely only get better."

Greg nodded and walked away. Derek saw him make his way over to Angela who was still staring out across the lake. As he walked up behind her he didn't call out and instead placed his hand onto her shoulder. She screamed loudly. As all eyes turned in her direction, Angela pulled the terrified, young man over her shoulder and laid him out flat on the ground. As her hand reached for his throat Greg screamed out,

"I was wondering if I could bother you for a few seconds."

Chapter 11

It was a quieter group that made their way to the pond area behind the main house. Angela had been very apologetic to the frightened young man but told him he should never sneak up on someone like that. While Derek agreed, he'd still thought it a slight over-reaction, seeing as Angela wasn't walking down some dark alleyway alone somewhere but was instead, sat with a group by a lake in the grounds of a stately home. She'd tried to laugh it off with them all as they walked off but something definitely wasn't right with her.

Once they were all sat down again on a couple of wooden benches beside the large, rectangular pond with the rock garden waterfall at one end, the group began chatting and the atmosphere lightened. There was a bit of entertainment as they watched Maureen pass by with her group. She kept frantically turning round, making sure the three more able-bodied residents were still with her, which meant she didn't so much push the wheelchair containing the fourth member of her party than jerk it forwards haphazardly. When the old lady was almost thrown out of it as Maureen tried to manoeuvre around the pond, she stood up.

"I haven't been bounced around like this since my wedding night," she said, indignantly, "I'll be safer walking."

She headed off at quite a pace, down the path leading to the dry garden with Maureen chasing after her, shouting at the rest of her group to hurry up and follow her, their walking frames crunching rapidly through the gravel. Derek noticed Dora with her notebook out.

"What are you up to?" he asked her.

"Just a little sweepstake Derek," she told him, "On what time today we see Moron start crying."

Derek turned back to Angela sat beside him and shook his head.

"Can you believe her," he said, "She'd bet on the daily growth of the shrubs in the Home's gardens if I gave her the idea."

There was no response.

"Angela!"

She jumped.

"Bloody hell, Derek. You scared the shit out of me then."

"Well perhaps if you were here with us and not, God knows where in your head, you wouldn't be so jumpy. What is wrong with you?"

"Nothing."

"Come on, something obviously is. Why won't you tell me?"

"I did. I'm worried about my responsibility at work."

"Oh please, you don't attack a poor, defenceless, young man and then make him cry just because you're worried about work. It's not that stressful a job. You guess a price for a vase someone's brought in and stick it in the sale."

Angela stood up.

"Oh thanks, Derek," she said, "I'm sorry my job isn't as stressful and complicated as gardening."

Derek sighed.

"Let's not start arguing again," he told her, "You know I didn't mean it like that."

"I know. I'm sorry. Look it's hot. I'm going to go buy some

ice creams for everyone. You stay here."

She walked off. As she passed Sir Jasper he dropped his stick. His eyes lit up as Angela's shorts rose up her thighs as she bent over to retrieve it.

"By God, Derek," he said, as Angela walked off, "You're a lucky man. She's a damned fine filly and no mistake. Firm set of fetlocks and a nice shapely rump. Bet she's fun in the old saddle, what?"

"Well, lately there's not been much of...actually, Sir Jasper, that's not really any of your business."

Derek turned away and looked at the rolling countryside that stretched out in undulating hills beyond the gardens. He could just make out the copse where he and Angela had attempted to have some al fresco fun back on the coach holiday. Okay so it hadn't ended quite the way they'd expected but it had still been an enjoyable experience, just the two of them together. Where had it all gone wrong? They hadn't made love for a while. Having two of their parents living in the house with them did make that tricky but certainly not impossible. He'd thought, after chatting together on Sunday that things were about to improve but Angela had soon become distant again and for some reason she was brushing him aside. Surely, if she had a problem, he should be the first person she turned to? Derek sighed to himself. In her current state there was no way he could bring up Leanne's request with her.

*

Angela wasn't handling her stress very well. She dreaded Max, or one of his cronies, showing up at the most inopportune time and had realised, as she stepped out of the minibus in the car park, that today was the perfect opportunity, when she was with a group of people who knew her but didn't necessarily know about her past. She knew she wasn't hiding her fears well, especially when she screamed and attacked that poor man. Still, he had come up behind her and put his hand on her shoulder. It could have been Max or one of his contacts. At least she still remembered everything from that self-defence course she'd taken years before.

Poor Derek though, she shouldn't be shouting at him. He obviously knew something was wrong but she couldn't blurt out what that was. No, she had to get a grip on herself and try and behave normally for the rest of the day. Being scared and irrational was exactly what Max wanted. He wanted her to feel trapped, nervous and to lose confidence. It was causing more friction between her and Derek and she wouldn't put it past Max to try and break the two of them up as well. Mind you, that probably wouldn't be too hard to do at the moment. When was the last time they'd had a conversation about their relationship without it ending in an argument? No, she couldn't allow Max to make it any worse. She couldn't let him win, not again.

Heading off for ice creams was a good excuse to pull herself together. Max was a slimy creature but he wasn't an idiot. As she stood in the queue she realised that he may keep tabs on her but he wasn't about to reveal himself and tell everyone about her past, that would defeat the object. Angela's past was his trump card. No, he wanted her to stew. He was out to play the slow game. Angela just had to start playing it too. Today should be an opportunity to take her mind off of him. She was meant to be watching the residents after all.

And they certainly needed watching. The cafeteria served

bottles of beer and small bottles of wine. Neither Angela nor Derek could prevent their group from purchasing them at lunchtime and residents that could afford to live at the Whispering Wood Retirement Home weren't too worried about the cost of several bottles. Raucous laughter ensued, usually at poor Maureen's expense, who was sat with her group several tables away. She'd told Angela she was hoping for a quiet hour or two while her charges enjoyed a leisurely lunch. Getting bits of cheese and apple flicked at her wasn't part of the plan. The thing was she hadn't a clue who was doing it and Angela was beginning to think her nickname suited her. When she was trying to shuffle her group outside once they'd finished eating, Maureen managed to slip over on a pickled egg that Dora had deftly rolled across the floor in a move any crown green bowler would have been proud of. After helping her up and checking she was alright, Angela couldn't help a smile escaping onto her face. Dora's table was falling about laughing. Derek wasn't joining in. He'd just taken a phone call from Ash and Angela had overheard him say,

"No, you don't need to water the dry garden. Yes I know it's dry, it's meant to be. What's that noise? It sounds like the hose running. You haven't watered it already have you? What was that crash? It sounded like something breaking. Sorry? How can you possibly shatter a galvanised watering can?"

Sir Jasper's clumsiness with his stick seemed to be annoying him too. Angela didn't know why. It was always her that kept picking it up after all.

The afternoon saw the group make their way slowly round to the rose garden. Angela noticed the one called Flossie kept looking at her watch. What could she possibly be in a rush for?

The rose garden was beautiful. The pergola walkway had

roses trained along the sides of it, resembling hanging garlands and there were an abundance of beds and borders awash with a heady scent and looking beautiful in the sunshine in all colours of the rainbow. It was a popular spot and had a large seating area beside a coffee kiosk. They managed to get two tables of four beside each other for them to sit down at. Derek went up to the counter to buy the coffees and teas. He took Sir Jasper's stick with him. Angela worried the old man was getting too much sun. Every time she'd handed it back to him today he'd seemed hot and flustered.

"What time is it?" Flossie asked, shaking her watch and then lifting her wrist to her ear, "Is it late?"

"It's half past three," Angela told her, "Don't worry, we're due to leave within the hour."

"Must be back for eight," she said to herself.

"Why's that?" Dora asked.

Flossie looked up from her watch.

"Must be back for eight," was all she said.

Dora tutted and turned to Angela.

"Right," she said, "What's happening with you; you've been jumpy all day?"

"Nothing's wrong," Angela replied.

"You can't kid me," Dora told her, "Is it Derek? Do I need to lamp him one?"

"It's not Derek. It's something else. Don't worry, I'm getting it sorted."

Dora patted her arm.

"You know you've got friends," she said.

Angela felt the urge to cry. She smiled and nodded.

Derek walked carefully back down to the table with a tray of hot drinks in polystyrene cups, Sir Jasper's stick hanging off his wrist. Just as he neared the table so Maureen came rushing over. She bumped right into him. The stick slipped between Derek's legs and he tripped, sending all seven cups tumbling onto the grass.

"Oh for fuck's sake!"

Maureen didn't seem to hear or see him.

"Have you seen Brendan?" she called out, to the group, "He's been trying to wander off all day and now he's managed to do it. Should I call the police?"

"Calm down," Derek said, "There's no need for that. Besides I just saw him up by…"

Before he could say he'd just seen him at the counter, Dora cut in.

"Oh Brendan does love his fish. He's probably off looking for some. Is there somewhere close by that has them?"

A look of horror appeared on Maureen's face.

"Oh my God," she said.

She turned and sprinted off, rather quickly for a woman her height and shape.

"Drag the koi pond," they heard her shout.

"Dora, that's wicked," Derek told her, although he was smiling seeing as Maureen had just made him spill seven drinks and hadn't checked to see if he'd burnt himself.

"Well he does like fish," she replied, with a twinkle, "Breaded, battered, in sauce, he's not fussy."

For those that saw it, Maureen did an amazing swallow dive into the large, rectangular pond although it took four members of staff to pull her out. Dora was jubilant on the way home. She'd won the sweepstake for the first time that day they'd witnessed the matron cry.

*

Arriving back at the Whispering Wood Retirement Home, the residents were in a buoyant mood after their day out. The same couldn't be said for the staff that had been watching them. Poor Maureen rushed off home to bathe and scrub the pond weed off of her body. Margaret was in a happy mood as she counted the residents back in.

"I take it the meeting went well today," Angela said to her, once the residents were all safely inside.

Margaret gave a shy smile.

"Yes," she said, "Mr Riley is going to arrive here next week."

"And?"

Margaret giggled.

"Well, his son, Jeremy was very nice. We chatted away while I showed him round the Home. It was like we'd known each other for years."

"Ah, that's sweet."

"He stayed for coffee afterwards and, before he left, asked me out to dinner on Friday."

"Perhaps he's after a discount," Derek said, without thinking.

The smile dropped from Margaret's face and Angela smacked him on the arm.

"Derek! Margaret is a lovely woman and that's why this man asked her out."

"Oh sorry, I didn't mean to suggest he didn't find you attractive," he told her, his face getting hot, "I just meant..."

The two women were staring at him.

"Actually I don't really know what I meant."

Angela tutted and rolled her eyes at Margaret.

"I'll take this one home," she said, and grabbed Derek's arm.

"Honestly," she told him, as they walked back down the driveway, "I don't believe some of the things that come out of your mouth."

Angela smiled as she said it and Derek smirked too. They both started laughing. Derek wanted to tell her it was great to see her laugh but didn't want to remind her of whatever the reason was that she'd been distant today. He took hold of her hand and they continued walking.

Back at the coach house everything seemed quiet. As Derek passed the door to the third bedroom he heard voices.

"I'm sorry, Bert," Ursula said, "But I don't think your tool is going to fit."

"I agree," he replied, "It is a bit too large for your box."

Derek threw open the door.

"Alright, what's going on in here?"

Ursula and Bert both looked up at Derek, confused. Bert had a screwdriver in his hand.

"We're trying to fix the loose screw on my sewing box," Ursula said, "I got fed up keep asking you so Bert offered to assist me. Unfortunately his screwdriver is too big."

"Perhaps I could use yours Derek," Bert said, "Do you have a toolbox?"

Ursula laughed.

"Yes he does," she told him. "It's pristine; never been used. Derek's never been that way inclined when it comes to DIY tasks."

"Oi, I'm regularly called on at the Home to sort out DIY matters," Derek told them, indignantly.

"Poor residents," Ursula said, "Honestly Bert, he put up some shelves for me once that were classified by the Skiing

Authority as a black run."

The two old people laughed. Angela leaned in over Derek's shoulder.

"How about we order in some Chinese food for dinner," she asked them, "It's been a long day."

"Ooh lovely," Ursula said, "Oh by the way Angela, you had a phone message earlier. I didn't catch the name but I think it's to do with work."

"Oh yes?"

"Yes," Ursula continued, "It was a man's voice and he said, 'the clock is ticking.'"

The colour drained from Angela's face.

"I assumed it was to do with some antique clock at the auction house. Anyway, if its working that must be good news mustn't it."

"Mmm," was all Angela managed to say.

How on earth had Max got their ex-directory, home phone number? He must know where they lived. Well, why wouldn't he if he'd been planning her downfall for months. Was he close by now, spying on them? Was he around the corner, laughing at her? What was he going to do next? Who else in her family was he planning to hurt? Angela didn't feel hungry anymore.

Chapter 12

Angela looked at her watch. He'd be back soon, with the photos. What else might he return with; knowledge that could ruin her?

The paranoia had taken over again but knowing she was being paranoid didn't mean she could just switch it off. The guy that took all of the photos for the auction house catalogues was down at Max's place, taking shots of all the items for sale. There were a lot of fine pieces and Angela's boss, Ben Jacobson, was ecstatic with the deal she had made.

"This will make a huge commission for us," he'd told her, the day she'd returned from valuing the items, "This is a client we really want to keep sweet."

"Yes, I think he knows that," she'd replied.

Ben was so happy that he'd told Angela he wanted her on the rostrum the day of the sale, on her own; taking the lead in the auction.

"You're more than capable," he'd said, "You've learned so much from everyone here and its time you did a whole sale rather than just selling the odd item here and there."

"But this is such a big deal," she'd replied, "Surely one of the more experienced auctioneers should do it. I wouldn't want them resenting me. I can do a smaller one sometime."

"Angela, calm down. I have complete faith in you. This is your time to shine."

Or my time to crash and burn, she'd thought.

Since Ursula had taken that phone message two days ago,

Angela had been on tenterhooks, wondering when and how Max was going to strike. She suspected the photographer was going to come back today with a message from him. She really should be excited at the prospect of leading her own sale but all she felt was fear. She hadn't been able to concentrate on her work while waiting for the photographer's return so had escaped into the main room where the general sale was on. At least she could pretend she was gaining vital experience from the auctioneer. Not that Craig was someone she wanted to emulate particularly. He banged his gavel.

"Sold," he called out, "To the lady with the bingo wings."

Angela looked at her watch again. Surely the photographer should be back by now. There were a large number of items to be sold but even so, it shouldn't have taken this long. The waiting and wondering what Max was going to do next was awful.

"Next up we have a pair of very chipped and cracked cast stone garden planters. I've got commission bids starting here at seventy-five pounds. Someone's got more money that sense. Do I hear eighty? I have eighty from the lady wearing the outfit of a much younger woman. Can I get ninety?"

With a start, Angela saw her boss, Ben Jacobson walking over to her with the photographer, Matt in tow. Why was Ben here? Had Max decided to go straight ahead and ruin her career by spilling the beans now, or maybe he'd decided to pull out of the auction altogether. That would be his style. He'd asked for Angela by name. If he pulled out, Angela would be seen by her boss as having unreliable acquaintances. Mind you, in Max's case that was true.

"Sold, to the man with the humongous zit on the end of his nose. Sorry? No, there's no way you can call that a beauty spot, sir."

"There you are," Ben said to her.

He smiled. Ben was thirty-six. His long, floppy fringe hung across the top of his oversized, black-framed glasses but on him, with his attractive, perfectly symmetrical face, the look seemed cool rather than odd. He wasn't aware of his looks though and never noticed the admiring glances that always followed him.

"Matt's just got back," he told her, "And he's shown me some photographs."

In her current frame of mind Angela wondered what sort of photographs they were. She couldn't ever remember posing for anything sexual for Max but twenty years was a long time ago.

"They look great," Ben continued, "That porcelain bust is particularly exquisite."

Well if they were photos of her, they were good ones, Angela reasoned. Then she recalled that Max's mum had that beautifully painted, Paul Duboy bust of a lady in a plumed hat going into the sale.

Up on the rostrum Craig was in full swing.

"I have one hundred and fifty pounds from the woman with the sweaty cleavage. Do I have one seventy-five? Yes, I have one seventy-five from the man with the itchy bum. Can we burn that bidder card after the sale?"

"I wondered if you wanted to see the photos before we put the catalogue together," Ben continued, "This is your baby really."

Angela shook her head.

"No," she told him, "I'm happy for you to go ahead with whatever you think is best."

"Fine," he said, "We'll get on to it straightaway."

He nodded at Matt, a sign for him to leave and get on with his work. Alone, he gently took Angela's arm and turned her away from the crowd in the salesroom.

"I'd like to throw out all the stops on this and get the sale ready as soon as possible," he told her.

"I totally agree with you."

The sooner it was over the better, as far as Angela was concerned, whatever the outcome. At least it would be over with…wouldn't it?

Ben grinned.

"Between you and me, we're going to have a TV film crew here soon from that new digital channel dedicated to programmes about antiques."

"You mean Timeworn Television?"

"That's right. They've got a new series about rural communities coming out and want to film an auction here. I've had to keep silent about it until it was definitely happening. This will give us some free advertising and I think this sale is just the one for them to record."

Angela turned cold.

"You mean you want me to do my first auction in front of TV cameras?"

Could this situation get any worse?

"You'll be fine," Ben told her, "You're a natural at this game. Now you don't have to worry about being camera shy. I've met the programme's producer. She's a lovely woman. I'm sure she'll help put you at your ease."

He looked at his watch.

"Ah, I've got a meeting now. Anyway, mum's the word for now regarding the TV show."

He stared at Angela for a second, still smiling.

"I must thank you again for this contact," he said, "I don't suppose you know any more people like Mr Saunders do you?"

"Thankfully no," she said.

Ben's forehead creased into a look of puzzlement but then he remembered his meeting and headed off. Angela let out a long sigh.

Oh my God, she thought to herself, now what do I do?

It was bad enough that Max could ruin her life by telling her boss, one person, about her past, but now he could humiliate her in front of millions of people. She had to get out of this auction and definitely out of this TV thing. Perhaps she could get Charles to do it, a last auction before retiring. It would make it special for him. Yes, that was a good idea. She'd go see him now.

Outside she bumped into Matt again.

"Glad I caught you," he said, "That Max, I mean Mr Saunders; what a great guy he is, isn't he."

Angela didn't reply.

"He was such a laugh. That's why I got delayed. He kept telling me stories. He told me you were old, old friends."

Matt took Angela's continued silence as a sign he'd offended her.

"I don't mean you're old, or anything. I just meant you've been friends for years."

"I knew him twenty years ago," Angela told him.

Matt whistled.

"Wow," he said, "I was only three."

She was starting to go off of Matt.

"Anyway," he continued, "He gave me a message for you."

Her stomach began to turn somersaults. Matt half-closed his eyes as he tried to recall the message.

"He told me, 'Tell Miss Jenkins that I'm sorry I didn't speak to her at Tenham House on Wednesday.'"

A cold shiver descended through Angela's spine.

"Then he said, 'But I'll catch up with her in Baddlesbury soon.'"

Matt smiled; pleased he'd remembered the entire message. He expected Angela to thank him but instead she barely nodded before rushing off.

*

Derek was up early on Saturday morning. He wanted to put a couple of hours in at the Home. Although the hot weather meant the dry grass didn't need cutting, he still had to make sure the plants were watered. The areas around the lawn at the back of the house were on an automatic sprinkler system so they were fine. He'd given the beds out the front a good water last night once the temperature had cooled and his experimental dry garden behind the outbuildings was doing what it was supposed to and thriving without water. However, he wanted to go and check on the plants in the Victorian glasshouse and then hose the beds in the formal garden inside the yew hedge, which were next on the list to be added to the automatic water system. Ash was coming in this morning too, after taking yesterday afternoon off. Derek wanted him to clear one of the large beds out the back of the house. The one on the right-hand side of the path was looking particularly stunning, but it put the one on the left to shame and Derek wanted to replant the whole bed. With Ash clearing it today, Derek was looking forward to replanting it on Monday after he'd been to the garden centre.

He wasn't breakfasting alone. Ursula and Bert were both

early risers and appeared to be in as good a mood as Derek was this morning. Angela was up too. She hadn't slept all night but was fed up of lying in bed, staring at the ceiling with all manner of worrying thoughts passing through her mind. Her mood didn't match the others.

The four of them were sat round the dining table with bacon sandwiches and coffee. Angela hadn't touched hers. She was staring out at the garden, barely listening to the conversation going on around her, although snippets kept reaching her and whatever she heard seemed to annoy her. One moment they were discussing the dress Ursula was making for Theresa Jennings and the next they'd somehow moved on to art.

"Bert and I saw some paintings in a small gallery when we were out yesterday, didn't we," Ursula said.

"And bloody awful they were too," he replied.

Ursula giggled.

"Oh Bert," she told him, "You were funny yesterday. The gallery owner told us the paintings we were looking at were based on the Expressionism Movement."

"And I told her that they were creating movements in my stomach," Bert added, "She got shirty but as I told her, I was just expressing myself."

Ursula laughed.

"She said perhaps we'd rather see some nineteenth century Naturalism and Bert told her we weren't interested in nudes."

Angela tutted.

"Naturalism," she informed them, her gaze remaining on the garden, "Was painting landscapes in a more realistic way. Think John Constable."

"Well he was someone who could paint what was in front of him," Derek said, "That's my kind of art. I'm not one for this modern stuff. Angela dragged me along to a modern art exhibition once. It was dreadful."

Angela let out a sigh but didn't say anything. Derek continued talking to Ursula and Bert.

"There were all these weird paintings. It was all meant to be representative or something. I think it just showed that these people couldn't draw properly."

Angela closed her eyes but was unable to shut the conversation out.

"And you should have heard what some of the pretentious snobs around us were saying. They were all pretending they 'understood' it and tried to show off to the rest of the crowd. Everything was 'powerful' and 'had movement.' They knew bugger all."

"Derek, please," Ursula scolded, "No swearing at the breakfast table."

"Sorry."

Derek took a sip of his coffee but quickly swallowed it as he remembered something else from that evening.

"There was this small canvas that the 'artist' had covered in Tippex. What was it meant to represent, Angela?"

"Hmm? Oh, woman's struggle to break through the glass ceiling."

"That was it. Honestly, what a load of rubbish."

"It wasn't rubbish, Derek," Angela told him, forcefully, "The artist had used the little brushes in each pot of Tippex to paint the picture, rather than using one big brush, which was meant to signify the length of time woman has struggled to be seen as man's equal. The individual brush strokes could be seen all over the canvas."

"Well I couldn't see them," Derek said, "It was just a canvas painted white. I still don't see what made that art."

Angela sighed again.

"That whole evening was about representational art, Derek. It was art because no one else had thought or done it before."

Derek huffed.

"I've never shat onto a dining table before," he said, "If I did it wouldn't make it art."

Bert laughed.

"Derek!" Ursula admonished.

"Sorry mum. But I don't understand how some people pay millions for things any idiot could come up with."

"More money than sense," Bert agreed.

Angela tutted.

"If you don't understand it then stop moaning about it," she snapped.

While Ursula and Bert looked embarrassed Derek kept talking.

"I don't think anyone really understands it," he persisted, "Like those people at the event who were trying to look knowledgeable and cool. When you went to the Ladies I sat down on a seat by the exit and waited for you. A woman and a child walked past and the child sneezed, right onto the fire extinguisher. Thirty seconds later the crowd were surrounding it saying loudly that it was 'expressive' and 'had movement.' It had movement alright. The contents of the sneeze were running down the outside of the canister."

"Oh Derek that's disgusting," Ursula told him, collecting up the breakfast plates, "Hmm, I think this is the last of the bacon. I'll pick up some more today if you like. I'm driving Bert into Cunden Lingus so that he can go to the bank again."

"You're not wearing a balaclava are you?" Derek asked.

Bert laughed again. Ursula looked puzzled.

"In this heat?" she asked, "Why would you say that Derek?"

"It was a joke," he told her.

"Well I don't get it."

Angela's mood had been steadily getting darker while the conversation about art had been going on. She turned now to face them.

"Oh God, it's a reference to my dad being a thief," she said, "Derek's suggesting he's going to the bank to rob it. Not that he probably needs the money, living here rent free for over a week."

The atmosphere of the whole room darkened to match Angela's mood.

"You only have to say if I've outstayed my welcome," Bert told her.

"You did that the night you arrived," Angela threw back at him, "Why are you here, dad? Usually you want money. You know we haven't got any to spare so why are you still hanging around? You'd better not be trying to get at Ursula's money. That's for her own place. Not that she's exactly been in a rush to move."

"Alright Angela," Derek whispered, "Calm down."

Ursula had just sat back down again after putting the plates into the dishwasher. She took a tissue out of her cardigan pocket and blew her nose.

"I looked at a place yesterday," she said, "That's where Bert and I were. That's why we're going to the bank today instead."

Angela felt bad.

"I'm sorry," she told her, "I'm not being fair."

"I want to find the right place," Ursula continued, "I'm sorry I've not been quicker about it."

"It's fine, really," Angela told her, "I'm sorry. What was this place like that you saw?"

"Oh, it was down in Ryan Harbour," she said.

Angela's stomach turned over.

"Yes, it was actually a two-bedroomed house. Victorian, very nice but it was in a road that was up a rather steep hill. I think a more modern apartment would suit me better. They had some lovely-looking ones on the harbour front, didn't they Bert? We had a walk along there. That's where the gallery was."

Ursula smiled as she recalled her lovely day out.

"We had lunch in a beautiful restaurant right next door to the gallery. Bert really liked it, didn't you? You'd seemed anxious earlier when we were out walking, kept looking behind you, like you thought someone was following us."

"It was nothing," Bert said, but he looked a little worried.

Angela felt sick. It had to be Max. The two of them had gone down to the town where he was living of their own accord. She could almost hear him laughing.

"How easy," he would have said, before following the two old people around, making sure they realised they were being followed. The man was a monster. What should she do?

"So the house there is probably a no," Ursula said, "I'm sorry about that."

"Honestly we're not rushing you," Angela told her, "Forget what I said. I didn't mean it."

"Good," Bert said.

"I didn't mean you. You're still on borrowed time."

"Well that's nice," Bert turned to Ursula, "Kids; you bring them up and they turn on you."

Angela snorted. She was just in the mood to argue with her

dad.

"When did you ever bring me up?" she said, "I had to fend for myself **and** look after my brother after mum went off. You were in prison most of the time."

"I did my best by you."

"What, by staying away?"

"I only went inside twice when you were a kid," Bert reasoned.

"Yes, once for three years and once for five. Eight years is a lot of missed childhood dad. If you weren't such an incompetent burglar you might have been around to see your children grow up."

"I wasn't incompetent," Bert snapped.

She laughed, mockingly.

"You stole a builder's tools and equipment from his yard."

"Expensive stuff to replace."

"Exactly. You tried to sell it back to him. It was coded. He knew it was his."

Bert shrugged his shoulders.

"A mistake anyone could make."

"And another time," Angela continued, "You stole from that stately home. Security chased you and you hopped over that two foot wall, forgetting there was a ten foot drop the other side. You were in court on crutches."

"That could have happened to anyone."

"No dad, it couldn't."

Bert leaned over to Ursula.

"I wasn't that bad a person," he told her, "But once the police think you're a wrong'un, they won't leave you alone."

"Is that right?" Ursula asked, looking startled.

Bert nodded.

"They were forever turning my house over, looking for stolen goods."

"They knew what you were dad," Angela said, "I think it was called 'doing their duty.'"

Bert ignored her.

"It's no fun, Ursula," he said, "I bet you've never had the police wake you up in the middle of the night."

Ursula's hand flew to her mouth and tears appeared in her eyes. She stood up.

"Excuse me," she said, and fled the room.

"What did I say?" Bert asked.

Derek sighed.

"That's exactly what did happen to her, the night my father died," he told him, "He'd been out on his boat that day and hadn't returned home. Mum was woken in the night by the police, telling her they'd found him. They think he'd struck his head accidentally. He was found hanging over the side of the boat, his foot caught up in some rope."

"That's awful. Poor Ursula," Bert said, looking out into the hallway where she'd fled.

"Congratulations dad," Angela was still fuming, "You've now managed to upset the only person in this house who still wanted you here."

Derek thought that was a bit strong but felt it wasn't the right moment to contradict her. Bert stood up.

"I guess it's time for me to move on then," he said.

"You do that," Angela told him.

Derek didn't know what to do. He stared down at the table. Bert mumbled something about doing what he came for and walked out of the room and off to his bedroom. Angela held up a hand to Derek.

"Don't say anything," she said, "He's my dad. I know what he's like."

Derek nodded and squeezed her other hand, comfortingly.

"Right," he said, standing up, "I really should be heading off to work, once I've checked mum's okay."

"Actually Derek I might come with you," Angela said.

Derek raised an eyebrow.

"I want a word with Margaret."

She had to talk to somebody about all of this. Max was driving her crazy.

"Ah, of course. Find out how her date went last night," Derek said.

Angela had forgotten about that but it was a good excuse to use.

"Yes," she told him, "That's it exactly."

*

Derek felt bad about Bert. Yes, he was worried about the amount of time his mum was spending with him but he hadn't wanted the old man thrown out like that. The past week hadn't really been much of a burden. He'd got quite used to Bert and his mother being there when he came home from work. Still, Angela knew him better than he did. Although it was selfish, Derek was actually quite glad that Angela's wrath had been directed away from him for once. Something was definitely wrong and he was still hurt that she wouldn't confide in him. He wanted to make his own confession about seeing Leanne so that he could discuss the situation with Nathan but right now, in her present mood, Angela would probably bite his head off. Hopefully she would confide in Margaret this morning and maybe things could move on. In the meantime he was going to take the Home's van and go out and buy some paint for the apartment once he'd finished his gardening chores. Maybe he'd head down to the apartment next weekend and get a good start on the decorating. Hopefully there'd be time to see Nathan too.

While Angela went off in search of Margaret, Derek got busy with hosing the flowerbeds in the formal garden. He quite liked coming in on Saturday mornings. It was too early for visiting relatives and, with Ash out the back, he could concentrate on his own jobs.

He'd barely started watering his seedlings in the glasshouse in the walled garden when Ash came bounding in through the door, entangling himself in one of the tomato plants. Derek had to reluctantly cut off several stems to free him.

"Honestly Ash you need to be more careful. That's a lot of tomatoes we're not going to get off of this plant now. *Sweet Cluster* this one is called. I was looking forward to trying them."

"Sorry," Ash said, grinning lopsidedly at his boss, "I've finished clearing the flowerbed like you asked me to, the one on the right."

"What?" Derek looked aghast, "That's the wrong one."

"Are you sure?"

"Of course I am," he replied, "That was the one I wanted you to keep."

Ash tutted.

"You know, I thought it looked a bit too nice to clear."

Derek tried to control his temper. He spoke slowly.

"Then why didn't you come and check with me first?"

"Well I didn't want to bother you. Besides you'd given me instructions."

"That you didn't listen to."

"I did," Ash told him, looking a little hurt, "I listened to every word."

"You couldn't have. I told you the one on the right, needed to be left; oh."

Ash looked confused. So did Derek. Saying it out loud he could see where the confusion had occurred.

"I think I need to go get a few things back off of the compost heap," Ash said, dejectedly.

Derek sighed.

"No," he told him, "Don't worry. Why don't you clear the bed on the left now and we'll replant both of them together on Monday."

Ash's grin returned. He looked excited.

"Really?" he asked, "You'll let me plant up? You don't usually."

Derek was starting to regret saying that.

"Yes, okay," he said, with a feeling of dread, "I'll let you plant up too."

Ash rushed off to clear the flowerbed on the left, but not before catching his t-shirt in the *Sweet Cluster* tomato plant again. Derek returned to his watering. A few moments later he heard the door open once more.

"If I turn round and find you tangled up again it'll be your own *Sweet Cluster* I lop off this time.

"Excuse me?" said a voice that Derek didn't recognise.

He span round and came face to face with a smartly dressed man he didn't know.

"Oh I'm sorry. I thought you were someone else."

The man smiled and pointed at him.

"Are you Derek?" he asked, in a well-spoken, gentle voice.

Derek nodded. The man gave him a warm smile and walked in. He held out his hand in front of him as he said,

"I'm Jeremy Riley."

Derek looked blankly at him. The man blushed slightly.

"I'm a friend of Margaret's," he said, "We went out for dinner last night."

"Oh yes, of course," Derek replied, shaking the man's hand, "Are you lost or…"

Jeremy shook his head.

"No I've been banished," he told him, "Margaret is having some kind of meeting with your other half I believe. It's not a problem. I turned up unannounced. Margaret dropped an earring in my car last night and I just brought it back. She told me to come and pester you until she's free."

"Did she?"

"Well she didn't say pester but I know I'm going to do just that."

Derek grinned. Jeremy seemed very nice. He gave off a warm, friendly vibe. His black hair was streaked with grey around the temples and he was wearing a plain, light pink shirt and, what looked like, suit trousers. Derek got the impression that this was Jeremy in relaxed mode and his tie and suit jacket weren't far away.

"I believe your father is joining the residents here next week," he said.

Jeremy nodded.

"That's right, on Thursday. I'm his only son and had to move to Tenhamshire with my work about a year ago. Dad's in a Home in Manchester and it's been difficult trying to get there and see him each weekend. I finally persuaded him to move out this way. Well, it's a big thing moving, especially when you're ninety-two. I've been scouring the county, looking at all manner of Homes but I must say this one seems perfect."

"Oh, so it's not just Margaret then," Derek teased.

Jeremy blushed again.

"An added bonus, shall we say. No, actually it's the grounds here that really stood out. They're amazing. Dad always loved his garden at his old house. He had a couple of acres. Here he can enjoy then without having to do all of the work."

Derek smiled.

"Yes, he can leave that up to me."

"Well, what I've seen so far is a credit to you."

Derek felt rather proud of himself.

"Would you like another look round," he asked, "I've pretty much finished in here. I can tell you about the plans for the new area we're going to develop, if that's something that would interest you?"

Jeremy beamed.

"I'd love to," he said.

Derek found Jeremy very easy to talk to as they walked around the grounds of the Home. He had a number of stories about his own life but he didn't force them on Derek although they were all interesting. After he'd left university ("Almost thirty-five years ago. I can't believe it's that long") he'd gone travelling and wound up working as a gardener himself for a while in the United States.

"I can't say I was very good," he told Derek, as they walked along the back terrace on their return to the glasshouse.

Several residents were sitting on the terrace, relaxing in the shade after their breakfast.

"I remember one day taking some young saplings out to plant up. They'd been grown from seed in peat moss compost.

Well, it was a blistering hot day, much hotter than this. I hadn't taken appropriate clothing and was wearing a borrowed pair of very baggy shorts."

Willy Jenson had just emerged from the back door of the conservatory and was slowly making his way to an empty wicker chair beside where Derek and Jeremy were talking.

"I wasn't wearing a hat and fainted. Of course I had to fall right into the rose bed didn't I."

Mr Jenson picked up a newspaper and passed by the back of the two men.

"When I came to," Jeremy continued, "I was covered with pricks and had peat stuck up my bottom."

Mr Jenson's eyes widened. He gasped, clutched at his chest and collapsed into the wicker chair. Fortunately a nurse was close by.

Chapter 13

Angela found Margaret in the dining room having breakfast with Dora, on a table that also included Sir Jasper. His eyes lit up when he saw Angela and he pushed his stick onto the floor. Kenny got there first and picked it up for him, annoying Sir Jasper but making Dora's day.

"It should be illegal to keep buns that firm and round covered up," she said.

"Mum, stop it."

"What? I'm only admiring beauty."

"You're sexually harassing the staff."

"Chance would be a fine thing at my age," she told her, winking at Kenny.

Margaret smiled as Angela approached but the smile very quickly dropped as she realised something was wrong. She stood up.

"Let's go into the front lounge," she said.

Dora stood up as well.

"I didn't mean you too."

"Oi, you're not leaving me out. I knew something was wrong on Wednesday when she floored that irritating volunteer at Tenham House."

"I didn't actually floor him," Angela told her, her face reddening, "Just scared him."

"Yeah right," Dora laughed, "That's why he walked off limping afterwards. I'm coming with you. No, you stay here Sir Jasper. This is girl talk, not girl on girl action. You're not missing anything."

She indicated the next table along.

"Continue with the assignment to find out what Dental Flossie gets up to at eight o'clock each night. I think we're getting close now."

Sir Jasper saluted her orders. Before they could step away a nurse entered the room and came over to Margaret, whispering something into her ear. Margaret blushed.

"Is he here now? Oh, erm, okay, I'll come out."

She turned to Angela.

"I'll be two ticks," she said, "Jeremy has shown up."

"Oh, last night's date."

Margaret giggled.

"Perhaps he's after what you didn't give him last night," Dora said.

"Oh mum!"

"I've told you, at your age you can't afford to be coy. You've got to put out as soon as you can."

Margaret tutted.

"I'll be back in a couple of minutes," she told Angela, and headed off towards the hallway, patting at her hair as she went.

Dora took Angela's arm and they made their way to the front lounge through the connecting double doors. The room was empty, the residents of the Home preferring the east facing conservatory or back terrace to sit in after breakfast to enjoy the morning sun.

The front lounge was a large, square room with a lovely bay window which had floor to ceiling glass. The focal point was an impressive white, marble fireplace. With the central heating it was rarely ever lit but when it was, invariably windows had to be opened to cool the room to a comfortable temperature.

Above it was a large, ornate, gold-framed mirror that Angela had always admired. The room would have been used as an entertaining area back in its heyday and with its elaborate cornicing it still hadn't lost that splendour.

Dora led the way over to the window where several wingback chairs were placed together, facing out to the grounds at the front. Margaret came in a few minutes later, still red-faced and grinning.

"I've sent him off to chat to Derek," she told them, "He's usually round in the walled garden when he's here on a Saturday."

"I'm sorry," Angela told her, "I didn't mean to ruin your plans."

Margaret shook her head.

"You haven't," she said, "I wasn't expecting him anyway. He found my earring in his car."

"Where you dropped it on purpose last night?" Dora enquired.

Margaret giggled.

"Actually I didn't but it's not a bad idea to remember."

She instantly became more her business-self when she turned back to Angela.

"So," she said, "What's happened."

Angela felt tears spring to her eyes and it took a couple of deep breaths before she could speak. She told her two friends about Max being the new client at work and what he'd threatened her with.

"What a bastard," Margaret said, "Have you told Derek?"

"No," she replied, "He'd be angry. He'd probably want to go and see him and Max knows some dangerous people. I don't want him getting hurt."

"What about the police?"

"What could they do? Besides, that would still end up with the auction house discovering the truth."

Dora tutted.

"I don't see what all the fuss is about," she said, "**We** know you used to be a prostitute and it doesn't bother us. Why should it bother anyone at work? If it does, well, tough on them."

Angela sighed.

"It's not as easy as that, Dora. There's the reputation of the auction house to consider as well. How would it look if potential customers discovered they had an ex-prostitute valuing antiques? Besides, they'd also wonder how I'd managed to get a role there. It would all go back to Alistair, the man that got me a job in the first place. He was a sweet man, a true gentleman and even though he's dead, I wouldn't want his reputation tarnished. He has children and grandchildren."

"I still think you ought to tell Derek," Margaret said.

Angela bit her bottom lip.

"There's a problem with that," she admitted, "You see, when we bumped into Max two years ago on the coach trip I just told Derek that he was a mistake from my past. When he discovered I was a prostitute on the last night of that holiday he assumed Max was an ex-client and I…well I didn't correct him."

"You mean he wasn't a client."

"Well, yes and no."

Margaret looked at Dora and then back at Angela.

"This is intriguing," she said.

Angela took a deep breath as she tried to find the words to explain.

"I told you I started prostitution to help me get through university."

Margaret and Dora both nodded.

"Well, I planned to stop once I'd got my degree. It was towards the end of my course that Max…used my services a couple of times. (He'd heard about me through a friend of his at the university). He was charming, fit and very attractive. He was fifteen years older than me. To a twenty-one year old, thirty six seemed so mature and exciting. I wasn't sure why he wanted or needed to pay for sex. He exuded sex appeal and could easily have got any woman he wanted."

"Whereabouts did you say he lived?" Dora asked.

"Ssh," Margaret admonished.

"Mind you, he did have some, well, special tastes in the bedroom."

"Ooh, like what?"

"Mum, I won't tell you again, keep quiet!"

"I knew he was married," Angela continued, "He told me that himself. He had two children as well, daughters I believe. Well, even though I'd spent almost three years charging men for sex, I was a very naïve twenty-one year old when it came to love. I told him that I was giving up prostitution once I'd got my history degree and said that I'd saved enough money to be able to do a Master's. He was very complimentary, told me I was worth more than what I'd become and I fell for him, hook, line and sinker. We began dating and I'd never felt so happy. He moved me into his apartment that he owned in town. He told me he'd leave his wife once the kids were older and I believed him."

"What? You believed that?" Margaret said, "That story's as old as the hills."

Angela stood up.

"I know, I know," she said, looking out of the window, "I

told you I was naïve about love. I'd never had a relationship before. I'd never had a proper job before. Well, who'd give Bert Jenkins' daughter a Saturday job in their shop? The mother had run off years before. You couldn't trust him so you shouldn't trust his kids either. That's what they all thought where I lived. He was a thief so I'd be a thief as well. All I really knew when I headed off to university was that I had a brain, but I had to sell my body to be able to use it."

Angela fell silent. She stared out at the grounds beyond the parking area. Two colourful flowerbeds edged the car park with an expanse of dry, yellowing lawn beyond. It was her Derek that had made them beautiful. He made her feel beautiful. So had Max, early on. Behind her, Margaret and Dora sat patiently, waiting for their friend to continue. Eventually Angela turned round and sat back down again.

"So there I was, living in a luxury apartment, waiting for my exam results and planning my future. Then dad paid a visit."

Angela could feel the anger of the morning return to her.

"He said he just happened to be in the area. This was Colchester in Essex. I was brought up near Market Harborough in Leicestershire, over a hundred miles away. I doubt he was just out for a walk and thought he'd pop in and see me. Anyway, he stayed at the apartment for a few days. He even met Max a couple of times who was very cordial to him. After he left I found that the money I'd put aside to complete my Master's degree had gone. That was the first time he stole from me. My God I've been a mug letting that man keep coming back into my life. I was so right to throw him out this morning."

Margaret and Dora shot each other a look, both realising they needed to stay silent on that topic until after Angela had finished her story.

"I was so distraught," she continued, "Even obtaining a first for my history degree couldn't lift my spirits. Max arrived at the apartment while I was crying and I told him everything. He took me in his arms and said everything was going to be fine. He'd support me while I continued my education. I told him it was too much but he said he loved me and that I could do him the odd favour when he needed one."

Angela paused. This was coming to the difficult part of the story; something she'd never told anyone before and tried not to think about.

"Well, I obviously had the summer to look forward to before starting the next part of my degree. I was hoping Max and I would be able to spend lots of time together but that didn't happen. I knew his children were on school holiday so I had to content myself with Max's occasional visits. I sat in the apartment waiting, just in case he was going to turn up unexpectedly."

Margaret couldn't help a snort of disgust escaping. Saying this all out loud Angela could understand why, but twenty years ago she'd been a very different person. She carried on with her story.

"Then the first of his 'favours' came my way. He told me he had a difficult, rather dodgy business client who needed sweetening up. He wanted me to go to dinner with him and if he wanted more, to give it to him."

Margaret gasped. Angela shrugged her shoulders.

"I didn't feel I had a choice and it wasn't like I hadn't done it before. Max told me that if I didn't help him then he might end up getting hurt. I was totally obsessed with him and thought that if it meant I was helping Max, then surely that was a good thing. But then it happened for a second time, with someone else; then a third and then more frequently. It took me the summer to realise I was, to all intents and purposes, still a prostitute and Max had become my pimp, giving me money each week to live on. When I told him I didn't want to do his favours anymore the mask slipped and I saw the real Max appear. He said I was going to continue with the favours for as long as he wanted me to. It was really scary. The man I'd fallen in love with had gone. His shell was there but someone evil had taken it over. I didn't know what to do. He was providing me with food and lodging and I had nowhere else to go. I rarely went home anyway but since dad had taken my money, Max owned me and he knew it. He had me over a barrel."

"Ooh is that one of the extras he liked you to do?"

"Oh for God's sake mum!"

It didn't look like Angela had heard. She was staring over Dora's shoulder, towards the fireplace. A second later she shook her head and continued on.

"Then that first client came back again, the one Max had told me to be nice to otherwise he'd get hurt. I didn't want to see him again but Max got angry and I found myself going out to dinner with him once more."

Angela sighed.

"I made the mistake of refusing this guy sex only once he was back inside my apartment. Well, he didn't like being told to go. He said he wasn't going to leave without getting everything he'd already paid for."

Fresh tears sprang to Angela's eyes.

"I found out then how dangerous Max's acquaintances could be. The guy was so angry and violent. A neighbour heard the commotion and found me in a mess in the lounge. I was rushed off to hospital. It was that attack that left me unable to have children."

Angela pulled a tissue out of her jeans pocket and blew her nose.

"I told Derek I was sterilised. I lied to him and yet lately all I've been telling him is it's not good to have secrets. What a hypocrite I am."

Margaret moved across to Angela and held her while she cried. A resident tried to come into the room but Dora told him loudly to fuck off and he left. Once composed, Angela continued with her story.

"Max came to see me in the hospital," she said, "He didn't even ask how I was. He just sat there, fuming because I'd hurt him by not sleeping with this guy. He talked as if I was going to resume my 'favours' once I was back at home again. Well, that wasn't going to happen. The attack had been awful, but it had given me a kind of strength. I suppose I'd hit rock bottom and felt I couldn't be hurt any worse than I had been already. My love for Max had turned to hate. I told him it was all over and that I was going to tell the police everything. He laughed, said I was being dramatic and that they wouldn't believe me."

Angela's lips quivered at the edges, as if she was trying not to smile.

"I sat myself up in the bed. God, it hurt but I did it so that I could face him at the same level. I told him that maybe the police wouldn't believe me but that wouldn't stop me telling them. Perhaps they'd investigate further and talk to his wife. I told him I could talk to her too. I knew where they lived. Maybe I wouldn't be believed but mud sticks. I said that I had absolutely nothing to lose now as I had nothing left. Was he prepared to risk everything he had?"

"What did he say to that?" Margaret asked.

"He was so angry but he couldn't touch me, not there in the hospital. Actually he wouldn't have anyway, he was just a bully. It was always someone else he got to do his dirty work for him. He stood up, told me I was a filthy whore and always would be and then left. I didn't hear from him again and then someone told me later that he'd moved the family to Spain. I got on with my life."

Margaret scratched her head.

"That's quite a story," she said, "But what I'm having trouble with is, after you were attacked, how could you have possibly returned to prostitution?"

Angela looked at her matter-of-factly.

"A very low feeling of self-worth and a raging anger at what had happened," she told her, "The man that attacked me said he'd paid Max a lot of money for me. Well, I thought I might as well make that money for myself. I swore never to trust a man again and I started becoming very picky with whom I slept with. Obviously it was difficult to start with but I now had the strength I hadn't had before. I was going to be the one in charge. Sex with me was on my terms now. The plan had been to earn the money back to do my Master's but after a while I realised I was making big money. I was being recommended and I took on a lot of escort work. I was an intelligent woman that a man could talk to as well as have sex with. I was taken on business trips around the world. I was seeing new places and learning from life. I didn't need to return to university. The money earned gave me a life to live and I started to enjoy myself. The one thing I always made sure of was never to fall in love again. I found that rather easy; until I booked up to go on a coach holiday two years ago."

Dora sat forward in her chair.

"So why is there still a problem," she asked, "You either tell this Max to go to hell or you let him walk all over you again. Is there really a decision there that has to be made? If you let him walk all over you, you might as well return to your old life. There are plenty of rich, old men in here that would pay a hefty price for a piece of your tail."

"For goodness sake, mum!"

"What? If this Max is just a bully why is she letting him get to her?"

Angela sighed.

"Because this time I have too much to lose, that's why. I fear for what he could do to others around me. Well, not him personally but another of his dodgy contacts. I mean, Ursula and my dad went to Ryan Harbour yesterday where Max is staying and dad felt they were being followed. Max knew I was at Tenham House the other day as well. He phoned our house and spoke to Ursula. That must be how he discovered who she was and how he managed to have them followed yesterday. I'm really scared."

"Calm down," Dora said, "Let's get this into proportion. If this piece of shit is such a bully then he's using bullying tactics. Now then, when did you find out he knew you were at Tenham House?"

"Yesterday at work. He gave the auction house photographer a message for me."

"Well, there you go then," Dora said, "He phoned your house on Wednesday (and a phone number is easy to get hold of) and he spoke to Ursula, who told him you were out. She'd have told him where as well. That's how he knew about Tenham

House."

"Mum's right," Margaret added, "You know Ursula; she probably told him where you were, what time you were coming back and what colour knickers you were wearing that day. You said Max could be charming and Ursula loves a good chat."

Angela nodded.

"Yes, you could be right," she admitted, "But even so, he knew about Alistair too."

"Who's Alistair?" Dora asked.

"Alistair St John Pilkington, the man that got me my first auction house job. Max knows all about that."

"I've heard that name before," Margaret said, trying to recall where from.

"Yes, well he was well-known in antiques circles," Angela explained, "He was also a director of several companies. He used to hire me a few times a year to attend events with him."

"Well there you go," Margaret told her, "That's how Max found out about you and him. You were at public events with Alistair. You said he was well-known in certain circles. If Max didn't know him he probably knew someone who did. I mean, I've heard of the man and if I checked, I'd probably find someone I know who was also an acquaintance. It's not so unlikely. There must have been photographs taken at these events which will almost certainly be on the internet somewhere now. All that information coupled with your biography on your firm's website, it wouldn't take much for Max to work out what Alistair did for you. You're getting too wound up over this. You said yourself Max is a manipulative bully, that's all he's doing, manipulating you."

"And he's doing a good job of it. I'm frightened," Angela admitted.

"Why?" Dora asked.

"Sorry?"

"Why are you frightened of him?"

Angela frowned.

"Did you nod off while I was talking just now?"

"There's no need to get huffy with me," Dora told her, calmly, "What I mean is, this Max has had twenty years to get his so-called revenge on you. Why now?"

"Because he saw my photo online while he was looking for an auction house to sell his mother's things through."

"Yes but you keep telling us that he has some dodgy contacts. Well, if that was the case, why did he walk away from you twenty years ago? Surely if he'd wanted to get back at you he'd have known someone who could have added you to the foundations of a new office block?"

"Oh mum!"

"You know what I mean. I'm trying to help here. This poor woman is frightened of a bully but I don't believe he does have dangerous acquaintances."

"It wasn't a respected businessman that attacked me," Angela told her, quietly.

Dora took Angela's hands in hers.

"I know that love," she said, kindly, "But that was a nasty man that got angry and attacked you. It wasn't some planned event and there's been nothing else done to you in twenty years. You saw this Max the next day in hospital and he wasn't hurt was he? He told you that guy would hurt him if you didn't sleep together but you were the one attacked. You're allowing this guy to manipulate you. Now, think about what we've just said. Do you really think this man is some kind of criminal genius with murderers and thieves in his back pocket?"

Angela shrugged her shoulders.

"Maybe not," she said, "But can I afford to take the chance that you're right. I've got Derek and Ursula to worry about, perhaps even you two as well. I want to keep everyone safe. Max is going to cause trouble."

"Well then," Margaret said, "Let's give you some ammo to fight him with."

"Sorry?"

"She means we'll all go round to his house together and beat the crap out of him," Dora told her.

"That isn't what I mean, mum. No, we'll use some of his tactics. He's been looking at your past, let's look into his. Perhaps he's got a lot to lose as well. I can't say I would be able to find out if he has some dodgy contacts, although I agree with mum and think he's just bluffing, but I can certainly look into his business history."

"Really?"

"Oh yes, it's simple, especially with the internet now. I've also got a contact in Spain, one of dad's old acquaintances who retired out there. He was an expert in company law. He'll be happy to do a bit of digging for me. We'll find out what we can about Max."

"He won't get into trouble will he, your friend?" Angela asked, "Or you?"

Margaret laughed.

"Of course not," she said, "This is simple stuff really. Besides, how do you think my father made his business so successful? He had to be aware of what was going on with his competitors. He had to grease a few palms when it came to getting permission to extend premises. There's a lot of 'knowing the right people' that goes on. I'm still in touch with a lot of dad's old contacts."

"With what, a Ouija board?" Dora asked.

"They're not all dead," Margaret replied, "I made some contacts of my own as well."

Dora sighed.

"Can we still keep beating the shit out of this guy on the table as well?" she asked, gripping her walking stick tightly.

"Well let's leave it as plan B for now, mum. First we'll find out about this Max's life. What's his surname?"

"Well, he's using Saunders now," Angela told her, "But when I knew him it was Trelawney. He used to own a number of properties around the Colchester area I believe. Besides the apartment I was living in I think there were a few business premises, you know, high street shops, that sort of thing. He was always talking about his business empire."

Margaret nodded.

"Right," she said, "And he is, or was living in Spain. You don't know whereabouts?"

Angela shook her head.

"No worries. It might just take a bit longer to track down the information. Leave it with me. I'll make a few phone calls."

Angela smiled. For the first time in days she felt some relief.

"Thanks," she said, "I really appreciate this. Now if I could only be sure that he doesn't have any dodgy contacts I'd feel like me again."

Dora leaned forwards, resting her hands on the curved handle of her stick.

"Don't **you** know anyone who could help you with that," she asked, "I mean, in your line of work you must have met lots of different people."

"As a valuer?"

"No, I mean whorring."

"Mum!"

Dora waved her hand.

"I wasn't being nasty," she said, "I couldn't think of another word. Surely you met a few dodgy people yourself in your time, or even someone high up in the police force. A Chief Constable's salary could afford you surely."

Angela shook her head.

"My contacts tended to be wealthy businessmen who were very into the arts," she explained, "They took me on business trips, well away from any wives or girlfriends. I never mixed with anyone from the police."

"Shame," Dora said, "You'd think they'd be into the sort of things you could provide, you know, uniforms, handcuffs, truncheons, role play?"

Margaret sighed, shaking her head at her mother.

"I need to start rationing late night television," she said.

She turned back to face Angela.

"Now then," she said, "Why don't you, Derek and Ursula come up here for dinner this evening? It might be a bit tense at home, you know, with Bert so recently gone. That's as long as you don't mind eating at about eight o'clock. The residents will have all left the dining room by then."

"That sounds lovely," Angela told her, "I'm sure we'd all love to come."

"Me too?" Dora asked.

Margaret grinned.

"Would you stay away if I said no?"

Dora shook her head.

Angela laughed. It was amazing how much better she felt already, having been able to trust in her friends. She couldn't help thinking that she should trust Derek with this information as well but in truth, she was just trying to protect him.

"I must admit, I've got an ulterior motive about tonight," Margaret said, "I want to ask Derek another favour. We've got Tommy Jefferies funeral on Thursday."

"Have we," Dora asked, her face brightening, "I love a good funeral. That's happened quickly."

Margaret nodded.

"I know. He already had it all planned and paid for and he's got a plot in the churchyard next to his wife. You should see the outfit he's being buried in, all rhinestones and white leather."

"Kinky," Angela said.

Dora laughed.

"He was into Elvis," she told her.

"That's right," Margaret said, "He's being brought into the church to his and his late wife's favourite song, 'The Wonder of You.'"

"And going out to, 'A Little Less Conversation' I suppose."

"Mum!"

"Not that he was ever much of a talker."

"Anyway, Thursday morning is the only day his great niece can come to a funeral. She only lives in Tenham but apparently has important meetings the rest of the week."

Dora tutted.

"She never came to see him while he was alive. Why's she bothering now?"

"The will," Margaret told her, "Not that she's getting much. After paying for the funeral and leaving enough for some drinks for his fellow residents afterwards, Tommy left the rest of his money to charity. The great niece is only getting a vase she's always liked apparently but Tommy stated that she'd only get it if she turned up for the funeral. I'm meant to go along to ensure she's there but that's the day Jeremy's dad is arriving. I was hoping Derek could take my place instead."

Dora tutted again.

"I bet that vase will turn up at your auction house on Friday," she said to Angela.

Angela grinned.

"I'm afraid the vicar is tied up elsewhere on Thursday as well," Margaret continued, "So his curate is going to perform the service."

Dora clapped her hands and laughed.

"Oh great," she said, "Nervous Nigel. This is going to be a scream."

"Mum, it's a funeral!" Margaret chided, before turning to Angela, "I try to go to as many of the residents' funerals as I can but I also like to greet all new residents as well. I'm hoping Derek will be okay with representing me at the funeral. I know a couple of the nurses will be there but they need to concentrate on making sure the residents get there and back safely."

"I'm sure he won't mind," Angela told her.

"Mind?" Dora said, "He won't mind. Not with Nervous Nigel in charge. Oh this will be great. This'll get Tommy back for my losing a tenner on him dying."

"What was that?" Margaret asked.

"Oh, er, nothing."

Chapter 14

Angela was pleased they were going up to the Home for dinner. Ursula had seemed very subdued during lunch.

"I must say, I'm going to miss Bert," she'd told them, "I've rather enjoyed going out and about with him this past week. After visiting the bank today he was going to treat me to a sixty-nine."

"What!"

Derek had looked stunned.

"We were going to go into that ice cream parlour next to the bank," she'd explained, "And have an ice cream with a chocolate flake in it."

"That's a ninety-nine mum!"

"Is it? Oh well, it doesn't matter now does it."

Although she thought it had been the right decision to make her father leave, Angela couldn't help feeling a tad guilty for Ursula's sake. When she and Derek were changing for dinner that evening she asked him,

"Do you think your mum is happy with moving to Tenhamshire?"

Derek finished buttoning up his shirt.

"What do you mean?" he asked.

Angela walked across to him, holding her sliver necklace with the sapphire pendant up to her neck. As she turned, Derek took hold of the ends and clipped it up for her.

"Well she seems very down about dad leaving. The way she keeps talking about the various villagers around here I assumed she was settling in. Well, let's face it, I was worried that she was settling in a little too well but now I'm wondering if those other people are just acquaintances, you know, people you speak to in passing but not actual friends. Is she lonely here? Was dad her chance at making a new friend? I know she wanted to live closer to us but we're out at work each day. We've got each other and are sorting out a new life together. What is your mum doing? She's left her life behind her. Perhaps we've not given her enough attention."

Derek tucked his shirt into his jeans.

"You might have a point," he admitted, "But I think perhaps she's waiting until she finds a place of her own before settling down. I mean, it's not worth her making friends in Baddlesbury if she ends up living in Ryan Harbour."

At the mention of Ryan Harbour, Angela instinctively felt a knot in her stomach. She had to remember Margaret was going to help her try and sort that situation out.

"I think mum will make friends wherever she settles," Derek continued, "Still, perhaps we ought to do a few more things together, especially with your dad gone. I must admit I've got used to coming home each day to a meal waiting for us. I'd hate to take her for granted. We should go out more."

"Starting tonight."

Derek grinned.

"Yeah, what a great start. We're taking my mum to a Retirement Home."

Angela smiled.

"Yes it doesn't actually sound like a good night out, does it. Sorry I threw my dad out Ursula but don't worry, we've found a place where you can make lots of new friends."

They laughed. It felt good, to both of them.

The pleasant mood changed once they were back downstairs. Ursula was in her room. For a split second Angela worried that she may have shut herself in there, refusing to come out until Bert was brought back to the house. However when Derek called out, she opened the door. She was wearing a white blouse over a grey skirt and had applied her make up but she seemed perplexed.

"Sorry I've been so long," she said, "But I can't find my emerald bracelet."

A startled look passed between Angela and Derek.

"I know we're not going anywhere fancy," Ursula continued, "But I had it on yesterday when I went out with Bert and he so admired it I thought I ought to wear it more often. Goodness knows where I've put it."

They took Angela's car up to the Home. It wasn't that long a walk but there had finally been some rain forecast for later. They drove in silence. It didn't seem to have occurred to Ursula that Bert could have stolen her bracelet and neither Angela nor Derek wanted to tell her.

At the Home they made their way to the dining room. Dora was in there alone, looking at something on her iPad. Margaret followed them in. She was looking a little stressed.

"Honestly," she said, "I've never known someone get so riled about a sticky door."

"Who has?" Dora asked.

"Florence Fitzpatrick. She says the hot summer and now the damp in the air has made her door stick so that she can't lock it. She's been paranoid about locking her door since she said someone had been inside her room."

Derek cast a glance at Dora who maintained her innocent expression.

"I told her it's the cleaner that goes in each day but she's adamant someone else has been in there," Margaret continued, "I think the poor dear may be worrying too much and is becoming confused. She's always staring anxiously at her watch. Perhaps I ought to have a word with the doctor."

"That's probably best," Dora told her.

Derek thought Dora must be immune to guilt. She'd told him herself that she and Sir Jasper had managed to get into Dental Flossie's room.

"I've told her I'll get the door fixed tomorrow but she went into a bit of a panic," Margaret said, "It's taken me ages to calm her down. In the end I told her if the door sticks and makes it difficult to open, why is she worried about it being locked. It's practically the same thing."

"And that calmed her down?" Angela asked.

"Well, that and a promise that if it's not fixed tomorrow she'll get a reduction in her monthly bill."

"Ooh, I'll have to get my door to stick," Dora said.

"You don't pay anything for your room, remember?"

"Oh that's right, I don't," Dora said brightly.

Margaret did a double-take as she looked across the table at her mother.

"Why have you got your iPad with you? That's very rude."

"Calm down. I'm not using it now. Sir Jasper told me earlier that he's going to send me an e mail tonight that I won't want to miss."

"He told you he's going to send you an e mail," Margaret queried, a puzzled expression on her face, "But you live in the same house."

Dora shrugged her shoulders.

Derek was sat in the seat beside where Margaret was

standing.

"Would you like me to go up and see if I can do something about the door?" he asked.

"No, you're here as a guest," Margaret told him, patting his shoulder, "Besides, I've got another favour to ask you."

"Angela mentioned it already," he replied, "It's fine. I can go to the funeral. The weather forecast isn't meant to be too good next week, lots of rain. I know we need it but I won't be able to do as much in the garden as I'd like anyway."

"That's another thing," Margaret said, "With the weather such as it is, I was going to say; after representing me at the funeral on Thursday morning, why don't you take the afternoon off and head down to your apartment. You could have Friday as an extra day to get on and finish that decorating. I hate the thought of you losing income on that property. The sooner it's decorated the sooner you can have tenants in there again."

That idea pleased Derek. A long weekend meant he could get painting done **and** go and visit Nathan. Of course, Leanne would expect him to have spoken with Angela about the guardianship by then. He could say she'd had trouble with her father and it hadn't been the right time. That wasn't a complete lie.

"I'll go check on dinner," Margaret said, "Monique, bless her, stayed on to prepare it for us."

She headed off towards the kitchen door.

"Perhaps you should take Angela with you this weekend, Derek," Margaret called back, over her shoulder, "Help get the job done quicker."

She disappeared into the kitchen. A look of horror appeared on Derek's face that wasn't missed by the three women sitting across from him at the dining table. Fortunately Angela just laughed and said,

"Don't worry Derek, I won't be coming. You've seen my attempts at painting walls."

He smiled with relief.

"Yes," he said, "That's true."

"But perhaps Ursula would like to go with you?"

"What?"

Angela turned to Ursula.

"Would you like to go back and visit some old friends?" she asked.

This could ruin his plans.

"No I don't think I'll bother," she replied.

Derek's relieved sigh was louder than he expected it to be.

"Well that's nice," Ursula said, "Anyone would think you didn't want to spend time with your mother."

"No, no, it's not that," Derek spluttered, before seeing the glint in his mum's eye.

She was only joking and he grinned back, but Dora was looking thoughtfully at him. She never missed a thing. He was sure she was pondering what he was getting up to at the weekend. Margaret returned to the room.

"Dinner's going to be another ten minutes," she told them, "Monique said she'll serve. She's such a treasure. I hope a roast chicken is okay."

Derek stood up.

"In that case why don't I head up to see Dental Flossie?"

"Who? Oh, Florence. Well, only if you're sure," Margaret said.

"It's fine."

"She's room twelve, second floor."

Derek hurried out of the room. While he didn't think Dora

was about to ask him straight out what he was up to, she might have started asking some awkward questions about the weekend. Unlike her, Derek found it very easy to feel and look guilty.

In the dining room Dora's iPad pinged.

"Oh it's the message from Sir Jasper," she said, "He's sent me a link to open."

At that second, Sir Jasper himself rushed into the room, his stick dragging along the floor behind him. He had a laptop balanced across his arms. He was grinning away to himself but pulled up sharply when he saw Dora wasn't alone.

"Oh," he said, "I didn't realise you had company."

"Well what did you think I meant when I said I was dining later this evening?"

Sir Jasper shrugged his shoulders.

"Anyway," Dora said, her eyes back on her iPad, "What is this link all about? GrannyGrinding.com?"

"Perhaps you shouldn't look now," Sir Jasper told her, putting his laptop down onto the table behind where the group were sitting.

Dora wasn't listening. She'd opened the link and laughed.

"Oh my God," she said, "Sir Jasper, I know you've not got any lately but even for you this is sick."

"It's not for me," he cut in.

"What is all this about?" Margret asked.

Across the table from her, Angela and Ursula leaned in to look at the screen of Dora's iPad. Ursula gasped and quickly stood up, walking away from the table with a tissue to her mouth. Angela was smirking.

"Granny porn is it, Sir Jasper?" she called over to him.

Margaret whipped round in her chair. In an instant she was

standing beside Sir Jasper, looking at the screen of his laptop. On it were several live feed screens of old ladies, lying on beds wearing very little.

"Oh Sir Jasper," Margaret said, disappointedly, "You've a very sick mind haven't you."

"It's not for me," he whined, "Look."

His cursor pressed one of the individual screens and the image filled the laptop. Margaret gasped.

"Oh my God, it's Florence."

The small, grey-haired old lady was sat on the end of her bed, a vision in a black leather basque and nothing else. The outfit had detachable cups and one of them was hanging open, a wrinkled, flat, old tit dangling out of it, looking like a deflated balloon. She'd gone mad with her compact and the white powder on her face showed up every wrinkle. With the bright red lipstick, she looked like a hundred year old kinky ghost.

Dora began laughing on the other table as she too found the right screen.

"Dental Flossie," she said, out loud, "So that's what you get up to at eight o'clock each night, you little strumpet."

Flossie had her camera angled so that the mirrored doors on her wardrobe were in shot. The camera equipment couldn't be seen in the reflection, just the door into her bedroom and the back of Flossie herself, spilling over the top of the basque, all back fat and liver spots.

"She must be making a fortune," Sir Jasper said, "You have to set up an account to pay for a private show."

"So that's how she can afford to live here," Dora said.

Sir Jasper nodded.

"Although I've found you can just type odd things onto the screen without an account and she'll sometimes do what you ask. I suppose it's a way to try and entice you in. Watch this."

He spoke as he typed.

"Stick a finger up your arse."

"Oh God Sir Jasper," Margaret said, while Angela gasped as the instruction was carried out on screen.

Dora was still laughing.

"No wonder she was worried about her door being stuck," she said, "No one wants to burst in on that."

Margaret's hands shot to her face.

"Oh my God," she said, "I've sent Derek up there."

As everyone looked back at their screens, a knocking could be heard on Flossie's door.

*

Derek wouldn't normally have waited for the lift to take him up to the second floor but one of the residents was using the stair lift and from past experience he knew he couldn't get away with rushing past them up the stairs, but would instead be expected to walk behind them at the same pace and have a natter. When the lift door finally opened he was met by Maureen, wheeling one of the residents out into the hallway.

"Sorry Mr Brady," she said, "But I just can't remember the name of the seventh dwarf. Now then, let me see, we've had Dopey."

Mr Brady rolled his eyes at Derek.

"I'm stuck with Dopey," he said.

Derek grinned. Maureen was concentrating too hard to hear.

"Perhaps you could help Derek," she asked him.

Once they'd located Sneezy, Derek was able to get into the lift and go up to the second floor. Number twelve was down the far end of the corridor. Outside he knocked gently. There was no answer. He knocked a little louder; perhaps Flossie was hard of hearing. He called out to her. Silence in a care home wasn't good. Maybe something was wrong. What if Flossie had hurt herself trying to force the door shut? Surely it constituted a fire hazard if she couldn't open her door. Margaret was being a bit blasé about it. He tried the handle. It turned but the door didn't open. If it was stuck he may need to get his body behind it. He readied himself and lunged.

*

On the screens downstairs they watched as the door in the reflection of the mirror suddenly burst open and a body flew into the room. The figure disappeared from the wardrobe mirrors and reappeared in shot as Derek fell forwards on top of Flossie. She screamed and a set of teeth flew through the air.

"The lying cow!" Dora shouted, "They're not her own after all."

"That's what you're focussing on at the moment, is it?" Margaret called over to her, incredulously.

Angela was now standing beside Margaret, able to see more on the larger screen of Sir Jasper's laptop. She watched as Derek struggled to right himself on the bed, Flossie's wrinkled tit hanging across his eyes like a blindfold. He grabbed it and peeled it from off his face. Opening his eyes he yelled as he realised what he was holding and saw who it belonged to. Turning away from her he looked right into the camera.

"Ooh look," said Sir Jasper, reading the messages under the image, "Someone called 'BigD' has just asked her to strip the guy beside her."

Margaret looked up over the top of Sir Jasper's screen.

"Mum, get off of your iPad."

"You mind your own," was the response.

Back on the screen Derek was trying frantically to get off of the bed but Flossie had accidentally got him in a neck hold as she tried desperately to fasten the rubber cup back over her breast. The messages of the viewers were coming through thick and fast. Some were asking who the man was, others were offering to pay for a private sex show between the two of them, 'BigD' told Flossie to start spanking the guy's arse.

Derek eventually managed to release himself from Flossie's vice-like grip and bounced his way down to the edge of the bed. As he put his hands down onto the mattress to brace himself for standing up, a confused expression appeared on his face. As he raised his left hand into shot, everyone saw he'd managed to grab hold of a very large, and very realistic-looking, whirring vibrator. His expression changed to one of horror.

"Oh bugger," Flossie said, "Has it fallen out again."

Derek screamed and threw the vibrator over his shoulder.

"Not out of me," Flossie called after him, as Derek disappeared from view, "Out of its box."

A second later his profile was glimpsed in the reflection of the mirrored wardrobe door as he darted out of the room. A moment later the screen went blank. It was a good few minutes before Derek entered the silent dining room, white as a sheet.

"Erm, I don't think it's the right time for me to check Flossie's door," he told them, quietly.

Angela walked over to him and led him back to his seat.

"We know," she said, "We saw it all on the internet."

"What?"

"Congratulations Derek," Dora called over to him, "You've

just made your debut on GrannyGrinding.com."

"Oh God!"

Derek put his head in his hands. Angela patted his back.

"I saw and touched things in that room I never want to see or touch again," he whispered.

The kitchen door opened and Monique staggered in with a roast chicken on a large tray."

"Dinner is served," she called out, brightly, placing it down on the table right beside Derek, "Who's ready for a piece of lovely, plump bird?"

"Derek's just had one," Dora told her.

Monique didn't seem to hear. She tapped Derek on the shoulder.

"I bet you wouldn't say no to a nice bit of breast," she said.

"I'm sorry," Derek replied, looking up at her, "But I've just become a vegetarian."

Chapter 15

When Max arranged a meeting for Thursday morning to talk through the sale, Angela wasn't unduly worried. Margaret had already managed to work her magic. Angela assumed her Spanish contact must have been a great admirer of her father's as, on Wednesday, Margaret was able to give her a complete history of Max's business life. So much for the so-called 'business empire.'

When she'd first known Max, Angela had been impressed with his talk about the number of properties he owned and the businesses he was involved in, but only now did she see that it was just talk. At the time they met he actually only owned his family home. Property prices were increasing but Max had over-stretched himself and had had to sell all his rental properties to cover debts, including the apartment Angela had been living in, which he'd later rented back from the new owner. His 'other businesses' had been half-owner of a pub in a tiny, Essex village which closed due to a lack of custom, and an investment in a small restaurant in Colchester that was forced to shut down due to its continuing failure to meet basic hygiene standards.

His move to Spain was described by Margaret's friend as 'hasty.' There were a number of debts left behind. He made several other attempts at businesses there, mostly bars and restaurants for tourists, and while there was success for a while Max had once again over-stretched himself with property purchases and lost everything in the last recession. No wonder he was keen to sell off his late mother's belongings.

While this brought some relief a shadow of worry still remained. Angela knew that this was just a record of Max's legitimate businesses. What else had he been getting up to? She was pretty sure he hadn't declared his income from pimping her out that summer to the Inland Revenue so perhaps he had other hidden earnings. It was probably unlikely. After all, his so-called business empire that he'd boasted about didn't exist, so why should his dodgy lifestyle with dodgy acquaintances not just be a work of fiction as well? Both Margaret and Dora thought him a fraud but then they hadn't been the ones lying in a hospital bed after being attacked. Angela needed to be certain.

Margaret's contact had also managed to provide one other piece of information for her. Max's wife had left him a number of years before. She'd met and married a Spanish bar owner and, with her two daughters in tow, had moved to the Canary Islands and opened a hotel. Apparently the place was thriving. Knowing Max, Angela was aware that his wife being the one to leave would have been damaging to his ego, but there was no evidence that he was trying to sabotage her new life. While he was now trying to disrupt Angela's, she had to admit that she had been safe from his clutches for the last twenty years.

Perhaps he didn't have a network of dodgy contacts at his beck and call, ready to do his dirty work for him. Maybe he did just get lucky, stumbling over her photograph on the Jacobson & Lee website. Even so, that didn't necessarily make the situation less of a problem. He was alone, penniless and desperate, which was a dangerous combination. There was no telling what someone was capable of when they felt that way. Angela knew that feeling first hand. It was how she'd felt that day in the hospital, when she'd stood up to Max because she had nothing else to lose.

Of course in her case, Angela hadn't cared who knew how desperate and pathetic she felt. For someone like Max, where appearance was everything, he'd be devastated if the truth about the loss of his business empire or how his wife had left him for another man was known. That was the only thing Angela had to play with at the moment. Her boss, Ben was leading this meeting. Somehow she had to make Max understand that she knew everything and try and gain the upper hand.

In the meeting room beside Ben's office, Max sat staring at her, sneering while Ben chatted away. Angela stared right back at him.

"So this is the catalogue; hot off the press, so to speak," Ben said.

He handed a copy to Max.

"It looks great," Max replied, throwing it down on the table without even glancing at it.

"Aside from the catalogue, we've also been advertising the items online," Ben continued.

"Good of you."

"And they're creating a lot of interest. With Ms Jenkins up on the rostrum leading the sale I'm confident we'll be selling at the top end of her estimates."

Max grinned.

"Yes I'm sure you're right. Ms Jenkins will enjoy being the centre of attention that day. And she's always been marvellous at selling the goods to the highest bidder."

Ben chuckled.

"We're known for getting a fair price and at a very reasonable rate of commission compared to a lot of other auction houses."

"That's right," Angela said, smiling sweetly at Max, "Our commission rates give the customer a little extra in their pockets. It's great for those of you that are desperate for those extra few pounds."

"And we all enjoy an extra little bit every now and then don't we," Ben added, brightly, before realising how that sounded. He fell silent.

Max's eyes had narrowed slightly.

"I'm just sorry that we can't take delivery of the items until the day before the auction," Angela continued, "As this is an extra sale that we're putting on for you it does mean our storerooms are already full at the moment. I hope that doesn't inconvenience you with getting your mother's house onto the market. I'm sure you're desperate for a quick sale."

Max turned his gaze away from Angela for the first time. A frown had appeared and Angela knew he was puzzling over what she was saying. Ben was ignorant of the messages passing between them.

"I'm afraid we can't help you with that one," he said, "We only auction antiques here, not houses."

He looked at Angela.

"Perhaps we should extend our range," he joked.

Max's grin returned.

"Oh you'll be surprised at what she can sell," he said.

"Yes, well, Ms Jenkins is a very experienced lady."

"You can say that again."

Max was enjoying himself too much for Angela's liking.

"I haven't led a whole auction on my own before," she threw in.

"But you've still clocked up many happy hours performing

on the rostrum with Charles," Ben told her.

Max's eyes widened.

"Well that's one way to get a promotion," he said.

Ben chuckled again.

"Oh Ms Jenkins is a valued member of staff. You should have no worries about the amount of items in your sale. Once she's sold the first item she'll be away, and at it for hours."

"Yes her stamina is good."

"I promise you, she'll be banging that gavel down non-stop."

"That sort of thing usually cost extra."

"Pardon?"

"Perhaps," Angela interrupted, "We should discuss the actual day of the auction. I'm sure Mr Saunders is eager to get his cash and leave…I mean return to his home in Spain and to his…well, no one really."

The smile left Max's face. Angela smirked.

"Of course," Ben continued, "We're going to auction off the items next Friday. We were going to wait a couple of weeks but, confidentially, we have a TV crew filming us and they've brought the filming date forward to next week."

The smile now fell from Angela's face. She'd forgotten about the bloody TV programme. Max saw her expression change and he laughed.

"You want to film the auction of my goods," he said to Ben, "Well I think that's a marvellous idea."

Ben beamed.

"I'm so glad you agree," he told him.

"Oh yes, I think that sounds perfect. A large audience with all eyes on Ms Jenkins. How wonderful. I shall look forward to it."

"So you are coming to the auction," Ben asked, "We often

find a lot of our clients that are selling a large number of items find it rather stressful."

Max leaned forwards and rested his folded arms on the table in front of him, staring straight at Angela.

"Oh I wouldn't miss it for the world," he said.

The meeting at an end it was up to Angela to show Max out. They stopped by the front entrance and, for anyone watching, Angela had to be seen to shake her client's hand. She felt sick touching him.

"So," he said, "It's all working out well for me isn't it. You're up on the rostrum selling my items in front of an extra-large crowd. Wouldn't the TV people love a story about a whore auctioneer?"

"They're not going to get one though, are they," she whispered back, "I can still refuse to sell your items you know; and we both know how desperate you are for a bit of cash. Your business empire isn't up to much these days is it? Well, it never was really."

Max laughed.

"Been doing a little digging have you, my love? That's so cute."

"Don't call me 'love,'" she told him, "Not if you want your sale to go ahead."

Max's demeanour changed.

"Listen sweetheart," he hissed at her, "Don't try and threaten me. I hold all of the cards. You want to cancel my sale, go ahead. Your boss will want to know why. Yes I need the fucking money, so what. My bitch of a mother hardly gave me a penny while she was still alive but she's come up with the goods now."

He took a step closer to her and it was all Angela could do

not to flinch.

"Isn't it convenient that she died just when I needed money the most?"

"One of your imaginary friends again is it," Angela mocked, "You're so loved by these dodgy mates that they'd kill for you would they? Am I supposed to believe that?"

Max moved his head so that he could whisper in her ear.

"Who's talking friends? It's quite easy to pay the right person to create a little accident," he told her, sinisterly.

Angela was starting to lose her confidence.

"How can you afford to pay them," she said, realising her voice didn't sound quite as assertive as before, "Aren't you broke?"

Max sighed pityingly at her.

"My dear, you above everyone know the sort of money I'm about to make next week. Besides, an insignificant accident for an old woman doesn't cost much; a little push here, a snapped brake cable there. How is your mother-in-law by the way? It's Ursula isn't it? Still driving is she?"

Angela's heart began thumping loudly in her chest. She wasn't controlling this situation as she'd hoped. It was one thing to threaten her, but Ursula? She was always out and about in her car. Max's contacts suddenly seemed very real again.

"Just what do you want from me?" she asked.

Max looked pensively at her.

"You know, I'm glad you asked. Perhaps it's time I did get a little something from you."

"Like what?"

"I must admit," he continued, "I don't particularly want to appear on TV if I don't have to, and I have missed the delights of your services. I think it's time you returned to your old ways."

Angela's mouth dropped open.

"If you think I'm going to…"

"I won't take no for an answer," Max interrupted, "Why should Derek be the only man to enjoy you? How about Thursday? Yes, next Thursday, the day before the auction. You'll come over to see me that night and will show your appreciation for the amount of commission I'm giving you and for not spilling the beans about your past on national television. If you don't come then I'll be forced to appear here on the Friday…and I will."

Angela felt sick.

"There is no way I'm going to do…"

Max leaned in again, sharply.

"You don't have a fucking choice in the matter, sweetheart," he spat, "Now you bring your tight, little arse to my house next Thursday and we'll rekindle a few magical moments. I'll supply the accompaniments. I assume you had a ritual burning of all your straps, tassels, toys and outfits when you met your Derek, didn't you. All you need to bring with you are your moves."

He looked her up and down.

"And for God's sake wear something enticing will you?"

He winked at her as he put on his raincoat.

"I'm looking forward to it already," he said, "Aren't you? Here, press against me and feel how excited I am?"

Angela gasped in disgust and stepped away from him. Max laughed.

"You'd best get that out of your system now," he told her, "Because next week you'll be showing my body a bit more appreciation, otherwise it's all over for you."

He leered at her before turning and leaving the building. Angela felt the need to shower. She returned to the valuing room, hoping a bit of normality would help calm her down but all she saw was the world she loved, the world that Max was about to take from her. She collapsed into her chair in the ceramics area, ignoring Charles who was looking disgustedly at a Tupperware box a woman had just unwrapped.

"No madam," he said, "This is not a piece of Lalique."

Angela closed her eyes. This had gone beyond a game to Max now. He was acting like some kind of madman. What could she do? This was no empty threat. She either provided him with sex or waited for him to tell everyone about her past. Either way, Max was going to humiliate her.

Chapter 16

Be careful what you wish for Derek, he thought to himself, as he tried to tiptoe round the copious amount of muddy puddles that had formed on his route up to the staff entrance of the Home.

He'd wanted rain for ages but not this much. This June had been one of the sunniest on record but now it seemed to want to be one of the wettest as well. It had rained almost constantly since Sunday and he was fed up with it after four days. It had been handy on Monday when he and Ash had been able to replant the two empty flowerbeds at the back of the house into soft earth, but now the ground had turned to mud. The grass had regained its colour and begun growing with abandon. Ash was itching to be allowed to use the sit-on lawnmower. Derek had caught him sitting on it this morning inside the outbuilding as he passed by, making car noises as he turned the steering wheel left and right. He left him to it. There wasn't a lot else to do at the moment anyway.

He'd changed into his suit in his tiny office area and now headed into the Home to see Margaret for any final instructions regarding Tommy Jefferies funeral today.

"I spoke to the niece again this morning on the phone," Margaret told him, after Derek had sat down in her office.

She tutted.

"Three very short phone calls I've had with that selfish bitch and that's three too many."

Margaret passed over a carrier bag.

"Here, this is the vase that Tommy left her. She wanted to make sure someone was taking it to the church as she said she wouldn't have time to come up to the Home afterwards to collect it. She's heading back to work straight after the service. She's doing the minimum she can to get her hands on that vase. If I was Tommy I'd have left it to someone else but I think he wanted to do this. Knowing the sort of person his niece is I bet he had a good laugh adding this stipulation to his will, making sure she had to show up for his funeral."

Derek wished he'd known Tommy Jefferies better. He sounded like a very astute man. He looked inside the bag.

"This is only wrapped in a couple of sheets of newspaper," he said.

"Too right," Margaret told him, "I'm not going out to buy bubble wrap for her. She's lucky I'm not charging her five pence for the carrier bag."

"I'll head down now then to meet her outside the church, unless you want me to take any of the residents with me?"

Margaret shook her head.

"No, you go now Derek. Kenny is walking the able-bodied group down and the minibus is coming to take the others. It should be here any minute."

Derek walked down the main driveway of the Home and along the narrow lane that led up to the church. It was an impressive building for so small a village. He and Angela had visited it on their coach holiday two years before and he knew it was built by the local landowners who'd become rich through the wool trade, all hoping that doing this for the community meant they could gloss over that part in the bible that said it was easier for a camel to pass through the eye of a needle than for a rich man to enter the gates of Heaven.

Derek walked through the avenue of yew trees to the main entrance of the church. Fortunately the rain had decided to take a break although the cloud above was still dense and the day rather dreary. He found the curate, Nervous Nigel in the porch way, bent over taking some deep breaths. Derek cleared his throat and the man shot up straight.

"Oh excuse me," he said, "I didn't hear you coming."

Derek wasn't a church goer and only knew Nigel was a curate because Margaret had told him, otherwise he'd have assumed Nigel to be the vicar. He was dressed like one with the dog collar and the long white smock with the full-length black scarf around his neck. (Derek was pretty sure 'smock' and 'scarf' weren't the correct terminology to use). The vicar was in charge of several parishes in the local area and getting an appointment with him these days was becoming harder than getting an appointment at the doctors. Baddlesbury often had to rely on Nigel. He looked to be in his late twenties and was pencil thin. His dark brown hair was already thinning but he thought keeping it long meant it didn't notice so much, whereas his congregation always made reference to his 'comb over' behind his back. He glanced at his watch.

"Am I behind schedule," he asked, "I thought the funeral wasn't for another fifteen minutes."

"You're okay," Derek told him, "I'm just the advance party. The congregation are only just heading out from the Home."

Nigel smiled with relief.

"Good," he said, "I've still got time to finish my breathing exercises. I hate doing funerals. I always get the urge to laugh, isn't that terrible? I don't know what it is."

"Perhaps you don't like seeing sadness," Derek suggested.

Nigel pondered the response.

"No I don't think that's it," he said, "I don't ever get the urge to put on a red nose and throw a bucket of confetti over the congregation to cheer them up."

He giggled but instantly put his hand over his mouth.

"Oh dear," he said, "That's all I'm going to think about now."

"Sorry."

Nigel nodded.

"I think I'll just go and finish my breathing exercises in the vestry."

He turned and walked through the entrance, banging straight into a tall, floor-standing candelabrum, sending it crashing loudly to the floor. By the time Derek had helped him stand it upright and placed all of the candles back into their holders, the minibus had arrived, dropping off the less able-bodied of the Home's residents. A couple of nurses saw them into the church. The walking group arrived not long after, led by Kenny. Dora stopped beside Derek.

"Is the bitch niece here yet?" she asked.

Derek shook his head.

"No, I'm still waiting."

Dora tutted.

"Well I'm going to go inside and get a good seat. I'll save you a place next to me. We can sit back and enjoy ourselves."

"It's a funeral Dora."

"If it was the vicar doing it, it would be a funeral. With Nervous Nigel it's going to be a circus."

She winked and was about to walk inside when she spotted the carrier bag Derek had stood down in the porch area while helping Nigel with the candles.

"I'll take that inside," she said, "We don't want the

avaricious, old cow to take it and run. She can sit through the service first, that's what she's meant to do."

Dora picked up the bag and headed inside. A taxi pulled up by the gate at the other end of the yew tree path and a woman stepped out of it. She was wearing a black skirt suit, with the skirt barely coming halfway down her thigh. She had to keep pulling it down as she bent over to talk to the driver through his side window. She must have told him she wasn't staying long as, when she turned round and began tottering up the pathway towards the church, the driver remained where he was.

Her stiletto heels were very high and her long curly blonde hair bounced from side to side as she walked. When she got closer to Derek he saw that she was actually older than her figure had suggested at a distance. He'd thought Tommy's niece was going to be about thirty but now on closer inspection he had to go with late-fifties. Perhaps the permanent scowl on her face aged her?

"Right," she said, looking Derek up and down, "Are you something to do with the Home? That woman I spoke to first thing this morning told me to look out for a man."

Derek smiled.

"I'm Derek," he told her.

She didn't take his proffered hand so he dropped the smile before he continued talking.

"I'm here representing the owner, Margaret. She's very sorry she couldn't be here in person today. She usually likes to attend all the funerals of her residents."

The niece pulled a face.

"Sounds like someone needs to get out more," she said.

She took a silver compact mirror, with the word Cartier written across it, out of her Prada handbag and checked her reflection. Derek couldn't help wondering if she actually had one.

"Right," she said, "Have you got it?"

"Have I got what?"

She tutted.

"Uncle's vase."

"Oh that, yes."

Derek was glad now that Dora had taken it inside. This woman probably would have snatched it and run off back to the cab, as fast as her stilettoed heels would allow. Is that why the driver had left his engine running?

"It's safely inside the church," he told her.

She sighed. Derek noticed the hearse pull up.

"Ah, here's your uncle now."

The woman whipped round and then clutched her chest.

"Oh my God," she said, "I thought he was still alive for a moment. You almost gave me a heart attack."

"Sorry."

She checked her gold watch and tutted.

"I said I wanted the body here at eleven o'clock sharp. It's typical of him to be late."

"Who?"

"Uncle."

"Oh, well I don't think he had much say in the matter."

The niece tutted again.

"Honestly this is all such a waste," she said.

"Of time?"

"Of money. Why even have a funeral? I'm the only relative left. He could have at least given me the money from the cost of this. I can't believe he left everything else to charity. Of course he wasted the majority of his fortune."

"On what," Derek asked.

"On Auntie Pearl. Paid for private care after her Alzheimer's diagnosis. Put her in the best nursing home he could afford. A complete waste of their money, she was quite gaga by the end. Wouldn't have appreciated the surroundings she was in. Meanwhile I've had to take out a bridging loan on the St Tropez apartment."

Derek had never hated anyone so much on first sight before.

"You're not coming up to the Home afterwards," he said, "Your Uncle's paying for the party so you might as well get your money's worth."

The niece looked at him sharply, lips pursed, wondering if he was taking the piss. Eventually she smiled and said,

"Sweet of you to ask but really, I don't want to waste my time chewing on a dried-up, old sandwich from the local supermarket, standing with a bunch of whiffy, old people talking about their aches and pains. Besides, I have an important meeting at twelve back at the office," she looked at her watch again, "I'm going to be cutting it very fine as it is. Right, I'd better get inside."

"Don't you want to follow the coffin in?"

"Good God, no."

She pushed past Derek and tottered into the church. Not sure what to do he followed.

The church was vast on the inside. During tourist season the place was often full of people but the recent rain had kept them away from the whole village. There were rows and rows of pews and even a gathering of two hundred people would still look tiny in the space. The twenty or so congregation today seemed paltry and Derek felt a little sorry for the late Tommy Jefferies. Still, after meeting her, Derek was glad that Tommy had decided to spend money on a funeral rather than give it to his niece. She'd made her way to the front and was sat alone in the first pew. Derek noticed Dora sitting two rows back and he sat down beside her.

Nigel was already stood in the pulpit, mopping his sweaty brow. He'd looked nervous enough before the service but now he seemed on the verge of a panic attack. He cast terrified glances down at the niece in her short skirt and then crossed himself. He nodded at someone at the back of the room, which Derek presumed was the undertakers with the coffin. Nigel cleared his throat.

"Could we all rise?" he squeaked.

For a congregation made up of members from a residential home this wasn't the quickest or quietest of requests.

"Here we go," Dora whispered, "A fiver says he gets the wrong Elvis song."

Derek saw Nigel fiddling about with buttons behind the pulpit.

"You're on," he whispered back.

The buttons pressed, Nigel faced the congregation again. The opening bars of 'Return to Sender' filled the church. Nigel's face looked aghast and he bent down and frantically began pressing buttons again. Dora started giggling. As Derek got a five pound note out of his wallet he turned round and saw the undertakers backing up the aisle with the coffin, waiting for the correct music. He could understand now why Nigel got the urge to laugh.

'The Wonder of You' began and Tommy Jefferies was finally brought to the front of the church.

"We are gathered here to…" Nigel began, before realising he hadn't switched off the music.

Once done he began again.

"We are gathered here today to join this man…"

He looked down at the coffin.

"Oh, sorry, wrong page."

A rustling sound came through his microphone as he flipped over the pages of his notes.

"We are gathered here today to mourn the loss of," he squinted at his writing, "Is that Timmy?"

"Tommy Jefferies," Dora shouted out, "You stupid fart!"

Nigel jumped.

"Sorry," he called out, "Tommy Jefferies. That's right. We remember him today and although it's a sad passing he is now in heaven with his wife, John and his late brother, Pearl. Jesus wept, that's not right. You know what I mean."

Nigel turned over the page.

"Timmy only had one remaining relative, his beloved niece, Silly…Sally; but he had many friends at The Whispering Wood Retirement Home who remember him fondly and have taken the time to write down some of their memories of him."

He picked up a separate piece of paper and read from it.

"Bill Henderson recollects his love of all things Elvis, Percy Fanshawe recalls Timmy's kindness and warmth, Pissy Cissie remembers him as a terrific shag."

Nigel's eyes widened in horror and there were several gasps in the congregation. A voice hissed,

"I'll get you for that Dora."

Dora laughed loudly, her voice echoing through the wide, open space. Derek closed his eyes. Surely funerals weren't like this when Margaret came to them. Should he do something, take Dora outside? That would just cause a scene. Although not a particularly religious man, Derek offered up a little prayer that this travesty of a service would soon be over.

Perhaps his prayer was heard as Nigel abandoned his speech and moved straight on to the hymn, 'Abide with Me,' which went off without a hitch.

"Before we move round to Timmy's final resting place beside his beloved wife," Nigel told the congregation, after the hymn had finished, "We'll say together the Lord's Prayer."

A silence followed.

"How does it start again?" he asked.

Once reminded, Nigel flew through the prayer at lightning speed. The congregation rose as Nigel headed down the steps of the pulpit to lead the coffin out. Unfortunately at the bottom he tripped over a stray hassock and staggered forwards, right into the coffin, knocking it off its stand. Sally, the niece, screamed but fortunately the lid didn't fly open. Nigel, with one hand holding the side of his head that had banged into the coffin, tried to apologise to her but managed to get hold of the hem of her short skirt with his other hand. As his balance went again he fell to the floor, taking the skirt with him.

The undertakers deftly picked up the coffin and began to take it outside. The rest of the congregation followed while Sally rushed off to the vestry to put her skirt back on. Nigel followed her, still apologising until she told him to fuck off and leave her alone. It was only then he remembered he was supposed to be playing another song, Elvis's version of 'Blue Eyes Crying in the Rain.' He rushed back up the stairs into the pulpit and Tommy Jefferies actually left his funeral service to, 'All Shook Up.' It seemed more appropriate.

The burial plot was round the back of the church at the far edge of the graveyard with beautiful views across open fields. The gravediggers were standing at a respectable distance, ready to fill in the hole afterwards. The congregation were all in place around the grave by the time Nigel rushed round to join them. They waited a few minutes more for Sally to appear. Derek was holding the bag containing the vase and knew she wouldn't leave without it.

She tottered over, all eyes on her. Nigel was standing at the end of the grave. She gave him a look of disdain and a wide berth before coming to stand beside Derek and Dora on the right hand side.

"Oh damn," she said, looking down at the floor, "I've got mud on my grey suede Louboutin's. Honestly, is there anything worse than that?"

"Yes," Dora told her, "How about death. You're at a funeral love."

"I'm at a farce," she replied, "Is that the vase Eric?"

"Erm yes it is," Derek replied, handing it over.

It was the first time he'd seen her smile all day.

"Good," she said, clutching the bag to her bosom, "Royal Worcester. Now then, let's get the old bugger in the ground. I've got a meeting at twelve o'clock."

Nigel got on with the rest of the service without a hitch. There were a few tears as the coffin was lowered but none came from the niece.

"Right," she said, looking down into the grave, "That's it then. I'm off."

"Are you not coming back to the Home?" Dora asked, "Your Uncle arranged a spread."

The niece laughed.

"As I've already told Derren here, it's hardly my scene. I've got better things to do than hang around with a bunch of people who'll all be in the same place as my uncle within the next six months."

She made to leave. To the rest of the congregation it looked like Sally stumbled on her stilettos. Only Derek, standing right beside her, saw Dora's quick movement with her walking stick. Sally let out a squeal and as she twisted round, trying to get her balance, she found herself teetering on the edge of the grave.

"Save the vase, save the vase," she called out, trying to pass the carrier bag forwards to someone.

No one came to her aid and she fell backwards with a scream into the hole, a pleasant tinkling sound of breaking pottery coming directly after a loud thump.

"I think the vase is broken," Derek said to Dora.

"And hopefully her bloody neck too," she replied.

She grinned and then looked over to where the gravediggers were standing.

"We're all done here lads," she called over to them, "Start filling it in."

*

It was left to Nigel and the gravediggers to rescue Sally from the grave. She appeared unhurt but was inconsolable, clutching a carrier bag full of broken pieces of pottery to her bosom and sobbing hysterically.

"I bet that was the closest her and her uncle have been in years," Dora said to Derek, as they made their way back onto the path that led round to the front of the church.

"Do you think she's going to create a fuss about the vase?" he asked.

"I don't see how she can. It was an accident after all wasn't it. It's her own fault for wearing such high heels," Dora winked at him, "No she can't do anything. She has to live with the fact that Tommy left his money to charity rather than to her. He was pretty wealthy you know. He had the measure of who she was."

She smiled.

"He'll be having a good laugh up there today. We did him proud."

"It was a disaster," Derek said.

Dora chuckled.

"I know. He'd have loved that. Are you walking back with the rest of us?"

Derek looked about him.

"No," he said, "I'll give you all a head start first. After that funeral I could do with a bit of fresh air."

Dora laughed again.

"Suit yourself," she said, "There's alcohol don't forget. I won't leave any for you."

Derek smiled.

"I'll only be five minutes," he told her, "I'm sure even you can't clear a table full of alcohol in that time."

"Is that a challenge?"

Dora grinned before heading off to join the rest of the group at the front of the church that were walking back up to the Home. From where he stood, Derek could still see Nigel trying to calm Sally down beside the grave. For anyone passing who hadn't been to the funeral the scene looked touching, aside from the chief mourner shouting out, 'fetch me some glue.'

He headed off in the opposite direction, through the graves on the right hand side of the church to an area full of trees and shrubs. Walking amongst these, Derek could remain hidden from view. He ambled along beside a beautiful, old stone wall that formed the boundary of the churchyard. Through a gap he spied the old rectory. From the main road only one side of the house was visible through the wrought iron gates of its driveway. From this angle Derek could see how striking the large, Georgian property was, sat in its picturesque grounds. It was made of a creamy yellow brick and of the three large, ground floor, mullioned windows along the side, the far one was a vast bay with French doors leading out onto a patio area. It was the sort of house Angela would love to live in. Derek had a nagging feeling that she'd compromised with the coach house after seeing how excited he'd been about it. She would definitely have liked a house with a bit more character on the inside.

Derek remembered that this was the house where the lady lived that his mum was making a dress for. What was her name again, Terri, no Theresa, that was it, Theresa Jennings. And her husband owned an antiques' shop up on the square. Derek thought about his mother. Had Angela been right when she said Ursula might be lonely? She'd seemed to jump at the chance to move to Tenhamshire but Derek hadn't really considered what she was leaving behind. Perhaps she hadn't either in her rush to be nearer to him. Friends were no longer just around the corner. Seventy years old was quite an age to be embarking on a fresh start.

No matter what Angela says, Derek thought to himself now, I'm not going to rush my mum into buying anything, especially if it's a long way from here.

He looked at his watch. He really ought to be heading up to the Home now. He needed to tell Margaret about what had happened, in case Tommy's niece did try and make a complaint. He'd have a quick drink with Dora and then take the van and drive down to his old apartment. He planned on starting the decorating first thing in the morning, unless Leanne said he could go and see Nathan.

Derek crept further along the wall and came out onto the main path beside the gate at the front of the church. The taxi that had been waiting for Sally had gone, hopefully with her in it. He crossed the road and walked back up the narrow lane, turning off at the entrance to the Home.

Inside, he discovered Margaret was still busy with Jeremy, showing his dad his new room and taking him around the rest of the Home. Derek headed through to the rear lounge that opened up onto the conservatory, where the party was taking place. The drink had already started flowing and everyone was laughing as those that had been to the funeral were telling those that hadn't, everything that had happened.

"I wish I'd been there," Sir Jasper said.

"You hated Tommy Jefferies," Dora reminded him.

"I know, but that niece of his sounds like a damned fine filly."

"She's only interested in money."

"I could have given her some of that for a quick roll in the hay."

Sir Jasper began trembling at the image that formed in his mind and he flopped down into the nearest chair. Dora waved Derek over.

"Have you heard," she said, "'Not so Dental' Flossie has gone."

"Really?"

Dora nodded.

"Apparently my Margaret helped her find a new Home to live in. She moved out this morning while we were at the funeral. It's all a bit cloak and dagger isn't it? No one's actually seen her since that night you and she put on a sex show."

"I did not put on a sex show!" Derek replied, a little too loudly.

The room fell silent and everybody looked at him. A second later and they were all laughing again, only at him now rather than at Tommy Jefferies' funeral.

"Thanks for that Dora," he said, "What rumour can I start about you?"

"I'm too quick for you Derek," she told him, laughing, "Anyway, come and have a drink. There's plenty of it, God bless Tommy."

"I'll have a small one," he replied, "I'm driving later."

Although he only had the one alcoholic drink, Derek stayed longer than he was planning to. It wasn't often that the retirement home burst into life like this and it was fun to watch. Pissy Cissie told everyone she loved them before living up to her nickname, Sir Jasper danced with Rose Delaney, until his hand wandered and she smacked him round the face, sending him flying into the damp chair Cissie had only just vacated. Everyone found that funny too.

"Right, it's time for a song," Dora called out, and she stood in the centre of the lounge, facing the crowd in the conservatory.

Dora's dirty songs were legendary. This was a new one on Derek, all about a woman called Tiffany, who had a personal freshness problem. 'Whiffy Tiffy' tried a number of remedies and while the group all laughed loudly, Derek felt rather embarrassed. Just as Dora reached the line, *she was embarrassed when the vicar caught her, splashing her chuff with holy water*, the door to the lounge opened and Margaret walked in with Jeremy. He was pushing a smart but very old-looking, white-haired man in a wheelchair.

"And this is the main lounge," Margaret said, "Mum, shush will you."

Dora was in full song so Margaret had to call out loudly,

"Everybody, please meet our new resident. This is Leonard Riley."

Dora's voiced cracked and she fell silent. As she was still facing the crowd, Derek could clearly see the look of horror that appeared on her face. She slowly turned round to face her daughter and the new resident.

"Oh my God!"

Dora's hands flew to her face. The old man in the chair let out a whine.

"No," Dora said.

She staggered backwards and fell into the first chair she found. Margaret and Derek both sprang to her side.

"Mum, what is it?" Margaret asked her, concerned and patting her hand, "What's wrong?"

Behind them, Jeremy was tending to his father. Dora took in a huge breath and glanced across at them. Her face creased and tears sprang to her eyes.

"What is it mum," Margaret asked again, "What is it about Mr Riley?"

Dora's gaze found her daughter's face. She'd turned deathly pale.

"He's your dad," she whispered.

Her eyes rolled upwards and she passed out.

Chapter 17

Derek felt bad leaving all the trouble behind him and heading back to his old apartment but there wasn't much else he could do. Dora was rushed off to the hospital while Margaret had fled the scene in her car, heading no one knew where. Jeremy had taken his shaken father back to his own house so suddenly all the main players in the scene were gone, leaving Derek and the residents wondering what was really going on. What was the truth? Had Dora just got confused? Surely not; she obviously knew the name 'Leonard Riley' and she and the old man had definitely recognised each other. Could he really be Margaret's father? What about Billy? Poor Margaret, she'd idolised the man.

While the residents of the Home all started gossiping, Derek phoned Angela at work and told her what had happened. She'd seemed rather distant at first, as if her mind was elsewhere and it took her a while to grasp what Derek was saying. Once she had though, she told him to carry on with his plans and that she'd phone Margaret's mobile and go and visit Dora at the hospital if she was being kept in. Derek felt relieved, as well as a little guilty, that someone else was taking control of the situation. Angela was much better at dealing with upset people than he was anyway and he knew she'd do whatever she could to help.

Back at his old apartment, a world away from Tenhamshire, he felt calmer. Angela would keep him posted about events and he could always cut short his weekend if needs be. He texted

Leanne to say he was back for a few days painting but hoped they'd be able to meet up. He even offered to babysit again if she wanted him too. She replied saying she was free tomorrow night and why didn't he come over for dinner.

That Friday morning while painting, Derek felt the familiar excitement rising inside him and realised he was very much looking forward to dinner that evening. Being in Leanne's company he could forget everything else that was going on in his life and just discuss what was going on in hers. At lunchtime he nipped out and bought some wine and flowers for her and a big toy car for Nathan.

Leanne looked immaculate that night as always, in a pair of shiny, black leggings and a long, white, silk blouse. Derek had made sure to pack a couple of shirts this trip and a smart pair of trousers so that he wouldn't look like a scruff. He'd taken a taxi tonight. He didn't want to get drunk, certainly not in front of Nathan, but at least he would be able to enjoy a second glass of wine.

Leanne accepted the flowers and wine with a smile and showed Derek into the lounge diner at the back of the house. Nathan was sat inside a large playpen that was made up of colourful fence panels, which had some activity centres built into them. When he saw Derek he pulled himself up and held his hands up to him. Derek's heart melted again but he looked at Leanne first and, when she nodded; he picked the boy up.

"He can play outside of that while you're here," she said, "I just put him in there while I was cooking."

Leanne went out to the kitchen and Derek held Nathan to him in a hug, until the boy got bored and began to struggle. He put him down on the carpet and gave him his present. They spent a very pleasant ten minutes driving the car around the living room floor, Derek making car noises just like Ash had while sat up on the lawnmower at the Home.

When Leanne came in to take Nathan upstairs to bed he started crying. Derek watched the little boy reaching out over his mum's shoulder as she walked out of the room. He chose to believe Nathan wanted to play with him some more but knew it was really the new toy car he was upset about leaving.

"Pour us both out a glass of wine, Derek," Leanne called out, before she headed upstairs.

Derek did as he was told and walked out to the kitchen. Dinner smelled great but as Derek threw the screwcap from the top of the wine bottle into the bin, he noticed rather a lot of flattened, ready-prepared food containers in the recycling section behind it. He smiled.

Some things don't change, he thought.

He poured two glasses and took both them and the bottle of wine into the lounge, setting them down on the dining table. By the time Leanne came back downstairs he'd already topped his glass up.

"Little bugger didn't want to go down," she said, picking up her glass and taking a healthy swig.

"Sorry, that was probably me playing cars with him," Derek replied, "I got him too excited."

"You're still a little red in the face yourself there, Derek," she told him, "Did you get too excited as well?"

He grinned.

"Well it has been a while since I played with cars," he admitted, "It was rather fun."

Leanne laughed.

"I'll go serve up dinner," she said.

It was a very pleasant meal, lamb shank in a red wine gravy

with vegetables and herb-coated new potatoes. They talked about Leanne's work, as always, and what Nathan had been up to the past couple of weeks. After she'd taken the plates out to the kitchen and topped up both of their glasses, Leanne sat back down and said,

"So, I assume you have some news for me."

Derek's first thought was of Dora's revelation but as Leanne didn't know her she'd hardly meant that.

"About being Nathan's guardian," Leanne prompted.

"Oh right, yes…well no actually, I don't at the moment."

Leanne sighed.

"I know I said there was no rush, Derek," she told him, "But I thought you would have made a decision by now."

"I have," he replied, "I mean, I would love to do it, it's just that I haven't got around to asking Angela yet."

"Why not?"

"It's not been the right time."

That sounded familiar. Wasn't that his excuse for not telling his mum about Angela's past?

"A friend of ours has just received some shock news," he told her, "And, well, mum's been a bit down since…"

Leanne laughed.

"I knew Ursula would get a mention somewhere along the line."

Derek looked puzzled.

"What do you mean?" he asked, "I was just going to say, and Angela agrees with me, that I'm a little worried that perhaps mum was too quick in moving down to Tenhamshire."

Leanne nodded, knowingly.

"Of course," she mocked, "I can see why that would stop you discussing something important, such as the welfare of my son."

Derek was beginning to get ruffled.

"You think my mother isn't important? Just because your parents would rather spend time playing bridge with friends than come and see you, doesn't mean you have to mock my relationship with my parents. You were always jealous of that, weren't you?"

Leanne threw her head back and laughed loudly.

"Oh my God, Derek," she said, "You're still playing the same record. I can't believe it. I've never been jealous of your relationship with your mother. I have a good relationship with her myself. I told you she stays in touch. It's your overweening protection of her that's the problem. It's what ended our marriage."

Derek's mouth dropped open. Was she really about to blame him for the divorce that only she'd wanted in the first place?

"I think your shagging another guy was the cause of that," he told her.

Leanne shook her head.

"I didn't start dating Rick until after we'd split up."

"I know that's what you said at the time."

"It's the truth Derek," Leanne took a sip of her wine, "I had no plans to find someone else but Rick came into my life and well; it was meant to be just a fling but then I got pregnant with Nathan and…"

She tailed off and shrugged her shoulders. She saw Derek's confused expression.

"Did you really believe an affair ended our marriage?" she asked him, "Come on, you must have known the marriage was over for a long time before that."

Derek took a big gulp of his wine.

"I knew we'd drifted apart a little," he admitted, "But we'd been together for over twenty-five years. Shouldn't we have talked things through first, you know, if you were just unhappy? I mean I thought you'd been having an affair and that's the reason I agreed to the divorce."

Leanne emptied the remainder of the bottle of wine into both of their glasses.

"I'm sorry Derek," she said, "But I knew it was over."

"And you blame me and my mother for that?"

Leanne sighed.

"Of course not," she told him, "Not really. A marriage doesn't end because of one little thing. It was just one of the issues; something that had really started getting on my nerves. That's the problem isn't it? We never talked about things. We never sat down together to say how we felt."

"Well that's because you were hardly home," Derek threw at her, his voice angry. If she wanted him to tell her how he felt, he'd do that right now, "Your bloody precious career always came first. You were never satisfied with it. Whenever you got a promotion you always started looking for the next one. I wasn't given a second thought. You hated that I was happy where I worked and mocked me for not trying to get a better job. What you always failed to remember was that I began working in that job straight after I left university, supporting you while you continued your studies; your Master's and then your PhD. Don't you think I was owed a bit of gratitude once you'd got your doctorate?"

"I was grateful."

"Well you never bloody showed it!"

"And what was I meant to do?" Leanne was angry now too, "Get pregnant straightaway after we married so that you could have your precious baby? There wouldn't have been any point to my education then would there?"

"It wasn't all about babies," he told her, "A 'thank you' now and then would have been enough but I never even got that. Everything always had to be about you and be on your terms. You were a selfish cow throughout our marriage. Yes, I wanted to have children. Most couples do. You knew I did but instead of saying you didn't want them you kept telling me to wait. And I did. I waited years for you to be ready to start a family and then you go and have a baby after we broke up. How do you think that made me feel, Leanne?"

"I didn't plan on having a baby," she said, "I just realised it was my last chance. It wasn't like before when I…"

She stopped talking as she realised what she'd just said. Derek frowned.

"Are you telling me," he said slowly, his voice a whisper as he tried desperately to control his anger, "That you got pregnant during our marriage."

Leanne closed her eyes. Derek saw her purse her lips together, as she often used to do when she was upset. She nodded.

"What!"

Derek's voice echoed around the room. Upstairs Nathan began crying. Leanne rushed out of the lounge. In the five minutes she was away Derek went through so many emotions, anger, regret, hurt. He'd calmed somewhat by the time she returned, carrying two plates of lemon cheesecake. He almost laughed. Here they were, about to continue a serious conversation and Leanne had brought something to snack on. She put the plates down in front of them and sat back down. They stared at their uneaten slices of dessert. The silence was unbearable.

"I'm sorry Derek," she eventually whispered, "I never meant for you to find that out."

Derek didn't look up.

"When," he asked?

"It was eight years ago, in the September. We'd been away with friends to the South of France."

"I remember," he replied.

"It was only when I discovered I was pregnant that I realised our marriage was broken. My first thought had been that it wasn't the right time for a baby, but then I understood that it never would be the right time. It shocked me."

Derek looked up.

"That was five years before we split up."

"I know. I should have said something then but I felt so guilty, going off and having an abortion, that I let the marriage continue on."

Derek's anger had gone, replaced with a feeling of despair.

"Why didn't you want to have a baby with me?" he asked.

Leanne sighed. She took a deep breath before replying.

"Because I couldn't be the mother you wanted me to be," she told him, "I couldn't be another Ursula."

"What? Oh come on…"

"It's true Derek," she interrupted, "You put your mother on a pedestal. You always used to talk about what a great upbringing you had and how brave Ursula was after your dad died and how she turned her life around. That's who you wanted me to be."

"Rubbish!" he told her, "You think if I'd wanted to marry someone similar to my mother I'd have married you? I always knew you were ambitious but I didn't think that would have to get in the way of our having a baby together. I mean, what do you take me for, some out-dated male chauvinist who wanted the little wife at home ironing nappies? I wouldn't have asked or expected you to give up your career after having a baby. We'd have raised him together."

Leanne picked up her spoon but didn't start eating.

"You say that now but I know you, Derek. I know the romantic image you have in your mind. You always talked of babies and about coming home from work each night to play with them before bathing and putting them to bed with a story. You never thought about the best schools they should go to or even pictured them growing up. And I don't think you'd have been happy with us having a full time nanny either."

"Rubbish," Derek said again, although quieter than before.

"Really? What did you think when I asked you to babysit the other week? Did you think I was being irresponsible because I was so desperate to go to a dinner that could help my career that I left my baby in the care of someone he'd only met once before?"

Derek couldn't respond and Leanne nodded, knowingly.

"Exactly," she said, "I left him with you because **I** knew you and could trust you but I know how your mind works. Admit it Derek, together we'd have been stressed-out parents, constantly arguing over our opposing views on how our children should be raised. I'd have been angry with you for not taking the same interest in their education as I did, while you'd have accused me of not spending enough time with them because I was always working late. We'd have ended up creating an awful, and probably hurtful, negative atmosphere for our kids to live in."

"Well if I'm such a bad role model as a parent, why do you want me to be guardian to Nathan?"

"I never said you would make a bad parent. I'm trying to

say **we'd** make bad parents together. I can't think of anyone better I'd want Nathan to go to if I was no longer here."

Derek couldn't stop a warm glow spreading through him.

"I still don't really understand what you meant about my mum breaking us up," he said, "All I've tried to do is be there for her since my dad died. I don't feel she's ever faced up to what happened."

"Derek, she's continued living her life. I think you'll find she's doing okay. It's been what, twenty-seven years since it happened; just before we first met."

"But I don't think she's ever got over it. She never talks about the accident and gets upset if it's ever mentioned; well, you remember that."

Leanne put down the spoon she was holding.

"It's okay that she doesn't want to talk about it, why should she? Your dad had a tragic boating accident it's not like he died after a long illness. I'm sure she misses him every day but she's had to move on. Not wanting to talk about it doesn't mean she hasn't dealt with it. Besides, she may just not want to talk about it with you. Perhaps she's worried about upsetting you. For all you know she spoke with friends about it at the time. You were away at university. She kept you out of it. Ursula's a brave lady, a mum. She'd do anything to protect her child from hurt, no matter how old he is. It's only since having Nathan that I've really understood that."

Derek conceded the point.

"Was it really the way I thought about mum that broke up our marriage?"

Leanne shook her head.

"I told you, it's never one thing that ends a marriage," she said, "We'd grown apart, we both knew it, didn't we?"

Derek half nodded.

"The fact that neither one of us made the effort to talk things through with the other one shows that we were heading for the divorce courts," she continued, "We couldn't be bothered to make an effort to save the relationship. All I mean when I talk about Ursula is that she often came between us in our marriage."

Derek opened his mouth to respond but Leanne quickly continued.

"I don't mean Ursula herself, just your overprotectiveness. How many times did we have plans cancelled because you'd spoken to your mum on the phone and 'thought' she sounded low; so around there you went and she was always perfectly fine. You're doing it now too, worrying that she's made a mistake rushing to live in Tenhamshire. Don't you think she would have thought about that before she decided to make the move? Ursula isn't an idiot, you know that. You sing her praises often enough. She's a great woman. You just need to stop overprotecting her. Don't make the same mistake with Angela that you did with me. Don't allow your opinion of your mother to ruin a great relationship."

Derek remained silent. How many people had told him he was selling his mother short; Angela, Margaret, Dora and now even Leanne. He hadn't realised his protectiveness of his mother was such an issue. He'd always blamed Leanne totally for the failure of their marriage. How could they have been together so long and never really talked? Angela wasn't like that. She always wanted to talk things through and Derek often found that difficult, probably because he wasn't used to it. He and his mum didn't discuss his father and now he realised that he'd never discussed the state of his marriage with Leanne.

Perhaps that was why he and Angela argued so much. He wasn't one to talk through his feelings and Angela became frustrated by that.

Leanne, sensing she'd got through to Derek, picked up her spoon again to start eating her dessert.

"Angela used to be a prostitute," Derek blurted out.

The spoon clattered onto the plate.

"Sorry?"

Derek looked across at his ex-wife.

"Angela used to be a prostitute," he repeated, "I thought you ought to know that before you decide about Nathan."

Leanne opened her mouth to reply but then closed it again, not knowing what to say. She thought for a moment or two and then opened her mouth again.

"You dated a prostitute?" she said, "Did you meet as her client?"

"No!"

"Then how?"

"I told you before, we met on the coach trip to Tenhamshire two years ago. I found out about her past on the last night of the trip."

"That must have been a tough conversation."

Derek nodded.

"It was. We almost broke up over it. Well, we did actually but we got back together and worked through it. She wasn't on the streets or anything. Really, she was more of an escort."

Derek began telling Leanne what he knew about Angela's past life, only stopping to allow Leanne to go and open another bottle of wine."

"And so you see," he finished, "She's a very clever woman and has turned her life around."

Derek took a healthy swig from his glass.

"But I'd understand if it changed your mind about Nathan."

Leanne remained silent for a few moments but eventually shook her head.

"No," she told him, "No, I can't see that being a problem. She sounds like an amazing lady. You must tell her about the guardianship though. And I'd like to meet her some time too."

Derek smiled.

"Of course," he replied, "I'll tell her when I get back. I really think she'll be happy with the situation. Why don't you get your will papers sorted now, save some time?"

Leanne was smiling to herself.

"What did Ursula say when you told her?" she asked.

"About Nathan?"

"About Angela."

"Ah."

Derek's face reddened.

"Oh my God she doesn't know, does she?"

Derek shook his head. Leanne groaned.

"Derek Noble, why do you make every situation more complicated than it needs to be?"

"It's a gift."

"You've been with Angela, what, two years? Your mother is currently living with you but she doesn't know about Angela's past. How have you even managed to maintain that?"

"It's been difficult," he admitted, "We had one of her ex-clients round for dinner the other week."

Leanne's eyes widened.

"What, for old time's sake?"

"No, he was dating a friend of ours and none of us realised."

Leanne burst out laughing. Derek felt she was channelling

Dora. He hoped the old girl was okay. Angela hadn't contacted him about her or Margaret.

Leanne wiped her eyes with the cuff of her blouse.

"Oh my God," she said, "That sort of thing could really only happen to you Derek. You know sometimes I do miss you."

They grinned at one another.

"But you've got to tell your mum the truth."

"I know, I know," Derek said, "You're not the first to tell me. I will, it's just that…"

Leanne sighed.

"No," he continued, "It's not overprotection…well a part of it is but, to be honest, I'm frightened."

"Frightened?"

"Yes. Of course there's the element of shame and embarrassment about what Angela did, I've never denied that, even to her, but what if mum can't accept the truth? What if she doesn't want to see Angela ever again? That's my fear. I can't choose between these two women. I want them both in my life. I mean, mum is mum, and Angela, well Angela is the best thing that's ever happened to me."

He realised how that last bit sounded.

"Sorry," he added.

Leanne smiled.

"I can't tell you what to do Derek. Personally I think Ursula will want anyone in her life if that person makes her little boy happy."

Derek laughed.

"But you'll only find out her opinion by telling her."

He nodded.

"You're right," he said, "I do need to tell her. I just need to find the right time."

Leanne groaned again.

"No, I'm not trying to put it off," he told her, "It's just that we're dealing with another problem at the moment. A friend of ours, the same one who was dating Angela's ex-client, has just discovered, at fifty-eight, that her late father wasn't her real dad."

"My God," Leanne said, reaching for the wine bottle, "And they say things are quiet in the countryside."

Chapter 18

Angela had to admit to a very selfish feeling when Derek phoned her up and told her about Dora's bombshell. She'd been worrying herself silly about Max after their meeting that morning but now someone else had a crisis which she could focus on instead of her own and it provided her with a bit of relief.

It also gave her the excuse to leave work early where she was having trouble concentrating anyway. She tried several times to contact Margaret by phone but it kept going straight to voicemail. She left her a couple of messages and switched her focus onto Dora instead. Derek had told her on the phone that she'd been taken to the hospital.

Angela was glad she'd told him to carry on with his plans and head down to the apartment. She'd been jumpy enough recently since Max had reappeared and had mostly taken her anger out on him. She was especially upset after today's threat, demanding that she provide Max with her 'old services,' but at least now Derek wouldn't be around to be on the receiving end of her wrath. Angela could spend some time working out her next move.

The fact that Max had given her a week before going to see him was no accident. He used to use the same ploy when they were together; not phoning her for a week so that she became anxious with worry about him and was therefore so pleased and grateful to see him when he did eventually show up.

This time he was hoping she'd spend the next seven days

squirming and worrying and fretting about what to do. He wanted her desperate to protect her job and to have such a low opinion of herself that she'd let him do whatever he wanted to her. He obviously didn't know her. Actually Angela believed he didn't understand women at all. No wonder he was alone.

Perhaps it was the news about Margaret and Dora that helped her put Max's threat into perspective. Driving home, Angela realised Margaret's problem was much worse than her own. Max could ruin her career but he couldn't destroy her, not like Dora's news could destroy Margaret. Max had tried to ruin her twenty years before yet she'd survived that. He thought he could do the same thing to her now but she was much stronger. The initial shock of seeing him again **had** made her remember the young, innocent, unconfident woman she used to be but if Max thought she was still that woman then he was sorely mistaken. She wasn't going to spend the next seven days squirming and worrying and fretting. She was going to spend it planning a revenge attack to make the bastard pay for what he'd put her through. Right now though, she had to concentrate on Dora.

Angela thought it best to drive up to the Home rather than the hospital and get the latest information about the situation. Still concerned that Ursula might be lonely, she decided to stop by the coach house first and see if she wanted to come along with her. Okay so it wasn't exactly a day out somewhere nice but with Derek back at his apartment, Margaret missing and with the possibility that Angela might have to spend the evening up at the hospital with Dora, she didn't want to leave Ursula on her own for that long.

She pulled into her parking space outside the coach house and got out of her car. Angela retrieved her briefcase from the back seat and as she stood up, felt a hand grab her shoulder. Her reaction was instant. She screamed but then grabbed hold of the hand and bit it, right at the base of the index finger. A loud howl emanated somewhere near her ear. She turned round, ready to floor whoever this person was…and came face to face with Bert. She let go of him.

"Jesus Christ, Ange," he said, gripping his hurt hand in the other one, "What's wrong with you?"

"I thought I was being attacked," she told him, angry yet relieved. It was Tenham House all over again, "You should never creep up on someone like that."

"I didn't think I was creeping," Bert replied, "And I didn't expect my own daughter to attack me. Look at these teeth marks. My God, have you got fangs in there?"

He put his sore hand into his mouth and sucked on it, before saying,

"Where did you learn to do that?"

"Self-defence classes. In my old line of work I had to be prepared."

The hospital she'd been taken to after her attack had run a six week course. Angela signed up as soon as she could.

"What are you doing here dad?"

"Calm down, I'm not staying," he told her, "I just wanted to ask a quick favour before I head off."

Angela sighed.

"Look I don't have any spare money and…"

Bert held up his hands.

"Calm down," he said again, "I don't want money. I've got a little bit put by anyway. I just wanted to say that, well, if the police call, and they probably won't, you haven't seen me."

"Oh my God, what have you done now?"

Bert looked affronted.

"Nothing," he said.

Angela raised an eyebrow.

"I'm only ever surveillance these days," he told her, "It's great. I get paid by someone else to check out a place and then I disappear. No one suspects an old man like me to be casing a joint. Old people are practically invisible. I'm known as The Shadow."

"I've heard you called other things."

Bert grinned.

"Hang on Shadow," Angela said, confused, "If you're invisible, how come you're worried about the police calling here?"

The smile dropped from her father's face and he looked rather sheepish.

"Well, I got a little bit cocky this time and I may have been seen. I had a feeling I was being followed in Ryan Harbour. I really should have left here that day but I've been hanging around hoping to see Ursula again before I go. She doesn't seem to have been going out as much recently so that's why I stopped by here today. I was just about to knock at the house when you pulled up in your car. Ursula's been so kind to me I hated not saying a proper goodbye."

Angela's eyes narrowed.

"I think taking her emerald bracelet was enough of a farewell greeting."

"Eh? I never took that," Bert told her.

Angela sighed.

"Come on dad," she said, "We both know what you're like. I know she showed it to you and then she couldn't find it after you'd left."

"I never took it," Bert told her, indignantly, "I've never taken anything, not off of a loved one anyway."

His face reddened.

"I don't mean 'loved one' in that sense," he added, "I mean family."

Angela couldn't believe what she was hearing.

"How can you say that?" she said, "You've always stolen off of me."

Bert's expression showed complete shock.

"I've never taken anything from you," he told her, "The only money I've ever taken is what you've offered me. How can you say I stole from you?"

Angela could feel her eyes prickle and she blinked several times to prevent tears forming, all the memories of twenty years ago were in the forefront of her mind.

"What about that time just after I'd finished university," she said, "When you visited me at that apartment? Don't you remember?"

Angela realised she'd never had it out with him before. She'd swept every aspect of that time in her life under the carpet and tried not to think about it again. That theft was the reason she'd allowed Max to control her. That was why she'd been attacked and left unable to have children. That was why she'd returned to prostitution. She could feel all the anger and hurt inside her trying desperately to break free. Bert was looking thoughtful.

"Wasn't that the apartment that older guy you were seeing owned?" he asked, "The one who always walked with a bit of a swagger, good-looking but fancied himself a bit, confident?"

"Yes."

Bert nodded.

"Yeah I remember him. He was a bit like me in many ways."

"God, don't tell me that!"

Angela was fretting enough over Max without worrying her attraction to him had been some psychological replacement for her own father.

"I was bothered about you living there," Bert admitted, "Being kept by an older man in his apartment; I thought it was asking for trouble."

"Forget about the apartment," Angela shouted at him, "I'm talking about the money I'd saved up to complete my Master's degree. You left there with that money."

Bert appeared both hurt and puzzled.

"I never took any money," he told her, shocked, "Why would I do that? If you had money then that was yours. I was proud of you, you know. My little girl was getting a degree. Okay so I wasn't too happy about the way you earned your income but…"

Angela was astounded by what she was hearing. When had Bert ever cared about her?

"How can you say that?" she asked him, "Don't you remember when I told you about the disgusting Denny propositioning me when I was fifteen?"

"Of course I do," Bert told her, "And he was dealt with."

"What?"

Bert was baffled by his daughter's confusion.

"He was dealt with," he repeated, "He was shown, in no uncertain terms, that you didn't treat a fifteen year old girl that way, especially Bert Jenkins' daughter."

Angela struggled to reply. Bert shrugged his shoulders.

"Okay so it wasn't an actual lesson, more a beating up, but he certainly learned something."

"But...but you laughed about it," Angela said, "With me. I told you what had happened and you laughed. 'That's Denny for you.' That's what you said."

"Well of course I did," Bert replied, "What else was I supposed to do? I didn't want you feeling scared and anxious and blaming yourself for what had happened. It wasn't your fault. I tried to make light of the situation. Was that wrong?"

"Of course it was wrong!"

Angela's reply came out in a loud screech, shocking both of them. Bert looked all around him frantically, worried about being overheard.

"Of course it was wrong," she repeated, much more quietly, "I thought you didn't care about me, that it didn't bother you that men were ogling your young daughter."

"Oh Ange."

Bert made to step forward, as if to hold his daughter but stopped. They'd never really had that sort of relationship and he suddenly felt awkward.

"I'm sorry Ange," he said, "I did what I thought was right. Your mum had long gone and I was trying to be a relaxed parent to a teenage daughter. I tried to treat you as a grown-up. You were my eldest and you didn't come with an instruction booklet."

Angela leaned up against her car.

"I can't believe this," she whispered, more to herself.

"You really have a low opinion of me don't you," Bert said.

Angela looked up at him.

"Can you blame me?" she asked.

To her surprise, Bert nodded.

"Yes," he told her, "Yes I can blame you. Look I know I've been in and out of prison for most of my life, particularly when you were young, but you can't blame me for that for ever. I did the best I could when I was there and even when I wasn't I made sure there was someone looking out for you. Okay with hindsight, Denny shouldn't have been one of them but as I say, he was dealt with. I've always looked out for you Ange, I promise. Why do you think I keep turning up?"

"Because you have a 'job' on nearby?"

"Not always. I turn up because I want to see my daughter. You'll always be my little girl. I love you Angela."

"Do you?"

"Of course I do!" Bert snapped.

Angela jumped.

"You think I don't worry about you all of the time," Bert continued, "I've always wanted what's best for you. I've always accepted your prostitution and never once questioned you about it, even though I hated it."

"Really?"

"Of course, what father wants to see his daughter cheapen herself like that?"

Bert realised how that last sentence sounded and fell silent. It was a few moments before he spoke again.

"I'm sorry, that came out wrong."

Angela snorted.

"No it didn't," she said.

Bert smiled.

"Okay, I suppose it didn't. You've made a life for yourself Ange and I would never judge you for it, but I must say, this visit is the first time I've ever seen you happy. Truly happy I mean. There's a glow about you, even when you're moody. You're in a good place here with your job and young Derek. You two really suit one another."

Angela felt a sob rise up through her body. She swallowed it, not wanting to cry again.

"So you honestly never took my money when you visited me after I finished university?"

Bert shook his head.

"I didn't. I swear it on your mother's grave."

"Dad we don't know she's dead."

"No but here's hoping."

"Dad!"

Bert grinned again.

"Sorry. I honestly didn't steal your money though."

Angela sighed.

"Oh God, it must have been him then," she said, "I can't believe I didn't think of that before."

"Who, that chap you were living with?"

Angela nodded.

"Yes," she said, "Max. He's…"

Angela didn't really want to tell her dad about what had happened to her, or to tell him that Max had resurfaced.

"Well, I've only lately come to realise what a con man he was," she finished.

Bert laughed.

"I could have told you that," he said, "I remember going for a pint with him back when I visited you. What a muppet! He tried all that old spiel about knowing dangerous people on me. Load of old bollocks. I told you he was like me. I invented that speech."

Angela remained silent but looked thoughtful.

"My old mate, Bobby Dawson knew him," Bert continued, "He was the guy I was doing some work for when I came to see you in Colchester. Now he really does know some dangerous people. Oh, maybe I shouldn't have told you that."

"I won't pass it on, dad," Angela said, "Tell me more about the connection."

"Oh, well that Max used to own a building in a parade of shops on the edge of town that housed a café. Bobby needed somewhere to meet his…well, let's call them his friends. This café place was great, not in a busy area so not too many eyes watching you, but still public enough so that a group of blokes together weren't going to be noticed."

"How do you know all this?" Angela asked.

"I used to go there myself, to get my orders off of Bobby. He told me all about Max, once he knew he was knocking off my daughter."

"What a lovely turn of phrase you have."

Bert ignored her and carried on with his story.

"By the time I was going there the place was owned by Bobby himself. Max had got too big-headed. His tenants that ran the café during the day didn't know about the evening meetings. It was always Max that let the guys in and cleaned up when they left. He was never part of the meeting. Once he'd opened up he was given his money and told to piss off upstairs. Anyhow, soon it came to Bobby's attention that Max was talking; not about what was said in the meetings but about who was there. He was trying to act the big man, making out that he was mates with guys in the criminal underworld but he was showing off to too many people. Those guys he saw at the meetings, he'd call out to them whenever he saw them elsewhere, out on the street, in the pubs. It was bloody stupid because he was linking different blokes together and also linking them to Bobby. Some of these guys weren't meant to be in contact with Bobby, if you get what I mean. They were meant to be his enemies in rival groups. If they were known to be in contact with him then they couldn't be trusted by their own…acquaintances, and it could spoil all of Bobby's plans."

"So what happened?" Angela asked.

"Well Bobby couldn't have this going on so he 'persuaded' Max to sign over the property to him. In return Max didn't get beaten up for talking but was told he would be in trouble if he wasn't discreet. He got the message and was a lot less vocal about his so-called 'friends' after that."

Not with me he wasn't, Angela thought to herself, sadly, I believed it all. Even now, when I know he can't be trusted, I've still believed his lies. He doesn't have any dodgy contacts, never did. My God I even accepted that he had his elderly mother killed. How can I have been so stupid?

"Ange?"

Angela jumped. Bert was staring at her, looking concerned.

"Are you alright?" he asked.

She nodded.

"Yes, I'm fine. Or at least I will be, very soon."

One week to plan, she told herself. Max was so going to pay for what he'd done to her.

Angela smiled at her father. For the first time she noticed he was getting old. Here he was, over seventy, probably without any type of pension and still working; going all over the place to do surveillance work in all types of weather. Now that she knew he hadn't been stealing from her she found herself worrying about him.

"Why don't you come inside? You can bathe that hand and say a proper goodbye to Ursula."

Bert looked at his watch and shook his head.

"I'd love to," he said, "But I can't now. I really must be

going. I've got a friend waiting in a car up the road. I just wanted to ask you to pretend you hadn't seen me."

"I can't do that dad," Angela told him, "Too many people know you've been here. Ursula knows and she…oh my God, you were using her on your surveillance work weren't you?"

Bert looked very sheepish.

"You had her driving around the county in her car so that you could check out places to be burgled."

"I didn't think it would be a problem," he told her, "I'm usually out of the area before anything happens. I was enjoying driving round with Ursula, telling her some of my stories. Like I said, I got a bit cocky. I thought it would be okay to use Ursula's car. I'm normally careful but I think we may have been seen on the security cameras of the house next door to the one that's just been burgled by my contact."

"What?"

"It's the contact's fault really," Bert continued, sounding as if he was trying to convince himself, "He shouldn't have burgled it so quickly. He was meant to leave it at least another week. It'll probably be okay though. I mean it wasn't the house with the cameras that was burgled. Still, if the police do look at the neighbour's CCTV…"

"Well if the police do come knocking on my door," Angela interrupted him, "I'm not going to lie for you if it's going to get Ursula into trouble."

Bert conceded the point with a nod of his head.

"Fair enough," he said, "I wouldn't want you to do that either. But if it doesn't involve Ursula, you will do your old dad a favour won't you?"

"Yes okay," she told him, "And if Ivan and Sergei show up from the Russian mafia, I'll tell them I haven't seen you in months."

Bert laughed.

"Thanks Ange," he said, "I'll head off now. It's probably best if I don't tell you where I'm going."

Angela felt a sudden surge of affection for the man standing in front of her.

"Take care of yourself dad," she said.

Bert smiled and then nodded.

"Right, well I'll best be going," he told her. "I'll have to stop off somewhere on the way and buy some decent food, your brother never has anything good in his fridge."

"You're going to Neil's?"

Bert groaned.

"Shit, I shouldn't have said that."

He sighed, shrugged his shoulders resignedly and walked off with a cheery wave to his daughter. Angela watched him make his way down the driveway towards the high street. At the bend in the road he threw himself against a wall and peeped carefully round it. If he was trying to be inconspicuous he was failing miserably. Angela couldn't help smiling.

"Silly old bugger," she said out loud.

She locked the car and headed into the house. Ursula was sitting at the dining table at the back of the house, hand sewing. She grinned up at Angela.

"Look what I found in the boot of my car earlier," she said, waving her wrist, "It must have come off when I was picking up the shopping bags last week."

Her emerald bracelet shimmered in the sunlight.

*

Up at the Home Angela was told that no one had heard from

Margaret. The place was abuzz. A funeral, a party with alcohol and then a tasty bit of gossip had been too much for some of the residents and the nurses were running low on diazepam.

Maureen was staying at the hospital with Dora. She was being kept in overnight for observation but would probably be sent home in the morning. There wasn't really anything else Angela or Ursula could do for now. On the way out they bumped into a very merry Sir Jasper.

"My God that does a man some good," he told them, "Chancing upon two fine fillies such as yourselves."

Ursula giggled. Angela rolled her eyes.

"And where's young Derek disappeared to?" he asked.

"He's gone to London," Angela replied.

Sir Jasper leered.

"So," he said, "You two are without a man for the evening, what? How about a nightcap up in my quarters, eh? The night is young."

"And you're not, Sir Jasper," Angela told him.

"Don't let this exterior fool you, my dear," he said, "Parts of me may be sagging but other bits can still stand to attention when the situation calls for it."

Ursula looked aghast.

"How's about it then," he said, "The old ticker might not be up for a threesome but what a way to go, eh, eh?"

He elbowed Ursula in the ribs and then dropped his stick.

"We're not picking that up Sir Jasper," Angela said, before explaining to Ursula, "Derek told me he just wants to look at your behind while you're bent over."

Ursula tutted.

"You're a dirty, old man, aren't you," she told him.

Sir Jasper's whole body began shaking, excitedly.

"And at my age I can get away with it," he replied, "Come on now, I can be as dirty as you want me to be, you little minx you."

Angela grabbed Ursula's arm and led her towards the exit.

"Keep taking the Bromide Sir Jasper," Angela called, over her shoulder.

Sir Jasper watched them go. He sighed when the door closed and headed off to see if he could get away with goosing one of the nurses.

Chapter 19

Angela headed off to work as usual on the Friday. Ursula told her that she'd go back up to the Home to check on Dora's return and would let Angela know if she was needed. Margaret still hadn't responded but Angela wasn't unduly worried. Margaret was too sensible to do anything silly and probably just needed some time alone. Still, she'd wait to hear from her before she updated Derek.

It was a selfish thought to have but Angela hoped Margaret wasn't going to stay away for too long as she wanted her help with her revenge on Max. Now that Bert had confirmed Max's dodgy contacts were pure fiction, Angela's plans were going full steam ahead. That man had had too much control over her entire life and he really needed to pay for what he'd done to her. Perhaps he'd done the same thing to other women as well. She wouldn't put it past him. Well, justice was just around the corner and with Margaret's help, Max was going to learn that women were a lot tougher than he thought.

Angela sat at her desk going through the e-mail valuations but her mind kept drifting. She was so angry at herself for not seeing Max for the man he really was when they first met. Why had she believed everything he'd told her? Wasn't she an intelligent woman? Still, it was easy to see things clearly with hindsight. Twenty years ago Angela had thought herself in love and love really was blind. She wouldn't have seen Max for the liar he was at the time, even if someone had pointed it out to her. No one believes the person they adore could ever hurt them...until it actually happens.

It was difficult not to think of what her life could have been like if only a few decisions had been different. If only she'd realised Max had taken the money she could have had a better relationship with her father. If only she'd decided not to return to prostitution after the attack she could have got a proper job somewhere. If only she hadn't refused to sleep with her attacker she would still have been able to have had children. She could have given Derek a child. Derek; she loved him so much. All of their arguments lately had been about her past. If the prostitution had never happened they'd be so much happier now.

Angela shook her head. She couldn't think that way. If her life had been different then she may never have met Derek Noble on a coach holiday to Tenhamshire. The past was the past. It happened and couldn't be changed. But the future could be altered. It was time to put the past behind her and to do that she had to face Max next Thursday and put an end to his involvement in her life once and for all.

Derek was her future. Okay, so there was no chance of them ever having children together. They were too old to adopt a baby; not that they'd investigated that. What was the point? No one was going to hand over a baby to an ex-prostitute to bring up. But a baby wasn't everything. They could still be happy together, just the two of them, living out their lives here in Tenhamshire; Derek gardening and she working here at the auction house...provided next Thursday went according to plan.

Her thoughts returned to Margaret. Her friend needed to confront this crisis Dora had put her into, and sooner rather than later. Angela didn't want anyone to end up like herself, still trying to deal with a problem twenty years down the line. It was time to bring Margaret home to talk things through with Dora. Dora was eighty-seven after all. The shock of seeing this man at the Home could have killed her and then Margaret would never have been able to find out what had happened. Margaret and Dora, despite some of the things they said to one another, were actually very close. Angela didn't want this situation to drive a wedge between them that couldn't be erased. She phoned Margaret's number again. This time she left a different message.

"It's Angela. I'm done with the sympathetic messages. Stop feeling so bloody sorry for yourself and call me back. It's not right to scare a friend this way, you selfish cow."

Now that should get a response.

*

The response came that afternoon in a text message.

I'm on my way back. I'll come to your house. I can't face the Home yet. By the way, re your last message…you're a bitch. ☺ *Mx*

Angela arrived home at five o'clock and Margaret's car was parked in her space. Angela squeezed hers behind it, blocking the turning circle for her neighbours. Still, that was tough for now. She'd move it later. Once inside she heard voices coming from the kitchen, well, it was just Ursula's voice.

"And once I'd pressed the neckline I under-stitched it here, around the neck edge."

Ursula saw Angela first and smiled.

"I was just showing Margaret the dress I've been making for Theresa Jennings up at the old rectory," she got down carefully off of the stool, "In fact that's where I'm off to now, to do a fitting. I'll leave you two to it."

She left the room with the dress and a few moments later the front door closed. Margaret smiled.

"Bless her," she said, "She didn't know what to say to me so just started banging on about the dress. I'm glad you're here."

Angela stepped forward and hugged her friend. She heard Margaret sob and felt her body shudder against hers as she finally gave in to the tears.

Once Margaret had composed herself and refused a glass of wine, Angela made coffee and they sat down together at the dining table.

"Where did you go yesterday?" Angela asked.

"I drove around for ages; stopped somewhere for the night. A pub out in the sticks, I don't even remember the name of it now," Margaret shook her head, "Today I found myself over at Spratling Kershaw."

"Why?"

"I'm not too sure. I think it was because that was my first taste of Tenhamshire. It was where we all stayed on that coach trip a couple of years back. That was when I decided to make a fresh start in this county. I wanted a new project, a business. I thought Tenhamshire was going to make me happy and until yesterday, it had."

"Have you spoken to your mother yet?" Angela asked.

Margaret shook her head.

"No. I'm not ready to either. Ursula told me she's back at the Home. Apparently she's taken to her bed and is faking being at death's door."

"I'm sorry to say this Margaret," Angela said, tentatively, "But what if she is?"

"She's not. I know my mother. She's after attention. If she

was at death's door she'd have been kept at the hospital. I did phone them last night to check how she was. She was sent home today because there's nothing wrong with her, not because they can't do any more for her. No, leave her to stew in her room. She's got Maureen for company. That will piss her off."

Angela smiled.

"Maureen thinks she's dying," Margaret continued, "That's what she put in her text to me but that's just mum confusing her. Let's face it, you could confuse Maureen if you wrote 'push' on a door you can only pull."

She caught Angela's eye and the two laughed.

"Her hearts in the right place," Margaret said, "But sometimes I'm not sure where her brain is. No wonder mum calls her Moron."

She sighed.

"Oh mum, you've done it again," she said, "Why on earth did she have to start telling the truth now? She's never felt the need to before. She's always been convincing with a lie. I was twelve before I realised Santa Claus wasn't real."

"My God, twelve; really?"

"That's not what I want you to focus on, Angela."

"Sorry. Look, are you sure Dora's not just confused?" Angela asked, taking a sip of her coffee.

"Mum's never confused," Margaret replied, "No, she knew exactly who that man was."

She sighed again.

"I knew I was on the way when mum and dad married but I never dreamed someone else got her pregnant."

"Have you spoken to Jeremy?"

Margaret shook her head, tears forming in her eyes again.

"I can't, not at the moment. We're probably both feeling too embarrassed."

"What for?"

"What for? We went on a date and then found out we're brother and sister! I mean, we didn't do anything but we both... well, thought about it."

Angela gasped.

"My God, I didn't even think of that. I was too caught up in Dora's confession."

"It's typical of mum. She's always managed to thwart any chance of my being happy."

Margaret stood up and walked over to the patio doors. She stared out at the garden. Not that there was much of one, seeing as Derek hadn't got around to spending any time out there. It was really just a small, bare patch of lawn, muddy after all of the recent rain. Angela waited for her friend to speak again.

"I was never much interested in dating when I was younger," Margaret said, still facing the garden, "I was so focussed on my career. When I was born, dad's business was in its early stages. By the time I joined the firm it had tripled in size and was still in excellent shape. He made me start my career at the bottom, letting me see each aspect of the business and getting to know the people that worked for him. Dad always said a company was as good as its staff and you had to look after them. I loved working there and was dad's second-in-command by the time I was twenty-five. I was able to open up new avenues and we continued to thrive. I was so ready to take over but only once dad was ready to retire."

Margaret gave a little sigh and turned round to face Angela.

"When he was diagnosed with terminal cancer I was devastated, so was mum. I stayed late at the office each night, not only to keep the business running but also, I suppose, to avoid dealing with the grief. I was shocked when dad told me he was selling everything. I mean we came out very wealthy, mum and I, but that was no substitute to dad's passing."

She sat down at the table again.

"Before he died, dad told me to look after mum. He said she wasn't as strong as she made out. That was bollocks but I did what he asked. What else could I do, he'd sold the business and I had nothing except a load of money and an attention-seeking mother. Why did he sell the company? Didn't he think I could run it on my own? I never understood that."

"Perhaps you should ask your mum about it," Angela told her, "Wouldn't she know?"

Margaret tutted.

"I doubt it," she said, "Her only interest is herself. I did everything for her after dad died, as he'd asked me too, but I don't think she was grateful. I was so lonely. I'd never had many friends. Work was my best friend, my companion, my lover if you like. Only once I no longer had a job did I think a man friend would be nice to have. I tried to get in on the dating scene but that was difficult, what with taking mum here, there and everywhere. She always got in the way. When I bought the Home it seemed like the perfect solution. I could run my own business, go on dates and still make sure mum was being looked after. I've had a few disastrous relationships but then, just when I stopped looking, along came a man I really liked. We had such a lovely date, we felt like we'd known each other for years. Then mum manages to ruin everything by telling the whole world we're related."

Margaret reached for her tissue to wipe her nose. There were more tears but they were definitely angry ones. Angela waited for her to calm down a little before she spoke.

"Remember who it was who told you to stop trying so hard to get a date and let nature take its course," she said, "It was your mum, that night we met up for a drink in the pub. Since I've known you all Dora talks about are your relationships."

"She always asks if I'm getting any."

Angela bit her lip to stop herself smiling.

"Well yes," she said, "But that's just her way. It's obvious she cares for you. You need to talk to her. I don't care if you shout at each other but you really need to talk this thing through, tell each other how you feel."

Angela hoped she was getting through to her friend.

"The only way you're going to get any closure on this is to talk to her about it. You can't avoid the situation by bottling up your feelings. That will only delay it."

Margaret picked up her mug and took a sip of her coffee.

"I'm worried that I'm too angry to find out the truth at the moment," she admitted, "While I know mum's as strong as an ox I can't help worrying that I'll end up shouting at her too much and she'll pop off. That'd be just like her, dying so she can win an argument."

"It shows you still care about her."

Margaret groaned.

"That bloody, old cow," she said, "I sometimes wonder why I do still care. Let's face it, she's just told me my father isn't my father, the man I loved and admired so much. She's tarnished that relationship too."

Angela threw out her hand and grabbed hold of Margaret's across the table.

"No," she told her, "Don't think like that. Billy brought you up. He loved you. Of course he was your father."

Margaret smiled, gratefully.

"I just wonder what happened," she confessed.

Angela smiled.

"We're back where we started," she said, "You've got to go and speak to your mother."

Margaret nodded.

"Yes," she said, "You're right of course, but I don't want to go now, at least not tonight. I can't face the Home yet. Could I stay here?"

"Of course you can," Angela told her, "Now, how about we open that bottle of wine."

*

Derek was surprised that his summons back to Tenhamshire came from Maureen. He received the text message early Saturday morning, telling him that Dora wasn't long for this world and she was asking for him. Why hadn't Angela been in touch? Perhaps Maureen had only just sent her the same message. Maybe she was still trying to contact Margaret. Derek replied to the text, telling her he was on his way.

He had plenty to think about on the drive home, aside from concentrating on the teeming rain and busy, wet roads. Although they'd parted last night amicably, Derek was still shocked that Leanne had kept the abortion secret from him. He'd been awake most of the night. During the evening he'd been caught up in the idea of Leanne not wanting a baby with him but once back at his apartment, on his own, it hit him that he'd almost become a father. He and Leanne had conceived a baby together but she'd taken the decision on her own to get rid of it. He'd told her last night in anger that she'd been selfish throughout their marriage. Right now he couldn't help thinking that this had been another selfish decision.

But with Nathan, Leanne was being selfless. He came first in her life now and she wanted Derek to look after him in the event of her demise. She was trusting her ex-husband with the most precious thing she had. Maybe it was her way of making up for what had happened in the past.

Derek knew he'd have to get over the fact that Leanne had had an abortion to be able to move forward. After all, he did want to stay in contact with her and have Angela meet her and Nathan too. If the unthinkable did happen then at least Nathan would be going to stay with two people he knew. It wasn't the ideal outcome Derek had wanted in life but it was the nearest he was going to get to being a dad. It hurt that he'd come close before and never known about it.

Is that why he'd been so eager to keep seeing Leanne after bumping into her a few weeks back? They hadn't had a good divorce yet after one lunch together he'd decided to redecorate his apartment so that he could keep returning to the area. Things weren't so bad with Angela that he'd actually considered an affair. Okay, so he'd thought he was taking Leanne out for a meal that night he'd wound up babysitting, but that was a favour rather than a date.

No, it was because of Nathan that he kept returning. Angela had told him early on in their relationship that she couldn't have children and he'd told her it was fine, that he was just happy to have found love again but really, it hadn't been fine at all. Derek wanted to be a dad and thought it was still a possibility after divorcing Leanne. It was so much easier for a man as there wasn't an age limit to consider. Then, after falling head over heels in love with Angela, she'd told him it still wasn't going to happen. Had that played a role in their recent arguments? Was Derek resenting her for not being able to provide him with a child?

It was an awful thought to have but Derek had to face up to things. His recent attraction to Leanne had only been for her son. He was forty-seven years old and he wanted to be a dad. But he also wanted Angela and he realised now that he couldn't have both. He loved Angela more than anything and couldn't imagine life without her.

"I'm never going to be a father," he said, aloud.

It was no longer just the rain blurring his vision as he drove.

*

Derek felt a little better as he drove through Tenhamshire. He knew his future was with Angela and they could make it a happy one, a very happy one. He just needed a bit of time to accept the fact that children were never going to be a part of his life…unless Leanne fell under that bus.

He was glad to finally reach Baddlesbury. The wet weather and an accident on the motorway meant it had taken him a lot longer than normal to get home. He'd stopped for lunch on the way at a grotty, little service station. The coffee shop was shut, meaning the burger restaurant next door was packed full of people. Derek had bought a large black coffee and a blueberry muffin, choosing not to have something hot when he spotted one of the kitchen staff peeling a slice of pickle off of his shoe and adding it as a topping to one of the burgers.

It was late afternoon now and Derek decided to drive straight up to the Home. While acceptance of not being a dad was still at the forefront of his mind, he thought it best not to go and see

Angela first. While he knew it would be unfair of him, with his emotions still a little delicate, he feared starting an argument with her.

He parked up at the Home and switched off his mobile phone, not bothering to check it for missed calls or messages. He was about to make his way upstairs to Dora's room when Sir Jasper accosted him in the hallway.

"Are you off to see dear, old Dora?" he asked.

Derek nodded.

"Good," Sir Jasper said, "Good. Do tell me what she's like won't you. I haven't been allowed to see her. Moron is acting like a prison guard."

"I'll try and find out for you," Derek told him, saddened that Dora's friends hadn't been told how she was doing.

Sir Jasper smiled. He got a notebook out of his pocket.

"Great," he said, "I want to make sure I've selected the best slot in the sweepstake. It's a tricky one this time."

"You're running a death sweepstake on Dora?"

Derek couldn't believe his ears. Sir Jasper nodded at him innocently.

"Of course," he replied, "We do it to everyone in here."

Derek pressed his face right up against Sir Jasper's.

"Well I think it's sick," he told him, firmly, "You're meant to be her friend."

He turned and headed up the stairs. He had to get away from Sir Jasper before he hit him. Outside her room, Derek knocked gently on Dora's door. It opened a crack and Maureen's face appeared. When she saw who it was she smiled and opened it wide. She looked exhausted, with large black circles under her eyes.

"Derek," she whispered, sounding relieved, "I'm so glad

you're here. Please come in."

Derek walked in. This was the largest of all the residents' rooms; more a suite really with a good-sized bathroom and space for a seating area at the end of the bed. Dora had a large, three-seater sofa and a wingback chair in a matching fabric, and both faced a large, flat screen TV on the wall.

Dora lay in her king-sized bed, asleep. Without her glasses on and no scrap of make-up she looked every year of her age.

"How is she doing?" Derek asked Maureen, in a whisper.

The matron sighed.

"She drifts in and out of consciousness," she confided, "Bless her, I think she's still in shock. Her daughter hasn't returned yet but I haven't told her that. I'm trying to keep people away but she's been asking for you especially."

Derek pulled up a chair beside her bed and sat down.

"I'm glad you're here," Maureen said again, "If you don't mind, I'll pop out and get a shower and a change of clothes. Don't let anyone else in, will you."

Derek nodded and Maureen left the room. He stared down at the old lady in the bed.

"Has she gone," asked a croaky voice, in barely a whisper.

"Yes," he whispered back.

Dora opened her eyes. Suddenly she was transformed to her old self.

"Thank fuck for that," she said, sitting up in the bed, "I thought the stupid cow would never leave me alone. Pass me my glasses, Derek."

Derek was incredulous.

"Are you telling me you're fine? Maureen told me you were at death's door. I've just driven five hours in the rain to come and see you."

"Well I didn't know what else to do," Dora told him, "I know my Margaret isn't going to come and see me for a while and Angela would be the one trying to contact her. I had to get Moron out of the room, she was stifling me. And she was getting a bit whiffy too. My God, she could have killed me herself, lifting her arm up to stroke my forehead and giving me a full blast of her body odour."

Derek couldn't believe what was happening.

"You do remember what you said in the lounge on the day of the funeral, don't you?"

Dora yawned.

"Of course I do," she said, "And it was a genuine shock seeing that old bastard after all these years. I didn't want to blurt out what I did but well, it's done now and I've got a lot of explaining to do, but only to Margaret. I know her. She's upset now, of course she is, but she'll come and see me eventually. She'll want to know the truth and I'll have to tell her. Reach inside that bottom drawer for me will you."

Derek opened the drawer Dora indicated.

"Is there a packet of Hob Nobs in there?"

"Yes."

"Good, I'm starving. Bloody Moron has insisted on only soup being sent up to me and then she tries to feed me herself. Her aim with a spoon is about as accurate as a man's during a piss. I was drenched."

Dora took the whole packet from Derek and, after offering him one, began to devour the rest.

"Now then," she said, spilling crumbs down her nightdress, "The reason I've got you here is money. Have you seen Sir Jasper?"

Derek's face darkened.

"Yes," he said, "The bastard has started a new sweepstake."

Dora laughed and clapped her hands.

"Brilliant," she said, "Good old Sir Jasper. I knew I could rely on him."

"You mean you don't mind?"

"Mind? Of course I don't mind. I'd have been offended if he hadn't. It proves my acting skills when I was brought back from the hospital were good. I knew I could convince Moron I was at death's door. She wouldn't know a ruse if it bit her on her vast bottom."

Derek didn't know why he was surprised at Dora's behaviour. She threw the almost half-empty packet of Hob Nobs onto her bedside table and leaned forward in the bed, trying to look business-like.

"Now then," she said, "We've got a chance here to make a few quid."

"We?"

"Well I wouldn't leave my pal out of it now, would I?"

"Dora, you're worth a fortune already."

She waved her hand dismissively.

"That's all in investments and other stuff I don't understand. Actually most of it is in this place. I'm talking about cold, hard cash in your hand, ready money."

"If you're about to fake your own death I don't want any part in it."

Dora shook her head.

"Nothing as drastic as that," she told him, "I'm talking about a wager. Now, has Sir Jasper asked how I am?"

"That's what he was asking just now, downstairs."

Dora beamed.

"Perfect," she said, "All I want you to do, because I know

you're a wuss when it comes to deceit, is to tell him that you think Moron is right."

"That's all?"

"That's all…aside from then placing a bet."

Derek sighed.

"I've already told him I think the death sweepstake is sick."

"He won't care when you tell him you want fifty pounds on my living past Tuesday. You'll get great odds on that."

"Won't he smell a rat?"

"Not if you do it right. Just tell him you can't believe I'm going to die. Tell him you'd be lost without me, that the world will be a darker place without my light shining in it."

"He'll definitely smell a rat there."

Dora laughed, her usual roaring cackle.

"Okay, just tell him you refuse to believe I'm going to die. He'll think you're in denial and will take the bet."

Derek shook his head.

"I'm not sure," he told her, "I think it's wrong to take a lot of money from pensioners."

Dora sighed and looked at Derek. She straightened herself up in the bed.

"Listen to me Derek. Sir Jasper is a Baronet. His family owned this house and grounds before it was sold off and turned into a retirement home. At one time the family used to own the land Baddlesbury is built on, before they were forced to sell it to the Dukes of Tenham. Didn't you hear him tell us all that the day we visited Tenham House?"

Derek was surprised.

"I thought he was making most of that up," he confessed, "I didn't know it was this house and this village that his family owned."

"Well they did, but it was before the village was here. That's why Sir Jasper gets so angry about the Dukes. They became extremely wealthy because they rented and also sold off parcels of the land to the wool merchants who were becoming rich themselves and who wanted to build their own homes as status symbols. The land was right in front of the house Sir Jasper's family owned. There had always been rivalry between the two families. Sir Jasper's family were titled first but the Dukes soon followed and then surpassed them. Sir Jasper's family always believed the dukes sold the parcels of land just to rub their noses in the fact they were becoming wealthier while also ruining the view from the front of the house. It wasn't until the late eighteenth century that one of Sir Jasper's ancestors married a woman who came with a vast fortune and they were able to afford to demolish that other house and build this one further back from the village."

"How do you know all this?" Derek asked.

Dora looked indignant.

"Well I wasn't there to witness it before you ask," she told him, "Haven't you noticed the old books downstairs, on the shelves in the back lounge? The history is all in those. I like a good read."

Derek smiled.

"I never knew any of this," he said.

"Well you do now. Sir Jasper's family is worth a fortune after selling this place, even though it was pretty rundown at the time, but he's like me; his kids control the money and he gets an allowance. Still, a fifty pound bet is not going to put much of a dent in his savings. Will you do it?"

"Okay," Derek said, resignedly, "But I want the money up front. I know what you're like."

"Fine," Dora sighed, "Just reach inside my bra."
"Forget it, you can owe it me."
Dora winked.
"I mean the bra inside my top drawer."
"Oh, that's a relief."
Derek retrieved the money.
"Right," Dora said, "Now skedaddle. I'd like a bit of alone time before Moron comes back to fawn all over me again."
Derek nodded and turned to leave the room.
"Oh by the way," Dora called after him.
Derek turned back to face her.
"If you see my Margaret, tell her I'm sorry and I'll be waiting for her, when she's ready."
Derek thought he saw a tear slide down Dora's cheek. He nodded to her and left the room.

Chapter 20

Dora was right about Sir Jasper. He was very happy to take the bet. After leaving the Home Derek switched his mobile phone back on and saw that he'd missed several texts and an answerphone message from Angela while he'd been driving back to Tenhamshire. Margaret had been holed up at the coach house since yesterday afternoon. He phoned Angela up as he walked the familiar route home, hunched over to try and stay dry in the rain.

"Are you alright?" she asked, "I was starting to get worried when you didn't reply to my messages."

"Sorry, I switched my phone off without checking it before I went in to see Dora," he told her.

"You're here?"

"Yes, I'm just walking back home now. I had a summons from Maureen this morning. I'll tell you all about it once I'm in."

He told them everything over dinner, about Maureen's text, his horrendous journey home, the sweepstake bet and Dora waiting to see Margaret once she was ready.

Margaret nodded sadly at that (and rolled her eyes about the sweepstake).

"I think I'd better phone the Home and let them know I'm coming back," she said, "I should probably go soon."

"You're welcome to stay another night," Angela told her.

"Yes," Ursula said, "You can have my sewing room rather than the sofa, if you like. Bert and I found the airbed very comfy."

"What do you mean you both found it comfy?" Derek asked.

Ursula blushed slightly.

"Well we had a quick bounce on it together once it was pumped up," she admitted.

"What!"

"Hang on Derek," Angela told him, before saying to Ursula, "You mean you both sat down on it and then bounced up and down to test it, don't you."

"Yes," Ursula grinned, "We started laughing like a couple of kids. Up and down we were going, faster and faster, laughing and getting out of breath."

"Yes well I think that's enough description for Derek."

Angela was trying desperately not to laugh. Margaret was grinning too. She stood up.

"Thanks for the offer," she said, "It sounds like that bed can take a good pounding."

Derek winced.

"But I ought to get back and wrestle that fifty pounds off of Sir Jasper. I need to stop this bloody sweepstake, it'll only end in tears and it won't be mum's."

"She's going to hate me for telling you," Derek admitted.

"I'm afraid you're collateral damage," Margaret told him, and laughed.

To Derek she seemed on remarkably good form considering what she'd just found out about her father but perhaps that was Angela's influence over the last couple of days.

"Don't worry, I'll say I discovered it from another source," she continued, "Mum isn't the only one who is good at deceit."

She bit her lip as the thought of her mother's secret hit her once again.

"I'm scared of going back," she admitted.

"Would you like me to come with you?" Angela asked.

Margaret nodded gratefully. Angela turned to Derek.

"You don't mind, do you?"

"No, that's fine."

Derek hoped his reply sounded nonchalant rather than like some over-excited child the night before Christmas. He was desperate to discover what had happened between Dora and Leonard Riley and now Angela was going to be a witness to Dora's confession.

While Margaret popped into the downstairs bathroom and Ursula began stacking the dishwasher, Derek told Angela about painting the lounge in his old apartment but not that he'd had dinner with Leanne. He wanted to tell her all about it but knew it was probably best to wait until this thing with Dora and Margaret blew over. Mind you, that might even be this evening, depending upon what Dora had to say. If so, perhaps he could tell Angela all about Nathan later tonight. He was sure she'd be happy about it, once she'd got over the shock of Leanne being back on the scene.

"Give me a call when you're ready to come home," he told her, "The rain isn't about to ease off and the weather report on the radio in the car earlier said that storms are likely. If you're driving up in Margaret's car I don't want you walking back in it."

Angela smiled.

"My hero," she said, and kissed him.

Derek was pleased Angela seemed more like her old self again. It would make telling her about Nathan easier. Perhaps she'd talked her own problems through with Margaret these past two days. Both women were on top form. With her heading up to the Home for the evening it would give him the opportunity to sit down with his mother and ensure she was happy with her move to Tenhamshire. Hopefully she wouldn't talk anymore about bouncing around on the bed with Bert.

After saying goodbyes, Angela and Margaret headed up to the Home.

"This weather really is quite dreadful," Margaret said, leaning forwards and squinting through the windscreen, trying to see the road through the driving rain.

"Yes, Derek said storms were due," Angela agreed, "It's got so dark out there. Anyone would think it's the middle of the night."

"I hope this isn't an omen for what my evening is going to be like."

"It will be fine," Angela told her, "Well, maybe not fine but it will be better knowing the truth."

Margaret nodded.

They went to Margaret's office first where she sorted through some correspondence and spoke to a couple of members of staff over the internal phone line. Angela felt it was just a delaying tactic but she didn't say anything and gave her friend the time she needed to prepare for the talk ahead. Eventually, after standing up from her desk and taking a deep breath, Margaret said she was ready and the two of them headed upstairs.

Maureen had resumed guard duty. She was overwhelmed to see the two ladies and needed comforting. Margaret rolled her eyes as Maureen cried on her shoulder. Angela went into the room. Dora had her eyes closed and was looking frail again in the large bed. Knowing she was faking Angela whispered,

"It's me."

Dora opened one eye.

"Is Moron still there?"

"Margaret's trying to get rid of her."

"Margaret's here!"

Dora sat herself up in bed and retrieved her glasses. Outside they heard Margaret say,

"No it's fine, you get yourself off home for a rest. Don't come in tomorrow."

As Margaret appeared in the room a loud clap of thunder roared through the sky. The rain hammered against the window.

"There's a filthy night out there," she said.

"I can't see **him** now," Dora replied, "Besides Sir Jasper isn't a Knight, he's a Baronet."

"What? No, I was talking about the weather."

"Oh."

To Angela it was like nothing had changed between the two women and yet everything had. Would she be allowed to stay and hear what Dora had to say? She hoped so.

"Right," Margaret said, "I suppose we'd better get this sorted."

She sat down on the side of her mother's bed and indicated for Angela to take the chair Derek had sat in earlier.

"Don't give me your businesswoman persona," Dora said, "I know that person and she doesn't take shit from anyone. I want my daughter here."

Margaret took a deep breath.

"I'm not sure your daughter is going to be able to cope with what you have to say," she told her.

Dora leaned forwards and took Margaret's hands in both of hers.

"Please," she said, "Understand that both I and your father loved you. And of course I mean Billy. He was your dad love, not that man who trundled in here the other day. I'm sorry I blurted out what I did."

"But you did blurt it out though, didn't you," Margaret replied, controlling her voice, keeping it low, "It's not like you can take it back."

"I had to do it," Dora told her, "My God I'm always telling you to go and get some from a fella. I know it's a bit of a joke between us but when I turned and saw…that man, I realised in that split second that you'd gone on a date with your brother. That's what shocked me."

Margaret frowned.

"You mean you didn't faint because of Mr Riley?"

"Oh please," Dora said, letting go of Margaret's hands as she flung hers into the air, "I vowed years ago to never let that man affect me emotionally again and I've stuck to that. No it was seeing you and Jeremy standing beside each other behind the wheelchair that affected me. Of course I'm angry with the wizened, old buzzard too. Stuck in here with the missing link mollycoddling me for two days, all I've had to do is think over old times. If he hadn't turned up here I wouldn't have had to reveal my secret to you. Have you spoken to him at all?"

"What? No," Margaret said, "I'm too embarrassed."

Dora nodded.

"Good," she said, "Good. I wouldn't trust what the old man said. I wonder what he's told his son. I'm here to tell you the truth…if you're ready to hear it."

Margaret took another deep breath and nodded.

Dora was silent a moment, trying to get the words right in her head.

"Right, well I suppose I have to start the story with me," she finally said.

"Oh that will be a nice change," Margaret replied.

Dora ignored her and continued on.

"It will probably surprise you to know that I wasn't that interested in marriage and having children when I was younger."

Angela wasn't sure that telling your daughter a story about her dad not being her real father should really start with the mother saying she didn't want to have children.

"When I left school I got a job in a typing pool at an insurance company in London. I loved it. It made me feel grown up, although that feeling always disappeared as soon as I arrived home. My parents weren't bad people, just overprotective. Even after I'd been working for five years and had progressed from typing pool to secretary I was still on a curfew at home most nights of the week. I'm afraid I rebelled. Well, I was twenty-one and an adult. I began staying out past their curfews. I wasn't doing anything seedy, I was just enjoying myself. Well that led to a blazing row at home. My dad told me I couldn't behave like that under his roof so of course, I moved out."

Dora reached for her glass of water on the bedside table and took a sip.

"I moved into lodgings, still in South London," she continued, after replacing the glass on the side, "Well I say lodgings it was a grotty little room with a freezing cold bathroom on the floor below. I didn't have much money saved. My parents made me give them most of my wages while I lived at home, leaving me with barely pocket money. Now though, my wages were all my own. I saved what I could over the next few years and then I took the decision to move to Manchester."

"Why Manchester?" Angela asked.

The two women on the bed both turned to look at her, as if they'd forgotten she was there. Angela's face reddened.

"Sorry," she told them, "I was just curious."

"I moved there," Dora explained, "Because there were jobs, it was cheaper to live, and it was a long way from my parents' house. After I left home they tried to make peace with me but they still wanted to control my life. I wasn't having that."

She smiled to herself.

"I loved it up in Manchester," she said, "I rented a really nice room in a house with some other girls that also worked at the manufacturing company where I was based. We were out most nights, the cinema, the local dance hall, the pub. Oh, they were great days. I was so happy."

She looked up at her daughter.

"I did date but not seriously," she continued, "I wasn't looking to settle down. Why would I? I'd seen enough of my friends from school get married and have kids during the years I was working in London. They looked old before their time. No I wanted to kick up my heels for as long as I could."

Angela realised she was smiling. She could just picture the young Dora, the life and soul of every party.

"I was twenty-six when I moved to Manchester. Your dad, Billy worked for the same firm. He liked me straightaway, I knew that. I was still a big girl in those days, not as big as I am now but I was a looker and I had curves. I also think my happiness radiated off of me. I was loud and always up for a good night out. Your dad and I were the same age but he seemed older. He was cute but I thought him shy and reserved. I didn't realise how studious and determined he was back then to make a career for himself. We never dated but he sometimes came out as part of the group and we chatted and laughed together on those nights. I thought nothing of it. I didn't realise he'd fallen in love with me."

She sighed happily as she remembered that time, then a cloud passed over her face.

"Two brothers owned the manufacturing firm. I was secretary to the elder. After I'd been there three years he decided to bring his own son in to learn the business. That was when I first met Leonard Riley."

Angela saw Margaret tense up.

"He was the stereotypical only son of wealthy parents," Dora continued, "He was the wayward boy who'd been given everything. His father was strict while the mother spoiled him. He'd spent years doing nothing except spending his father's money and now his dad was taking him in hand. Of course I didn't know all this when he first appeared. All I saw was a very handsome thirty-four year old man. We clicked instantly. While I was always polite and professional with my boss, Leonard saw the real me outside of the office and he loved it. I fell in love with him and he fell in love with me."

Dora paused. Angela understood how difficult this must be for her, reliving a part of her life she'd tried to ignore for almost sixty years.

"Well of course I eventually found out I was pregnant. I was happy though. I was in love with a man I was sure would do the right thing and marry me. It all went wrong so quickly and horribly."

Dora pulled a handkerchief out from under her pillow and wiped her eyes.

"Mr Riley senior was appalled when his son told him. To give Leonard his due he was prepared to marry me but my boss was having none of it. He was a real snob and had arranged several meetings between Leonard and the youngest daughter of some local bigwig with a title. Mr Riley told his son he was to marry her and that was that. He told me I was dismissed and if Leonard went after me he would be cut off."

Dora sighed again.

"It turned out Leonard loved his money and lifestyle more than he loved me."

"You mean he just left you on your own?" Angela asked, shocked.

Dora trembled and a tear slipped down her cheek as she glanced up at her daughter. Margaret looked back. It was as if a thought passed between the two of them.

"Say it mum," she said.

Dora wiped the tear from her cheek.

"He offered to help me get rid of the baby," she said.

Dora began to properly cry now. Margaret moved further up the bed and put her arms around her. Angela felt tearful herself. What an awful thing to have to confess to your daughter. Eventually Dora composed herself enough to continue on with her story.

"Most of the staff at the company knew that I'd been seeing Leonard but they didn't know about the baby. It was only after I was told to leave that I began hearing the stories about Leonard's lifestyle, the drinking, the women and the getting up to no good. I didn't know what to do. I couldn't go back to London and face my parents. They'd have just told me I'd brought it on myself. This was the early sixties and there was still a stigma about unmarried mothers. All I did know was that I didn't want to get rid of my baby."

Dora smiled at Margaret.

"And then Billy came to see me at my lodgings. He'd heard

I'd been sacked. I found myself telling him everything that had happened. He was so calm. He told me he thought he could make things better...for the three of us and asked me to marry him. I said yes. At the time I couldn't see any other alternative. I told you I liked Billy. He was a kind man and I thought we could make a go of it."

Margaret fished a tissue out of her cardigan pocket.

"He went marching into Mr Riley's office. Mr Riley was a fierce man but Billy stood his ground. He began by telling him exactly what he thought about his treatment of me. He told him a few home truths about the things Leonard was getting up to and how, if word got out, it could threaten the marriage chances with the daughter of the local bigwig. Well, Mr Riley wasn't used to being spoken to in that way. I obviously wasn't there but I was told by a friend later that their raised voices could be heard across the entire office. Billy then told Mr Riley that he would help them out. He said he would take me off of their hands and raise the child as his own, providing they paid up for it."

Angela was stunned.

"You make it sound like you were a business transaction."

"Oh I was," Dora told her, matter-of-factly, "Billy understood business, probably better than anyone else there. He knew he could have run that company more efficiently than it was currently being run but also knew he was never going to be promoted into a position where he could instigate his ideas and plans. The price for his silence was enough money to set up a small manufacturing business in East London, well away from Manchester and the Rileys. I think Mr Riley Senior thought he was getting off lightly. It was all agreed and I believe there was some kind of contract signed, saying that neither I, Billy nor our child would make any more demands on the Rileys. Anyway, we moved down to London and got married by special licence. Everyone assumed Billy was the father of my unborn child. He opened his first manufacturing company and that was the start of his lucrative career. I gave birth to Margaret and Billy was named as the father on the birth certificate."

Dora laughed to herself.

"I must admit I was worried about the future in those early months after we married. Billy was very busy with starting up the business while I was stuck at home in our small, two-room, rented apartment, getting bigger and bigger. We didn't spend much time together. Then I went into labour and gave birth in the maternity home. Billy came in to see me that evening after work."

Dora looked into Margaret's eyes.

"He picked you up out of the cot and just stood there, smiling at you. It was at that moment that I fell in love with him. I knew then everything was going to be fine. We were a family, and a damned happy one."

All three women had tears streaming down their faces.

"I'm so sorry I had to reveal this," Dora said.

"No it's fine," Margaret replied, "You're right, we were a happy family. We still are."

She squeezed her mother's hand and the two ladies smiled at one another. Angela felt she ought to leave them alone.

"There's just one thing I don't get," Margaret said, before Angela could move, "Why did dad sell the business off when he became ill? Why didn't he let me take it over? I was practically running it for him anyway."

"That was the reason," Dora told her, "You were always at the office, never at home. He feared you'd be the same after he died and that I would be left alone. He felt so guilty that he was leaving me. Let's face it, he'd rescued me when I was struggling and had looked after me ever since. He wanted me to continue to be looked after. That's all."

"So it wasn't because he thought I couldn't cope?"

Dora smiled.

"Of course not," she said, "He knew how good you were. You were his daughter, a chip off the old block. We did try for more children but it never happened for us. He was so proud of you. I did tell him not to sell the company. I knew how much it meant to you. I told him that I'd be alright but he didn't listen. It's the one time that I think he made a wrong decision. Something in you died after the business went. Then dad passed away and you stepped up and did what he'd asked of you; you looked after me. A bit too much actually."

Margaret had been looking down, remembering, but her head whipped up.

"What do you mean, too much?"

Dora sighed.

"I mean that you didn't do anything else. You're very blinkered when you do things, did you know that? Your focus goes on that and nothing else. You spent all your time with me. I tried to snap you out of it and make you take me places each week; doing more than you should, desperately hoping that you'd turn on me and tell me where to go. I wanted to see that spark in you again."

"I just thought you needed me."

"Not that much," Dora winked, "Still, the spark did return eventually. You bought this place. You've come alive again running the Home, darling. I'm proud of you, and I know your dad would be too."

Margaret smiled.

"I mean Billy," Dora added.

"Yes I know that!"

They both laughed.

Angela was glad that the two ladies had talked through their issues but one problem area remained.

"What are you going to do about Jeremy and his father," she asked, "Will you allow the old man to stay here? Do you want to see Jeremy again; get to know him as a brother?"

Margaret shrugged her shoulders.

"I don't know," she said, "What do you think mum? Would you want Leonard Riley living here?"

Dora shrugged her shoulders as well. The expression on her face was the same as Margaret's and Angela wondered how she'd never noticed such a physical resemblance between the two of them before.

"I don't suppose it would bother me, not now," Dora said, "Let's face it, the poor, old sod probably isn't long for this world anyway. It's entirely up to you. It would be nice for you to have a brother but could you put up with having a man here who is your biological father?"

Margaret remained silent for a moment.

"It's like you said, Billy is my dad. This man is nothing to me. Perhaps he'd like to get to know me, perhaps he'd rather run back to his previous Home in Manchester. That's up to him. I think I could still offer him a place here if he wants it. I would like to get to know Jeremy better."

Dora smiled.

"If that's what you want," she told her daughter.

The two women hugged again. Angela smiled.

"I'm so glad you're friends again," she told them, "Now,

while I've got you together, I need your help with a spot of revenge."

Chapter 21

Derek usually enjoyed a trip to the garden centre but even buying four bags of compost and some packets of seeds couldn't improve his mood. It was Tuesday, three days since Angela had told him, but he still couldn't get over it.

It wasn't Dora's confession about Margaret's real dad that was troubling him. He'd been enthralled while Angela told him and Ursula all about that. It was her recent conversation with Bert that had got his back up. In bed that same night, Derek had been ready to tell her about becoming a guardian to Nathan. He was in a good mood. Ursula had told him earlier that she was very happy with her move to Tenhamshire, Dora and Margaret were friends again, and Angela was acting more like her old self. Before he'd had a chance to even mention Nathan, Angela had brought up Bert's surprise visit to see her, a couple of days before.

He'd almost had a heart attack when she announced that Bert might have got Ursula into trouble. When she explained that Ursula's car may have been seen on security cameras while Bert was eyeing up houses to be burgled, it didn't exactly make him feel any better. For some reason Angela was talking about her father with real affection in her voice. She didn't seem worried about Ursula at all.

"She'll be fine, Derek. It's not like she burgled the house herself."

"But she may be seen as an accessory."

"To what? It's dad on the screen looking at the houses."

"But mum can be quite nervy. If the police turn up and accuse her of stealing she'll probably admit to it."

Angela told him he wasn't giving his mum enough credit, which led on to his still not having told her about Angela's past and another argument began, ending with Derek sleeping on the sofa.

While he was now allowed back in the marital bed, relations between the two of them were still frosty. Derek felt like Angela was blaming him for the argument rather than blaming her criminal father for causing it to happen in the first place. Why was she now defending her dad, a man she herself had thrown out of their house? Why was everything always Derek's fault? He couldn't understand it. As well as being angry with Angela, Derek was also fretting about the police turning up unannounced on his doorstep, ready to cart his mother off to the cells.

The hot and sunny weather had returned after the storms of Saturday night but even this didn't help improve Derek's mood. Neither did having to swerve violently on the driveway on his return to the Home to avoid Ash, racing along on the sit-on lawnmower. He waved cheerfully at Derek as he careered round the corner on two wheels.

Derek parked the van and stored the bags of compost in the outbuilding. He was keen to take the seed packets of Foxgloves, Wallflowers and Sweet William round to the glasshouse in the Victorian walled garden and get them into seed trays so that they'd flower next year.

On his route through the formal garden he bumped into Margaret and Jeremy. They were both smiling and seemed so happy that Derek couldn't help but smile back at them.

"I've moved dad in today," Jeremy told him.

"Oh right," Derek replied, "Where is he now?"

"Mum's taken him off somewhere," Margaret said.

"Oh God, she hasn't pinched one of my shovels has she?"

Margaret laughed.

"No, it's nothing like that. She's not off to bury him. They're having a chat. They seem to be getting on very well together."

"As are we," Jeremy said, smiling at her, "In fact we were just heading out for some lunch. We're going to walk down to the pub and share a pizza."

"Make sure that's all you share," Derek told them.

The smiles fell from Margaret and Jeremy's faces.

"Oh God, I forgot you're related and not dating anymore," Derek said, his face reddening, "Sorry about that."

All three lapsed into an embarrassed silence. Derek looked down at the packets in his hand.

"Right, well I'd best be going then," he told them, "I must go and spread my seed…oh I mean these seeds, obviously…I wasn't talking sexually…I'll just go."

He turned and headed quickly away and through to the old Victorian garden. Derek was so caught up in his embarrassment that he burst through the door of the glasshouse without looking. He realised he wasn't alone by the grunting noises coming from up the back. As he looked up he let out a yelp. Dora was spread-eagled across a wheelchair, her back to him. All he could see of the occupant of the chair was a pair of skinny white legs wearing sock suspenders. His trousers were crumpled over a pair of tartan, felt slippers. Dora looked over her shoulder.

"Fucking hell, Derek," she called out, puffing slightly, "Can't a girl get a bit of privacy round here?"

Derek turned and fled outside. A couple of minutes later Dora hobbled out, leaning heavily on her stick.

"Christ," she said, "I haven't spread my legs that wide since my last smear test."

Derek couldn't believe she wasn't embarrassed.

"What the bloody hell were you doing in there?" he demanded.

Dora looked at him oddly.

"I should have thought that was obvious," she replied, "Blimey I assumed you and Angela would have been pretty adventurous bedroom-wise, considering her past."

"What!"

"It was just sex, Derek," Dora told him, "No need to go into one. We didn't trample on your seedlings or squash your tomatoes."

She giggled.

"I think I might have squashed Leonard's tomatoes. I am heavier than the last time we did it. Still, he's not complaining."

Derek stood staring at her, incredulous and unable to form a coherent sentence.

"Damn that man can still turn me to jelly," Dora continued, "He's still a looker for ninety-two."

"I can't believe you're behaving like everything is normal," Derek told her.

"What? Sex is normal."

"Not legs akimbo across a wheelchair in my bloody potting shed it isn't!"

Dora tutted.

"Well it takes a long time for an eighty-seven year old woman with a stick to push a man in a wheelchair back to her room. We couldn't wait."

Dora began rotating at the waist.

"I must say though, these new hips are a godsend. Mind you my legs are going to feel it in the morning. I'll have to get Moron to up my Ibuprofen dosage."

"I don't want to hear anymore," Derek told her, pushing past, "I'm going to go and pot up my seedlings."

"Hang on. I'm not sure Leonard's got it back in his trousers yet."

"Oh God!"

"Oh stop it!" Dora admonished, walking past him, "You're more of an old woman that I am. Leonard can't bend his fingers that well so struggles with some tasks. Let me go check on him."

Derek stood rooted to the spot. He couldn't believe what he'd just witnessed. And what was that cheap comment about his love life? He didn't want to know what Angela had done with her clients. For him it was all about making love, not having sex. They were two different things in his book.

It was a few minutes before the couple appeared, Dora breathing heavily as she pushed a grinning Leonard out into the fresh air, a cigarette stuck to his bottom lip.

"It's no good, I'm knackered," she said, "You'll have to push him."

Instead of planting up his seeds Derek had to push a ninety-two year old man with afterglow round to the conservatory. It didn't improve his mood.

*

Angela still felt irritable. It was a busy week at work and she was also trying to put finishing touches to her planned revenge attack on Max. She could really have done without having a sulking Derek to put up with as well. He acted like such a child at times. She wished now she'd never told him about Bert's visit. Did he really believe his mum was going to be arrested? Derek had been appalled when she'd mentioned that the car may have appeared on a security camera and she'd found herself having to defend her father.

To be fair, Derek wouldn't understand why her feelings for Bert had changed. That time she thought he'd stolen her savings was all tied up in the Max period of her life, which Derek knew nothing about. Still, he was definitely overreacting about Ursula…again.

It wasn't just Derek and Max that were getting on Angela's nerves though. The producer for the TV programme was in the auction house today and it was no longer a secret that a film crew were arriving on Friday. Angela already knew she was going to be the main focus of the programme and didn't need reminding of that fact every few minutes by another over-excited colleague. Charles was the only one not to share their enthusiasm, telling the producer that TV was full of garbage these days. Angela's hopes that Charles would take to the rostrum instead of her were dashed in that instant.

The producer was a very nice woman but she did tend to find everything fascinating and her gushing began to wear thin on an already agitated Angela.

"The acoustics in this salesroom are amazing. That two-piece, black trouser-suit you're wearing is divine. The toilet paper in the ladies is so soft."

Angela might have just imagined that last one, after the producer left the meeting to use the facilities.

The thought of appearing on television was frightening, especially if Max showed up as well. Her planned revenge attack was a risky strategy. If it worked then Max would be gone, but if it back-fired, and it very easily could, then he'd be here ruining her on Friday. Revenge was difficult to plan, Angela realised, especially when you were trying to keep within the confines of the law.

That last thought brought her back to Derek's sulking and his worry over Ursula. Angela sighed. He was too overprotective of his mother, why couldn't he see that? How could she tell him without causing another argument? She couldn't, that was the answer. Angela shook her head, resignedly. Derek was a kind, thoughtful man, but how could their relationship survive if he always put his mother first?

*

Dinner at the coach house that night formed the same pattern as the previous few evenings with Ursula leading the conversation, totally oblivious of the atmosphere in the room. Tonight she was talking about 'that nice young estate agent, Carla' whom she'd been speaking with on the phone that morning.

"She's just got engaged, isn't that sweet? She said she met her fiancé when she found an apartment for him. What a lovely way to meet. Apparently he'd said something to her about giving him a 'semi' and that's why she went out with him. I don't really understand what she meant by that. She found him an apartment, not a semi-detached house."

Just as they were stacking plates into the dishwasher the doorbell rang. Opening the door, Derek was shocked to be shown a warrant card. He could feel a cold sweat creeping down his back. This was his fear come true. So much for Angela trying to make light of the situation. Her bloody criminal father had got his sweet, innocent mother caught up in a crime.

"I'm Detective Sergeant Cheung and this is Detective Constable Knowles," the woman said.

Detective Knowles smiled warmly but his Sergeant maintained her 'face like a smacked arse' expression. Derek stood back to let them in. As he showed them through into the kitchen, Sergeant Cheung told him,

"We want to speak to a Mrs Ursula Noble."

Angela and Ursula both stood up from the dishwasher. Derek noted his poor mum's confused expression. At least Angela had the decency to look shocked.

"This is my mother, Mrs Noble," Derek told them, "Look, this is all a mistake."

"What's a mistake sir?" Sergeant Cheung asked him, calmly.

"Well, whatever you've come here for."

"Which is?"

"Murder!" Constable Knowles said, dramatically.

Ursula gasped but the constable chuckled.

"No I'm just joking with you," he said, "I've always wanted to say that out loud like that. Murder!"

Sergeant Cheung sighed wearily at her colleague.

"It's about a theft of a large amount of money," she continued.

Ursula's hand shot up to her mouth.

"Oh dear," she said.

The gesture wasn't missed by the obviously efficient Sergeant.

"You know about it?"

"I always suspected I'd be found out."

"Mum, don't say anymore. You're innocent of all this."

Ursula shook her head sadly at her son.

"I wish I was," she told him.

Sergeant Cheung smiled.

"It's always the quiet ones," she said, "Perhaps we should continue this chat down at the station."

"Oh no," Derek told her, "You're not taking her downtown to be booked and fingerprinted and thrown into some dirty police cell without the chance of a phone call."

"I think someone has been watching a few too many police shows on the television, sir," Sergeant Cheung told him, mockingly, "Now then, if you could…"

"Where exactly is downtown?" Constable Knowles asked.

"What?"

Sergeant Cheung looked confused. She wasn't used to being interrupted when she spoke.

"Where is downtown?" Constable Knowles repeated, "I mean, is it the town centre or is it somewhere on the outskirts? I've never really known. Of course if you're at one end of town, the other end will always be downtown. So then you've got two downtowns."

"It doesn't matter," Sergeant Cheung told him, firmly.

"It does if you're in Traffic Division."

"Oh for God's sake, why don't you go and wait outside?"

The sergeant returned her attention to the three people staring back at her. Angela stepped forward.

"Look," she said, "I think I know what this is going to be about, but why don't you tell us Sergeant. You're upsetting my partner and his mum is confused."

Sergeant Cheung looked straight at Ursula.

"Is that your silver hatchback parked out front," she asked her, and she read out a number plate from her notes on her mobile phone.

"Yes it is," Ursula replied, looking confused, "But I didn't own that back then."

"Mum?"

Sergeant Cheung continued.

"We're interested in it because it was seen parked up on security camera footage in front of a house on the Hereward development in Tenham; a house that was later burgled."

Angela nodded.

"Yep I can quicken this up for you," she told them, "You'll have seen a man get out of that car won't you?"

Sergeant Cheung didn't respond, waiting to see where this was going, but Constable Knowles, who hadn't moved away, nodded vigorously.

"That's right," he said, "Old geezer. Didn't look like he had it in him to steal from his own pocket, let alone disable an alarm and take a load of jewellery and cash from…"

"Danny!" Sergeant Knowles admonished, "You don't have to reveal all of the details of the case."

Constable Knowles looked down at his boots, like a naughty schoolchild scolded by his teacher in front of the class. Angela continued.

"That was my father," she told them, "Albert Jenkins. Look him up, he'll be on file. You're right, he's too old to burgle and too stupid to pull off something of that scale but I'm sure he'll know who did do it. Ursula knows nothing about him really. She's a kindly lady who drove him around when he visited us. The only 'crime' she's committed is being too trusting, that's all."

The two detectives looked at each other.

"Where is your father now?" the sergeant asked.

Angela shrugged.

"Your guess is as good as mine. He only shows up when he wants something. Other than that I have no idea where he goes to or what he does. As I said, look him up on your records."

This seemed to satisfy Sergeant Cheung who almost managed a smile. Perhaps being able to put a name to the man on the footage was a big step forward for her investigation. She took a business card out of her pocket.

"If he does get in touch, please call me."

She turned to Ursula again.

"Your car is lately registered to this address," she said.

"That's right," Ursula told her, "I'm only here temporarily until I find my own place but I thought it wise to alter my details."

"Yes, well don't move on without letting us know," the sergeant told her, a look in her eye that made Ursula shrink back against the dishwasher.

She and Constable Knowles turned to leave. Derek was about to let out a huge sigh of relief when Sergeant Cheung stopped and turned back again.

"What did you mean earlier about being found out someday and not owning your car at the time?" she asked.

Ursula looked startled. She opened her mouth but only a small whine came out. Angela stepped in front of her.

"It's nothing," she told them, trying to sound conspiratorial, "She was a day late paying her road tax one year, that's all. She gets confused easily."

She surreptitiously ushered the detectives out of the room as she spoke. Constable Knowles smiled at her.

"I know what that's like," he said, brightly, as they walked out of the kitchen, "These old ducks often get confused when they're taken out of familiar surroundings. My mum's the same when I take her to Asda instead of Tesco."

"Is she elderly," Angela asked.

The policeman nodded.

"Fifty-two next birthday."

"Oh God Danny, that's quite enough from you," Sergeant Cheung told him.

The voices faded and then the front door closed. A moment later, Angela walked back into the kitchen and let out a long, slow breath.

"Blimey, I thought they'd never go."

"Angela dear," Ursula said, "Have you just dropped poor Bert in it?"

"No," she replied, "He dropped himself in it and got you involved. Besides, there's no proof that he committed the burglary on that estate. Well, I know he didn't. Don't you worry Ursula, dad will be fine and if he's not, well, that's his hard luck. How about we all sit down and have a drink? I think we could all use one."

Angela walked over to the wine rack. Derek was standing in the way of it. He didn't move. He was looking puzzled.

"Derek?" Angela said, "Can you move out of the way?"

Derek stood his ground. He looked across at his mother.

"What **did** you mean about being found out?" he asked her.

Ursula pulled a couple of tissues from the box kept on the kitchen island and turned away while she blew her nose.

"When that moody sergeant told you about a theft of money you really thought she was talking about you, about something you did," Derek continued, "What was that?"

He and Angela watched Ursula's back. She finished wiping her nose and then stood up straighter. They heard her sigh before she turned back round to face them.

"Your father's death," she said, "It was a dreadful accident."

"I know. It was tragic."

"No I mean it was an accident. He wasn't meant to die. That wasn't part of the plan."

Derek was struggling to follow what his mother was saying but Angela had already put two and two together. She rubbed his arm consolingly.

"He was only meant to go missing off of the boat. That's why he'd been going swimming three times a week for the prior six months, to become a stronger swimmer."

"I didn't know that he had been swimming."

"Didn't you?"

"I was at university, remember?"

Derek finally moved away from in front of the wine rack and moved round the central island to stand beside his mother.

"What the hell was going on at home while I was away?"

Ursula shook her head.

"It was your father's idea," she told him, "I hated it but no matter how many hours your father worked, it wasn't enough to pay off his debts."

"What? I thought he only owed a few pounds here and there. That's the impression you gave me."

Ursula sighed again.

"It was worse than that," she replied, "It was gambling debts. Your father had a problem. Oh God, we owed so much money. Not that I knew exactly how much until he came up with the scheme."

"Scheme, what scheme?"

Derek was feeling more and more uptight with each passing minute. Why were there so many people in his life with so many bloody secrets? Ursula faced her son.

"The bank weren't interested in providing a loan. Your dad had taken out life insurance policies years before. It was the only way out, he said. He was going to go out on his boat and make it look like he'd fallen off and been swept out to sea. With him dead the insurance would have to pay out and the debts would all be cleared."

"What? How was that going to work?" Derek asked, incredulously, "He'd be missing, not dead. You have to be missing seven years before you're legally dead, don't you?"

"I don't know!" Ursula shouted back at him, clearly upset.

She walked away and sat down at the dining table. Neither Derek nor Angela had ever heard Ursula raise her voice like that before.

"He made all of the plans," she continued, "He told me what to say and do. I didn't know how it was all meant to work out."

She pulled a handkerchief out of her pocket and wiped her eyes.

"I had to wait for the police to come and tell me what had happened and then he'd contact me later."

Frustrated and struggling to find words to respond, Derek banged his fist down onto the worktop of the island, making both Ursula and Angela jump.

"Alright Derek," Angela told him, "Calm down."

"Calm down?" he said, "Calm down? My mum just tells me she's committed fraud and I'm supposed to calm down."

"But she didn't commit it in the end," Angela tried to reason, "That didn't happen."

She indicated Ursula with her head. Derek followed her gaze and saw his mother weeping silently.

"Your father died in that accident," Angela added, quietly, "That's the part to concentrate on."

Ursula looked across at them.

"I'd gone to bed," she told them, "Your father told me I shouldn't, that I should be up and worried that he hadn't come home, but after I'd reported him missing I took a painkiller to try and relieve the splitting headache that I had. You know how the weakest of painkillers make me sleepy. When the police woke me in the night I still felt groggy. I couldn't take in what they were saying. I was expecting them to talk about finding the boat but they were talking about finding a body. It was all wrong."

She began sobbing. It was Angela that rushed over to comfort her. Derek was unable to move again.

"It was all so awful," Ursula continued, through her sobs, "He'd actually died. I received the insurance money as he'd planned and paid off the debts but all the time I felt this awful guilt inside of me. Why did I let him do it?"

"Ssh," Angela consoled, "It wasn't your fault. It was nobody's fault."

"Except dad's," Derek blurted out.

"Oh Derek," Ursula said, "Don't blame your father."

"Who else? You always defend him. Why do you do that?"

In spite of her sobbing, Ursula managed a weak smile.

"He used to say the same thing to me about you."

"Me?"

Ursula sighed.

"Oh you were so alike," she said, "Too alike. You saw things in the other one that you could never see in yourselves. I wished you'd been closer."

"Well that was difficult when he was out at work all day, seven days a week," Derek told her, his anger worsening, "When the hell were we meant to become close?"

"Come on Derek that's not fair," Ursula said, "He worked hard to provide for us and he did his best but you were into different things. He wanted to take you to watch the rugby on Saturdays when he did have a day off but you always refused and either had your head stuck in a book or was out in the garden. He thought you just didn't want to spend time with him."

"Bollocks!"

"Derek!"

"No mum, it is bollocks. He only wanted to spend time with me on his terms. I don't like rugby, never have. Why didn't he come and join me in the garden instead? We could have chatted while digging or planting. No, he wouldn't do that. I wouldn't come to rugby so he sulked and went off into the garage to work on some project on his own."

"That's not fair love."

"Yes it is!"

"He kept on trying," Ursula pleaded, "That's why he bought the boat in the first place, for the two of you to go out on."

"Oh great," Derek said, pacing up and down the floor in front of the island, "So I suppose all this is my fault is it?"

"Derek," Angela said, gently, "Calm down."

Derek stopped pacing. They were the wrong words to say. He didn't want to calm down. His life was falling apart and at that moment, he was quite happy to blame it all on the person in front of him, the one telling him to 'calm down.' It was her fault that the police had come here this evening, she had the criminal family. It was her fault he was in a mood because she was on at him all of the time about being honest, even though his own mother had just turned out to be a liar. Everything was Angela's fault.

"Don't you start," he shouted at her, "I've had enough of being blamed for everything by you already."

"Derek."

"But you can't pin this one on me. You didn't even know my dad. But why am I surprised you're not standing beside **me** with a comforting arm around **my** shoulder. I'm only your partner. No, you stand over there and support the liar. You're also supporting my father. Well, why not, he was a criminal just like you and your entire family."

Angela moved away from Ursula.

"Don't you take your anger out on me," she told him, "I'm no criminal."

"Oh really; what you used to do was legal was it? Perhaps I missed that somewhere in the law when a woman accepts money for…"

He stopped talking.

Tears formed in Angela's eyes.

"And there we go," she said, "Even now, when you can't control your temper, you still can't bring yourself to say it, can you. You won't ever accept me, will you?"

"Oh fuck off!" Derek told her, "This isn't about you. You know, that's half the problem. I've just been told some devastating news but I'm not allowed to be angry about it. I've got to calm down. Why have I got to calm down, Angela? Is it so that the attention can be switched onto you? Why have you always got to be the victim?"

"Is that really how you see me?"

"Please, you two," Ursula called out, "Don't fight over me. Derek, I'm sorry I never told you this but your dad didn't want anyone else to know. He knew you wouldn't approve."

Derek turned his attention back to his mother.

"Wouldn't approve," he mocked, in her voice, "Wouldn't approve? Of course I wouldn't fucking approve! Why didn't you both tell me at the time? I could have helped out. I could have left university and got a job."

Ursula shook her head.

"No," she told him, "That was one thing your dad and I both agreed on. This was our problem, not yours. You were just starting out in life. We were proud of what you'd achieved. You had your life mapped out."

Derek tutted.

"Yeah right," he replied, "I was at university studying a topic I didn't care for. I only became an accountant because of what happened. I saw you struggling after dad's death and thought, 'that mustn't happen to me. Get a safe and secure job, Derek.' I had no idea that you weren't struggling with money but was instead, having a high old time on dad's insurance money."

"I wasn't. I told you, it paid off the gambling debts. I still had a few years left on the mortgage. I still had to up my workload just to cover all of the monthly bills."

Derek didn't appear to be listening. He was shaking his head.

"I've spent years trying to protect you," he said, "People have told me I was being too overprotective; Angela, Dora, Margaret, even Leanne. She blamed that as part of the reason we split up, do you know that? Only the other weekend she said to me…"

"Sorry, what was that?"

Angela interrupted Derek's flow.

"You saw your ex-wife the other weekend?"

"Oh well, yes, I did."

Derek's anger momentarily turned to a feeling of guilt.

"She wants us to…"

"You've been seeing your ex-wife behind my back and you have the nerve to stand there, wanting pity for having secrets hidden from you."

"It wasn't like that."

"You hypocrite!"

"Oh for fuck's sake, will you shut up being the martyr for one minute!" Derek shouted at her, "I've not been 'seeing' my ex-wife at all. We bumped into each other when I was back at the apartment. We got chatting, that's all. I was going to tell you all about it before Dora gave us her bombshell. Leanne needs to update her will and to provide a guardian for her son, Nathan. She wants us to be it."

"What?" said Angela, "You had one conversation and she asked you that?"

"Well no, I mean that was after I babysat and…"

"So you have been spending time with her?"

"Yes, but not in the way you're thinking."

"Well, that's great, isn't it," Angela said, more tears falling down her cheeks, "Your ex-wife is back in your life and providing you with a child, is she? Isn't that nice?"

Derek's anger flared again. Why was Angela making this about her? When had she become so needy?

"For God's sake, not again!" he shouted, "I'm going to say this one more time, this is **not** about you!"

"Oh that's nice. So Leanne doesn't want me around then, just you?"

"That's not what I meant."

"Why don't you fuck off back to her then," Angela told him, "You can have a wife and a child, all the things you've wanted that either you can't or don't want to have from me."

Derek opened his mouth to respond but saw the tears and the hurt in Angela's eyes. For a split second he almost ran over to her but a sobbing Ursula sitting behind her brought back the anger. Ever since he'd met Angela he'd been worried about his mum rejecting his relationship because of Angela's past. He'd feared reaching a stage where he had to choose between the two women he loved. Now, here they were, a team, both of them hurting him and giving no consideration to his feelings. Even at the end of their relationship, he and Leanne had never argued like this. Perhaps there was something to be said for keeping secrets and feelings hidden.

"Fine," he told her, "Why don't I do just that and go back to my old life. At least Leanne is no needy victim who craves attention all of the time."

He strode over to the door.

"You two can have each other," he called over his shoulder, "You deserve each other; two fucking criminals together."

"Derek," Ursula called out to him, but Derek ignored her.

He strode out into the hallway and a second later the two women heard the front door slam.

Chapter 22

Angela could feel her heart thumping in her chest as she drove down to Ryan Harbour on Thursday evening. So much had changed in the past week since Max had ordered her to come over tonight and sleep with him. She'd been disgusted by the thought and even more disgusted when she'd momentarily considered it as a possible option. Then there was her anger after the talk with Bert where she'd discovered Max had no dangerous contacts after all and he'd been the one to steal her savings, leaving her dependent on him. Revenge, that's what she'd wanted. That's what she'd planned, getting Margaret and Dora on board to help her.

"Have you spoken to Derek?" Margaret asked, from the passenger seat.

Angela shook her head.

"No," she said, "I've left him to cool off. Any contact from me while he's still upset will just end in another argument. Ursula texted him but he didn't respond until this morning. I think that was wrong."

"It must be tough on him though," Margaret added.

Angela sniffed.

"I don't think it's anywhere near as bad as what you have just been through but you've dealt with that okay."

"We're women," Dora called, from the back seat, "We're more mature than men."

"You've got that right," Angela told her, looking at Dora through the rear-view mirror, "Derek always runs off at the first sign of trouble. If he only stopped and faced up to things…"

She left the sentence hanging.

"We're all different," Margaret said, "And so we all react to situations in different ways. I don't think it's fair to compare Derek's shock and mine."

"Not fair?" Angela queried.

"That's right. We all live our own lives. Mum describes it as we're all on different paths in life. While I'm not a big believer in fate and destiny I understand what she means. We only live in our own shoes, not someone else's. How can we comment on other people's lives?"

Angela looked thoughtful.

"I guess I know what you're saying," she replied, "I was at school with a girl who was dating a boy in the next year up from us. I bumped into her a few years after university and they were married and had two lovely children. We became friends again for a while. They didn't know how I earned my money but saw that I had my own place, some nice things, and that I often travelled abroad. She was forever going on about how jealous she was of me and what a struggle it was having the kids and how lucky I was not to have any. She never once asked if I wanted them or whether I could have them. To start with I felt guilty for having a few quid but then I got angry. She was so wrong in her opinion of me and eventually I told her that I'd gladly change places with her. She assumed her relationship and children were a given in life, you know, part of the basics alongside food, shelter and clothing. She didn't realise how much she had to be happy about. She was too busy comparing her family life in her rented council house to my lifestyle in my privately-owned apartment. It didn't matter to her that I was alone; that I often cried in that apartment because I couldn't have what she had. I was glad when she stopped calling."

"Exactly," Margaret replied, "I became friendly with a woman in the office at work. Do you remember Sheila, mum?"

"Was she that emaciated-looking girl with the buckteeth and a mono-brow?"

"No."

"Then I don't remember her," Dora said.

Margaret tutted.

"Well anyway, we got on really well but then she lost her three year old child to Meningitis. I tried to be there for her, like so many of her other friends, and we all did what we could. Of course I'd never had children and knew I could never truly understand the level of pain she was going through but I did know what loss and bereavement felt like. She left the firm but we stayed in touch and she went on to have three more children. Obviously she still mourned the loss of her firstborn. The problem was that she was never able to reciprocate the support that each of her friends had given to her. It didn't matter what they were going through, she couldn't help comparing their situation to her own and telling them they didn't have it as bad."

Margaret sighed.

"That's not what someone wants to hear when they're trying to cope with their own tragedy. While we obviously couldn't feel the pain of what she'd been through, because we hadn't been through the same experience, we knew the death of a child was the worst thing ever. But knowing that didn't make our own tragedies any easier to deal with. It's like when dad died after his painful battle with cancer. At that moment I needed a friend's shoulder to cry on, not someone turning grief into a kind of competition."

Margaret shook her head.

"Most of her friends drifted away from her in the end, me included. It's a shame but if you can't count on a friend in a moment of crisis, then they're not truly a friend are they? I still miss her though. But that's what I mean about Derek. Don't be too hard on him. For him it must have been a travesty to discover his parents were involving themselves in an insurance scam. Derek's always struck me as quite naïve in the ways of the world."

"Really?" Angela said, surprised.

"Well perhaps that's not quite the right way of putting it," Margaret looked thoughtful, "I suppose I mean that I can't see Derek as ever having done anything wrong."

Angela snorted.

"You could have fooled me," she said.

Margaret sighed again.

"Dear me, I'm not putting this well, am I. What I'm trying to say is I bet, for example, Derek has never added a few extra expenses to his tax return to reduce the amount he pays. If he was given change of a twenty in a shop when he'd only handed over a ten pound note, he wouldn't put it in his pocket, he'd have to tell the cashier, or if he did take it, he'd be wracked with guilt for days. That's what I mean."

"You mean he's a bloody idiot?" Dora called out.

Margaret turned in her seat to face her.

"No, that's not what I mean."

"You mean," Angela said, "That he's too honest for his own good."

"That's it," Margaret replied.

"I suppose you're right," Angela conceded, "And he probably had that instilled in him by Ursula. Even though his parents didn't break the law in the end, the fact that they tried to, makes them guilty in Derek's eyes."

"That's right," Margaret agreed, "He must feel like he doesn't actually know who his parents are anymore."

Angela nodded.

"Yes," she said, "When you put it like that I guess it must have been hard for him to hear. Even so though, two days of the silent treatment still smacks of childishness."

"What did he say to Ursula in his text?" Margaret asked.

"Just two words, 'I'm fine.' He said more in the one he sent to you."

"Well that was work related," Margaret told her, "He was texting me as his boss, not as his friend. Anyway, at least you know he's okay."

Angela sighed.

"But he's not though, is he. He's holed up in his apartment on his own going over and over the argument in his head and staying angry about it. He should be here with me, talking it all through. That's the only way to move forwards," Angela made a huffing sound, "Ah well, let's see if his ex-wife provides him with a shoulder to cry on."

Neither Margaret nor Dora reacted to that comment. Angela had told them about Leanne wanting a guardian for her son. They knew Angela's anger was really just jealousy. Derek's ex-wife, in her own way, was giving him something that Angela never could. The conversation died.

Angela's thoughts returned to this evening. At least with Derek being away she hadn't had to lie about where she was going tonight. She'd told Ursula she was meeting Margaret and that wasn't really a lie. Not that Ursula seemed that interested. She'd been very withdrawn the last two days. It wasn't just Derek not talking to her, it was bringing that secret out into the open after all this time and having to face up to it that had hit her hard. Angela had had a good talk with her after Derek left and she hoped she'd helped a little. Margaret was right, Derek was a very honest person and Ursula was so like him. Why had she gone along with her husband's plan? How was it meant to have worked out?

Still, Angela thought, it's helped sort things out for me, and changed my own plans for this evening.

They drove down through the high street in Ryan Harbour and at the bottom of the road, Angela turned right and headed up to Max's house. She took a few deep breaths to calm her nerves. She'd planned out what she wanted to happen but that didn't necessarily mean Max would play ball. What then? She had no idea. She pulled up outside the house.

"This is it," she told them.

"Right," Dora said, rubbing her hand over the top of her walking stick, "You two keep him talking and I'll whack him across the head with this."

Margaret sighed.

"For God's sake mum, Angela's changed her plans."

"And that wasn't in Plan A in the first place," Angela added, "Although it's not the worst of ideas."

Dora grinned at her.

"Come on then," she said, "Let's go. Plan B, whatever that is."

"I think you should stay here, mum," Margaret told her.

"What? No!"

"I mean it. Let me and Angela go and check out how the land lies first. We don't know how this Max is going to react to my being here."

"I think Margaret's right, Dora," Angela admitted,

"Remember, he thinks I'm here to provide him with sex. He may have worked himself up into an excited frenzy."

"Well someone's got a big head about her bedroom prowess," Dora replied, moodily.

Angela smiled.

"I just mean he might get angry."

"Exactly, that's why you need me there," Dora told them, "I'm the muscle."

Margaret sighed.

"And that's what we don't want," she said, "Angela just wants to talk to him. I'm going with her so that she's not alone in the house with him, that's all. It's up to her whether you come in or not."

Dora looked pleadingly at Angela.

"I do just want to talk to him," Angela told her, "There's no revenge plan, not now; no actions, just a chat. I've realised that all of this isn't about my job at all."

Dora opened her mouth to respond but Angela quickly continued on.

"I mean it partly is, of course. I really don't want Max ruining my new career but it's mainly about closure. I've been hiding from my past in my new job, trying to pretend it never happened, but it did. Derek berated me for not telling my colleagues about my past and he was right to do so. I should have been straight with them from the start and if that meant they didn't want to hire me then so be it."

"But you love your job," Dora said.

Angela nodded.

"I know I do, but I love my relationship with Derek more and I've come to realise it's that, that I'm worried about, even though we're not talking at the moment."

Margaret looked confused.

"You've lost me now," she said.

Angela smiled.

"I've been going on at Derek so much about telling his mum about my past."

"We know that."

"Yes but the reason wasn't because I was worried Derek hadn't accepted me. I thought it was. Even two nights ago when we rowed I thought it still was. It was only when I spoke to Ursula about the insurance fraud after Derek had stormed off that I realised what all this was really about. She'd kept her secret hidden for twenty-seven years and I could see how much it had eaten away at her. She felt guilty and ashamed and always refused to talk about her husband's death with anyone because of it. She was so fearful of her secret coming out. As a result she's never grieved properly and it's probably stopped her from finding someone new."

Angela shook her head, sadly.

"That guilt prevented her from moving on with her life. I mean I know she's happy in her day to day existence but really, Ursula was only forty-three when it happened, a year older than I am now. I can't help wondering about what sort of life she could have had if she hadn't stayed silent and confided in someone. And yet, I've started doing the same thing, trying to keep my past a secret from my work colleagues and if I keep doing that I'm going to end up like Ursula; always on edge, scared of the truth coming out, not talking about the past. It's happening already. Derek and I have had so many arguments lately and it's because we've both been anxious, trying to keep things secret. Well it's time to put a stop to that. That's why I've come here tonight to talk to Max. I'm asking him not to tell my boss and colleagues about my past...because I'm going to tell them."

"You are?" Dora said, surprised, "When?"

"Once Derek and I have sat down together and told Ursula the truth. She needs to find that out first. That's why I don't want Max to talk, at least not tomorrow. With the TV crew and local press at the auction house it's highly likely that word would get back to Ursula before we got round to telling her ourselves. I don't want her discovering the truth that way and feeling upset because she felt we didn't trust her enough to be honest with her. Right now I don't know when Derek is coming back. We both said some nasty things to one another but I know he will come back, when he's ready. Until then I don't want anyone else finding out about my past."

"Why can't you speak to Ursula yourself, right now?" Margaret asked.

Angela sighed.

"Because that would only cause more friction with Derek. He'd see it as me going behind his back and it would just lead to another argument. No, as soon as he comes back I'll tell him all that I've told you, about Max, what he was to me, the attack, everything. I don't want there to be any secrets left between us."

Angela banged the steering wheel in anger, making Margaret and Dora jump.

"All these damned secrets," she said, "We've all had them. We think we're doing the right thing by burying them, telling ourselves it will only hurt someone if it comes out, but they don't disappear do they. They linger and fester and eat away at us. Old sins cast long shadows. Well I want to live in the light from now on."

Silenced ensued as all three women became lost in their own thoughts, thinking over all that had happened in the last few weeks. Eventually Dora sighed.

"Right then," she said, looking up at the house, "Let's go deal with this pervy, old shadow shall we?"

She was still told to stay behind.

Angela and Margaret walked up to the door together. Margaret gave her friend's hand a quick squeeze before Angela rang the bell. Max opened the door wearing a very tight, black rubber outfit. It resembled a vest top and shorts but the shorts part had a large hole in the crotch area and it was obvious he was looking forward to the evening.

"What kept you?" he leered.

His grin fell away when he saw Margaret.

"Oh Jesus Christ!"

His hands shot to his crotch and he turned away from them.

"There's a hole in the back as well," Angela pointed out.

"Fuck it!"

Max moved his hands backwards and forwards over the holes as he crouched over, trying to hide himself.

"What the hell is this?" he asked.

"It's a change of plan," Angela explained.

In the end Max sighed and abandoned trying to cover himself up.

"Ah, what's the point," he said.

He was no longer happy to see them. Footsteps on the gravel made the two women turn round.

"Mum! I told you to stay in the car," Margaret admonished.

"It's too bloody hot in there," Dora replied.

"I cracked the window for you."

"Great, thanks. What am I now, a bloody dachshund?"

"What is this?" Max asked again, "Who the hell invited Grandma Moses to the party?"

Dora raised an eyebrow as she came and stood beside Angela.

"That's some smart mouth for a man who's dressed like an overstuffed black pudding that's split its skin."

Max's mouth dropped open. Dora looked him up and down.

"This is him, is it?"

Angela nodded. Dora shook her head.

"No, I don't get it," she said.

"I'm going to ask one more time," Max told them, "What the fuck is going on here?"

"You watch your language, there are ladies present," Dora admonished, "You undersized fuckwit!"

"Mum! Go back to the car."

"Not a chance."

"Okay look," Angela interrupted, before an argument began, "I'm not here to sleep with you, Max. That's not going to happen, but before you get angry and before you turn up at the auction house tomorrow, I just want to talk to you. Give me ten minutes."

She could tell Max was trying to think quickly on his feet, now that he'd got over the initial shock of the scene. He was still standing there in his porch way with everything on show.

"Well now," he said, smarmily, regaining some of his composure, "Let me think about what I should do."

"Oh shut it," Dora said, stepping forwards. She shoved him aside on the porch, "It was a statement she was making, not a request."

She continued on into the hallway. The three people left on the doorstep watched her, all rather shocked. Max looked back at the two remaining women. He sighed and indicated that they should follow Dora.

Max showed them into the large lounge at the back of the house. It had a beautiful, original fireplace and decorative ceiling rose but it was devoid of the majority of its contents, which were now at the auction house, ready for tomorrow's sale. Only Max's mum's modern three-piece suite remained. Angela sat in one of the armchairs while Dora and Margaret took the sofa beside it. Max remained standing.

"Right," he said, "What do you want?"

"Well for starters," Dora told him, "You can cover yourself up. We don't want to sit here with that wrinkled, little todger winking at us all evening."

Max's eyes narrowed.

"I could throw you out, you know."

"And I could sit on you until your ribs crack, what's your point?"

"Mum! Will you shut up and let Angela speak."

Dora sat back on the sofa, obviously in a huff. Max left the room and came back with a towel around his middle.

"Is this better?" he asked sarcastically.

Dora shrugged her shoulders, staring daggers at her daughter. Max turned to Angela.

"So," he said, "Are you here to call my bluff? I will tell you know. I…"

"I know that," Angela interrupted, "I don't care anymore."

"Yeah, right."

"I'm just here to ask you to let me do it instead."

Max threw his head back and laughed.

"Oh my God," he told her, wiping his eyes dramatically, "You're not thinking straight. Time of the month is it, sweetie?

Well actually, it's probably more a menopausal thing for you now isn't it?"

"Let the lady speak or you'll get this stick up your jacksie!"

"Shh mum!"

Max absently rubbed his bottom through the towel.

"And why would I be stupid enough to think you would tell your boss everything?" he asked Angela.

"Because you've had your revenge on me already," she replied, "I know all about the money."

"What money?"

"The money I'd saved up to do my Master's degree. The money I thought my dad had taken."

Max rested himself against the window ledge and folded his arms, a look of amusement on his face.

"You've only just worked that out?" he said, "My God, I thought you were intelligent."

A small repetitive thud could be heard in the room. It only took a second to notice Dora, gently banging the handle of her walking stick against the palm of her other hand, staring menacingly at Max. Angela was pleased to see him look worried.

"I trusted you back then," she told him, "I thought I loved you and that you loved me. Why would I think you'd steal my money?"

Max didn't reply. Angela continued.

"So you see, you've already had your revenge on me. You ruined the relationship with my father, you left me with very little self-worth and you sent me back into prostitution. Isn't that enough?"

Max was silent for a moment.

"Of course that isn't enough," he told her, coldly.

"What?"

"You tell me I ruined your relationship with your father, but you were never that close anyway. You told me that at the time, crying into my shoulder after I'd fucked your brains out. You say you had little self-worth," Max shrugged his shoulders, "So what. Why should that bother me? You say I sent you back into prostitution. Well, you made a good career for yourself out of it didn't you. I found that out when I began researching you two years ago, after bumping into you in the high street up the road here. I haven't even begun to have my revenge on you, sweetheart."

Dora tried desperately to stand up but couldn't.

"You bastard," she told him, "How dare you…"

"Stop it mum!" Margaret told her, pushing her against the back of the sofa, "You're not helping."

She turned to Max.

"But mum's right. You are a bastard. You already destroyed this woman once. Why do you want to do that again? She doesn't deserve that."

"I didn't destroy her though did I," Max replied, "She bounced back. She stood up to me and threatened me. I had to run."

"Rubbish!" Angela spat, "You only had to leave me alone. I didn't send you to Spain, your creditors did that. That's why you're back here as Max Saunders and not Max Trelawney."

Max stood up.

"You were the start of all my problems," he shouted at her, "Don't you get that? My business failure, my wife leaving me with my girls, it all comes back to you."

Angela was shocked by this sudden rage but she wasn't going to take his lies.

"You can't blame me for any of that," she told him, "You cheated on your wife left, right and centre that's why she left. You were the one who made your own business decisions so any failure there was on you."

"And you've made all of your own decisions in life," he told her, "So why are you blaming me for your problems?"

Angela couldn't respond to that.

"You ruined everything for me," Max continued, "You were this incredibly beautiful, young woman when I met you. Okay so you were a prostitute but that didn't matter. You were doing it temporarily. Then you fell in love with me and I had to make sure I kept you; that you'd rely on me for everything. That's why I took your money. You were so upset and who did you turn to, me. I knew you were all mine then."

Angela couldn't believe what she was hearing.

"But you pimped me out to your acquaintances," she said, "You let everyone have me."

"But they didn't have you the way I had you."

"I'm not surprised," Dora cut in, indicating Max's outfit.

"Shut up mum! I won't tell you again."

"You were grateful to be with me," Max continued, "You could have had your pick of men and yet you wanted me."

Angela shook her head.

"And you thought treating me like that would make me stay with you? My God, you really don't know a thing about women do you."

Max ignored her.

"Then you turned on me," he continued, "You walked away. I was so angry and upset. The only consolation was that I found out you'd returned to prostitution. I knew why. It wasn't just me you hated back then it was all men. I understood you sweetie. You'd gone back to prostitution to try and pretend that you were using men rather than them using you. That was fine. I couldn't have you but no other man could either, not in a love way. Then I bumped into you again, two years ago and you were with that…Derek."

Max spat the name out in disgust.

"You were still beautiful, you were successful but now you were also in love with someone who wasn't me. It was so obvious how you felt about him that day and how he felt about you. Pathetic, that's what it was. What sort of man could fall in love with a prostitute?"

"You did," Angela told him, "When you first met me, I was a prostitute."

Max wasn't listening to her. He was too caught up in his confession.

"I couldn't have that. I couldn't allow you to be in a happy relationship, especially when mine had ended and I was all alone. That's when I swore revenge on you. I didn't know how I was going to do it but I was going to start planning. I've always been a patient man. I could wait for my revenge. Then mum died and I had to return to England again to sell her stuff. I was surprised when your face appeared on the auction house website but then I smiled because I knew what I could do. The tables had turned. I now had nothing and you had everything to lose. I could destroy all of your happiness and that's exactly what I'm going to do."

He walked over to her and leaned forwards, his face practically pressed against hers. Angela sensed Margaret and Dora tense beside her.

"Finally I can have my revenge," he hissed, "I'm going to walk into that auction house tomorrow and in front of the TV cameras I'll tell everyone that you're a whore. You were born a whore, you lived as a whore, you're still a whore."

She couldn't help herself. Angela's hand came swinging round and she smacked Max hard across the face.

"You bitch!" he shouted, and leapt on top of her.

The next few moments were a blur. Out of the corner of her eye Angela saw Margaret get up and at the same time felt Max's hands around her throat. Margaret was shouting and grabbing at his arms. He was practically snarling with rage. The next second there was a loud crack. Max slumped down on top of her and fell silent. The room came back into focus and Angela saw Dora standing in front of her beside Margaret, her stick firmly grasped in her hand.

"Sorry about the delay," she said, matter-of-factly, "It took me a few seconds to get up off the sofa."

Angela pushed Max off of her with a look of disgust. He slid to the floor. Margaret gasped.

"Oh my God mum, what have you done? He's dead!"

"He's not dead," Dora replied, "Just out cold. I didn't smack him that hard, although he deserved it."

"He's not moving mum," Margaret was starting to sound hysterical, "Oh my God!"

"Will you calm down," Dora told her, "I don't want to have to smack you as well. What's the worst that could happen even if he is dead? I get life in prison at eighty-seven; that's going to be a long stretch. Besides, I'll probably end up the leader of my wing; get myself a young, pretty girl to be my bitch."

"It's not funny, mum! What do we do now? Should we run?"

Dora sighed.

"You're a great businesswoman love but you're shit in a

crisis. Of course we don't run," she turned to Angela, "Now then, we need to prevent him going to the auction tomorrow. You go and find something to tie him up with. I'm guessing the dirty prick's got a set of handcuffs in his bedroom drawer and other bits and pieces for tying up. I'll stay here in case he wakes up and I have to give him another crack with my stick."

Nobody moved.

"Well go on!" Dora called out.

Upstairs Angela found Max's room. If she was already on edge regarding what had happened downstairs, the scene in the bedroom did nothing to make her feel calmer. Max already had handcuffs laid out on the bed, alongside some chains, rope and some weird type of mask gag. Anal beads were lying on an upturned cardboard box he was using as a bedside table, beside a paperback copy of 'Nicholas Nickleby.'

If you thought I was going to be a part of this, Angela thought to herself, you should have been reading 'Great Expectations.'

When she arrived back downstairs with the paraphernalia, Margaret was still distraught.

"She hit him again," she told Angela, on the verge of tears.

"Well he was starting to come round," Dora explained, "It was only a little tap."

"You might have brain-damaged him."

"Good!"

"Mum!"

"What did you find?" Dora asked Angela.

Angela couldn't speak and just threw the stuff down onto the floor.

"Good," said Dora, taking control of the situation, "Right, let's start with his arms. Get that towel off of him."

When Max came round again Dora was pleased to see that he couldn't move. His right hand was handcuffed to the fire grate and the left they'd managed to pin behind him with the chain, which was also attached to the rope that they'd used to tie his feet together behind his back.

"Trussed up like the chicken he is," Dora said, sounding very satisfied.

"You won't get away with this, you crazy bitches," Max snarled.

"He's right," Margaret whined, "What have we done?"

"Stop worrying," Dora said, "He's not going anywhere, are you sunshine?"

She kicked him with her foot.

"We're stronger than you," she told him, "You've lost. Accept that and you'll be okay."

"You fucking whores. I'm going to have the law on you."

"Oh shut up!"

Dora grabbed the mask gag that was among the things Angela had brought down. She lowered herself down onto the floor beside Max and deftly placed it over his head.

"There now," she told him. "Surely all this must be turning you on."

She looked down to the open crotch area.

"I guess not," she said.

"What are we going to do?" Margaret asked, in a panicky voice.

Angela was stood beside her. Outwardly she appeared calm but inside she was as scared as Margaret. What had they done? This hadn't been her plan, even when she was thinking about revenge. How had the situation got so out of hand?

"I wish you would stop worrying," Dora told her daughter,

"All we're doing is giving Angela some time to tell her boss about her past. Okay so she's going to have to do that tomorrow now, rather than waiting for Derek's return. Afterwards we can come back here and let this poor excuse for a man go."

She faced Max again.

"That's alright with you sweetheart, isn't it," she said, patting his shoulder, "You like being tied up. It'll only be for twenty hours or so."

Max was still making snarling noises through the mask.

"How will he go to the toilet?" Margaret asked.

Dora stared up at her daughter.

"Really, that's your main concern?"

"Well it just popped into my head."

"The man's dressed in rubber," Dora told her, "It's wipe clean. Besides it's probably something this dirty bastard is in to, pissing and shitting on himself. He's got holes in the right places. Actually I wouldn't mind a quick wazz myself before we leave."

She turned back to Max.

"Would you like me to do it all over you?"

Max's angry snarl turned to a fearful whine.

"Mum, that's enough!"

"Fine," Dora sighed, "Right girls, come and help me up will you. It's time we were getting home."

After finding a spare front door key in a kitchen drawer, the ladies left the house. Margaret was still letting out little gasps of terror every few seconds. Angela had been stunned into silence. Only Dora was cheerful.

"I must say," she said, as they pulled away from the kerb, "I really enjoyed Plan C."

Chapter 23

These recent trips to his apartment were proving costly for Derek. On the first one he'd bought a new suit when he thought he was going out for dinner with Leanne but had ended up babysitting, the time after that he came down with all the tins of paint ready for decorating; on this journey he'd arrived with absolutely nothing and had to go out and buy new clothes and toiletries. That was without the cost of all the petrol as well.

It was only after storming out of the house on Tuesday night that Derek realised he hadn't packed a bag. He was too angry to go back and, finding the keys to the van in his pocket, alongside his wallet, he decided to head up to the Home, retrieve the van and drive straight back to his old apartment.

After a sleepless night he spent Wednesday painting; the bedroom first and then the hallway. Channelling his anger into his brushstrokes allowed him to get both rooms done at lightning speed. It seemed ironic that the apartment was now ready to rent out when it was likely to become his main residence once again. He couldn't believe Angela had sided with his mother like that. She'd broken the law. He was the one in the right. Where was his support? He knew he'd said some nasty things the previous evening but he'd meant them at the time. Today, he was still too angry to want to take them back. He'd been worried about telling his mum about Angela's past and being forced into choosing between the two women. Now it appeared he'd lost both of them.

Derek sighed as he washed his brushes and roller out in the

kitchen sink that evening. Why did it seem his world was full of lies and liars? When they'd first met, Derek had thought Angela's job was something to do with history and museums. She didn't correct him until he discovered the truth and told him that she hadn't lied, but Derek felt she'd done exactly that. A person wraps themselves up in bandages they're still the same person underneath. Dora had lied about her daughter's father, Leanne had kept her abortion from him and now even Derek's kind, caring, innocent mother had revealed a secret side to her. Was he the only honest person in the world? That's what frustrated him the most. He felt like he was being blamed for everything yet he was the only innocent person among all of them.

He threw the brushes down onto the drainer. He was still so angry and felt he had every right to be. If only he'd been allowed to fully vent his anger the previous night but what had Angela told him to do? 'Calm down, Derek.' Well, he didn't feel like calming down. Why was it okay for her to rant at him but when he was angry she tried to stop it? All she had to do last night was to keep her mouth shout for five minutes, let him get the worst of it out of his system and then maybe they could have talked things through but no, she couldn't do that and he'd had to storm out of the house with just his anger for company. Did she really understand him at all?

Perhaps it was all for the best though, Derek thought to himself, while he sat in the silent apartment with a mug of instant coffee. Maybe he and Angela had got together too quickly after his divorce from Leanne. Leanne's new relationship hadn't worked out either. She and Derek had been married for fourteen years and had lived together for six years before that. Twenty years; that was a long time to rush headlong into another relationship. Leanne had told him over dinner that Nathan's father should have just been a fling. Perhaps that's what he and Angela should have had on that coach trip, a fun week together and then gone their separate ways.

Angela hadn't tried calling or texting him since he'd stormed off and that made Derek angry too. Obviously she still believed this latest argument was his fault, that it was up to him to make the first move. Well that wasn't going to happen.

He'd seen how upset she was when he only just stopped himself from revealing her secret past during his rant and knew Angela believed he was still ashamed of her but it wasn't that at all. The only reason he'd not blurted out the truth about her last night was because, even during that rush of anger, he knew he hadn't wanted to hurt his mother, and telling her Angela's secret at that moment would have seemed vindictive. Why couldn't Angela see that?

Because she's ashamed of her past herself, Derek thought, ever since she started working at the auction house. But she won't admit that so blames me for it instead. It's my fault, yet again.

The frustration for Derek was too much. He hurled his half-drunk coffee mug across the lounge and it smashed against the wall. He watched the brown liquid drip and spread down the Almond White paint. It would need another coat in the morning.

He took out his phone and looked again at the text Ursula had sent him the night before. She must have been worried about him as she hardly ever tried to send messages on her mobile phone and found predictive texts scary.

"It's like the phone can read your mind," she'd said, on more than one occasion.

She hadn't done too badly.

'I sorry Derk. Let me noo you fine. I loathe you. Bum. xxx'

He hadn't replied to it yet. He had too much to say to put into a text message and he was scared the anger would take over again if he tried phoning. He put the phone back into his pocket. He'd sent a text to Margaret to say he wasn't coming into work for a few days. She could read into that what she wanted. She was Angela's best friend and Derek was sure she knew about the argument now anyway but she was also his employer and he needed to let her know he was away.

After the full day of painting, Derek slept better that night. By the next morning his anger had subsided somewhat and he began to see his storming out of the house on Tuesday as embarrassing. While he still believed he had every right to be angry, running off and not speaking to anyone for two days did seem a bit childish. He read his mum's text again while eating breakfast at the small dining table in the bay window of the lounge. He really needed to give her another lesson on how to use her mobile properly. That sounded like he was going to forgive her. Who was he kidding? Derek knew he already had. This was Ursula Noble, the kindest woman he'd ever known. This was a woman who was mortified when she'd accidently hung up on a cold caller trying to sell her double-glazing. She hated hurting anyone, especially her own son. He finally replied to her text, letting her know he was fine.

He still hurt though, as well as feeling ashamed of himself. So many people had told him he didn't give Ursula enough credit, that she was more able and competent than he realised and they were right. They knew his mother better than he did, that was why he felt so bad. Tuesday night his mother had momentarily become a stranger to him and it was scary. This innocent, law-abiding woman that he'd tried to protect all of his adult life had been involved in an insurance scam. It still seemed unbelievable but really, she hadn't been the one who'd come up with the idea. She hadn't known how it was meant to have worked out. She'd gone along with it to save her husband and yet it had all gone wrong. His father had actually died while trying to fake his own death. He'd been found with his foot caught in some rope. Derek realised this must have happened just as he was about to dive overboard and swim to wherever he was aiming for. That was how he'd smashed his head and died without ever entering the water.

"You silly, old bastard," Derek said out loud, and for the first time, he allowed himself to cry over the loss of his father.

*

Later that Thursday, after giving the coffee-stained wall in the lounge a new coat of paint, Derek called Leanne. He was hoping to go and see Nathan again but realised he could also do with a good chat. While Leanne could be selfish he knew that she wouldn't interrupt him while he talked and would allow him to get all that he needed to say off of his chest before venturing a response. She wasn't answering her mobile so he left a message. She got back to him at eight o'clock that night.

"I've been in meetings all day," she told him, "I'm taking Nathan away for a long weekend tomorrow so I had to sort a load of stuff out today. Honestly, I'm only taking Friday and Monday off. You'd think they could cope without me."

Derek knew that Leanne secretly loved being seen as indispensable. Still, he was upset that she wasn't going to be around. He had no one else to talk to.

"Oh, right, okay," he replied to her, on the phone, "Not to worry."

"Something's wrong isn't it?" she said, detecting the note of sadness in his voice.

Derek was about to tell her everything was fine but he couldn't. He'd had enough of lies. It wasn't often he asked for help but now, he really needed someone.

"Yes it is," he told her.

There was silence on the other end of the line for a few seconds and Derek wondered if she'd hung up.

"Look," she eventually said, "Nathan and I aren't heading out until ten. Why don't you come over for breakfast, about nine?"

"Yes, thanks," Derek told her, relieved.

Friday morning was another hot and sunny June day but Derek barely noticed it as he drove over to Leanne's house. Angela still hadn't contacted him, which was frustrating. Surely his mum had told her he'd replied to her text? Was it too much for Angela to send one, saying she was glad he was alright? Okay so he hadn't contacted her either but he wasn't the one at fault. What was so important in her own life right now that she couldn't take a couple of seconds to make the first move and apologise?

Leanne opened the door holding onto a crying Nathan. When he saw Derek he stopped and held his hands out to him. Derek's heart melted, as it did every time he saw this little boy.

"Oh thank God for that," Leanne said, "Handing him over, "He's been ratty at me for changing his routine. I thought he'd enjoy a lie in on a Friday. Usually he's at the childminders by seven."

She headed off into the kitchen. Derek followed at a much slower pace, whispering and smiling at Nathan. Leanne was bustling around the kitchen. There was an opened cooler bag on the counter and several other holdalls and carrier bags on the floor.

"Afraid it's just toast," she said to him, "We're in a bit of a panic this morning."

"Where are you off to?" Derek asked.

"Oh a friend at work has a holiday cottage in Norfolk and asked me and Nathan up there. We haven't been away for ages so I thought it was a good idea. Thinking it's less of a good idea at the moment."

Derek laughed.

"Can I help you with anything?" he asked.

"You can keep His Nibs amused for ten minutes if you like so I can finish packing up these bags."

Derek took Nathan into the playroom at the front of the house and they played with his cars. Fifteen minutes later, Leanne walked in.

"Right, we're all packed up," she said.

She picked Nathan up.

"Come on back into the kitchen," she said to Derek, "I'll put Nathan in his play area in the back room. He'll be fine in there with the TV on for a while."

In the kitchen Leanne had made fresh coffee and Derek poured them both out a cup. When she entered the room she offered Derek toast but seemed quite glad when he refused.

"Right," she said, "What's up? Is it being Nathan's guardian? Has your Angela got a problem with it?"

"No, well yes, actually no, it's not that it's…"

Derek began by telling Leanne what he'd learnt about his

dad's death which led on to the argument of Tuesday evening. He didn't leave anything out. As he'd known, Leanne remained silent until he'd finished what he had to say.

"Wow," she said, once he'd stopped talking, "Good old Ursula. Who'd have thought she'd be up for a bit of insurance fraud?"

"It's not funny, Leanne," Derek replied, "I'm still in shock."

"Well of course you are. I told you, you've always put your mother on a pedestal. In your head she's suddenly a different woman, but she isn't really. Ursula's human, like the rest of us. She's still the same mum who loves her little boy."

"I understand that bit," Derek told her, "But it's more than that. This scheme cost my dad his life."

"Yes, and that's a terrible tragedy, but think how your mum must feel. I'll bet poor Ursula has been feeling guilty about that all of these years, trying to ensure her precious, little son didn't find out. She wouldn't want him hurt would she, he does so over-dramatize everything."

"Don't you start," Derek told her, "All I wanted to do after finding out what had happened was let off a bit of steam about it without being told to 'calm down Derek.' I was the one in shock. I was the one being told my parents didn't trust me. I don't think Angela knows me at all sometimes. Mind you I don't think I know her either. That argument was meant to be about my mum's secret but Angela somehow moved it onto her past."

Derek sighed.

"When did she become so needy," he said, more to himself, "How did she manage to turn the attention around to her?"

"Did she do that?" Leanne asked.

Derek looked at her.

"Of course she did," he replied, "I was in shock after what mum had confessed and Angela told me to calm down, which just made me angrier as she appeared to be siding with mum and then I almost revealed her secret in front of mum and...oh."

Leanne smiled at him.

"Sounds like you were the one that brought her past up," she told him.

Derek didn't reply. He was still replaying the argument in his mind. Leanne retrieved the coffee pot and topped up both of their mugs.

"To me it seems like Angela's past is the elephant in the room," she said, "It's going to keep coming up until you tell your mum the truth."

She grabbed Derek's forearm and he watched a look of shock come over her face.

"I just had the strangest feeling of déjà vu," she said, and then grinned.

"Yes alright, I know you've told me that before," he replied, "Thanks for mocking my life."

"I can't help it," she replied, "It's so easy to do. Look, you've had a shock and it's caused a big argument. Why don't you go back home, apologise for shouting and talk things through?"

"Why should I apologise?"

"Oh God Derek, you're not in the playground anymore. It doesn't matter if it wasn't your fault. I just said to apologise for shouting. You did shout didn't you? Surely the main focus should be on sorting out your relationship. If you apologising helps both of you to move forward then that's a good thing, isn't it?"

Derek sighed.

"I'm not sure the relationship is worth saving anymore," he confessed, "I mean I'm happy in Tenhamshire. I love my job, I like living in the coach house and the village is really beautiful. I love Angela, of course I do but…well I'm just tired of the arguing."

Leanne was about to reply but she stopped herself and remained silent for a few seconds. Another smile briefly appeared on her face. She stood up and walked over to the sink to empty out the dregs from the coffee pot.

"Perhaps you're right," she called, over her shoulder, "There's only so much effort you can put into a relationship without getting anything out of it."

"Exactly," Derek said, "Finally, someone sees it from my point of view. Still, we have had some good times together."

"Yes but not enough by the sound of it," Leanne added some washing-up liquid to the coffee pot and began cleaning it under the hot tap, "Relationships are a two-way street. Obviously Angela doesn't give you enough consideration."

"It certainly feels that way at times. Mind you, she is thoughtful…"

"And she's got a nerve blaming you for everything. She's the one with the issues after all. Well, it's not surprising she's got them really is it, with her past? Spending the bulk of your adult life as a prostitute must turn a woman into a hard-nosed bitch."

Derek drank the last drop of his coffee.

"You'd think so wouldn't you," he replied, "Mind you although Angela is strong she's more of a warm-hearted person really."

"No, that's all just a front, Derek," Leanne told him, grabbing a tea towel and drying the pot.

"You think so?"

She nodded

"Oh yes. She's got to have a separate personality for the punters hasn't she? I bet she can be a completely different woman to each individual client, eh; lots of different characters?"

"Well I suppose she must have had some sort of...I don't really like discussing actual details with her."

"No? Well I can't say I blame you. It takes a decent man to put up with their partner sleeping around. She ought to remember that. Perhaps she does. What character does she play for you, someone warm-hearted yet clingy? That's your type really isn't it Derek?"

"I wouldn't say clingy. Hang on; I wouldn't say I wanted a certain type either. Besides I'm with the real Angela. She doesn't play a role for me. She loves me."

Leanne shrugged her shoulders.

"If you say so," she told him, innocently.

"I do!"

"Good."

She placed the coffee pot back in the cupboard before turning round to face him again.

"Still, it doesn't really matter now anyway, does it?"

"What doesn't?"

"If Angela played a character for you or not," Leanne said, "You're not going to be together now anyway, are you?"

"Sorry?"

"Well, you just told me the relationship wasn't worth saving so I guess you've broken up."

"Oh well, I mean I know I said that, but erm well technically..."

"You're done with her, I can understand that," Leanne continued, "She's hurt you and doesn't even care. You can't be with a woman like that."

"I wouldn't say she doesn't care…"

"And you want me to take her name out of my will. That's fine. It was probably wrong of me to trust her with my child anyway."

"Actually Angela loves children."

"Just the males though, eh," Leanne winked.

"Well that doesn't sound right."

Derek felt confused.

"It's best that it's over though, isn't it? I don't know what I was thinking really, allowing a prostitute near my child," she shivered, "It doesn't bear thinking about does it?"

"But she's not a prostitute now," Derek explained, "Actually I think she regrets ever getting into it. It must be hard for her, feeling ashamed of something that was a big part of her life. She probably feels guilty for feeling ashamed. I never thought of that before."

"No, you're wrong there."

"Am I?"

"Of course. She's not ashamed. You can't go whorring around the world for twenty years and not enjoy it."

Derek stood up.

"Hang on now."

"Once a tart always a tart I say."

"Stop it Leanne!" he shouted at her, "Just stop it. Angela is not a tart. She is the warmest, kindest, sweetest woman I know. She's put up with so much shit in her life yet has achieved so much. She'd make a great mum. I can talk to her about anything and she doesn't judge me. Okay so she kept telling me to calm down the other night but that's just because she cares about me, more than you ever did! Quite frankly she's a huge step up from you. You looked down your nose at me all through our marriage. Angela treats me as her equal; she's happy for me if I'm happy. You've even told me that you wouldn't allow me to be a gardener if we were still married. How dare you! I'm sorry to disappoint you but that's the wonderful thing about Angela, she isn't disappointed by me. She loves me and I love her, more than anything."

Derek stopped talking and breathed heavily as he realised he'd barely taken a breath during his speech. Leanne stared back at him. A glint appeared in her eye and she grinned again.

"Well," she said, walking over to stand in front of him, "If Angela is as perfect as all that…"

She put her face close to his and said loudly,

"Why the bloody hell are you standing here talking to me? Go and sort out your mess Derek, you stupid prat."

Derek looked startled. He was about to say something back when he realised what he'd just said and what Leanne had been doing. He grinned, leaned forwards and kissed his ex-wife on the forehead.

"Got to go," he told her, and rushed out of the room.

"I'll leave her name on the will then," Leanne called after him.

She heard the front door close. She laughed and returned to the lounge to check on Nathan.

Chapter 24

Angela was so nervous and for so many reasons. It was her first auction being the auctioneer, it was her first time appearing on television, and there was a good chance that she could be arrested at any moment.

She still couldn't believe what they'd done last night. Okay so Max had attacked her and Dora knocking him out could be seen as a sign of self-defence, but all that happened afterwards, tying him up, gagging him and then walking away and leaving him there; would the police treat that as grievous bodily harm? If she hadn't gone to his house last night the worst thing that would have happened today was Max showed up here and Angela lost her job. Now, she could lose that and her freedom too.

She'd barely slept at all last night. Her first thought on waking had been to drive back to Max's house and set him free but Dora had insisted on keeping hold of his front door key herself.

"I don't trust either of you with seeing this mission through to the end," she'd told Angela and Margaret last night, as she placed the key inside her bra.

The morning at the auction house had been frantic with crowds of potential buyers turning up for the preview of Max's mum's things as well as the TV crew arriving and setting up their cameras and lights. Time flew by and there hadn't been a chance for Angela to take her boss, Ben aside and tell him about her past. He seemed more on edge than she was, running round the salesroom all morning in a panic, checking everything was straight and tidy, including the staff. Craig got his tie tightened, Sally's blouse was tucked in and sales assistant, Clive received a wedgie as his low-slung trousers were hoisted up to his waist.

In the few moments Angela had to herself her mind turned to Derek. She wished he was here with her now. Okay so if he knew what had happened last night he'd be panicking more than Margaret had yesterday and wouldn't be of much comfort to her, but he'd be here, her Derek. She missed him. When was he coming back? In her current panicked state she wondered if he **was** coming back. The look on his face when his mum had told him about the insurance scam, her heart had initially gone out to him. She'd tried desperately to keep him calm, knowing he was about to lose it, but it had backfired and he'd turned his anger on her instead. There'd been a real hatred in his eyes and then he'd started going on about her past and she'd lost it too. She'd still been angry with him on the journey to Max's last night but now she just wanted him here.

There wasn't time for a lunch break, not that Angela could have kept anything down anyway. She found it difficult to concentrate on what the director was telling her to do while a make-up lady tried to bring some colour to her cheeks. The woman had sighed when she first clocked the bags under Angela's eyes.

"Fetch the larger bottle of concealer from the car, Maxine," she'd called out loudly, to her assistant.

Before she knew it, Angela was stood in the salesroom, nervously biting her bottom lip as she waited for her turn on the rostrum. The room was packed. News of the TV show had leaked and there were plenty of people here that Angela didn't recognise as the usual dealers. The TV crew were currently filming the general sale and for some reason, Ben had thought the acerbic Craig was the ideal choice as auctioneer.

"We now come to a rather tatty-looking, wicker table, circa 1975. That was obviously a period that taste forgot. Who'll start me at fifty pounds? You sir, really? Well actually, looking at that jacket you're wearing I'm not so surprised. Do I hear sixty?"

All of Max's mum's beautiful items were displayed in the room and ready for sale. Angela wondered if he was okay at the house. What if he'd got into difficulty and died during the night? What would happen then? She couldn't allow Dora and Margaret to take the blame. They'd only gone there to help her out. No, Angela knew she'd have to take responsibility. A part of her hoped he was dead, if she was being honest with herself. Dead, he'd be harmless, alive and angry; he was more dangerous than ever. Mind you, he had every right to be angry with her this time. He'd never leave her alone again. Her losing her job would no longer be enough for him. It would just be the start. What else would he plan? She shivered. Charles was standing beside her and assumed she was trembling because of the auction.

"Don't worry my dear," he said, patting her arm, "You'll be fine. There's nothing to be nervous about."

Charles was officially retiring today. After all his years at the auction house, today should have been about him, not her and this bloody sale.

"I don't want a fuss," he'd said to Angela, after he'd announced his retirement, "I'm not someone that craves attention. But I am expecting a bloody decent leaving present. I hope you're arranging that."

Angela had shaken her head.

"No, Ben's secretary is in charge of the collection."

"What?"

Charles had looked crestfallen.

"What does she know about antiques? I told her once that I liked Majolica. She said she preferred Ibiza."

Angela had laughed.

"Don't worry," she'd told him, "Ben's selecting the gift. You won't be disappointed."

Now though, Angela was wishing Charles had wanted a fuss. It could have been him going up onto the rostrum next and not her. Craig was reaching the end of his sale.

"I have two hundred and fifty pounds for the painting by local artist, Emmeline Jackson. Are we all done?" he banged his gavel, "Sold, to the skinny bird with the big knockers…oh, I beg your pardon. Sold, to the flat-chested bird standing behind two large, silver, glass baubles."

The TV crew surely couldn't use any of his footage in their TV programme. It was all going to be about Angela.

"Right, lastly," Craig announced into the microphone, "There's this tired-looking figure to my right. It's seen better days, has lost its sheen and from here I can see quite a prominent crack. Who'll give me ten pounds for Clive? No, I'm only joking. Pull your trousers up Clive, this is on TV."

Angela's stomach was turning somersaults as she waited while the TV crew realigned one of their cameras. There was a distinct buzz in the room. A lot of people had been waiting for this auction. She was given the thumbs up by the director and stepped up onto the rostrum. All eyes were on her, the crowd, Charles, Ben and the camera crew. Even with the microphone her voice barely registered as she introduced the auction and the director asked her to repeat herself.

Angela took a deep breath and tried to focus on what she was meant to be doing. After she'd sold a couple of items she began to relax into the sale. She didn't have to work that hard to get the prices up. Max's mum had had very good taste and the items were selling themselves.

It was towards the end of the sale that she heard a commotion at the back of the room and an incredibly angry, yet familiar, voice shouting out to people to get out of the way.

"Will you let me through? This is my auction!"

Max appeared, barging his way through the dense crowd on the right-hand side of the room. He'd obviously rushed here as soon as he'd got free. The crowd parted as they stared at this oddly dressed person. Max was wearing a long, beige mac and a pair of smart black shoes. His legs were bare and his overall appearance said 'flasher.' The handcuffs were still attached to his wrist and to the black grate from the fireplace, which was dangling by his side.

"Stop this auction," he called out.

"Is there a problem?" Ben called over to him, a puzzled expression on his face.

"Yes!" Max shouted back, across the room, "I've spent the last twenty hours tied up to a fireplace."

"Ooh kinky," a voice from the crowd called out.

Max ignored them.

"It was only thanks to the cleaning lady coming round to collect her money that I'm here now. She had to untie me and rub me vigorously all over until I could feel myself again."

The people around him began to snigger.

"It's not funny," Max spat at them, "I had to pay the old bag extra! I had no circulation. I couldn't fucking walk until half an hour ago."

That part certainly wasn't going to make it into the final cut of the programme. He pointed up at Angela.

"That," he said, "That's the culprit. That woman is why I couldn't move, why I could barely breathe, and why I shat myself at half past three this morning."

The crowd moved further away from him.

"I wondered what that smell was," one of them said, "You dirty bastard."

"That woman isn't who she says she is," Max continued, "She's just a…"

Another commotion broke out to the left of the room and Max's words were lost in the murmuring. As Angela looked over her heart skipped a beat. Derek was pushing his way through the crowd towards her. To Angela it was like the end of a romantic film, the knight in shining armour coming to rescue his love, all shot in slow motion while a beautiful soundtrack played in the background.

In reality it wasn't quite like that. Derek slipped between two dealers who were chatting to each other before vaulting over an Ercol chair and disappearing from view as he lost his footing. When he reappeared he was limping but that didn't stop him vaulting a leather regency sofa. Unfortunately the old lady sitting in it received a hard kick to the back of her head, which sent her tumbling to the floor. After a quick apology Derek made his way to the front of the room, all eyes were on him. He smiled as he stepped up onto the rostrum. To Angela the room had become empty apart from the two of them. Derek took her hand

"Angela," he said. The microphone was still on and the whole room could hear every word, "I'm so sorry for hurting you the other night. I shouldn't have taken my anger out on you. I was upset about realising that you were right about mum. I have been overprotective of her. You're always right about everything. We need to go home now and tell her all about your past life as a prostitute."

People in the crowd began staring at one another, looking perplexed.

"Did he say prostitute?"

"It sounded like it."

"He said past life. Maybe she was a Victorian prostitute."

The two people on the rostrum took no notice of the crowd. Derek continued talking.

"I'm going to be proud to tell mum about your past because you know what, you are an inspiration to everyone. You've put up with so much in your life and yet you've overcome all of your problems. You're a kind, warm, generous, loving woman and I'm crazy about you. I've not been cheating on you with Leanne. I've been cheating with her son."

That sounded wrong and there were gasps in the crowd.

"I realised I was spending time with him because I hadn't faced up to the fact that I'm not going to be a dad."

People in the crowd smiled reassuringly at one another. Now they understood what he meant.

"But it doesn't matter," Derek continued, "I'd rather be childless with you than be in an unhappy relationship with a couple of kids. You are everything to me. I love you Angela and I could never be happier than I am when I'm with you."

Angela was beaming from ear to ear and tears were flowing down her cheeks, but Derek wasn't finished. Although it was difficult in the small space he managed to crouch down onto one knee.

"Will you marry me?"

Angela gasped. Only a short while ago she feared she was about to lose everything but now all those fears had evaporated. It didn't matter that Max was here in the room. It didn't matter that Derek had basically done what Max had been threatening to do all along and announced to the world that she'd been a prostitute. It didn't matter if she lost her job because of it. Derek was her world and she had everything if she had him.

"Yes, of course I'll marry you," she replied.

Derek stood up and kissed her. The room broke out into spontaneous cheering and applause. Still crying and laughing, the newly engaged couple turned to face the room and the cameras. They waved shyly at the crowd. As Derek looked around he spotted the gap on the right-hand side and a familiar figure standing in it.

"What's he doing here?" he shouted out, pointing at Max.

The crowd had momentarily forgotten about the smelly flasher that had interrupted proceedings before Derek appeared. All faces now turned in his direction.

"Max has been trying to blackmail me," Angela announced, through the microphone "He's been threatening to reveal my past unless I slept with him."

The crowd began jeering.

"You bastard," someone shouted.

"Somebody call the police," another voice called out.

"Sleeping with prostitutes, you ought to be ashamed of yourself," said another.

The whole room turned on him.

"Wait," Max said, "No, this is all wrong. I'm the victim here."

He span round on the spot, desperately looking for a way to escape through the throng. The fire grate attached to his wrist continued to spin after Max stopped and he lost his balance. As he stumbled, his mac flew open. There were gasps and screams as the rubber suit, complete with openings, was revealed to the whole room.

"My Bill's just had car mats fitted that look like that," a woman at the edge of the crowd said to her friend, a look of disgust on her face, "I hope he's kept the receipt."

Derek had leapt down from the rostrum as soon as Angela had mentioned the blackmail and he stood now in front of Max.

"It's not what you think," Max told him, "Really, it was all just a joke, my friend, I…"

Derek was in no mood to listen. He pulled back his arm and punched Max hard between the eyes. Max fell backwards, out cold again. As he hit the floor the room broke into another spontaneous cheer.

Derek walked back over to Angela, his hand throbbing like mad. She came down from the rostrum. The room was still buzzing around them. A very excited TV director was shouting to the camera crew,

"Did you get all that? Did you get it?"

"I love you," Derek said, placing his arms around Angela.

"I love you too."

They kissed.

"Happy?" he asked.

Angela nodded.

"Come on," Derek said, "Let's go tell mum the news."

"About me being a prostitute you mean?"

"Of course. What else?"

They laughed and walked out of the salesroom hand in hand.

"I suppose we could tell her we're getting married as well," he added.

Chapter 25

Angela had secretly always wanted a Christmas wedding and she got her wish. While it wasn't white outside, the Christmas Eve day was bright, cold, crisp and perfect. Actually, even if it had been blowing a storm outside, to Angela, it would still have been perfect.

It hadn't taken the whole six months to plan the day. Both she and Derek only wanted something small but a lot of things had changed in that time. Where she was sitting now, getting ready for her big day was one of the principal changes. Angela wasn't preparing in her bedroom at the coach house but was sat in the master bedroom of the old rectory beside the church. At their daughter's wedding back in the summer, Theresa Jennings and her husband had decided to sell up in England and move permanently to their villa in Spain. Alone, Angela and Derek could never have afforded to purchase the large, Georgian property but with Ursula putting her money in too, the beautiful house had become theirs. Ursula was happy living in the two-bedroomed annex where she continued making clothes for all of her friends in the village.

The coach house had proved to be an easy sale too. Jeremy Riley had been renting an apartment but wanted to settle down and buy his own place in Tenhamshire. He'd been more than happy to purchase the coach house for himself. It was very handy for visiting his dad and his sister.

Angela smiled to herself as she finished adjusting her lip liner. Jeremy had become such a good friend to them both and he was Derek's best man today.

"Are you ready to slip into your outfit?" Margaret asked, coming to stand behind Angela in her floor-length, A-line, claret bridesmaid dress.

"I think so."

"This is really beautiful," Dora called over, from the bed.

She was sitting on the edge and gently touched the ivory-coloured, sleeveless, full-length dress laid out beside her.

"The lace detailing on the skirt is exquisite," she continued, "Your mother-in-law is so talented."

"I know," Angela replied, "It's beautiful, as is the matching bolero jacket. I don't know how she does it."

"Are you sure you're going to be warm enough?" Margaret asked, looking concerned.

"I've not exactly got far to walk today," Angela told her, "I could leap over the back wall into the churchyard. Afterwards I've only got to walk up to the Home for the reception."

"The back lounge and conservatory look great," Dora said, "Moron's making sure the wrinklies stay out of the room and it's had a good dose of air freshener so there won't be any stale fart smells."

"Mum!"

"What? It's a retirement home. A retirement home without farts is like a kennel without barking."

Just to prove her point she leaned over and let one rip. Margaret tutted and gently picked up Angela's dress and took it off of the hanger.

"It's a shame Ursula didn't have time to make herself a new outfit too."

"She did, but she didn't want one," Angela explained, "Ursula makes so many outfits, buying off the rack is a treat for her."

Angela slipped into her dress and both Margaret and Dora sighed.

"You look beautiful," Margaret told her. She looked at her watch, "Time's moving on. Are you ready to get married?"

Angela smiled.

"I've been ready my whole life."

*

In the church Derek was feeling nervous. Ursula leaned forward from the pew behind and smacked his arm.

"Stop fiddling with your collar," she whispered.

"Sorry."

"Why are you nervous?" Jeremy asked him, "You're not worried she's not going to turn up are you?"

"Well I am now!" Derek replied.

Jeremy smiled.

"Just relax," he said, "She'll be here soon. You live next door for goodness sake. It's not like she's going to be late."

"I know."

Derek wasn't sure why he felt so nervous. It's not like this was his first time getting married. His ex-wife was here today. Leanne was sat with Nathan, beside Ursula. She'd visited them a couple of times in the last six months and Derek and Angela had been to see her too, staying in his old apartment before they sold it. Derek had decided to follow Angela's suggestion of buying an apartment somewhere nearby to rent out but that plan changed after Theresa Jennings and her husband's retirement plans were made known. Aside from the old rectory, Theresa's husband had an antiques shop up in the market square that he wanted to sell. Derek's apartment bought that and Angela starting running it, with the aid of some part-time advisory help from her old colleague, Charles.

Angela hadn't remained with the auction house after Derek's proposal. Although Ben had asked her to stay, Angela felt that the press interest in her past was detrimental to the reputation of the company. She saw the purchase of the antiques shop differently though and reignited the media interest in her after the sale had gone through. She told Derek it was a good way to get a bit of free advertising. She knew the attention wouldn't last long and it hadn't.

There'd been a lot of people who had visited the shop, keen to see the woman who had earned a living as a prostitute but who also had a good knowledge of the world of antiques. Derek was relieved when the press attention died down. Not all of it had been positive and Angela had received her share of nasty e mails and letters. She'd just laughed them off but he'd found that harder to do. That was probably the reason for his nerves today. Derek feared a reporter turning up at the wedding and the public interest in them starting again. He could just imagine the headline. 'Prostitute Finally Marries her Prince.' Actually he quite liked how he sounded in that.

Derek shook the image from his head. If an article about their wedding, with reference made to Angela's past, did appear in the local press then he and Angela would deal with it together as they always did. They were a team.

Derek thought back to the day he'd proposed. The two of them had headed back to the coach house and sat down with Ursula to tell her the truth about Angela's past. It had been a relief for him that his mother didn't have a problem with it. In fact she hadn't seemed shocked in any way.

"Why do you think I would have been?" she'd asked her son, "Do you think I've never heard of using sex before?"

Derek had blushed, hearing his mother use the word 'sex.'

"I mean," Ursula had continued, "Your Auntie Jean wasn't averse to using her charms to get what she wanted back in the day."

"Eh?"

"You think she paid cash for that extension on her bungalow and for all that plumbing work she had done? Of course she didn't."

That revelation had made it difficult for Derek to look his Auntie Jean in the eye today when she arrived at the church for the wedding.

While Ursula had been fine with Angela's past she did sometimes forget that Derek's original version of it had been a lie. When they'd revealed that they'd bought the antiques shop Ursula had looked concerned.

"Aren't you worried about the bottom falling out again?" she'd asked.

*

The wedding was beautiful, if a little unorthodox in places. There weren't many brides that followed an eighty-seven year old flower girl down the aisle. While Angela's father was able to give his daughter away, he did have to return to prison straight after the photographs were taken, where he was on remand. Nervous Nigel began the service by saying,

"We are gathered here today to mourn the loss of…"

As he realised his error his gaze fell upon old Willy Jenson in the fifth row, who let out a whine and slid off of the pew, much to the amusement of Sir Jasper, sat beside him, whose cackling laughter echoed around the vast space of the church.

Margaret really had pulled out all the stops on the Home's Christmas decorations this year in light of the wedding reception. The conservatory had a huge Christmas tree covered with lights and Victorian style baubles, and a local florist had made a living garland full of holly and autumnal leaves and berries that was draped across the mantelpiece of the huge fireplace. The rest of the room was covered with bows and ribbons, ornamental trees and festive statues but Margaret had only used the colours, sage green and white, which kept the décor tasteful rather than gaudy.

A bakery in Cunden Lingus had made a very appropriate wedding cake in the shape of a rather nice antique, eighteenth century dresser which had a pair of muddy-looking gardening wellington boots stuck on the top of it in green icing. The buffet was delicious and the drink flowed. As the evening drew on Dora announced it was time for one of her special songs. Derek grabbed Angela's hand and led her out through the conservatory door, pleased he was never going to find out what Annie from St Helen's did with her enormous pair of melons.

He placed his suit jacket over Angela's shoulders as they stepped out into the grounds. A cold night, there was already a light frost over the grass. They ambled in silence away from the house and walked round to the formal garden inside the yew hedge. It was dark as they approached but as they stepped past a sensor, lights hidden in the flowerbeds switched on and the garden was bathed in a delicate, warm glow; the shrubs and the central fountain casting shadows across the gravel paths.

"Ash and I put these in at the end of summer," Derek said.

"What, just for our wedding?" Angela joked.

Derek laughed.

"Of course," he replied, "It wasn't in case one of the residents wandered out here in the dark at all. Can you believe Ash is a whizz with electronics? The guy can't put one foot in front of the other without tripping over but he can lay cables, rewire plugs and design an entire lighting system without a hitch. He's wasted in gardening, he really is."

"Yes, well, we don't have to discuss work now."

Derek smiled. He placed his arm around Angela's waist and they stood there looking at the lit flowerbeds.

"So," he said, after a few minutes, "I suppose we should be heading off on our honeymoon soon."

"Yes," Angela replied, "I think I've remembered to pack everything."

"Insect repellent?"

"Of course. I know how tropical it is at the Manor Park Spa Hotel in Cunden Lingus at this time of year."

Derek laughed again.

"It seemed appropriate to book there," he told her, "That was the hotel we were supposed to stay in on that disastrous coach trip."

"It wasn't that disastrous," Angela said, "We met Dora and Margaret on it. We fell in love with Tenhamshire."

"And each other," Derek finished.

They smiled and kissed one another.

"Of course, one night away isn't exactly a honeymoon," Angela said.

"Well that's what comes of wanting a wedding on Christmas Eve but still wanting to share Christmas day with your family and friends," Derek told her.

Angela giggled.

"I know, I want it all don't I? But seriously, this is our first Christmas all together in Tenhamshire. I didn't want to miss that, especially after the year we've had."

"I agree with you," Derek replied, "Besides, who needs to go away on holiday? I've got all I want right here."

Angela grinned. She leaned in against her husband and rested her head on his shoulder. For a split second an image of Max appeared in her mind. After Derek's proposal back in June, the two of them had gone home and, after telling Ursula about Angela's past, they'd celebrated their engagement with Champagne. That night, once alone, Angela told Derek the whole truth about Max, what he'd been to her and how she'd been attacked. As she'd explained to Margaret and Dora on the fateful night they'd visited Max's house, she didn't want there to be any more secrets between them.

Max hadn't made contact again after the day of the auction. He'd been humiliated and Angela thought he'd gone home to lick his wounds. She was too happy to let him worry her anymore. Then, a few weeks later she read an article in the Tenham Herald. A man calling himself Max Saunders had been found dead at his late mother's home in Ryan Harbour. There was a reference to the day of the sale, when he'd shown up at the auction house in a rubber outfit. It had been explained away as a temporary mental breakdown; delayed shock for the death of his mother, brought on by the sale of her possessions. His death hadn't been suicide though. It was a case of erotic asphyxiation, where someone restricts the oxygen going to their brain to increase the pleasure of masturbation. It was an accidental death. He'd been found with a chord around his neck that had been tied to the doorknob of his bedroom door. He was naked except for a yellow washing-up glove on his right hand.

After he'd read the article, Angela could see that Derek was struggling with wanting to ask her about what Max had liked to do in bed while also trying desperately to forget all about it. He decided on the latter and Angela thought that was the right decision.

Max had been found by a local estate agent who'd popped round with a potential buyer for the property. Apparently Max was going to return to Spain. Would he have tried to hurt her again if he'd lived? Angela didn't know and didn't waste any time thinking about it. She'd got the closure she wanted and needed. All that was left was a kind of pity for the man he'd become; someone who was so obviously lonely and angry with the world.

She shook the image of Max away and snuggled further into Derek's shoulder.

"Are you cold?" he asked her, kissing the top of her head.

"No, just happy and contented."

"Well I'm bloody freezing," he said, "You've got my jacket. Come on, let's go back inside."

Angela laughed.

The two of them turned and, hand in hand, left the formal garden and made their way back to the reception where they could say goodbye to everyone before heading off. Back in the garden the lights in the flowerbeds switched off, extinguishing all of the shadows.

Printed in Great Britain
by Amazon